Plucking the Apple

Elizabeth Palmer's first job after leaving school, halfway through her A levels, was in a publishing house as a graphic designer. She then moved to the *Financial Times* where she met her husband. After the birth of the first of her three children, she started to work from home as a freelance book designer, and she and her family divide their time between London and Sussex. *Plucking the Apple* is Elizabeth Palmer's second novel. Her first, *The Stainless Angel* was published in 1992.

PLUCKING THE APPLE

Elizabeth Palmer

ARROW

First published in Arrow 1994

3 5 7 9 10 8 6 4 2

First published in Great Britain by Century in 1994

Arrow Books Limited
Random House UK Ltd, 20 Vauxhall Bridge Road, London SW1V 2SA

Random House Australia (Pty) Limited
20 Alfred Street, Milsons Point, Sydney,
New South Wales 2061, Australia

Random House New Zealand Limited
18 Poland Road, Glenfield
Auckland 10, New Zealand

Random House South Africa (Pty) Limited
PO Box 337, Bergvlei, South Africa

Random House UK Limited Reg. No. 954009

ISBN 0 09 919591 7

Photoset by Deltatype Ltd, Ellesmere Port, Cheshire
Printed and bound in Great Britain by
Cox & Wyman Ltd, Reading, Berkshire

A glimpse of golden breasts, a mat of hair
Thrown back from the eyes; a naked arm in a ray
Of sunlight plucks an apple. Because it is there.

The woodpecker, like a typist, taps away
Relentlessly; the record must be kept
Though the same larceny happen day by day,

The original and the final sin. Inept
Professors may reduce it to a case
And prove that Eve who brooded, burned and wept,

Was merely maladjusted; Queen and Ace
Survive, whoever deals, as Ace and Queen.

Louis MacNiece, 'Canto III'

For my parents

1

Looking back on it later, with the inestimable benefit of hindsight, Victoria Harting saw that the summer dinner party she gave for the Careys was when the events leading to the tragedy in Little Haddow began.

Sitting in her pleasant little house in Chelsea, blissfully unaware of what was to come, she pulled a pad towards her on which she wrote the word *List* and, under it, the names of those she would invite. In addition to the Careys, these included Tessa and Alexander Lucas, assuming their marriage held up until then, possibly Robert Wilmot, the editor of the glossy magazine *Modern Art*, and his wife, though according to her husband, James, this was another unstable marriage and too many of those around one medium-sized table was capable of capsizing the most well-organized of evenings. In the end she decided to ask Ginevra Haye instead. But who to ask with her? This was a tricky one. Perhaps no one was the answer. Thank God the graceless Kevin Haye, who was a builder, was safely stowed away in Saudi Arabia for the foreseeable.

Victoria's feelings towards her friend were ambivalent these days. At Oxford they had been close, the homespun Ginevra providing a flattering contrast to her own handsome vibrance. Then, they had all expected one of the cleverest students of her year to rise to the upper intellectual echelons of the civil service or something similar. And yet here she was, married to the thick and unalluring Kevin and living in Little Whatsit, writing some obscure book on the advice of her old tutor with a view to eventually getting it published.

In spite of all this, the strand which had bound them together did not break after university since Ginevra, whose brilliant English first had included the history and theory of criticism, then went on to the Courtauld Institute where, intent on broadening her scope, she did an MA in modern art, and soon after this wrote and published a couple of critical essays whose dry discernment and elegance of style had caused a stir of excitement and interest within the art establishment. Such a shame that she had not followed these successes up, but had embarked upon an unsolicited and, by the sound of it, turgid tome instead.

Every so often, calling to the fore the social callousness which must be the hallmark of any successful hostess, Victoria considered the possibility of dropping her old friend, and then magnanimously decided to give it one more summer. After all, she reasoned, with The Gallery now fashionably established as a showcase for the best and the brightest in contemporary art, once Ginevra's magnum opus was out of the way, they could be once more on parallel tracks, this time in the gallery world, where Ginevra's support and highly praised gift for critical analysis might, in the future, prove very influential. On balance, it seemed a good idea to let the status quo go on ticking over, certainly for the time being.

The next question was whether to expand a small supper party into a larger gathering. On the whole Victoria was disposed not to do that this time around, although it was true to say that Tessa and Alexander's fighting might have been better diluted. Thoughtfully she put her bare foot into the middle of what looked like a large and ratty old slipper which turned out to be Ho, her Pekinese dog. Ho, who bit everyone else, knew better than to bite Victoria. She rubbed his warm stomach with her toes. The sash window opposite her knee-hole desk was wide open and looked out onto a typical small Chelsea square of a garden, dominated by a mature tree. It was early summer and only the lightest of light airs stirred the shining leaves. Below, sitting in its deckchaired shade, wearing last summer's Italian straw fedora and reading the *Daily Telegraph*, was her husband. Beside him red, pink and white geraniums and petunias spilled brilliantly over the side of a terracotta Provençal urn. Listening to the faint hum of traffic from the King's Road, Victoria felt uncharacteristically peaceful, almost content. When she had organized her party she would go and disturb James. Herself a doer, she could not bear to see anybody else sitting down.

Surrounded by lush, buttercupped meadows in which stood

comatose cows, Little Haddow was the archetypal timeless English village where very little had changed in the last seventy years, and that included the residents. Comparatively new arrivals such as the Hayes were sized up, gossiped about and tolerated with gruff, reserved country courtesy which for the next twenty years would treat them as newsworthy outsiders.

In Pear Tree Cottage, turning Victoria's invitation over in her hand, Ginevra wondered what to wear. Her wardrobe was minimal and notable more for its serviceability than its glamour. And it would be a glamorous evening, of that she was sure, though the card gave no clue as to whether it was a party for six or sixty. *Mrs James Harting at Home*, it said, *8 for 8.30 p.m. Dinner.* Pompous, thought Ginevra, but then Victoria always had been incapable of just ringing up and saying come to supper. In the end she selected a black skirt, which had a button missing, and a salmon-pink pie-frilled blouse. With black stockings it would just about pass muster. Whether it did or whether it did not, Ginevra was quite determined to go.

All she could find to put on her feet were either Dr Scholl exercise sandals or the black lace-up shoes in which she bicycled. It would have to be the Dr Scholls. Hanging up her chosen outfit, which smelt faintly of mothballs, she put the whole thing to the back of her mind and went back to the computer.

2

Standing by the drawing room window uncorking the claret, James watched his wife's small Volvo, usually referred to as the Volvette, hit the kerb quite hard as she parked. Momentarily stopping what he was doing, he leant forward to try to get a better look at the front bumper. Surely she couldn't have? Not again! She had.

As she came in, the front door was slammed with enough force to shake the house and probably the ones on either side as well.

'Crashed the car again, I'm afraid, darling,' shouted Victoria breezily up the stairs. 'Sorry about that.'

He heard her, rustling with packages, proceed through the narrow hall and then descend the stairs to the kitchen and dining room. Waiting for the inevitable he heard her knock over something which subsequently shattered.

'Oh fuck it!' said Victoria. There was a shrill squeal. She must have trodden on Ho in the general confusion.

It was extraordinary, thought James, going back to the claret, that anyone could cause quite as much havoc as she could in such a short space of time. Her car was a joke it was becoming harder and harder for him to laugh at. The repairs were so expensive for one thing, never mind the fact that one day he was afraid she might really hurt herself. He recalled the houseguest who had been taken to see the latest exhibition at The Gallery, and who had spent the whole journey sweating with fear as she swept through heavy traffic with less than a millimetre to spare on either side. Trembling as he disembarked, he had said, 'Victoria certainly knows the width of her car.' Practically the day after, a lorry driver, oblivious to the gnat-like manoeuvrings of the Volvette practically beneath his front bumper, had taken half its side off. James couldn't think of anyone else they knew who had the wheels of their car regularly rebalanced the way they did, mainly because of his wife's extrovert and inaccurate parking.

The Volvette was four years old and there had been a debate about whether or not to replace it with a newer model. Here James had put his foot down, arguing that unless they replaced it with a tank, this was a pointless exercise. A dent was a dent after all, and what was the point of replacing a set of old dents with a set of new ones? Although her lack of contrition was famous, even Victoria had seen the sense in this.

She came upstairs with Ho. 'Who got trodden upon by Mummy then?' he heard her say. She put him down, and Ho, who was a wimp, limped whining to his basket and gingerly got into it. Victoria kissed her husband.

'How did you . . . ?'

'Prang the car? Oh, not sure really. I was parking forwards, if you know what I mean, and I clipped his wing.'

'Why on earth don't you park backwards like everybody else?'

'Yes, I should, shouldn't I? The other driver got very upset.'

'What sort of car did you hit?'

She had to think hard. He could see he was losing her attention.

'A Mercedes, I think. I said to him it's only metal after all. He kept saying that it was brand new and rabbiting on about the inconvenience. I said to him if your car spent even half as much time in the garage as mine does you'd know all about inconvenience.'

James was surprised a policeman hadn't been called to intervene at the end of this speech. A Mercedes! He anticipated the day when no one would be prepared to insure his wife and wondered vaguely what a chauffeur would cost.

Bored by this exchange which, with small variation, they had had many times before, Victoria enquired, 'Has the food arrived?'

'Yes it has, all you have to do is put it in the oven.' The food in question had been prepared by the Cordon Bleu girls who also did the catering for James's art gallery when they had a private view or party.

'Who have you got coming again?' asked James, who had been up to his ears trying to get Jack Carey's exhibition and, more importantly, Jack Carey himself organized, and had not really caught up with this particular dinner party.

'Um, the Careys, Alexander and Tessa, and Ginevra.'

'I suppose you did have to ask Ginevra.' He sighed. A vision of her in her usual shapeless, dateless clothes rose before his eyes. 'She's such heavy furniture. I know she's brainier than the rest of us put together, but she isn't at all amusing. And that unblinking stare of hers unnerves me.'

'That's really not fair,' protested Victoria, sounding a great deal more loyal than she actually felt. 'Her eyes are easily her best feature.'

James forbore to say that this was not a difficult challenge to meet. For the first time since university he actually thought about Ginevra's eyes, and had to admit that his wife was right. Resolutely he put aside the memory of them very close to his own the morning after the Commem. Ball all those years ago. He had woken up with a thundering headache and no idea of where he was, how he had got there and, worst of all, what he had or had not done during the small hours after his arrival. It was the only time he had seen his wife's unattractive friend without her glasses and he had been surprised by her eyes' blue darkness, fringed by thick shining lashes. Divorced from the rest of her plain face by their proximity to his own and extraordinarily beautiful they radiated intelligence, and something else as well which he couldn't quite put his finger on. Shortly after this he had got up and left her bed and her room, being very careful as he did so to make no reference to the night before beyond thanking her for whatever it was she had done for him. Ginevra, in a turmoil of both body and spirit, had found nothing to say. Neither of them had ever mentioned it again, and James had never told Victoria what had happened either.

Alexander and Tessa were the first to arrive and for once appeared to be the best of friends as well as married to each other. This was a relief and more than Victoria had dared hope for. She took them through to the garden where James was already reclining with his first drink of the evening. Brother kissed sister. They were very alike to look at.

Tessa, thought Victoria enviously, must have just about the longest legs in London and had the colt-like grace to go with them. She exuded the sort of confidence born of being exceptionally pretty and very spoilt. It was hard to separate Tessa from her own way. Wearing a skirt the size of a bandage, she was burnished by the sun and was the sort of girl for whom the phrase *jeunesse dorée* might have been invented. Even the long mane of hair was dark gold and artfully streaked, and, when she tossed it back, this, coupled with her straight nose and strong white teeth, emphasized her high-spirited equine look.

In contrast with her blonde assurance, her husband was willowy and dark, with a melancholic, almost nineteenth-century, air about him. Although elegant and much more intelligent than she was (not difficult), it was generally recognized by her family that she was in charge, and Alexander had even been unkindly referred to as Tessa's spare wheel. Tessa, who had done a little unexacting modelling, was always just about to get a job. Alexander, who worked in publishing, wrote poetry in his spare time. It was his passion and his solace. Their quarrels, which were frequent, were always about jealousy (his) and bad behaviour (hers).

Though like his sister to look at, James felt that, unlike her, he had found his own centre of gravity. In spite of her peccadillos, or maybe because of them, he honestly loved his wife. They both enjoyed running The Gallery, though it was true to say that without the enormous advantage of family money to draw upon, it probably would have had to close down long ago. Being moderately rich had not spoilt James. Used to money and the privilege that went with it, he was neither snobbish nor felt compelled to indulge in vulgar display to advertise his wealth.

They sat down, and there was a brief silence as all relaxed into the end of another blue summer day. The smell of jasmine pervaded the still warmth of the evening and, sipping his wine, James reflected that these golden, irresponsible days would not last forever and that he should not take them for granted while they did. Eventually children would come along together with all the clutter and mess of family life. When this happened he supposed he would enjoy it but until it did he was quite content with his life as it was.

'Oh, I brought you some mint chocolates, Victoria,' suddenly remembered Tessa. 'I think I've left them on the hall table.'

The door bell rang. 'Thanks, Tessa. That's probably Ginevra. Don't move, darling, I'll get it.'

She went up the garden steps. Tessa made a face at Alexander. Neither of them liked Ginevra very much but were forced to put up with her from time to time because of Victoria's inexplicable attachment.

Opening the door, Victoria discovered both Ginevra and the Careys on the step. Ginevra was wearing a most extraordinary get-up which did nothing for her at all.

Pink! Not even a shirt, definitely a blouse. And black. Dear, oh dear, thought Victoria, taking the proffered present.

'Oh lovely! More mints.'

She put them down on the table where they were upstaged by Tessa's flashier variety. More mints. *Embarras de mints.* Remembering a long wait to be served in the village sweet shop, whose dusty faded window was crammed with huge old ground-glass-stoppered toffee jars, and whose minute sawdusty interior smelt of liquorice and lemon sherberts, Ginevra, who could have done with the money they cost, resolved not to bother in future.

The two women kissed. Was it her imagination, Victoria wondered, or was there a slight frost?

'You do know Ellen and Jack Carey, don't you, Ginevra?'

'Yes, we have met. Hello.'

'Right!' said Victoria. 'We are all in the garden if you want to go on through.' Ginevra's large pale face on top of the pie frill looked as though it had been served up on a plate. Following her along the passage, Victoria noticed that her (woolly!) black tights had a hole in them, and she appeared to be wearing Dr Scholl exercise sandals on her feet. Pointing up this sartorial chaos, Ellen Carey gracefully stepped out behind her, wand slim in something long and fluid. Her loosely looped up hair was secured with a comb, and trailing her multi-coloured silk shawl she resembled an Augustus John gypsy. Jack brought up the rear. In baggy jacket, open-necked shirt, neckerchief and jeans on which he had apparently cleaned his paintbrushes, the ensemble finished off with espadrilles, he had made no concessions at all to Victoria's dinner party. The grandeur of Mrs James Harting at Home had completely escaped Jack.

As he passed her, Victoria caught the unmistakable whiff of whisky. Since he was supposed to be working hard on his next exhibition and therefore off the booze, this was alerting. I must tell James so that he can enlist Ellen's help, Victoria thought. She walked after them.

In the garden the languor engendered by the day drawing to its close had evaporated, and as the evening advanced her guests were all becoming wakeful and animated. Victoria saw with trepidation that Tessa looked sulky. Alexander was carefully not looking at her and trying to talk to Ginevra.

'So what exactly were you doing at the Courtauld?' Alexander was saying. Ginevra ate a peanut.

'Art and Patronage in Britain, among other things.'

Only minimally the wiser, Alexander persisted. 'But what does that specifically entail?'

'Oh, how it all works. The Arts Council, the ICA, the London gallery system et al.' For his benefit she paraphrased on from the prospectus as she remembered it. 'The role of the exhibition in structuring perceptions of art, and the writing and importance of certain leading critics. Berger, Read, Alloway, Sylvester and so on. That interested me particularly as I did the history and theory of criticism as part of my English degree course.'

Alexander, who had heard of Read, just, but not of either Berger or Sylvester, or Alloway come to that, and who would have liked to extract himself totally from the conversation if he could, said insincerely, 'Fascinating! What about the art itself?'

'Yes, we did that too. Thematically. The city, the body-in-landscape, Utopia. You know. That sort of thing.'

He did not. Silence fell. She ate another peanut. Noticing that her glass was empty, he said, 'Let me get that topped up for you,' and made his escape.

On the other side of the room, Jack and Ellen were deep in conversation with James. Victoria's feelings concerning Jack Carey were mixed. Although he was undoubtedly The Gallery's star, she sometimes privately wondered if he was worth all the trouble at the end of the day. By the time a Carey exhibition was actually hung, fingernails were usually bitten to the quick, hers included, and tempers frayed. What they would all do without Ellen to nanny Jack along and slap his wrist every time he reached for the whisky bottle, she dared not think. Jack wasn't even Jack's real name. Jack's real name was Reginald. He had struggled unacademically through school with the Reginald millstone round his neck, and by the time he got to art school felt enough was enough. 'Jack' then had arisen out of the fact that in his squalid student flat, or, rather, succession of squalid student flats, his bedspread had been his country's flag, bought for coppers off a rag-and-bone man. So much talent and so little discipline, thought Victoria, watching Jack, who was frankly ogling Tessa, with one arm around Ellen's waist.

Ginevra studied them all. The only one she dared not look at was James, in case her face revealed her confusion. Alexander, who had found her description of the book she was writing absolutely incomprehensible, was helping his hostess with yet more drinks. When, Ginevra asked herself, are we going to eat? While working on her project she frequently forgot about food altogether, and suddenly found herself ravenously hungry. Victoria seemed to be in no hurry even though it was now nearly nine o'clock.

I really don't like Victoria very much these days, Ginevra thought. She does have a brain, though not a brilliant one, and yet she doesn't use it. I don't believe she ever opens a book any more.

Ginevra despised this. Her friend had had one of the best educations going and for all she had done with it might as well not have bothered. But Victoria was her conduit to James.

Standing by the steps, a rather isolated figure with a bowl of peanuts in one hand and a drink in the other, Ginevra turned her glasses next on Tessa. Tessa, in Ginevra's view, was a spoilt brat, and dim with it. On the other hand she had no pretensions to brains as did her sister-in-law. Ginevra wondered what it was like to be so ravishingly good-looking that men fell down before you, and couldn't begin to guess the answer to this. If I looked like her, thought Ginevra, I wouldn't be married to Kevin and stuck in Little Haddow. I might even be married to James. The very idea made her heart lurch.

'Do I gather from Alexander that you are writing a book?' The speaker was Ellen Carey. With an effort Ginevra switched her attention from her secret obsession to the more mundane.

'Yes, I am.'

'What is it about?'

Ginevra repeated what she had told Alexander.

'Interesting,' said Ellen, meaning it.

'I didn't think Alexander Lucas was very interested.' Ginevra was determined not to be patronized.

How prickly she is, thought Ellen, one eye on Jack who had disappeared off, presumably in the direction of the loo. She pictured his frustration as he searched his pockets for his hip flask which was currently in the bottom of her bag. Keeping her husband away from his whisky during the run-up to an exhibition was an art form all of its own. Any minute now he would erupt into the room and accuse her of spoiling his fun. Mentally preparing for his tantrum, she reapplied herself to the unpromising conversation with Ginevra.

'I so much admire anybody who has the discipline to write. It's something I've always wanted to do myself.' She could have added, And have at last embarked upon, after all those years of thinking about it, but, daunted by Ginevra's reputation for extreme cleverness, was too diffident to say so.

'Discipline of that sort has never been one of my difficulties.'

'Well, lucky you! I've always worked to deadlines,' said Ellen, 'and I need to. They concentrate the mind wonderfully.'

Ginevra, whose mind had never needed concentrating but automatically functioned in top gear where anything academic was concerned, couldn't think of anything to say to this. She was vaguely aware that Ellen was a graphic designer, doing mainly large, lavishly illustrated books, and could see that with two children around plus Jack – who was so time-consuming that he basically constituted a third – carving out time for Ellen's own career must have presented problems. Still, she had succeeded and Ginevra respected her for it in a way in which she did not respect Victoria.

Sensitive to Ginevra's social unease, and her extreme isolation, which was emphasized rather than alleviated by Victoria's dinner party, Ellen, with her usual generosity of spirit, decided to help her companion to enjoy what was plainly something of an ordeal. Light and easy, she began to tease the other woman out of her shell. Unaccustomed to so much undivided attention Ginevra was at first suspiciously unsure how to react, and then found herself relaxing into it. She took off her glasses and cleaned them with the cuff of her blouse. Looking at her without them, Ellen thought, She could look so much better than she does. Almost handsome, in fact. She's one of those women who has absolutely no idea how to make the best of herself. If only I could take her in hand.

It was while they were discussing village mores, and those of Little Haddow in particular that, looking over Ginevra's shoulder, Ellen saw Jack appear at the top of the garden steps. Muscular and compact, he exuded disappointment laced with menace.

'*À table*,' cried Victoria, who had seen him at the same time, and recognized the symptoms. Positioning herself at the foot of the steps, effectively barring his way, she began to organize the others up them one by one leaving Ellen until last. Nevertheless he caught her.

'Where is it?' hissed Jack.

'What?'

'You know what.'

'No, I'm not at all sure that I do.' Moving away from her husband's restraining arm, Ellen positioned herself where Victoria indicated, to the right of James.

Like a time bomb dinner ticked on. Jack smouldered. Victoria cursed herself for not serving the food earlier. Chin held high, Ellen studiously avoided her husband's eye and continued her conversation. She decided that she liked Ginevra who now that she felt at one with her surroundings was conversing with cogency and spirit. Ellen, who had to listen to a great deal of drivel from clients of The Gallery interested in buying Jack's paintings, and, indeed, more and more from Jack himself these days, appreciated this. Suddenly seeing why his wife kept up with her old friend from Oxford, James joined in.

At the other end of the table Jack decided that if he and his whisky were to be separated then he would enjoy himself in a different direction, and began to flirt very openly with Tessa. Tessa, who had been annoyed earlier in the evening by a remark of Alexander's and who had been sulking ever since, revived, and vivaciously reciprocated in kind. Victoria saw her dinner party sliding out of control and was at a loss as to what to do about it. The high level of tension was putting her off her *boeuf bourgignon*. Desperately, in an effort to take his mind off his wife's behaviour, she engaged Alexander in conversation. Talking to her, fine eyebrows drawn together, he glowered at his wife.

Impervious to this, Jack thought Tessa very fetching. He wondered what she would look like without her clothes on, not that she was wearing very many now. It was, he mused, a long time since he had painted a nude, and decided that he would like to paint Tessa. They had, of course, met before but peripherally at one or two of The Gallery's numerous private views. Jack wondered if he dared put a hand on Tessa's yard of bare thigh, currently conveniently covered up by Victoria's white damask tablecloth. Sizing her up he decided not to do this. There was a very unpredictable quality about Tessa.

Instead he said, 'You must visit the studio sometime. Come and see the work I'm preparing for the exhibition.'

'I'd like to,' replied she, putting down her pudding spoon and looking him straight in the eye. By the way she said it, there was no doubt at all in Jack's mind that they perfectly understood each other. Alexander stood up abruptly and left the table.

Sitting beside his empty place Victoria felt like throwing up her hands in despair. Damage limitation was now the name of the game. Her eyes rested on the Jack Carey, which was the only painting in the dining room and took up the greater part of one wall. It was amazing to Victoria that someone as dedicated to life's earthier pleasures as Jack could produce something so ethereal. Thickly painted in different shades of shimmering blue, putting her in mind of this golden summer, its soaring elliptical shapes induced an impression of shining limitless space. I wonder what he's producing for this latest exhibition, thought Victoria, and then mindful of past brinkmanship on Jack's part, I wonder if he has started producing anything yet. It didn't bear contemplating.

'Who would like some coffee? Let's have it in the garden.'

They were all, with the exception of his wife, standing up as Alexander arrived back. Without ceremony he handed Tessa her small gold sling bag.

'Come on, get up. We're leaving.' He looked furious. For a moment they all thought she might be about to make a scene, but to everybody's relief she did not. Meekly she rose and prepared to follow her husband. Lecherously watching her, Jack longed to stroke her small firm bottom, which was barely concealed by the tiny skirt. Tossing back her long mane, Tessa said her goodbyes. When she came to him, Jack slipped his card into her open bag. Past master at this, he was fairly confident that no one had seen him do it. '*A bientôt!*' said Tessa.

Feeling exhausted, Victoria saw the Lucases to the door. They all kissed each other. 'Sorry,' said her sister-in-law, without sounding very contrite. She followed Alexander down the front door steps, and Victoria could hear them quarrelling all along the street until the sound was lost in the King's Road traffic.

Sitting in the garden with a cup of black coffee Ginevra saw that it was 11.30. If she was to catch the last train to Little Haddow, she would have to go.

James said, 'I'll phone for a cab.'

'That's all right,' replied Ginevra, who couldn't afford a taxi and intended to take the tube from Sloane Square, 'I'll pick one up in the King's Road.'

They both saw her off, watching as she strode along the tree-lined pavement and then turned left and was lost to sight. As she walked, Ginevra thought about the evening. She had seen Jack drop his card into Tessa's bag and was fairly sure that Ellen had too, though she had made no sign that this was so. Perhaps Ellen was used to this sort of thing. After all, the Careys had been married a long time and were older than the Hartings. It was Ginevra's private view that marriages were either made in heaven or in hell and that there was not a great deal in between. It was hard to understand how Jack could prefer the vacuous Tessa to his own delectable wife, in spite of the age difference. Ginevra felt protective towards Ellen whose dignity and good manners had impressed her and whose intelligent interest had significantly improved Ginevra's own opinion of herself. Ellen, she saw clearly, was a lady. Jack was a slob.

The night was warm and still. Although the hour was late

there was still a fair amount of traffic about. Ginevra loved the city, and in particular the feeling that she was part of some huge pulsating whole, a sensation which she did not experience in Little Haddow. An outsider all her life, she felt herself to be currently outside both her Oxford circle and her marriage. Passing the darkened windows of Peter Jones without interest, she crossed Sloane Square and entered the Underground.

Half an hour or so later, sitting on the last train to pass through Little Haddow that night, Ginevra tried to analyse her own hopeless passion for James Harting. He was not, she knew, anything like as clever as she was, nor was he particularly original, but rather a purveyor of other people's originality through the medium of The Gallery. And although he was handsome in a predictable blond, English way, so were many others. In the end she was forced to the conclusion that her enslavement was due to the fact that he had taken her virginity all those years ago during an unsatisfactory encounter that she was pretty sure he did not even remember. It was hard to believe that such a symbolic yet uncaring act could be quite so potent, and the knowledge that she was in the toils of something she could not rationalize and therefore dismiss made the intellectual Ginevra feel uncomfortably vulnerable.

By the time the train reached Little Haddow she was the only passenger. Outside the station her bicycle stood in its concrete wheel block where she had left it. Unlocking the chain, she mounted and set off through the lanes towards the cottage. Riding silently along without lights, Ginevra felt herself to be a part of the violet country night, another animal going home to its burrow through the sweet-smelling summer fields.

Pear Tree Cottage was a lot less pretty than its name suggested. Badly in need of a paint, it stood several hundred yards outside the village proper and had once been the abode of a pigman, a dour individual who had lived there by himself until he died. Since it boasted very few amenities of any sort and had an outside lavatory, the Hayes had bought it for a song. Interestingly, since Kevin was in the trade, they had then made no improvements to it whatever but had simply moved in and started living there. This earned universal approbation, change of any sort being regarded with deep suspicion by the village in general. There was less enthusiasm for the neglect of the garden, which quickly became a riot of unpruned roses and rampant bindweed, surrounding and encroaching on an unmown lawn through whose straggling tussocks the postman had to trip in order to achieve the peeling front door.

Inside, the rooms were tiny with minute windows. It was the sort of house where cupboards had to be cut in half to get them up the narrow, steep staircase at all. Not that the Hayes appeared to have very much furniture, and with the sole exception of the bedroom at the back of the house, no curtains of any description appeared anywhere. In the stone-flagged kitchen Ginevra Haye simply carried on where the pigman (who had been less than fastidious) had left off, never even bothering to clean the grimy old Belling before commencing to use it, and, rather than sweeping out the kitchen daily in order to keep the mice at bay, she imported a tattered, one-eyed tom-cat from the Animal Rescue in the nearest town, whom she called Captain Morgan, and let him get on with it.

The cottage did not possess anything so convenient as an outside light and it took Ginevra some time to find her door key and then to locate the lock. Once inside, she kicked off the exercise sandals and found herself assailed by a famished Captain Morgan. Moving across the hall, she put her foot on a small, soft lump and, flicking on the light switch, discovered that she had trodden on a dead and headless mouse.

After Ginevra and the Lucases left the house, Jack's aggression seemed to drain away. He had, or thought he had, a half-bottle of whisky hidden in the Docklands studio, which was where he and Ellen were going to spend the night prior to her departure for the country the next morning, and on top of this his chase now had a very desirable beast in view. He looked forward with relish to his seduction of Tessa, and to the way in which, because she was so much younger than himself, she would listen to his opinions and defer to his views, something Ellen did less and less these days.

When they had eventually gone, Victoria poured herself a stiff gin and sat down to drink it and regroup. In the garden she could hear James gathering up the glasses and putting them on a tray, ready for Mrs Pond to wash up in the morning. Feeling quite drained, she sat staring into space for at least fifteen minutes before wearily getting up and going out to help him.

3

The next morning Ginevra awoke to what sounded like a muted pneumatic drill. Opening her eyes, she found Captain Morgan's ugly battered face close to hers. He was purring with a rasping intensity which made his whole body vibrate. Sunlight streamed through the open window and filtered through the dirty closed one, exposing the faded bedspread and peeling wallpaper in Ginevra's bedroom. She must have forgotten to draw the curtains last night. Outside in the old pear tree from which the house derived its name she heard birds singing. What time could it be? It was, in fact, eleven o'clock.

Eleven o'clock!

Pushing Captain Morgan off the bed, she got up, pulled on her dressing-gown and went downstairs. Last night's dead mouse was still in the hall, lying beside what looked like a letter from Kevin. Picking it up by its tail, Ginevra took the rodent to the kitchen, and dropped it into the swingtop rubbish bin. Then she went back for the letter.

Standing holding this in her hand without opening it, Ginevra thought about Kevin. She knew that as one of the brainiest girls of her year at university, her marriage had surprised her circle, and could almost hear them asking one another, 'What *does* she see in him?' In exactly the same way, his mates probably wondered what he saw in her. The answer to this question was a straightforward one. It was sex. From the outset of their relationship it had been apparent that Kevin, who liked Junoesque girls (cuddly, he called them), had a lot of stamina, and that she, Ginevra, had a voracious sexual appetite. Junoesque she may have been but cuddly she was not, though it was by no means certain that Kevin had ever registered this.

With her intellectual capacity for marshalling and facing even the most unpalatable truths of the sort most people prefer not to confront, Ginevra's reasons for tying the marital knot were perfectly clear. Indisputably she was a large, plain woman. Her sturdy, thickset image topped by a lard-coloured face and round tortoiseshell spectacles reflected in the mirror in no way contradicted this unemotional summing up. Ergo, she was never going to cut a swath through the male population, and until Kevin came along, apart from the one-night stand when she lost her virginity, she had had no luck at all. So the question she had to address was whether life with Kevin was preferable to life without anybody. Mindful of the gnawing hunger which had afflicted her before they met, to the point where, while working during the day, she had been more or less able to put this dreadfully primal urge out of her mind, but alone in her bed at night she could think of nothing else, Ginevra decided in favour of life with Kevin, with one caveat.

As long as I don't have to talk to him too much.

In the event, apart from the nights when Ginevra's carnal abandon slightly shocked Kevin, even while he was making the most of it, they tended to lead separate social lives, and when she went to see her Oxford chums, which she did reasonably regularly, he stayed behind or went to the village pub. This arrangement bothered him not at all. He privately thought of her friends as a stuck-up toffee-nosed bunch of over-educated idiots, and much preferred playing darts.

The advent of the Saudi job had rather upset this curious arrangement and they talked more about whether he should or should not go than they had in the course of the whole of their marriage. Kevin reckoned he should.

'After all, Gin, we need the money, don't we?'

'Yes. Yes, we do.'

And I need you.

'How long do you think you'll be away for?'

'Dunno. Six months maybe.'

Six months!

Observing his furrowed brow as he tried to do his sums with a stub of pencil which, in the course of a working day, normally perched behind his right ear, Ginevra thought, Half a year without someone in my bed every night will kill me. If he insists on going I'll have to make alternative arrangements. But what? It's not as though in these days of AIDS I can start picking people up in bars. She shuddered at the thought of such casual liaisons and their possible consequences.

In the end he had gone, leaving her with only Captain Morgan for company.

Pulling herself together, Ginevra finally slit open the letter.

Hello, Gin, commenced Kevin in his round, backward-sloping hand. Her mind's eye saw his red perplexed face as he wrestled with the problem of what to pen next after this promising start. Six halting lines about nothing in particular were the upshot, at the end of which he had signed his name and drawn a line of kisses.

Kisses. The physical ache which she had suffered since he left became an acute pain. There had been no indication in it as to when he might be coming home for a day or two, as had been promised, before returning again. And even if he did, what use to her was that, she who needed sexual servicing on a more or less daily basis? She supposed she must be over-sexed since this need which obsessed her did not, so far as she could discern, afflict most other people to anything like the same inconvenient degree.

Starved of physical love, she turned her thoughts, as she had more and more lately, in the direction of James Harting. James and Victoria Benson, as her friend then was, had been a celebrated student couple in her year at Oxford. Intelligent enough, they had possessed the elusive quality finally pinned down by the American nation as charisma, and had acted, debated and partied their joint way through university, eventually achieving an unremarkable second each before going down, after which they married. James had been very, very drunk following a Commem. Ball and a quarrel with Victoria when he had taken Ginevra's virginity, after which he had been violently sick. Being relieved of this so-called valuable commodity was for Ginevra a definite relief, though it was doubtful that James remembered anything about it. It was, Ginevra realized later, by which time she knew more about these things, a minor miracle that he had been able to perform at all. Regardless of this and his unattainability, Ginevra had remained secretly and unrequitedly in love and as the days of Kevin's absence accumulated, during solitary Pear Tree Cottage nights in the lumpy double bed she began to indulge in more and more sexual fantasies which all revolved around this secret obsession of hers. James the First, as she thought of him.

With a profound sigh Ginevra dropped the sheet of paper into the bin, where it rejoined the mouse, and put the kettle on for some coffee. Today, she decided, she would work on her book.

In the event she did not do this. Her customary concentration seemed to have deserted her, and she sat inconclusively in front of the computer screen for some twenty minutes without producing anything. On impulse she stood up and went to the bookshelves in the alcove to the right of the fireplace. Running her finger along the spines of the books, she stopped it at the one she was looking for. Sitting down at her work table, she moved the computer keyboard to one side, put the book down and, taking care not to crack the glue of its spine, opened it. It was large, hardbacked and empty, with a dark blue and red marbled cover. Ginevra was addicted to such notebooks. She loved the crisp, pristine white pages which invited her to write. Buying such blank books was one of her few extravagances. Taking up her fountain pen, she unscrewed the cap, wrote today's date, and then, rather to her own surprise the words: *My Darling James*.

Used as she was to the country, Ellen was an early riser. The studio was a vast, airy room with north light, and smelt of oil paint. The floor had been stripped, sanded and polished and the walls were white, the better to enhance whichever of Jack's paintings he might choose to hang there. A luxuriant green plant, which Jack normally forgot about and Ellen watered when she stayed there, reached green fronds towards the window from its position beside a chaise longue strewn with Indian cushions. Jack's easel, which he had had custom-built for himself and the large paintings that were his current mode, stood in the middle of the floor, surrounded by painter's paraphernalia. Several canvases were stacked along one side, but otherwise the signs of industry were few. At one end of this pleasant room a door led to a bedroom, bathroom and kitchenette. In the bedroom Ellen was putting the final touches to her eyes, outlining them with kohl before making a miniature painting of each with the same cloudy shadow that she had continued to use since her days at art school. Her husband, who had succeeded in finding his secret whisky supply the previous night before Ellen got there first and poured it away, was lying on his back swathed in the Union Jack and snoring. Ellen was wearing a long black skirt with a flared fitted jacket designed like an Edwardian riding habit, complemented by a pair of high-heeled leather ankle boots. Carefully she folded up last night's party clothes, stowed them in a small holdall, and then sitting on one end of the bed she wrote a note for Jack. *Jack!* said the note, *you were asleep when I left and I decided not to wake you. As you know, the boys are home from school at the weekend and we all look forward to seeing you at Butterfly Cottage. Love, E.* This she tucked between his inert forefinger and thumb, before quietly closing the door as she left.

In their small house in Fulham, Tessa woke up as unobtrusively as a cat and, looking at Alexander through her curtain of hair, realized that he was still enraged. He was lying staring up at the ceiling, hands behind his head, expression set. Tessa, who had been here many times before, knew exactly what to do. Straightening her legs, she pressed herself lightly along the length of his body, at the same raising her blonde head and inclining it onto his chest. Then starting with the muscular roundness of his shoulder she ran her warm hand with its cool wedding ring down his torso, stopping only to caress his nipple en route before locating his sex. The response, in spite of himself, was immediate. Tessa's talents had always been tactile rather than academic.

Alexander moaned softly. 'Oh, Tessa. It's no good, we can't go on like this.' His voice died away. Whatever she was doing was quite exquisite.

'I know, darling, I know, but let's talk about it afterwards, shall we?' said Tessa.

In the kitchen of the Hartings' Chelsea house Mrs Pond, Victoria's daily, was in the process of clearing up the mess of the night before. Disapprovingly she held up to the light one of the glasses (Tessa's) whose lipstick imprint was proving surprisingly hard to shift. Like most people, Mrs Pond did the things she enjoyed doing very well and tended to skimp the rest. She did not enjoy washing and polishing glasses. A small woman, probably in her sixties, with frizzy permed hair dyed an unlikely shade of red, and her own lipstick out of register with her mouth, she had become a rather unsatisfactory fixture in the house. On the other hand, as Victoria had found out to her cost, finding and then keeping reliable cleaning help in Chelsea was not easy. Mrs Pond liked dusting and polishing, and superficial hoovering, which meant that she only pulled the beds and sofas out once a year, and when she did the spitting and crackling which resulted as the Electrolux tried to digest the accumulated rolls of dusty fluff sounded like a forest fire. Styling herself a domestic, she liked cleaning the silver but couldn't be doing with the brass, deeming it beneath her. When she had first arrived bearing a somewhat lukewarm recommendation from another lady for whom she 'did', Victoria had pursued her round the house with Brasso and new Electrolux bags, but in the face of a mulish determination by Mrs Pond to do it her way, eventually had been forced to give up the crusade. Still it was better than nothing, and although she was a mediocre cleaner, Mrs Pond was at least a reliable mediocre cleaner.

This morning, after the tensions of the night before, Victoria did not feel up to the endless minutiae of Mrs Pond's discourse, and was relieved that her daily was incarcerated for the time being in the basement kitchen, rather like a mole in a hole. Funnily enough, she reflected as she brushed her hair, the only person to have acquitted herself well after her misgivings about inviting her at all had been Ginevra. And Ellen, of course. But then Ellen went without saying. Ginevra's performance last night took Victoria back to their university days when they had talked about anything and everything, and she, Victoria, had been much more intellectually curious than she was now. I really must make more effort, thought she. Read more.

Aloud, she said to her husband, who was tying his bow tie, 'You don't find me boring these days, do you, James?'

Surprised by the question, which it would have been more than his life was worth to answer in the affirmative, he said that he did not. And, in fact, he really did not. Changing the subject, he pursued the problem of Jack. With the exhibition only three months away, it was uppermost in his mind.

'Did you get the impression that Jack is working hard at the moment?'

'He was certainly working hard on Tessa. Apart from that, I couldn't say. Why don't you drop in at the studio and see for yourself?'

'I keep trying to, and he keeps putting me off.'

'Why not ask Ellen?'

'Ellen seems to spend most of her time in the country just now. She has some project of her own which is taking up a lot of her time. And, of course, without the discipline of her presence, Jack is liable to become shambolic.'

'Liable to! Jack *is* shambolic!'

James thought for a minute. 'What I might do is invite Ellen to a crisis summit at The Gallery to decide what to do about Jack and then take her out to lunch. She'll just have to drop whatever it is she's doing and nanny him until the exhibition's out of the way. What is she doing anyway?'

'No idea!'

'Well, it can't be as important as this.' The spectre of a Jack Carey exhibition without a single Jack Carey on show rose before his eyes. 'I'll ring her today.'

As though a flood gate had been released, Ginevra began to write, and opened up her heart to the blank, white page. What she wrote began as a mixture of fact and fiction, a welling up of wishful thinking emanating partly from her own acute sexual starvation and partly from her underground obsession with the oblivious James Harting.

Looking at you the other night, I remembered the Commem. Ball when our affair first began. As we made love you told me I was beautiful. Before penning this line Ginevra took a deep breath. But then, she thought, why not? This is my fantasy, nobody else's. And if I want to be beautiful within it for the first time in my life, why shouldn't I? It's the only chance I'll ever get. Pursuing the alluring image of a besotted James, Ginevra continued, *and you said you had always secretly adored me.* So why had he married Victoria? queried a persistent alternative voice in her head. *Honourably, you insisted on marrying Victoria, to whom you had been secretly engaged for a year. She, of course, knew and knows nothing of this secret liaison of ours. I cannot pretend that, through the years, I have not felt hurt and diminished by this deception, though I understand perfectly the reasons for it. Perhaps it is because of this that I have decided to chart in this notebook the course of our passion for each other, so that when you are with her I can still feel close to you, and enjoy you sexually in your absence through these pages.*

Rereading all this, she was interested to note the direction it had taken. She also noticed, stringent critic of her own work that she was, a rather Mills-and-Boonish quality about the prose which was very unlike her own style, but supposed that when she got properly into her stride this would disappear. And anyway what did it matter? After all she was writing for nobody's eyes but her own. Picking up her pen again, she launched into a very explicit and satisfying description of their first fuck.

4

After she left Jack, Ellen caught the train to Sussex. An unremarkable figure in London, by the time she got to the country her attire was attracting curious glances. At the station she took a taxi, which short of walking or waiting an hour for a bus was the only way to get home. When she arrived at the cottage Mrs Phipps had been and gone, and Ellen was grateful for the empty house. Going upstairs, she put her holdall in the large low-ceilinged bedroom she shared with Jack when he was there, but did not bother to unpack it. From the pine wardrobe she chose a low-necked flowered Liberty print smock and changed into it, putting the London suit back in its place. Feeling cooler and more at one with herself, she went to the kitchen where she filled up the kettle and put it on the Aga, and then, noticing that it was now lunch time, changed her mind and poured herself a glass of white wine instead.

Sitting alone on a loveseat in the garden, Ellen found herself taking stock of her life. Now thirty-six years of age, for the first time she frankly acknowledged to herself that what she had wanted at twenty-two was not necessarily what she wanted now. This disenchantment with her current situation had been incubating for some time, she recognized. And yet, thought Ellen, I am so fortunate. I have two sons, both of whom I love and like as well. Jack is now famous and for the first time we are not short of money. So what is my problem?

She let her mind range back over the years with her husband. They had met at Chelsea Art School where even in those early days Jack's extraordinary talent had been remarked upon. Ellen herself had been a gifted student but without his vein of genius, and had been content to be one of his flock of female admirers until he had singled her out. Even in the early days of their marriage he had been unfaithful. Then, as now, one of his favourite epithets had been the word bourgeois. Monogamy, pronounced Jack, was bourgeois. She must not mind his other women, said Jack, for she, the mother of his sons, was the one he loved. At the time, short of leaving him, there had not seemed to Ellen a great deal she could do about the situation. Sometimes, given his view of marriage, she wondered if he had only married her to spite her formidable and disapproving mother. When both of them were in the room together Ellen felt as though she was between the hammer and the anvil. Mrs Braithwaite insisted on calling Jack Reginald. It was, after all, she said, his name. Jack called Mrs Braithwaite the old bat, though not to her face.

As the marriage went on, Ellen's confidence grew. It became apparent that Jack needed its solid base and his sexual wanderings with nothing to wander from would not have had the same naughty excitement. When the boys were born with three years between them the pattern of things to come began to emerge. Jack had wanted to christen the elder one Merlin. Ellen, who now felt secure enough to put her foot down, baulked. 'No.'

'No?'

'No!' She sounded very firm. Uncharacteristically so. He hoped she was not going to make a habit of it.

'Why not?'

'Use your common sense. Can you really imagine a five-year-old starting school with the name Merlin Carey? It's just not fair, Jack.'

When the second child arrived he tried again.

'Casimir?'

'No!'

This time, heavily embroiled in a hot affair with his favourite model, for this was in the days when he still painted nudes, he really couldn't be bothered to insist. So in the end the boys had been christened David and Harry and the two cats of the day Merlin and Casimir, which seemed a satisfactory compromise. Still later there had been a rather similar exchange concerning which school they both went to. Jack found it almost impossible to make up his mind between Holland Park Comprehensive and a progressive and unstructured boarding school. Ellen had vetoed both. As far as the first was concerned she wanted the boys to board. It had become apparent to Ellen that when one took into consideration the inordinate amount of time she was forced to spend looking after Jack, who seemed to be getting more demanding as he got older, if she ever wanted to get back to her own work and carve out some time for herself this was the only way to do it. On the subject of structured versus unstructured she was equally down the line.

'But I want them to learn to express themselves,' proclaimed Jack.

'They can learn to express themselves later,' had been his wife's reply. 'For the moment I want them to concentrate on learning how to read and write. And anyway Mother is paying the school fees, and I can't see her allowing you to launch them into some progressive experiment with her money.'

This was indubitably true. Jack was then making his name but had not yet made it, and neither he nor Ellen could have afforded to put the boys through school. So they both went, courtesy of Mrs Braithwaite and her cash, to a traditional boys' boarding school where they appeared to thrive and neither showed any aptitude for, or indeed interest in, art of any sort. Perhaps they got enough of it at home. Jack secretly blamed Ellen for this but these days, as the balance of domestic power had almost imperceptibly tilted in her favour, was more circumspect concerning what he said to his wife, and kept these views to himself. Maybe he would get a chance to punish her with them at some later date.

So their marriage had ground on. And it was true to say, Ellen reflected, that despite his philandering and his thoughtless, chaotic progress, life with Jack had been fun in the early years.

It was hard to put a finger on when things had begun to deteriorate. The purchase of Butterfly Cottage, on which they had both agreed, had been the first hairline crack, because after it Ellen had not been quite so available, and had compounded this by announcing that she intended to resume work as a freelance designer. Jack was in two minds about this new development. On the one hand it meant that he could conduct his affairs with very little interference, but on the other hand the worshipping students with whom Jack habitually went to bed were mostly unable even to boil an egg, so that when Ellen was away, which was more and more, there was no one to look after him and his creature comforts. Selfish, had been Jack's verdict on this. Ellen was very, very selfish. He had been surprised at her. She remembered that he had tried to have a row about it, but she would not. Rowing was not Ellen's style. She had, however, been immovable and, baffled and maddened by such calm intransigence, Jack had gone out and got extremely drunk. This heralded a new phase in their relationship. She began to earn money and was surprised at the feeling of confidence and freedom this engendered. Ironically it happened at the point in his career when Jack hit the big time and at last, after all the years of scrimping and saving, they were no longer poor. Jack had pointed this out.

'There is no need for you to work,' Jack had finally shouted, feeling himself to be getting nowhere. She had taken no notice. It had become apparent to Ellen that whereas when they had met she had been totally reliant on, and dominated by, Jack, something approaching the opposite was now true. Even so, the thought of leaving the marriage was one that she had put to the back of her mind. The boys were only ten and thirteen, and on exeat weekends nearly always came to Butterfly Cottage, which meant that they did not see a great deal of their father. Unless Jack organized himself down to see them, as she hoped he would this weekend.

Even though the loveseat was in the shade of an apple tree, she had gradually become uncomfortably warm. This was one of those stifling, brash days of hot yellow and bright blue. Like those summers we used to have when I was a girl, Mrs Braithwaite would have said. Thinking of her reminded Ellen that her mother was due to turn up on Sunday for lunch, ostensibly to see her two grandsons. This would not be popular but Jack would just have to put up with it.

She became aware that the telephone was ringing. Draining her wineglass, Ellen walked into the kitchen, where the tiled floor felt cool beneath her bare brown feet, and picked up the receiver. It was James Harting. Listening to what it was he had to say, Ellen felt exasperated. She was sick to death of wetnursing her husband. At the end of his speech there was a long unnerving silence.

'Ellen? Ellen? Are you still there?'

'Yes, I'm still here. Look, I've just arrived in Sussex from

London and I honestly don't want to travel back again this week. I'm sorry, James, but you must appreciate that I do have my own work to do.'

'Yes, yes, of course I do, but couldn't you possibly make an exception? *Please*, Ellen.' His voice had a note in it which was closely akin to panic.

She had an idea. 'Look, I'll tell you what. Why don't you and Victoria come to lunch here at the cottage on Sunday? Jack will be around, but there's no reason why we shouldn't have a private talk. He'll be very taken up with the boys anyway as it's their exeat.' And she could have added that the presence of other guests would damp down the Braithwaite/Carey war and might even, if the combatants were feeling particularly mature that day, lead to good behaviour all round.

'What a brilliant idea!' He sounded pathetically grateful. Poor old James! And then, 'Oh Christ, I'd completely forgotten. We've got Tessa and Alexander coming to lunch.'

'Bring them along too.'

'Could I? Are you sure you don't mind? Thanks, Ellen.' Any minute he would tell her she was a brick.

'Why don't you plan to turn up at eleven thirty? And bring tennis racquets. We might as well make a day of it.'

'Marvellous! Absolutely marvellous! See you then.' He sounded altogether calmer, clearly sure that if he could only see her face to face he would be able to persuade her. He was probably right.

For a brief moment Ellen considered the prospect of Tessa's presence at Butterfly Cottage. She had seen Jack slip his card into the little gold bag. If Tessa was not already his mistress then no doubt she soon would be. Ellen was well past the days when she would have eaten her heart out over such an incident. The skewer of sexual jealousy, once so agonizingly painful, had been neutralized by time and custom and had lost the twisting power to stab her to the heart. In her bed at night she was no longer tortured by visions of Jack and his women and what they might be doing with each other. Sometimes it seemed to her that she had no heart left, but only a husk, so indifferent was she to her husband's excesses. Given this fact it really made very little difference whether Tessa came or not, though no doubt Jack would enjoy himself. Dismissing the subject from her mind, Ellen put on a wide-brimmed straw sunhat, unhooked a trug which habitually hung from a brass hook imbedded in one of the kitchen ceiling beams, and went out into the vegetable garden to pick some parsley and some chives.

In the Docklands studio, Jack woke up, groped around for his wife and, on discovering that she was not there, lay where he was for at least another hour thinking about getting up. When he did finally gain a standing position he slid his feet into a pair of moccasins and went in search of her.

'ELLEN!' roared Jack. No answer. He looked on the table in the kitchenette. No note. Finally he found it lying on the floor by the bed. Reading the message he felt sorry for himself. Who would make his breakfast? Returning to the kitchen he opened the fridge and made the depressing discovery that there was nothing to make breakfast with. So that was that. *Au naturel* apart from the slippers Jack cut the forlorn figure of an unministered-to male chauvinist. Without a submissive female in tow he felt reduced. Shambling through the studio, he sat down on the chaise longue where his reflection in the large old dressmaker's mirror that he and Ellen had bought years ago in Camden Passage confronted him. Considering his age and, more importantly, his life style, Jack was in reasonable physical shape apart from a slight paunch, and had probably achieved this by letting everyone who had anything to do with him do his worrying for him. Of medium height and muscular, with a pair of strong shoulders, Jack had what could only be described as a heroic head. Proportionally almost too large for his body, it was reminiscent of a Caravaggio and was crowned with thickly waving hair of a suitably painterly length.

The telephone rang. Eyeing it warily, for he was currently avoiding James Harting, Jack finally picked up the receiver and, preparing to be someone else if necessary, cagily said, 'Hello?'

'Tessa Lucas speaking.'

At the very sound of her voice he noticed with interest that his penis had slightly stiffened.

'You asked me if I would like to drop round and see your work and I'm phoning to say that I would.' She certainly didn't prevaricate. 'What about later on this morning?' Or waste any time.

'Sure,' was Jack's response, and then, ever the opportunist, 'When you come do you think you could bring with you a pint of milk, some bread, some butter and some Marmite?' He would have liked to add, 'and a half-bottle of whisky', but decided that he didn't know Tessa well enough to do this.

Sounding distinctly irritated, she said, 'Are you sure you wouldn't like me to do a week's shopping for you while I'm at it?'

Jack ignored this sarcastic shaft. 'What time do you want to come?'

'Eleven o'clock would suit me.' She did not, he noticed, ask if it would suit him.

'Eleven it is.'

Replacing the receiver, he realized that he now had a problem on his hands, since he had not yet got round to doing any work for The Gallery exhibition, and beyond a few preliminary drawings he had literally nothing to show her. On the other hand this was hardly the point of the exercise – at least he hoped it wasn't. Bearing this in mind it hardly seemed worth getting dressed, but he did anyway and in her honour even shaved and put on some L'Égoïste. Fishing around in the plan chest, Jack discovered some lithographs which he had forgotten about. He could display those. He supposed he really would have to get down to some serious painting pretty soon. Putting off James was getting harder and harder, and there were sounds of desperation in the copious messages from The Gallery which Jack found on his answer phone when he bothered to switch it on, which was hardly ever. The phone rang again and this time he let it.

Eleven o'clock came and went. He was beginning to wonder if she was going to stand him up, when there was a knock on the door. Opening it, he stepped to one side to let her in. Tessa was wearing a very short denim dress whose faded blue mightily became her Nordic beauty. On her feet were sturdy, rather biblical sandals and in contrast her manicured toenails were painted a vivid pink. There was no sign of any shopping.

By now very hungry, Jack said, 'Did you bring the food?'

'Oh, the *food*. No, I forgot.'

This was a disappointment, but one he would obviously have to rise above and it might not be the only one. Tessa had an air of containment about her. *Noli me tangere.* Jack began to see that this was only a preliminary skirmish and that he probably would not succeed in getting her into bed this morning. It looked like being a day of denial.

She wandered on into the studio.

'What a marvellous room!' Standing in the sunlight, she seemed to absorb it into herself, as though its golden radiance and her blondeness flowed in and out of each other.

Imagining her without her clothes, Jack thought, I'd like to paint her like that.

'Can I offer you anything?'

This was rash, since there wasn't anything. Luckily she said no.

'Where do you work?'

'Here, of course!'

'I only ask because there doesn't seem to be any about.'

'No. In fact I'm just about to start.'

Like Tessa herself, Jack spent a great deal of his life just about to start.

'What! You mean you haven't yet produced a single painting for the exhibition? James will have a fit! Does he know?'

'No, and I'd rather you didn't tell him.' Jack began to feel that this encounter for which seeing his paintings had been a flimsy excuse was getting out of hand.

She didn't answer, but changing the subject completely, said, 'What did you think of Victoria's dinner party?'

It was hard for him to remember through a Scotch mist what he had thought of it.

'It was all right. Ellen talked to Ginevra Haye for a lot of the time.'

Tessa grimaced. 'I can't think why Victoria keeps up with her. She's married to a bricklayer, you know. She's very clever. They met at Oxford. Ginevra and Victoria, I mean, of course, not Ginevra and the bricklayer.'

Jack, whose own origins were just about as humble as Kevin's, registered the fact that Tessa was a snob.

'Did you go to university?'

'Heavens no. I'm much too thick.'

Well at least she had no intellectual pretensions. Jack found clever women threatening. By now Tessa was sitting on the sofa leaning back against the ethnic cushions. One long leg crossed over the other had caused the minuscule skirt to ride up even further, exposing yards of bronzed thigh to Jack's lascivious gaze. He speculated that she might be expecting him to pounce and was asking herself why he didn't.

Tessa put an end to all this self-examination. She said, 'I may not be brainy, but I do know what I want.'

'Which is?'

She looked at him as if he was an idiot.

'You, of course. But not today. Today I have a hair appointment.' She stood up, repositioning the enormous sunglasses which had been resting on the top of her head on the bridge of her nose and picked up her bag, which was a small leather one with a gold chain. He didn't feel there was much he could do to stop her. At the door, she paused.

'Do you still make love to your wife?'

Tripped into truth, Jack, who normally told his mistresses that he did not, said, 'Yes, I do.'

'So do Alexander and I. Just so long as we all know where we stand.' She kissed him on the lips.

'*A demain*. Eleven o'clock again, I think, don't you? Try to be more organized next time. Get in a bottle of wine or something.' Blowing him another kiss, she went. She was clearly a very naughty girl indeed.

It wasn't until some time later that he realized she hadn't even seen the lithographs.

5

Sunday dawned promising to be another peerless day. This was useful because it meant that they could all eat outside under the white *ombrollone* which the Careys had bought one year on one of their Italian holidays. Sunday being one of Mrs Phipps's days off, Ellen had poached the salmon herself the night before and, having skinned it, was now in the process of decorating it with lemon and fronds of dill. Both her cats, who were not permitted on the work surface, patrolled the floor, watching hungrily. She completed her task by covering up the glaucous eye with a twist of peel and then carried the fish on its oval dish down to the cellar where the marauding animals could not get at it.

Returning, she consulted her check list. It was probably a good idea to lay the table next, especially with her exacting parent in the offing. Ellen had discovered long ago that her mother took up all her attention when present and consequently had got up early in order to get organized. Since Olivia Braithwaite had a reputation for leading with her chin, it was very important that her daughter should be free to calm down confrontation when it threatened to erupt.

A designer to the marrow of her bones, it was apparent to Ellen that with ivory-coloured tablecloth and napkins, the existing bowl of flowers would not do. Taking a pair of secateurs from the kitchen drawer, she went out into the garden to cut some more. Peach, cream and apricot roses would do it, together with some glossy evergreen. Getting the rose bed to flourish had been something of a problem since the soil in this area was very stony, and, on top of that, the heart of Mr Phipps, who did the gardening, was not really in flowers at all, which he considered to be drones, as opposed to vegetables which were useful. At this time of the morning it was cool enough to be enjoyable in the sun. Attended by her cats, Ellen selected her blooms, which still retained droplets of dew, and took them into the house. Consulting her watch she saw that it was already ten o'clock and decided to put some Bach on the record player, choosing the Brandenburg Concertos for mental fortification.

To this accompaniment, calmly and methodically Ellen worked on, and was just completing her preparations when she saw Mrs Braithwaite's taxi bumping up the lane. It drew to a halt. Noticing some sort of altercation taking place apparently over the fare and wanting no part of it, Ellen refrained from going outside to greet her mother, but waited to be summoned by a bossy double ring on the door bell.

Olivia Braithwaite kissed her daughter then, standing back, her opening salvo was, 'You're looking peaky, Ellen. I've always said you don't eat enough. Where's Reginald?'

'He collected the boys from school yesterday to take them to some London exhibition and he's bringing them down with him today. Mother, please, *please* don't call Jack Reginald. You know he doesn't like it.'

'Why ever not? It is his name after all.'

'Yes, but he didn't choose it, and, as I've just said, he doesn't like it.'

Dismissing the subject, Mrs Braithwaite said, 'There's nothing the matter with it. It's a perfectly good name. You had a great uncle called Reginald.'

Impossible to explain to her that names went in and out of fashion and, especially for an artist, Reginald was currently right out. Ellen gave it up.

'Can I get you a drink?'

'At eleven o'clock?'

'Of tea!' She's only been here ten minutes and already I feel like strangling her, thought Ellen. 'Or coffee, if you prefer.'

'Neither, thank you, Ellen. I shall go and sit down in the garden. Do you have a Sunday paper? And perhaps you would be good enough to bring me a glass of Perrier water with ice and a slice of lemon.'

A tall, stout, floral-printed woman with a chest like a bolster and a massive handbag on her arm, she made her way towards the open French doors. Feeling that a good scream might help relieve her feelings, Ellen made the drink and followed her out, collecting a newspaper as she went.

'I see you are expecting other guests.'

'Yes. I have the Hartings coming and the Lucases. Tessa Lucas is James Harting's sister.' It had occurred to her to ask Ginevra too, but in the end she had decided against it. For different reasons Ginevra was another person who needed careful handling, and Ellen felt that with her mother there as well she would be spread too thin to cope with this. 'I thought after lunch we could play croquet and maybe some tennis.'

At the prospect of croquet, Olivia Braithwaite's face lit up. Highly competitive, with enough beef to hit the ball very hard indeed, and not above cheating, she terrorized unsatisfactory partners. Jack had a theory that death must have come as a welcome relief to Lionel Braithwaite, poor bugger, since it had let him off being just that. Within the family but unknown to Olivia, the game was known as Cut and Thrust when she played it.

Hearing another car coming to a halt outside, Ellen went to see who it was, and found Jack putting his key in the door, while the boys unloaded. Hardly noticing that he had done so, Jack kissed his wife.

'Jack – ' began Ellen.

Interrupting, as was his habit, he said, without troubling to lower his voice, 'No sign of the dragon yet!'

'For God's sake keep your voice down, she's here.'

'Where's her car?'

'Being serviced. Mother came by train.'

'*She* needs servicing. Cheer her up a bit.'

'Jack, I want your assurance that you'll behave. She's an old lady, after all.'

'She's an old battle-axe. Where is she anyway?'

'In the garden. Now remember what I say!'

'Yes, all right.'

The boys rushed up to her.

'Hi, Mum.'

'Hello, Mummy.'

Hugs and kisses. There was no doubt about the warmth of their welcome.

'Good heavens,' said his mother to David, 'you are soon going to be as tall as I am! And you, Harry, are catching him up. How shall I ever discipline you? Put those bags in your rooms and then come on through to the garden.'

Sitting on the loveseat, Mrs Braithwaite was reading the business section of the *Sunday Times* through horn-rimmed spectacles. She raised her eyes as Ellen and Jack arrived.

'Granny Braithwaite,' said Jack, kissing her powdered cheek. Looking at her husband in disbelief, Ellen thought, You know she hates being called Granny.

His mother-in-law gave him a glittery-eyed look. 'Reginald!'

'I need a drink, Ellen.' Waiting for the inevitable 'At eleven thirty?' which did not in fact come, Ellen decided that she must be keeping her powder dry for later.

'Need?' said Mrs Braithwaite.

'Yes, need,' said Jack.

Ignoring them both, Ellen said, 'Would you mind coming and fixing your own, Jack, and getting one for Mother if she would like one?'

'At eleven thirty?'

'It's actually nearly twelve o'clock.'

Following his wife into the kitchen, Jack enquired, 'How long is she staying?'

'Only till tonight. She has to get back for some soirée or other.'

'Thank God for that. I've bought you a present, by the way.'

He must have got a new mistress. Perhaps he had succeeded in getting Tessa Lucas into bed already.

Here Ellen was wrong, because Tessa had in fact cancelled the next day's assignation with Jack, rescheduling herself for the following week, much to Jack's frustration.

No point in being curmudgeonly: 'How lovely! What is it?'

'A computer.'

A computer! Ellen, who had been tapping out a novel on a twenty-year-old portable, and who had always regarded herself as a Brontë when it came to the new technology, looked at her husband doubtfully.

'Jack, I won't have a clue how to use it. What sort is it?'

'It's an Amstrad. You've been typing and retyping for a year, and if you carry on with the Olivetti you'll still be typing and retyping in four years' time.'

'It must have cost a fortune! Thank you, darling.' She kissed him. 'Where is it?' It suddenly struck her that Ginevra Haye had said that she herself had just acquired an Amstrad. Perhaps she would agree to give Ellen a teach-in.

'Upstairs in your work room. I got the boys to take it up.'

Voices and laughter and her mother's stentorian tones saying, 'I can't *think* where Jack and Ellen have got to,' indicated that the Hartings had arrived, and possibly the Lucases with them. Jack, she noticed, looked fugitive.

Arriving in the garden with chilled Chablis and glasses, Ellen found that they had all introduced themselves, and even her mother appeared to have been seduced by the easy charm of the Hartings. Catching her sons, who looked as though they were both about to slide off, Ellen instructed them to wait on the guests, and, leaving Jack in charge of the drinks, a function he could always be relied upon to fulfil, she herself went back to the kitchen to make a mayonnaise and boil some Jersey potatoes.

Lunch was a relaxed and informal meal, and it was not until Mrs Phipps's Tenby cream arrived that James casually enquired of Jack, 'How's the work going?'

Aware of Tessa's green eyes watching him closely and praying that she would not let him down, Jack replied, 'Fine, fine,' in an expansive, vague sort of way.

Not deceived by this response, which rather confirmed his own fears, for after all he had known Jack Carey for five fraught years, James said, 'You do realize that it's only twelve weeks until the exhibition?'

'Of course I do. Don't worry about it. You know me, I won't let you down.'

That was the trouble, mused Victoria – amazed that he had had the nerve to make this speech and noticing that she had started to bite her nails again, a sure sign of a forthcoming Jack Carey exhibition, they did know him and that, given half a chance, he would. She looked in Ellen's direction, but Ellen's face was a careful blank. Tessa, on the other hand, seemed to find the whole thing amusing, though Victoria could not think why.

James pursued it. 'I don't want to disturb you while you are working, but I'd very much like to drop by the studio just to see what you've got so far. One evening, perhaps.'

'Sure,' said Jack easily. 'Let's fix it up next week.' He could see that he was finally going to have to get down to it.

Bored by the whole subject, Olivia asked, 'Who's for a game of croquet after lunch?'

Wondering why the entire Carey family, even including the insouciant Jack, looked suddenly apprehensive, Alexander said, 'That's a great idea!'

Mindful of previous games of croquet with Granny, David and Harry chorused, 'We'd rather play tennis.'

'Why don't you all start to walk over there now,' suggested Ellen, clearing away the plates, 'and I'll follow you as soon as I've thrown this lot in the dishwasher.'

Watching them go, and anxious to enlist her invaluable help in coping with the Problem of Jack, James said to Ellen, 'Shall we just let them get on with it while we have a stroll around the garden?'

'All right.'

Standing on the croquet lawn, Olivia Braithwaite sized up the talent, prior to selecting a partner. On offer were Alexander, Tessa and Victoria. Jack had declined to play in the interests of having frequent nips from his secret whisky cache which he kept in a tree near the tennis court. On balance she decided Tessa looked the most likely. Tessa would be able to achieve a good swing between those long legs, unimpeded by any skirt at all to speak of. There was also, she noted, a certain air of determination about Tessa which should bode well where winning was concerned.

'Tessa, you can partner me,' she announced. Recognizing her desire for her own way reflected back tenfold by Ellen's mother, who was clearly a master at it, Tessa complied.

'Reginald, could you straighten that hoop, please?'

Kicking it into position, and watching the laugh on Tessa's face at the same time, Jack thought, If she calls me Reginald once more, I'm going to lay her out with her own mallet.

'Thank you, Reginald.'

Gales of giggles from Tessa. On second thoughts he decided to vanish into the bushes for a swig of Scotch.

*

Walking around the paddock in which the Careys had once kept a pony in the days when the boys had been interested in riding, James was saying, 'After all, you know what the problem is, Ellen.'

How, reflected Ellen, could I not?

Aloud she replied, 'Yes, of course I do, but it doesn't alter the fact that I have my own little life to get on with.' This sounded more than somewhat tart, and the moment the words were out Ellen regretted them. After all, she liked James very much, and if it hadn't been for The Gallery she and Jack would still have been living hand to mouth in some disgusting one-bedroomed flat. The other thing worthy of consideration was the fact that their latest bank statement had arrived, bringing with it the depressing news that the joint account had very little in it.

'I'm sorry, I didn't mean that the way it sounded.'

'I know.' James smiled at her. He really was very handsome. 'Please say you'll help, Ellen.'

Taking a decision, she said, 'Look, if you can cope for the next two weeks or so while I sort things out down here, I'll undertake to come to London to concentrate his mind for as much of the time that remains as I can. But it really is the last time, James.'

She thought about adding, Because I'm seriously thinking of leaving my husband, and after that it really is down to you, but did not.

Having no idea that this was in her mind, James was puzzled by her obvious reluctance, since a successful Carey exhibition would bring in a very great deal of money which, no doubt, Ellen would enjoy spending as well as Jack. Still, whatever the state of the Carey family finances, he had achieved what he wanted and so decided to drop the subject before she changed her mind.

'Shall we go and find the others?'

'Yes, but let's have a quick diary session first, shall we, because the summer holidays intervene, and that means the boys will be home.' She extracted her diary from a carpet bag.

'Can't you farm them out?'

'They don't come home from school to be farmed out, James, they come home expecting to spend some time with Jack and me. It's called family life.' Bemused she thought, Of course

James and Victoria don't have any children yet, so he really hasn't thought through that sort of thing.

'What did you do other years?' He vaguely remembered Ellen being there most of the time.

'Other years, except when they were very small, I travelled up and down between London and Sussex like a yoyo, coping with them, coping with my work, coping with two houses and coping with Jack. For Jack, as I don't have to tell you, can't even look after Jack.' Just listening to herself, Ellen felt suddenly extremely tired.

Sifting through his diary, James was silent.

Opening her own, Ellen said, 'Got a pen? Okay. Today is the seventh. The boys go back to school on the tenth, which means Jack will be back in London from then on. I could come up on June the twenty-ninth for a fortnight, but then I have to be back here on July the eleventh to collect both of them from school for the summer holidays. The following week they are at home but after that you are in luck for the next fortnight, because Harry is going to sailing camp, and David is going to Greece with the school. So I could spend that period encouraging Jack, but I should have to be back from August the second until the fifteenth. After that, Mother is having them for a week, and then I shall need a day or two here to get them ready for school. Which takes us up to August twenty-sixth. And, according to my diary, Jack's exhibition opens with the usual private view on the first of September. By then we hope there will be something for everyone to look at.'

Fervently endorsing that, and writing it all down, James reflected that although it wasn't as much as he had hoped for, it was certainly better than nothing.

'Thank you, Ellen. Thank you very much. And if there is any way in which The Gallery could make life easier for you, like paying for extra help, you only have to say so.'

'Extra help wouldn't really solve my problem,' said Ellen, then, mindful that there might by now be a riot on the croquet lawn, 'Shall we go?'

As the game developed, Alexander Lucas was watching Mrs Braithwaite very closely indeed. He could have sworn that he had seen her cheating, but, because she was a mistress of the diversionary tactic, could not be entirely sure. As it was, with Tessa in tow, she was in the process of roqueting her way around the lawn, awarding herself one extra shot after another.

Able to stand it no longer, and, in spite of Olivia's advanced years, Victoria decided to mount a challenge.

'Mrs Braithwaite, I'm sure you're not allowed to do that!'

'Butterfly Cottage rules,' smartly replied Ellen's mother, undeterred, as, having hit Alexander's ball, she placed her own next to it and, securing this by means of her foot, with a mighty blow shot his into the rough.

'Your turn,' she said graciously to Alexander.

As he strode off towards the undergrowth, he reflected that Tessa, who was currently meekly following all Mrs Braithwaite's copious instructions, appeared to have been telling the truth when she had assured him that there was nothing going on between herself and Jack. Studying them together, and on the alert for any sexual vibration, he had been unable to detect one.

Reaching his ball, which was the yellow one and nestled treacherously in a small hole which might have been tailor-made for it, he called, 'When this happens we normally allow the ball to be placed a mallet's length inside the lawn!'

Currently, with Tessa's help, trying to knock the post into the iron-hard earth, Olivia assented grudgingly. In spite of its helpful point the post made no further impression on the ground and still slanted precariously, looking as though it might fall over at any minute. His mother-in-law looked around for Reginald, who was nowhere to be seen.

Catching Harry, currently retrieving a tennis ball which had shot over the wire netting, she ordered, 'Go and find Daddy, would you please, Harry.'

This was tricky. The whole family, with the exception of Granny, knew about Daddy's whisky bottle in the tree. Instinctively Harry recognized that now was not the moment to parade his self-indulgent parent in front of Mrs Braithwaite. He hesitated.

'Well, come along now. Chop chop!' She sounded very impatient.

Wishing his mother would reappear, he turned reluctantly in

the direction he knew to be the right one. On the way he stopped at the gate to the tennis court, ostensibly to hand his brother the ball which he would normally simply have thrown over, and in fact to ask David for advice.

'What am I going to do?'

'Go and look for him,' replied the more sophisticated thirteen-year-old, 'and then come back and tell her you can't find him.'

Eyeing his grandmother who was watching him, arms akimbo, he set off. As he disappeared among the rhododendrons, Mrs Braithwaite turned back to the game. Alexander had had his go and so had Tessa. Victoria knocked her ball through the hoop and prepared for her second shot.

'That was *hopeless*,' Olivia said to Tessa. 'Quite hopeless! Whatever made you do that?' With Tessa sulking, they played on. There was no sign of the return of Harry. Scenting insubordination, his grandmother decided to go in search of him. In the event it was not her grandson she found but her son-in-law, who was sitting on a tree stump apparently meditating.

In a hurry to get back to the game, for Tessa's judgement was clearly not all it might be, Mrs Braithwaite said imperiously. 'I need your help, Reginald. Follow me!'

Turning on the heel of her peeptoed shoe, she led the way back to the lawn. Jack, who was now very drunk indeed, followed her, weaving unsteadily. Attempting to negotiate his way around two of the hoops to address the problem of the post, which seemed to be exercising the old bat's mind, he caught his foot in one of them, and, as though he were wearing a suit of armour, fell rigidly and heavily, immediately passing out as he did so.

It was at this moment that James and Ellen arrived. A small awed group was standing silently looking down at her supine husband.

Stepping over him, Mrs Braithwaite remarked, 'It appears that is that for the day as far as croquet is concerned!'

It was plain to Ellen that it would require nothing short of the sort of hoist used to put the knights of old on their horses to heave her husband upright. She felt like stepping on him rather than over him.

'I'm afraid,' announced Ellen, 'you'll either have to play round him, or abandon the game.'

Gratefully, Victoria said, 'Oh, I think we should abandon the game. But what are we going to do about Jack?'

'Nothing. I suggest we leave him exactly where he is.'

Later that evening, back in Chelsea, Victoria said to James, 'You really have got a problem on your hands with Jack. It's the worst he's ever been. I honestly don't know how Ellen stands it.'

'Nor do I.'

'Does she think he has done any work at all?'

'She said she *knows* he hasn't. But there is something odd going on there. Ellen seemed distant, almost as though what he does or doesn't do is no longer any real concern of hers. Still, the main thing is that she has agreed to move to the studio and get him going.'

'You don't suppose she's thinking of leaving him, do you?'

Thoughts veering away from such a dire possibility, her husband answered a question with a question.

'Where would she go? Not home to mother I shouldn't have thought.'

Heavens, no!

On another tack she observed, 'Tessa seemed remarkably subdued.'

Knowing his sister much better than his wife did, James replied, 'Not subdued, merely biding her time before she pounces.'

'What! On Jack?'

'Let's put it this way, it was a day of lulling Alexander into a false sense of security.'

'Poor Alexander!'

'One day he'll throttle her,' said Tessa's brother. 'And she'll deserve it. Poets can be very violent.'

Wondering what evidence he based this on, Victoria enquired, 'What are you going to do about Jack?'

'I'm going to go and see him, but, short of breaking and entering, unless he lets me into the studio, there's not a lot I can do. I'm pinning all my hopes on Ellen.'

Feeling that he had had enough of Jack Carey to last him a

lifetime, and needing to blot out the memory, James walked across to stand behind the chair on which his wife sat, brushing her hair. Leaning over her, he stared at their faces reflected in the oval mirror. Dark and fair. Striking rather than pretty, brush suspended, Victoria smiled at her husband through the medium of the mirror. Suddenly craving the marvellous oblivion that making love to her gave him, he slid his hands over the smooth roundness of her breasts and touching her nipples felt them harden, all the time watching her reaction in the glass.

Kissing her neck, he murmured, 'Do you want to make love?'

Standing up and turning round to face him, statuesque as her robe slipped silkily to the floor, she said, 'Yes please.'

In Sussex, on the croquet lawn, Gulliver-like Jack woke up to find himself covered with ants and chilled to the bone. For a moment he could not think where he was, but did register the fact that he was very cold and – he felt his hair – dewy. Looking at his watch, he discovered that it was one o'clock in the morning. Where was everybody? Struggling to his feet, he discovered that he ached all over, and in an effort to keep warm started to jog back towards the house, which made his head throb.

From his bedroom window David saw him burst through the rhododendrons.

'Here he comes,' he said to Harry. Ellen had left the outside lights on and together they watched Jack's erratic progress up the hill, the optimistic jog having deteriorated into an uneven trot.

With trepidation Harry anticipated Daddy's eruption into Butterfly Cottage. It had been obvious that Mummy had been very upset, and Granny, who had left along with the other guests at six o'clock, hadn't been exactly tactful either. Harry loved both his parents, but this did not prevent him wishing that they were more like other people's.

'Shouldn't we go and fob him off?' he suggested. 'Stop him disturbing Mummy?'

'I think we should leave them to it,' said his worldly-wise brother. 'After all they are supposed to be grown up.'

Standing on the landing, they could hear their father having two shots at putting his key in the lock, succeeding at the third attempt. At least Mummy hadn't locked him out. Harry felt as though his stomach were in knots. It was true to say that his parents' marriage had always been an up and down affair, but he sensed that in some indefinable way it had gone one stage further than that, mainly because Mummy, who was normally the peacemaker, appeared to have lost patience with Daddy. Stiffly, their father began to mount the stairs, and they both fled noiselessly into their respective bedrooms.

Proceeding along the passage, Jack reached his and Ellen's bedroom door and turned the handle. This door was locked. Jack stood irresolute for a few seconds. Observing him through a crack in the door, Harry's heart was in his mouth. He hoped his unpredictable parent was not going to try to force his way in, which would have led to a row. In fact, Jack was no longer drunk enough for this sort of precipitate behaviour, and eventually turned and walked off in the direction of the spare bedroom.

Lying in bed awake, but with the light off, Ellen heard the handle turn and then, after a pause, steps receding along the corridor. Thank heaven he had gone. Unable to get back to sleep, she reviewed her options. The first was simply to leave. But what with? She supposed she could always raid the joint account, except for the fact that there was currently next to nothing in it. There would, on the other hand, be something in it if she could concentrate Jack's mind sufficiently on the forthcoming exhibition.

And then there were the boys. She was well aware that she was their anchor in the choppy, unsettling waters of her husband's irresponsibility. For the last two years she had earned nothing in the interests of pursuing her dream of writing a novel. Given the fact that an unsolicited book was a gamble which would probably never come off, maybe what she should do was abandon it and resume freelance designing. That way at least she could support herself, assuming her mother went on paying the school fees.

But then there was the problem of where David and Harry stayed during exeats and holidays and so forth. Presumably Butterfly Cottage would have to be sold, unless Jack was prepared to let her have it to live in while he retained the studio.

Ellen, who did not feel vengeful, had no desire to deprive Jack of that, or of anything else for that matter, but simply desired an honourable withdrawal. How to achieve this without ending up in the workhouse was the question. Jack was not mean, he was generous, which was one of the reasons the joint account cupboard was bare, but who knew how he would react to the news that she wanted a divorce? Ellen had heard legion stories of atypical behaviour in the face of such a proposal. Switching on the light, she suddenly saw that the thing to do was to ring old Edward Montague, a family friend and Mrs Braithwaite's solicitor until he retired five years ago. That way she could obtain some advice on her position without going public.

This left getting to sleep as the most pressing problem. She picked up Elizabeth von Arnim's novel *Vera*, which was one of her favourites, from the bedside table. Reading about the dreadful Wemyss always made her feel well off. Fifteen minutes later, still propped up against the pillows with the book in her hands, Ellen was asleep.

6

Ginevra arrived back from the village post office, which doubled as a wool and haberdashery shop, to find a letter from Kevin on the doormat. It was hard to generate much enthusiasm for this since what she really wanted was Kevin in her bed, rather than literary Kevin.

Slitting it open with a bread knife, she read, *Dear Gin, How are things with you? It is like an oven here and no sign of the job getting finished. They keep changing their minds.* 'They' must be the Saudis. *The food is fucking awful. What I wouldn't give for a steak and kidney pie. One of those ones from the Spar. I hope the money is going into the account every week.* It was. She had checked. There was a surprising lot of it. *I would like to get home for a few days but they say no chance at the moment. I miss you (you know what I mean!) Luv, Kevin. PS You can give that cat a kick from me.*

There followed the usual row of crosses. Coming from the inarticulate Kevin, it verged on eloquence. Normally Ginevra threw his letters away, but, in recognition of a sterling effort, this one she promoted by tucking it behind a chipped mug on the mantelpiece, which celebrated the wedding of Prince Charles and Lady Diana Spencer. These days, heavily involved in her paper affair with James Harting, which grew more and more explicit as time went on and which was proving surprisingly satisfying to her starved sexual appetite, she thought less and less of Kevin. Every morning with her customary discipline she worked on her thesis manuscript, and, unless travelling up to London to do some research, quite often every afternoon too. In the evening after her usual frugal meal, she got out the marbled notebook and, with a generous glass of brandy by her elbow, courtesy of the new healthy bank account, added in her careful, even script another few pages to what was rapidly turning into a Little Haddow Kama Sutra. That it was all fantasy made no difference to Ginevra's enjoyment at all. In fact this enhanced it, for what could he and she not do? In the pages of her own prose she felt, probably for the first time in her life, both loved and lovely.

Sitting in the play tree house designed for them by Jack and built by Mr Phipps, David and Harry savoured the early promise of another blue day. The leaves of the huge beech which, legend had it, dated from the time of Napoleon, formed a translucent green bell all around them, insulating both for the time being from the complicated world of grown-ups.

'Yesterday was a complete disaster,' announced David into the limpid morning air.

'What do you mean?'

'Don't be a dork! You saw what happened.'

'Mummy was very upset.' Harry, who adored his mother, tried to put out of his mind the memory of her stricken face.

'Mum *always* gets upset when Granny and Dad are together.'

This was true, and Harry, a sensitive little boy, more susceptible than most to the tensions which appeared to be endemic to adult life, fell silent.

His brother, who was a pragmatist very much in the Braithwaite mould, opined, 'I think Mum should leave Dad.'

Harry's heart contracted.

'Why do you say that?'

'Well, he makes her unhappy. And everything we do is done Dad's way. He never considers her. Know what I mean?'

'No! No! Not always! If Dad had had his way we would have been called Merlin and Casimir, instead of the cats!'

A two-minute silence ensued while they contemplated this awful near miss.

'Do you remember,' reminisced David, 'when Dad said he wanted us to call him Jack?'

Harry did remember. The whole thing had made him distinctly uncomfortable. It had been as though Daddy had wanted to make himself into a brother rather than a parent. Mummy had thought it a silly idea and had said so.

David, whose capacity to shock seemed to be almost limitless today, said, 'I think he's been having it off with that blonde. Tessa.'

Harry's heart looped the loop all over again.

'She's practically our age. And anyway she's married to someone else.'

Giving his little brother a patronizing look, David said, 'You really *are* a dork, aren't you? That doesn't make any difference to anything.'

'Why would he want someone else when he's got Mummy?' Harry thought his mother beautiful.

'All men do,' replied the thirteen-year-old man of the world.

When I get married I won't, thought Harry, saying aloud, 'What about women?'

'They don't count.'

'I think Mummy has more say than you think. And anyway, look at Grandma.'

Harry knew he had scored a point here. Mrs Braithwaite was a powerful woman, and deferred to no one, male or female. To his relief this shut his brother up for a short while.

Then David said, 'Do you think they do it together any more?'

Playing for time, although he was frankly baffled by his brother's drift, Harry asked, 'Who?'

'Mum and Dad.'

'Not sure.' Harry tried to sound sophisticated and then gave up on it. 'Do what together?'

'You know. Sex.'

Apart from a rather sketchy dissertation on the subject by Jack to both of them at Ellen's instigation, and some wildly erroneous information authoritatively passed on to him by his best friend at his prep school, Harry's knowledge of the subject was limited.

'Oh. I don't know. Aren't they too old?'

'Hugo Prendergast,' (David's best friend) 'says that after a certain age they do it with other people. His parents do anyway.'

Mystified, Harry asked himself: Why do it with other people when you've married somebody specially to do it with?

To his relief a fallow deer, hesitant and graceful, passed beneath the branches of the tree on its way to have a drink from the pond. Finger on lips, he pointed it out to his brother. They both stopped talking.

When it had gone, David said, 'Have you been reading Mum's book?'

Harry flushed. He had, of course. Evading the question he asked, 'Why? Have you? She told us not to.'

'Course I have. After all, she does leave it lying around.'

'What do you think of it?'

'Well, you know the way she harps on about no swearing and good manners? Her book isn't like that. And it's rude too.'

Harry had registered this fact as well, but had assumed that Mummy's novel was directed at other adults rather than himself, who shouldn't have been reading it anyway, and so had loyally suspended judgement.

Voicing what was really troubling him, he asked, 'If Mummy left Daddy, what would happen to us?'

'We'd stay with her. After all everybody knows Dad can't organize his way out of a paper bag.'

This at any rate was true, and was a relief. Harry, on the other hand, was an old-fashioned little boy who liked the idea of both his parents living togther, however unsatisfactory an arrangement this might be for them. Unquiet in mind, he began to negotiate the rope ladder.

'I'm going back to the house now.'

In spite of having had a disturbed night, Ellen rose early. Going in search of Jack, she eventually ran him to earth in her work room, where he was setting up the computer for her. Apparently penitent, he gave her a shame-faced look when she entered.

'Sorry!' said Jack.

'Par for the course, really, wasn't it?' replied his wife, unmollified.

'You shouldn't have left me there,' he accused. 'You should have woken me up.'

'Woken you up? You were practically in a coma.'

'I hoped we might make it up, and you've just thrown my generous attempt to do so back in my face.'

'That's not the way it looks to me! It seems to me that you've just delivered the most minimal apology I've ever heard, and then started telling me that your bad behaviour was all my fault. Well, I'm not having it! I was mortified, if you must know. And you've supplied Mother with enough ammunition to keep her going for years!'

Cheeks flaming with anger, Ellen, wearing a cheesecloth shift, her eyes not yet painted, suddenly looked absurdly young again, and very desirable as well as very cross. It took him back to the days when they had been students together, and he had first noticed and been attracted to her quality of repose, in an instinctive way recognizing that if he was ever to achieve anything he needed a centre of gravity, and that she might be the one who could provide it.

With a sudden rush of sad self-knowledge, Jack said, 'Ellen, what has happened to us? We used to be so close.'

'Only as close as you allowed us to be.'

She sounded defeated, remembering all those easy girls, and all the lonely nights, especially when the children had been small and she had been too poor to afford help and was tied to the house, while her husband enjoyed himself.

Soon, thought Ellen, he will begin to cry. Usually a man ended up imploring a woman not to cry. In their case it was the other way round and it was generally she who mopped up her husband's maudlin tears. Unable to face the prospect she turned on her heel and walked out.

Putting down the screwdriver with which he had so far achieved very little, Jack followed her along the passage and into their bedroom, one wall of which was dominated by a painting of his wife, regarded by himself as one of his best pieces of work. In it Ellen lay modestly naked on the chaise longue which now stood in the Docklands studio, her gravely beautiful face calmly observing the artist. Her right hand was in the act of removing a full-blown scarlet rose from a bowl of garden flowers which stood on the floor, and on the back of the sofa sat Casimir, her favourite cat, whose feline good looks reminded Jack of Ellen's own. The sight of this luminous oil revived in him the desire to paint. He suddenly saw with great clarity that Ellen was his muse and that without her he would probably accomplish nothing.

She was standing apart from him, looking out of the window. Falling on one knee beside her he took her hand, saying, 'Darling Ellen', as he did so.

Disregarding this extravagant gesture, she said only, 'Oh do get up, Jack!' Like a huffed cat she exuded prickly displeasure.

Faced by an intransigent woman, Jack employed the only

solution he knew, which was to take her in his arms. Ellen did not push him away but, to his consternation, burst into a torrent of weeping.

'Oh Ellen, don't cry. Please, please don't cry.' The sight of her tears unnerved him, for if his still centre, as he thought of her, could not fight the fight, how could he be expected to? Lifting his unresisting wife onto their bed, Jack slipped the cheesecloth shift over her head and began to make love to her with more gentleness and consideration than he had displayed for years.

Later, as they lay together, he stroking her hair, he thought, I shall never be unfaithful to Ellen again. And then, with an unwitting echo of St Augustine: but not yet. After I've had Tessa Lucas.

Kissing his wife, he whispered, 'I love you, Ellen. You know that. And I need you. You'll never leave me, will you? Promise you'll never leave me.'

Ellen did not answer.

Walking away from his office along the cool grey pavement of St James's in search of a sandwich for his lunch, Alexander Lucas mulled over his marriage. Intelligent and cultured, he had married an upper-crust primitive, which was probably one of the reasons why she was so good in bed. It had proved impossible for him to disentangle intellectually the two follies of infatuation and love. He suspected that he was infatuated with Tessa, but not in love with her, which might have made the whole thing viable. On the other hand, the thought of her in bed with somebody else caused him agonies of jealousy, a poetic emotion but, at the same time, a very inconvenient one since it often occupied all his thoughts and therefore frequently prevented him doing what he enjoyed most, next to making love to his wife, which was writing verse.

Though he had never actually caught her at it, Alexander was pretty sure that Tessa was unfaithful to him. Some days, no, *most* days, there was a satiated sheen about his wife which alerted him. Being almost sure was worse than being one hundred per cent sure since it meant that he felt obliged to watch her like a hawk whenever they went out together. Observing her flirt, as she had flirted with Jack Carey the other evening, made him wonder what on earth she did when he was not there putting a brake on the proceedings. It didn't bear thinking about. The intellectual side of his brain recognized that he should never have married her. Fucked her, yes, but married her never. For they had nothing in common. And what would be left of Tessa when her beauty had gone, a beauty so potent that it currently transcended the emptiness of her head? Nothing for her and even less for him.

O let not time deceive you,
You cannot conquer Time.

In his heart of hearts Alexander knew he should leave her now, his blonde Aphrodite, while she still had her looks and could marry somebody equally brainless, and before she destroyed, once and for all, all his illusions. And yet . . . and yet . . .

He wished that like the Hartings he had been born with an income of his own. An honourable and proud man, Alexander would never have dreamt of living on his wife's money, and so was forced to work in publishing, which was at least reasonably congenial, and write his poetry when he could.

After queuing in a small delicatessen, he bought himself a prawn and cream cheese sandwich and a can of beer, intending to have his picnic in the park. In his pocket was a small volume, a selection of the verse of W. H. Auden, whose work he very much admired and proposed to read while he ate his lunch. The grass was crowded with lunch time lovers, tourists and little old ladies walking shortlegged spotted dogs. It was very hot. Locating somewhere peaceful and shady to sit was clearly going to be difficult. Wondering, as he spent so much of his time doing, what activity his wife was currently engaged on, he eventually found a park bench inhabited by only one person, probably because he was talking animatedly to himself, and began to eat, shelving for the moment the problem of what to do with his private life.

Unaware that she was the object of all these troubled thoughts,

Tessa was wrestling with her own doubts concerning the marriage. Most of the time there was an uneasy truce, and even Tessa could see that this was not a marriage of minds but rather of bodies only. To her this did not matter, but it probably did to Alexander, she conceded. Why did I marry him in the first place? she occasionally asked herself.

Probably because he was attractively older than she was and elegantly cleverer than she was. Brought up within an intellectual family, as one of its dimmer members Tessa had felt almost obliged to hitch herself to brains in order to redress her own imbalance. And she had been flattered by his romantic view of herself and the way in which he had apparently equated, at the beginning anyway, beauty of face with beauty of character. Of course, when they met she had been younger and softer. Five years and a lot more affairs than that later on, Tessa had begun to wonder if this was all there was to it. A new lover assuaged this boredom for a while, but not for good. One day, no doubt, Alexander would find out about these sexual excursions and then, she thought, with a shiver of foreboding mixed with a frisson of perverse pleasure, the balloon would really go up. A very hot temper was one of Alexander's less lovely characteristics, and had often in their tempestuous relationship been provoked by Tessa, though never to the point where he had actually hit her.

Picking up the silver-framed photograph which sat on her dressing-table, opposite a similar one of herself, she studied her husband's face. With its Celtic combination of blue eyes and dark hair which brushed his shirt collar, it was an attractive though introspective face whose aquiline nose indicated a certain fastidiousness. Effortlessly stylish, there was at the same time a world-weary languor about Alexander, which in his role as poet became him. Together, Tessa knew, they formed an arresting couple. She also knew, or thought she knew, that he had never been unfaithful to her. The sum total, then, so far as she was concerned, was that she still found him attractive and sexually stimulating, so what was missing? For something was, otherwise why was there this constant compulsion to play away? Never very analytical, it did not occur to her to wonder whether her own inability to rise even marginally above the relentlessly physical had not atrophied her self and, in its turn, her marriage.

She replaced the photograph in its customary position, sprayed herself with scent and proceeded to get dressed.

Looking at her watch, she saw that it was already 10.30. Always a late riser, Tessa was never ready to launch herself into the day much before eleven. Getting out a fat, well-thumbed little Filofax, she dialled her sister-in-law's number, and on hearing Mrs Pond's corncrake tones said, 'Is Mrs Harting there?'

Knowing perfectly well who it was, Mrs Pond said, 'Yes, who is it?'

'Tessa Lucas, Mrs Pond.'

'I'll just get her, she's in the garden.' Throwing the telephone receiver down with an ear-splitting crash she shuffled off in search of her employer. Mrs Pond did not approve of Tessa, considering her hoity-toity, and it was with disapproval that she called, 'Mrs Harting! Mrs Lucas on the phone for you,' before returning and switching on the Electrolux.

Half deafened by the din, Tessa wondered how Victoria put up with her daily.

Arriving at the phone, Victoria shouted, 'Hello, Tessa, could you hang on a minute?' and then, 'Mrs Pond.' No answer, only the sound of the vacuum cleaner sawing on. 'MRS POND! COULD YOU PLEASE DO THE CLEANING IN HERE LATER.' The machine slowly ground to a halt, and Tessa could hear whipping noises as Mrs Pond, now in a temper, gathered in what sounded like fifty feet of flex.

'Thank you,' she heard Victoria say, and then with something of a sigh, 'Sorry about that. Where were we?'

'Nowhere as yet,' said Tessa. 'But I wondered if I could come and take lunch off you today.'

'Yes, of course. Any particular reason? Not that you need one,' she added hastily.

'I want some advice.'

'Not about your marriage.' Impossible to refuse, but nevertheless Victoria's heart sank. The roller coaster progress of Tessa's marriage was almost as exhausting to contemplate as the prospect of gearing up for another Jack Carey show.

'Yes, how did you guess? Anyway never mind about that, I really do need someone to talk to,' (Talk at, she means, thought Victoria, with uncharacteristic sourness) 'and you are such a good listener.'

Well aware that however good the advice she doled out, Tessa never took it, Victoria was not deceived by this, and suspected hidden agenda.

'Why don't you come at one o'clock? Mrs Pond will have gone by then. You'll have to take pot luck though.'

'That's all right, a lettuce leaf will do me. See you later.' She rang off.

Preparing a salad, Victoria reflected, Because Tessa does nothing, she always assumes that the rest of us have nothing to do either. I wonder what she really wants.

Over lunch this did not become immediately apparent. There was a certain amount of the usual grumbling about her husband's suspicious mind, and the fact that he did not pay enough attention to her.

'But, Tessa, he has to work. You know that, unlike you and James, Alexander has no private income. And if you're at a loose end, why don't *you* get a job?' Not at The Gallery though. Tessa under her feet at The Gallery would be the last straw. She need not have worried.

Tessa looked at her as if she was mad. 'Get a job? Oh no, I couldn't possibly. I have far too many other things to do.'

Like what, I wonder? Aloud: 'Couldn't you do some modelling? You could fit it around the rest of your busy schedule.'

The mild sarcasm implicit in this last suggestion was lost on her sister-in-law, who had not the faintest intention of doing any such thing. Suddenly very impatient with Tessa's evasion of all responsibility for her own problems, real or otherwise, and sensing that they were circling a very different topic, Victoria decided to go for the conversational jugular.

'Do you have *lots* of lovers, Tessa?' she casually asked, sipping her Frascati.

Frontal attack was usually Tessa's gambit and worked almost every time. Now she discovered that she herself was no exception to her own tactics.

'Yes I do. Oh shit, I didn't mean to tell you.'

Had Victoria said 'a lover' Tessa would probably have denied it, but her question somehow implied certain knowledge.

Trying to recover the situation as well as she could in the circumstances, she amended, 'Well, not lots exactly, and not all at the same time.'

'Who?' asked Victoria, carefully expressionless, aware that even the merest hint of censoriousness would dry up this astonishing wellspring of revelation.

Concentrating her mind with a frown, and pulling out the Filofax at the same time, Tessa began to tick off what looked like being a long list.

Listening to it (by now her sister-in-law was up to D in the address book), Victoria thought, It's amazing that she hasn't caught something awful. That's assuming she hasn't. Alexander will murder her if he ever finds out about this. He must never know – although given the length of her list it must be about the biggest open secret in town.

Noticing with relief that at least Jack Carey's name did not appear, Victoria swallowed and said, 'Do you think Alexander suspects?'

'No, I don't think so, though he is *very* suspicious. Flies into terrific rages when other men take any notice of me. Like the other night. Remember? He was really unreasonable.'

'Yes I do, and no he wasn't,' came the terse reply. 'Oh come on, Tessa, you must know there isn't a man on this earth who could sit by and watch his wife putting on that sort of blatant display without becoming homicidal. Between you, you managed to wreck my dinner party.' She did not mention Jack's role in all this. 'What's your intention? Just to go on as you are?'

'Well, lots of people do. After all, look at the Careys.'

'That's different. I think Ellen knows all about Jack's promiscuity and simply turns a blind eye. But, according to you, no such arrangement exists between you and Alexander. And take it from me, Tessa, if he finds out from somebody else, he's going to be very, very upset.'

Not liking the word promiscuity at all, though it had not actually been applied to herself, Tessa had to agree with this prediction. She pushed a slice of cucumber inconclusively around her plate.

'Perhaps I should tell him.'

'No! No, I don't think that would be a good idea at all.' Victoria felt quite panicky at the thought of the mayhem which would result from extreme honesty on a subject so sensitive to the male ego. 'If you want to freelance on quite such a grand scale, why don't you just leave him? No need to destroy him by telling him the real reason why you're going.'

For Tessa the conversation had taken a path down which she had not wanted to go. Her main aim in coming had been to see if she could extract information on the state of the Careys' marriage. Should her own marriage fold, the idea of being married to a famous painter, such as Jack was, appealed to Tessa. There would be parties and first nights and fun, and, like Jack himself, no one would expect her to be conventional the way they all did now. Looping back the shining veil of her hair, and unaware that Jack, like most male philanderers, applied one set of rules to himself and quite another to the women in his orbit, she decided that was what she would aim to achieve.

Watching her and unable to divine what she was thinking, Victoria felt as though she had trawled a promising field with a metal detector to find only a disappointing deposit of scrap iron. She had always assumed Tessa to have been unfaithful to Alexander somewhere along the line, but to have uncovered this Catherine the Great-sized catalogue of misbehaviour took her breath away. And with a Carey exhibition in the offing too. It occurred to her to wonder whether perhaps she shouldn't book into Forest Mere for a week in order to tone up for the fray.

Faintly, she said, 'It's very hot in here, wouldn't you prefer to sit in the garden?'

'No, thanks all the same, I think I'd better be on my way. You won't tell anyone else about this conversation, will you? Especially not James.'

'No, of course not.'

But of course she did. For Victoria to keep something like this from James would have been out of character, and, she decided, justifying her action to herself, out of order since it affected the rest of the family.

He arrived home that evening looking harassed. Pouring

him a glass of his favourite Chardonnay, she followed him out into the garden with her own gin and tonic. Sitting down, he loosened his tie and unbuttoned his shirt collar.

'Christ, it's hot!'

'Had a good day?'

'Not particularly. I had a fax from Maybrick this morning enquiring about the exhibition and what might be suitable for his museum.'

Harold Maybrick was an American collector who had purchased four of Jack's paintings already and was keen to buy some more.

'Whatever did you say?'

James shrugged. 'What could I say? I just played a dead bat. Said Jack was currently in the country, and that I planned to have a session with him at the end of the week, when he gets back. And that I'd ring him as soon as this had taken place.'

'But, James, the way Jack is carrying on that will be never.'

Feeling that he needed it, he took a deep swig of his wine. 'I know. But once Ellen's back things will look up. Anyway let's not talk about Jack. Frankly I don't think I can *bear* to talk about Jack.'

'No, quite. I don't want to talk about him either. I want to talk about Tessa.'

'Tessa?' Surprised, he looked at her. 'Why, have you seen her today?'

'She came to lunch. Now be a good rabbit and listen, and don't interrupt.'

At the end of it he was stunned into silence, then said, 'I've never heard of anyone being quite so massively unfaithful. But then Tessa never did do things by halves. I'm also amazed that reverberations of all this frenetic activity haven't reached Alexander. What do you think we should do?'

'Nothing to do. But I thought you should know, since it looks as though we may have a family explosion on the point of detonating.'

'Strikes me that Tessa's marriage, like an iceberg, has been conducted mainly beneath the surface. Hopefully she'll keep it that way. After all she's twenty-five. She's a big girl now, and with all the problems I've currently got with Carey I simply feel I can't get into it. I always thought she would drive Alexander mad.'

'It's possible she may leave him but without telling him why.'

'I should have thought that would have been a relief, poor devil. Was that your advice to her?'

'Yes.'

'Has she ever taken your advice on anything before?'

'No, never. Though she has wasted an awful lot of my time apparently listening to it.'

'Tessa's tough as old boots,' said her brother. 'Whatever happens she'll be all right. He's the one we'll have to prop up.'

'I'm not sure you're right. Underneath that languid air there is something quite steely about Alexander. And I think he would have left her in the end anyway. Tessa is like a fire in the blood, evanescent because there is no substance, nothing to go on burning. They should have had a hot affair instead of a marriage.'

'They had that too. Anyway, listen, I think I'm going to add the Lucases to the Careys and refuse to talk about them as well when I'm supposed to be relaxing.'

'Poor darling, why don't I get you another drink?'

He kissed her. 'I'll get you one.'

'No, *I'll* get you one.'

'You get me one.'

7

As had been arranged, it was Jack who drove the boys to their
respective schools on his way back from the country, leaving
Ellen clearing up behind them with the aid of Mrs Phipps.
Apprised of the timetable drawn up by James and Ellen, he had
worked out that it should be perfectly possible to conduct an
intermittent affair with Tessa, which would be very therapeutic
while he worked. And Ellen would look after him, so that there
would be Marmite in the cupboard and milk in the fridge. No
whisky, though, if she had anything to do with it. Maybe Tessa
could help out there.

The impetus to get down to some painting which had
manifested itself while he looked at his own portrait of his wife,
was still in evidence, though he inclined towards a nude of
Tessa, to start with, rather than the abstracts which The Gallery
was anticipating. Thinking creatively for the first time for
months, he let his mind range over the possibilities, and
kaleidoscopic colours and shapes began to form in his mind's
eye.

Sitting side by side in the back seat, both listening to
Walkmans through headphones, David and Harry watched the
countryside rush past them. It was Jack's intention to drop
David off first, and then Harry, who currently boarded at a prep
in London.

Bumping slowly over the sleeping policemen all the way up
the tree-lined drive to the fine Palladian house which was
David's school, Jack wondered *how* he should treat Tessa on
canvas. In spite of her youth, there was a sophistication about
her which put him in mind of certain of Lucas Cranach's
worldly Venuses. Perhaps he should portray her wearing a hat
and nothing else. The idea appealed to him though it was
possible she would not go along with it, and also raised the tricky
question, what sort of hat?

Parking the car in the headmaster's space, Jack got out.

'Dad! You can't park here.'

'I'm only going to be five minutes. Get your tuck out, could you?' Together they heaved it into the house. Fishing about in his worn leather wallet, Jack said, 'Here's a tenner, old son. Should help to keep you going until the end of term.'

'Oh! Thanks, Dad!'

They embraced, and Harry moved into the front seat of the car hoping that Daddy, who could be absent-minded about that sort of thing, didn't forget his tenner when the time came. He was still wearing his earphones. To the accompaniment of their tinny jangle, father and son drove in silent companionship the rest of the way to London. After he dropped off his younger child, Jack made his way back to the studio, stopping off en route to buy himself some Scotch and some food in that order.

Once inside, noticing that it smelt stuffy, he threw open the windows, remarking with appreciation how this altered the quality of the light, and then brushing past the drooping green plant, and causing it to send up a cloud of dust, he made his way into the tiny kitchen. Putting down his shopping, Jack poured himself a slug of whisky prior to unpacking it. He swallowed his drink down, then opened the fridge door. Within, right in the middle, was something which looked very like a shrunken head, with an aureole of hairy tendrils of mould flaring around it. Whatever could it be? Jack and the head stared at one another, and then he began to pack his purchases carefully around it, leaving an inch to spare between them and it. Getting rid of it himself never occurred to him. That was women's work.

After making himself a sandwich, he ambled back into the studio, dropping large wholemeal crumbs as he went. Sitting on the chaise longue, he switched on his answering machine. There were several messages. The first was a tearful one from his current mistress, about whom he had completely forgotten what with half term and his general lather over Tessa. It appeared that he had stood her up. Outside a cinema. Racking his brains he vaguely recalled some arrangement to go to the MGM in Baker Street.

'I didn't even *want* to see that film,' quavered the voice, dissolving with grief and then reforming only to dissolve again. 'I was only going to see it because *you* wanted to.'

He wondered how to tell her that she was now redundant. Jack was a coward where matters like this were concerned. It would have to be a letter, he decided, otherwise, as he knew from past experience with others, she would clutter up his answer phone for weeks on end with lachrymose messages.

He passed on to the next.

'James Harting speaking,' said the voice. 'Wednesday, six p.m. I tried to reach you in the country, but you must have already left. Maybrick came through from America and wants to know what's in the pipeline. So do I, come to that. Could you make it a matter of top priority that you ring me first thing tomorrow so that we can set up a meeting, preferably at the studio, during the course of which I can see what you already have?'

Jack despised Maybrick, though this did not extend to the Maybrick dollars. Knowing what Maybrick liked, which was his minimalist stuff, Jack thought, I can knock off two of those in a morning. Perhaps I should do that tomorrow. At least it would shut them all up for a while.

The last communication of any interest was from Tessa.

'Hello, Jack, or should I say Reginald?' (Minx!) 'Time we got together, don't you think? What about tomorrow morning? Not too early though. I really am incapable of getting out of bed before ten. Shall we say twelve? *A demain*.'

Forgetting all about the Maybricks, Jack went and selected one of his prepared canvases. Tomorrow he would fuck Tessa, and then he would paint her. Or maybe the other way round.

That same evening Alexander and Tessa went to a party. Tessa loved parties. Alexander preferred dinner parties. It always seemed to him that at drinks parties no communication of any sort took place except at the top of one's voice, which was exhausting. Since Tessa only communicated on the most superficial level anyway, this bothered her not at all. She seemed to know a great many of the people there, which was more than he could say he did. Multitudinous men came and kissed her, one or two giving him speculative looks as they did so. Noticing this, Alexander was at a loss as to how to account for it.

Bringing Alexander into this milieu was a calculated risk, but it had been either that or not come at all. Tessa was in her element. In sparkling, sequined black bustier, and the usual bandage, though tonight it was a black satin one, she cruised the room followed by interested looks.

When he finally caught up with her, Alexander said, 'Whose party is this, Tessa?

'I'm having such a good time I feel as though it's mine.'

'No, seriously.'

'Honestly, I'm not sure. I was asked by Charlie Inchcape over there, but I don't think he's giving it.'

Alexander noticed that she said 'I' not 'we'.

'Where did you meet all these people?'

Scenting a jealous scene in the offing, Tessa said blandly, 'Oh, round and about you know, round and about. Why don't you come and meet Charlie? He'll know all about it.'

Alexander followed in her spectacular wake, wishing he was anywhere but here.

'Charlie!'

'Tessa, darling!'

In the ridiculous modern fashion, a much longer embrace than Alexander thought strictly necessary took place.

Finally extricating himself, Charlie said, 'You haven't introduced me to your friend.'

'This isn't my friend, this is my husband. Alexander Lucas, Charlie Inchcape. Charlie Inchcape, Alexander Lucas.' Tessa was aware that this sentence had not come out as she intended.

'Your husband?' He looked very surprised. 'I didn't know you . . .'

'Yes, my husband.' Tessa gave him an intense, loaded look.

Charlie's eyes flicked around the room and then back to Tessa. Both men noticed at the same time that the third finger of her left hand was bare.

'Where's your wedding ring?' Fine dark brows drawn together, Alexander sounded accusatory.

'I must have taken it off when I washed my hands. It must be in the bathroom at home.' The ring in question was family jewellery, formerly the property of Alexander's great-grandmother, and had a large fine stone which tended to get in the way. Tessa had formed a habit of taking it off when she made love, as her husband well knew.

Hell and damnation, she must have forgotten to replace it at the end of that afternoon's dalliance. It must be still sitting in Sam Jessop's flat. He was supposed to be coming here tonight, though looking round the room Tessa could not immediately see him. It was just possible that he would have had the wit to bring the ring with him.

Anxious to find him as soon as possible in order to retrieve it, Tessa realized that she would have to shed Alexander for a while in order to do this. At the same time she was unwilling to leave him talking to Charlie.

'Would you mind getting me one more drink, darling, while I go off to the loo? And then I think we should go, don't you? Bye, Charlie.'

Firmly she steered her husband in the direction of the bar. Leaving him there, she trawled the room which was large and by now very crowded, and eventually she found Sam sitting on the stairs, talking to a brunette. He did not look very pleased to be interrupted.

'Hello, Tessa.'

'Sam, have you got my ring?'

As he raised his hand she saw that he was wearing it on his little finger. Noticing out of the corner of her eye Alexander approaching with two glasses of red wine, she said urgently, 'May I have it?'

The ring was very distinctive, and it would be catastrophic if he saw it in its present position. For an awful moment it looked as if Sam was not going to be able to remove it. Tessa was just about to say, 'Never mind, forget it, I'll get it some other time,' when he succeeded. She just had time to drop the emerald into the same little gold bag into which Jack had dropped his card before her husband caught up with her.

'This is my husband, Alexander,' said Tessa.

Her husband?

'This is my fiancée, Celia,' said Sam.

His fiancée?

Slipping her arm through that of Alexander, she announced, 'I'm afraid it's hail and farewell, we're due somewhere else for dinner, aren't we, darling?'

How did he propose to explain away the emerald ring to Celia, she wondered.

'Are we?'

'Yes, we are.'

They left. In the taxi, going home, she noticed he was very silent. From experience Tessa knew that he was either composing a new poem, or that he was absolutely furious. The way he slammed the door after them left her in no doubt.

Going into the bathroom he said, 'It isn't here!'

'No, I found it. In my bag. Look.' Fishing out the emerald, she put it on her finger. Then, in an effort to get off the vexed subjects of wedding rings and tonight's party, and on to the commonplace, 'What would you like to eat? What about an omelette? Or shall we grab a snack in the King's Road?'

'I'm not hungry.'

His expression, she saw, was thunderous.

'It seemed to me that a lot of men at that party were very surprised at the news that you are married. Especially Inchcape. Is he your lover?'

The sight of his black-browed, aggressive anger caused all lofty ideas of confession that she might have entertained to evaporate. Victoria had been right. Normally a very civilized man, Alexander's rage when aroused was almost uncontrollable. Heaven knew what he might do if she said yes.

On rather firmer ground than she easily might have been, for Charlie was one of the few who had not been, Tessa haughtily protested, with justified conviction, 'Of course he isn't. How could you suggest such a thing? Sometimes I think you don't trust me at all.'

'Too bloody right I don't!'

This finished Tessa's high-minded resolution to attempt to turn away wrath with a soft answer.

'How dare you speak to me like that!'

'Bitch!'

'Bastard!'

Swinging back her hand to slap him, she winged their wedding photograph, which toppled and fell, glass smashing, into the fireplace. Trying to defend himself, Alexander caught her wrist swinging her round as he did so and causing her to lose her balance. Together they fell onto the sofa and then toppled off it onto the floor where they rolled over and over, still struggling. A good tennis player and swimmer, Tessa was surprisingly strong. Biting and kicking and scratching, she suddenly became aware that her husband was no longer fighting her but kissing her so savagely that it was hard to tell the difference. Peeling off the bustier and the skirt, as one might skin a perfect peach, and with them her silk knickers, he drove a massive erection very hard between her long polished bare legs. By now wearing nothing but a pair of silver high-heeled shoes, Tessa began to enjoy herself.

In Little Haddow it was so hot that even Ginevra, who would not have described herself as an alfresco person, had been forced out of the house into the garden. Since this meant being without the computer, she was sitting on a very old-fashioned striped deckchair of the sort that graces English seaside resorts, with her notebook and pencil on her lap and a fraying sunhat on her head. Used to operating within the airtight confines of the tiny sitting room, Ginevra found working like this to be surprisingly noisy. There was an air of commotion about the country which was distracting. Bees buzzed, birds sang, trees rustled, and the rookery was particularly raucous. In the midst of all this uproar, Ginevra was peripherally aware of the eye-level flighty progress of butterflies and the indefatigable industry of hundreds of ants around her Dr Scholl sandals. It was very hard to concentrate. In the end she decided to put the book aside, and take the day for what it was. Sensing her capitulation, Captain Morgan jumped onto her lap, and, after deeply scratching one tattered ear, settled down there, purring loudly at this unaccustomed privilege.

Absently stroking his coarse fur, Ginevra surveyed her small estate. Starred with celandine, speedwell, campion and butter-cups, the grass was now so long that it was in danger of turning into hay. In what remained of the borders, the roses were fighting a rearguard action against greenfly. Looking at the cracked, parched earth, Ginevra thought, I feel as dry as this ground on which I'm sitting. The only time I feel stimulated and at one with myself is when I am writing at night in the marbled notebook. And that is nothing more than a mirage in the middle of my own physical desert, at the end of the day.

She suddenly became aware that the telephone was ringing. The Pear Tree Cottage phone, which was of the old-fashioned black variety, had a curiously hesitant bell. It began and then faltered apparently uncertain of its own ability to transfer a voice hundreds of miles through the ether.

Plucking the receiver from its perch, 'Ginevra Haye speaking,' said Ginevra loudly, compensating for the machine's insecurity.

'Ellen here, Ginevra. Ellen Carey. I haven't rung at an inconvenient time, have I?'

It was interesting, noted Ginevra, that no man in her experience ever asked this particular question, but all assumed that if the time was right for them, it must be right for her.

'No, of course not.' An image of Ellen as she had last seen her rose before Ginevra's eyes. Graceful, pretty Ellen, but more to the point, *kind* Ellen. All too often a dismissive quality emanated from the beautiful and successful towards those less favoured than themselves. Almost as though they considered themselves to be a caste apart.

'Am I right', Ellen was saying, 'in thinking that you work on an Amstrad? Because if so it's just possible that you may be able to help me out. Jack has just given me one, and since I'm not a child of the computer age, I don't have the remotest idea how to even start. I do have a daunting pile of instruction books, however.'

'Most of those are specially designed to drive first-time computer users to drink! May I ask what you are going to use it for?'

'Yes. I'm writing a novel. Nobody outside the immediate family knows, by the way, so I'd be grateful if you could keep it under your hat. It's unsolicited, so it will probably never see the light of day anyway. What I intend to do is to have a shot at the computer by myself first, using the idiot's guide that they thoughtfully supply along with the main book. At least that way I'll get some sort of grip on the basics, but if and when I run into the sand, I wondered if I could come and see you for a teach-in. I know you are busy, and that it's a lot to ask, so do feel free to say no, Ginevra. I shall understand.'

And she would have understood too, reflected Ginevra, for that was her nature.

Heart lifting at the prospect of a visit from Ellen, she said, 'No problem. In fact you'll be word processing more than computing, and once you get the hang of it nothing could be easier. Or more convenient,' she added. 'What is the number of your Amstrad?'

Ellen had had the forethought to write this down. 'PC1640 HD30.'

'Brilliant, it's the same. If you like I'll come to you.'

'Oh no, I wouldn't dream of putting you to the trouble. Look, leave it with me for the present. When I've got as far as I can, I'll give you another ring, if I may, and perhaps we could sort out a day. I really am enormously grateful, Ginevra. Thank you.'

When she had rung off, Ginevra sat for a few minutes staring out of the window and thinking how much she would like to be able to claim Ellen Carey as a friend. It suddenly brought home to her how lonely her current existence was.

I really am turning into a solitary. If I'm not careful, before I know where I am I'll be one of those mad women shunned by everyone who talks and gesticulates to herself in the street. And it will all have happened without my being aware of it.

On impulse, putting the kettle on for some coffee, she decided to go to London soon, during the course of which she would combine lunch with Victoria Harting with a visit to the library for some research. It would do her good to get out of Pear Tree Cottage.

Waiting for Tessa to arrive, Jack had become almost business-like. Before painting her he had decided to execute some preliminary sketches. Nothing had been done about the May-brick paintings, nor had he contacted James Harting. The studio still had a neglected, slightly forlorn air about it, and would have until Ellen appeared in a week or so to sort it out and employ a new cleaner. Remembering Tessa's instructions, he had placed a bottle of white wine in the fridge, and for the first time since he arrived, made the bed. He hoped she would not put him off yet again. She did not, and, unusually for her, arrived right on the time she had suggested. She was carrying a bag, which she handed to Jack.

'It is already cold,' she said.

Examining the contents, Jack found a bottle of champagne, which drink he normally referred to as cat's piss. It did not seem politic to use this term today, however, and making suitably grateful noises, he placed it in the fridge, where it reposed to one side of the shrunken head. It was a pity it wasn't Scotch. Clearly he would have to educate Tessa.

Going into the studio, he was astonished to find that she had taken all her clothes off and was standing immobile in the centre of the room, a gilded unselfconscious figure enveloped in the sun which poured like molten gold through the window. Jack was momentarily dazzled. Her body, for all its slimness, had a voluptuous quality about it, probably because her breasts, which were round and high, were rather larger than the current ectomorphic fashion dictated. To Jack she was like certain bronzes he had seen, and his painter's eye registered a fluidity of line that was quite breathtaking.

The telephone began to ring. Without taking his gaze away from Tessa, he waited until it subsided, and then took the receiver off its cradle and left it off. It was probably James Harting.

'Where's the champagne?'

'You want me to open it now?'

'Absolutely! Why do you think I brought it?'

Emerging eventually from the kitchen, he handed her a glass.

'To us!'

'To us!'

'Do you want to paint me first, or fuck me first?' enquired the blonde goddess. Reflecting that he had never got anywhere near taking the initiative with Tessa, and disquieted by this fact, Jack was tempted to say, 'Paint you first,' but, lacking the strength of character necessary for this, said instead, 'Are you always this forthright?'

'Always. If you know what you want, what's the point in beating about the bush?'

Jack, who had never beat about the bush much either, but had never until now met a woman who did anything else, was forced to agree.

'But before your next move, assuming you are going to make a move, I should like some more champagne.'

When he returned she was no longer in the studio, and he found her in the bedroom standing looking at an engraving which Ellen had bought in some junk shop or other. It was entitled at the bottom, on the left, *Venus Gratiarum artibus exornata*, elucidated on the right as *Venus attired by the Graces*. In it a fleshy Venus reclined with a rather silly expression on her face, a fact that Ellen had not failed to point out, while one of the Graces placed a jewelled fillet in her hair, another tied her sandal and a third clipped a bracelet on her wrist. Between her open thighs stood Cupid, who had dropped his quiver full of arrows at her feet, and who was helpfully proffering an earring. The Graces, though bare breasted, were as dressed as they were probably ever going to be, but no one had as yet got round to putting any clothes on Venus herself, except a wrap of some sort which, while it covered nothing else, was artfully draped to conceal her pubic hair. At the top of the chipped, gilt frame someone – Ellen, presumably – had tucked a large burnt-orange silk rose which looked as though it might have adorned somebody's wedding hat at some stage. Tessa was full of approval for this sybaritic scene.

'*That* is how I should like to live.'

'It's from a painting by Guido Reni,' announced Jack, momentarily distracted from the task in hand, as he handed her the refilled glass of champagne. With the amount of ministering he was doing, he was beginning to feel like one of the Graces himself.

Lying back luxuriously sipping it, Tessa said, 'Well, come on then.'

She was, he soon learnt, enormously inventive. This came as a surprise to Jack, who had assumed that at her comparatively tender age he would have something to teach her. Disconcertingly it seemed that the opposite might be the case. At the end of it all, sated, they lay side by side, not touching each other.

Suddenly noticing the time, Jack said, 'I'd like to make some drawings before painting you.'

'Yes, all right. Where?'

'In the studio. The light is better.'

As he worked, he marvelled at her complete lack of inhibition. Such relaxation affected his own drawing, and produced a purity of line which he had possessed in his art school days, but which he thought had long since deserted him. By no means thin enough to rival a Klimt model, Tessa nevertheless expressed on the page, through the medium of himself, a similar dissolute sexual vibrance as old as time itself, which, going hand in hand as it did with her youth and beauty, had enormous power.

'Why do you stay with Alexander?' Jack asked, rapidly sketching her as she lay, legs apart on the chaise longue.

'I need someone to look after me, I think,' she replied vaguely.

Like hell she does, thought Jack.

'Why do *you* stay with Ellen?'

Opening his mouth to say, 'In spite of the way it must look, I still love Ellen,' Jack closed it again, the words unspoken. He knew that without her he would be unable to work, and with Tessa he would be equally unable to work. There was a rampant selfishness about his new mistress which was set fair to overtake even his. So, like the others who had gone before her, although indubitably in a class of her own, Tessa must perforce remain an unofficial delight, and when she became too demanding, as in Jack's experience they all did sooner or later, he hoped he could rely on Ellen's presence as his wife to see her off. But not yet.

At last, he said, 'We go back a long time, Ellen and I. I have come to depend on her.'

'Same thing then really,' pronounced Tessa. Getting up, she began to put on her clothes which consisted of the tiniest pair of knickers he had ever seen and what looked like, and in fact was, a man's white shirt which she clinched at the waist with a brass-buckled belt. Sliding her narrow painted feet into leather sandals, she began to search in her bag for her car keys.

'I must go.'

'Must you?'

'Yes.'

'When shall I see you again?'

'Not sure. I have a very busy week ahead of me.'

Replacing the telephone receiver, which he had forgotten about until now, and watching her leave, still firmly in charge, Jack thought there was very little he could do about it, though as the door closed softly behind her, it did occur to him to ask himself if he wasn't perhaps playing with fire.

8

Several days after his fight with Tessa, Alexander still felt ashamed of himself. She, on the other hand, seemed unaffected by the whole episode.

Perhaps, he conjectured, watching her as she brushed the honey blonde fall of her hair, humming to herself as she did so, she likes being insulted and then thrown to the ground and raped.

It was characteristic of their marriage that they had not talked about the incident since it happened. Tessa had not brought the subject up because her practical outlook recognized that whereas she should have been outraged by his use of force, she had, in fact, rather enjoyed it. She supposed she could still have objected, but did not feel disposed to do so. Water under the bridge was Tessa's view. Alexander had not raised the subject because of the remorse and guilt he felt at the way in which he had treated his wife. He simply felt he could not talk about it. Since she was never up in the mornings when he left for the office, they met for the first time each day at dinner, during the course of which they were scrupulously polite to each other. Afterwards she watched interminable television soaps, to which she appeared to be addicted, and he sat in his study, trying to write his poetry and failing. He felt depleted and sometimes it seemed to him that it was his wife who plugged into him and siphoned off his energy.

At the end of a week of it, on 19 June, he rang his old friend Marcus Marchant with whom he had been at school, and whose first marriage had been as unsatisfactory as he currently felt his own to be, and suggested lunch.

Sitting in the cool shade of a tree in the back garden of a fashionable Chelsea restaurant, he talked. Listening to him, Marcus, whose sharp ears had picked up some gossip about Tessa on the social circuit, was only surprised that none of it had as yet reached Alexander himself. Knowing her fairly well, he had immediately recognized her particular combination of beauty, stupidity and driving will to be a lethal cocktail. And whereas it was clear to Marcus that the Lucases probably should separate, it was equally clear at the same time that the moment was not yet ripe for this to happen. Alexander was still obsessed and would need to catch his wife in the act of being unfaithful, rather than just suspecting it, so that he could conclusively cut the cord that bound them and get on with his life with someone who was more suitable. Unlike Marcus himself, who had cynically observed his own first wife's infidelity for years before finally getting round to doing something about it, Alexander was a romantic.

'Do you ever see Diana these days?'

'Occasionally. As you know, we don't have children in common, only a childhood, so there really isn't any need.'

'Has she remarried?' Alexander had lost touch with Diana since the divorce.

'Yes, to a pompous prig called Philip Gresham.'

'I've heard of him, haven't I?'

'Probably,' said Marcus, sipping his wine. 'He's a well-known psychoanalyst, who opines on radio and television when he isn't mentally dissecting his patients. He put her together again after the riding accident and the divorce. He practically breathes for her.'

Getting off the subject of his first marriage, which no longer exercised his mind much at all these days, he said, 'Do you *want* to go on being married to Tessa?'

Alexander briefly brooded. 'Yes. No. I don't know. The problem is that while I recognize that she's no good for me, I still can't get her out of my system. I think of her constantly when she's not with me, and wonder what she's doing. And yet,' he added, emotion crystallized by the frankness of the question, 'most of the time these days I really don't even like Tessa very much any more. So how do you explain that?'

Marcus observed, 'Quite easily. You are in the grip of a fixation, though judging by what you've just said, taking the first steps to detachment.' Then, uttering a great truth, 'And there will come a time when you absolutely do know whether you want it to carry on or not. Until that happens there is nothing to be done. If you anticipate it you'll only crucify both of you by endlessly leaving her and going back to her again, until you finally do go for good,' at the same time reflecting that by all accounts Tessa's behaviour was now so indiscreet this looked like happening sooner rather than later.

'You're probably right.' Alexander sounded resigned. And then, changing the subject, 'How's Jane?'

'Pregnant again. You really must come to Marchants for a weekend. It's far too long since you last stayed with us.'

'I'd like to, but with all the emotional detritus we are currently carrying with us, it really wouldn't be very relaxing for you. Besides which, as you know, Tessa isn't very keen on the country. Prefers to set up her deckchair in Harvey Nichols.'

'Come on your own. Sit in the summerhouse by the lake and write some poetry. We rebuilt it after the hurricane, you know.'

'I'll think about it.'

Later, as they drank their coffee, Marcus enquired, 'What's happening on The Gallery front?'

'Limbering up for another Jack Carey, God help them.'

Out of nowhere the thought came to Marcus: Tessa and Jack has to be an affair waiting to happen. The day those two get together there will be spontaneous combustion. Unaware of his own clairvoyance, he drained his cup, at the same time signalling for the bill.

Sitting in her work room in the country, with all the windows thrown wide open, Ellen and the computer faced one another. It appeared to be impenetrable. Jack had promised her that it would revolutionize her life by lightening her load, and to date she had wasted two whole days on it and was no further forward. Jack's a fool, she thought crossly and ungratefully, and I'm a fool for listening to him.

There were six manuals in all, two for the printer, and four for the computer and its keyboard. So far Ellen had managed to display the disk manager, but such sophisticated exercises as opening a file and creating a document were proving elusive. She was amazed at the extent of her own frustration. The manuals seemed to have been designed to confuse the issue further, rather than elucidate, and every step Ellen looked up appeared to refer her to yet another part of another manual. Sighing with irritation, she thought, *If David and Harry were here they would sort me out.*

Aloud she said to the intransigent Amstrad, 'You're a brute, an absolute brute, do you know that?'

Oh heavens, now I'm talking to it as though it's a human being. Soon it will be organizing the house, picking the boys up from school and, hallelujah, running Jack. The one thing that won't be happening is my book.

Steeling herself she reopened the tutorial manual, and by the end of the morning had not only wrested a file out of the computer, but had succeeded in giving this a name. It was when she came to try to format a disk that Ellen met her Waterloo. It was not that the manual was incomprehensible, but rather that following the instructions did not appear to produce the desired effect. After three or four fruitless attempts to master it, and becoming aware of creeping paranoia, she abandoned the attempt.

What is the matter with me? I'm a reasonably intelligent person, I have the instructions, which wouldn't even stump Harry, and still I can't do it.

Deciding that achieving something printed would improve morale, Ellen turned her attention to that instead, resolving for the moment to stay with the hard disk.

She typed, *I will learn to use this bloody machine even if it kills me!* At that moment the telephone rang. Stretching out her arm to lift the receiver, she inadvertently leant on the keyboard, pressing who knew what keys, and sending the screen into spasm, at the end of which primadonna-ish tantrum it threw up the message *ERROR IN*, and thereafter stubbornly refused to do anything she asked of it. The phone call was a wrong number. By now the urge to throw the computer, printer and instruction manuals (especially the instruction manuals) out of the window was almost overwhelming. Feeling that she might be about to burst into tears, Ellen exiled herself to DOS (what was DOS, anyway?) and rang Ginevra Haye.

In the event the Little Haddow telephone broadcast its hesitant ring to an empty house, for Ginevra was in London that day, having lunch in her pleasant Chelsea garden with Victoria Harting.

*

'Tell me about the Careys,' Ginevra was saying.

'Well, you knew them slightly already, didn't you?'

'Very slightly.'

'What can I say? Jack was an infant prodigy, and at the age of thirty-nine still is. He is a marvellous painter, when he isn't squandering his time and his talent elsewhere, and, in my view anyway, a case of arrested emotional development. He philanders.' Victoria said this rather in the way she might have said, 'He collects stamps.'

'What about Ellen?'

'Ellen's rather mysterious. I've known Ellen for years, but the shallows, I suspect, rather than the deeps. She has never, to my knowledge, complained publicly about Jack, and has always been on hand up until now to discipline him into actually doing some work. This time, though, she was altogether less co-operative, saying that she had her own project on hand and therefore couldn't guarantee to spend as much time as usual on Jack.'

Without mentioning the novel, since she had been asked not to, Ginevra observed, 'But Ellen *does* work. She does freelance design.'

'Oh, but she will bring in peanuts compared with the sums Jack can earn.'

'What does that matter? That shouldn't invalidate what she does.' Ginevra suddenly felt irritated. If people were to be measured by the amount they earned, rather than their potential, what hope for anything creative but untried ever seeing the light of day? Like her own book, for instance.

Aware that she had upset her prickly friend, for the atmosphere had become glacial, but unsure how to correct this, Victoria soldiered on. 'You talked for a long time to Ellen at the dinner party. Did she say anything to you about it?'

'Not really. But I couldn't help noticing Jack flirting with Tessa Lucas.'

'Everyone flirts with Tessa.'

'He slipped his card into her shoulder bag as she was leaving.'

'Oh no! Are you sure?' Victoria was visibly upset.

'Absolutely sure.'

'Did Ellen see it?'

'Yes, I think she did.'

Rallying, Victoria said, 'I'm positive it doesn't mean a thing.' Would it were so! 'Gentlemen's cards rain down on Tessa like confetti, wherever she goes.' And not just cards either.

'Really?' Feeling envious, Ginevra sounded dismissive.

'Yes, really.' This was said starchily. Victoria felt thoroughly unsettled by the story of the card. Remembering that Ginevra was her guest, she followed it up with, 'I'm sorry, Ginevra. I didn't mean to snap. It's just that if Jack takes his eye off his easel now we'll *never* get an exhibition out of him.'

And what of Ellen in all this, reflected Ginevra. Nobody cares. They just use her. Victoria, who used to have great generosity of spirit, really has become a silly, selfish woman, unable to think beyond her own interests. I think marriage has addled her brain.

Concealing her contempt, she asked, 'What are you going to do when it's all over?'

This was a question Victoria had been asking herself. It was all too easy to fritter away whole days, and nothing to show for them at the end. Perhaps children were the answer. She found herself wishing she had the same intellectual ardour for her subject, which had been History, as her friend had for hers.

'I might go for another qualification. Art History would be useful.' Her voice trailed away. They both knew she would not.

'After all, you don't have to do anything.' Ginevra took off her glasses in order to polish them, and stared at her chum. Without them her eyes revealed more than they otherwise would have, and Victoria was conscious of a sudden jolt, like a small electric shock. In the depths of them was a spark of something inimical. It might even have been hate. Unnerved, she looked away, and when, seconds later, she looked again, Ginevra had replaced her spectacles and whatever it was Victoria had seen was once again veiled.

Feeling uneasy she stood up.

'It's really very hot out here. Shall we go inside for coffee?'

Standing in the kitchen as she made it, they talked about the absence of Kevin. Unable to ask the question to which she most wanted to know the answer, namely why on earth did you ever marry him, Victoria said instead, 'He's been away quite some time now, hasn't he? You must be missing him.'

'No. No, I'm not.' This was delivered so unemotionally that it had the ring of truth. It was difficult to know how to respond. In the end she decided not to do so directly.

'Does he write very often?'

'No, not very. Writing anything above the level of a bill has always been a struggle for Kevin.'

Silence.

Stickier and stickier.

'Do you want him back?'

As an effort to ginger up a flagging conversation, this failed dismally since it was greeted with the lacklustre response, 'Not particularly.'

It is beginning to sound as though Kevin is about to receive his marching orders, thought Victoria with interest. That is, if he has the wit to find his way home from Saudi Arabia.

'You'll probably feel differently once he's home.'

Thinking of James Harting and the exotic sexual athletics between the pages of the red and blue marbled notebook, Ginevra was sceptical.

'I don't think so.'

'Don't you think you should write and tell him how you feel? I mean it seems only fair.'

Ginevra, who had already said more than she intended, as had Tessa before her, nodded absently. 'Maybe.'

They went upstairs, Victoria carrying the coffee on its tray. Mounting behind Ginevra she was able surreptitiously to look at her watch. Two o'clock. She had a desperate desire to get out of the house, and out of this conversation, which had the feeling of something not quite right about it, as though it were operating on two levels at once.

Pouring out the coffee, she said, 'When we've finished this, I really must take Ho out for his walk. Why don't you come with us to the park?'

At the mention of the word walk, Ho put back his ears and whimpered his way into his basket, where he lay very still, hoping that she would forget. Labrador-sized walks, when his short, fat legs became a blur in an effort to keep up with his mistress's fast, heedless stride, were torture for him.

To her inexpressible relief Ginevra refused.

'Thanks all the same, but I really do have to spend some time in the library.'

Her eyes rested on the framed wedding photograph of James and Victoria. She had been there, eating her heart out in the background. Standing looking at it, she experienced one of the internal dialogues which were becoming more frequent these days. The voice of fantasy averred, If Victoria were no longer there, I could have James Harting. This was countered by the voice of sanity saying, No you couldn't. You know he isn't interested in you. Fantasy continued, If you want things enough you can will them to happen. Never underestimate the power of the mind. This at any rate was occasionally true, though whether it applied in this case was doubtful. The voice of sanity said as much.

Watching Ginevra's immobile, entranced stance, Victoria was struck by it. I really do believe that living in Little Haddow is affecting her mind, she decided. Ginevra has always been eccentric, but just lately her behaviour has been getting odder and odder.

Putting down her cup with a clatter in order to break the spell, she briskly announced her intention of getting Ho's collar and lead.

'Who's coming walkies with Mummy?' she enquired stepping over his basket.

He rolled his eyes at her.

Listening to this Ginevra thought, No wonder that dog is as daft as it is if that's the way she talks to it.

She could hear Victoria rummaging around downstairs in the kitchen. Noticing a coloured silk scarf lying stranded over the arm of one of the chairs, on an impulse she could not explain Ginevra picked it up and crushed it into her bag. She recalled having seen it before but could not think exactly when. It must be something Victoria wore quite often.

She was about to put it back when Victoria reappeared. They walked downstairs together, Ho dragging his feet. On the hot June pavement they said their farewells.

'You are sure I can't give you a lift anywhere? I'm going to Battersea Park.'

Ginevra declined. 'But thank you for lunch. I enjoyed it. I'm rather too isolated these days.'

Reassured by the fact that she had at least recognized this, Victoria replied with a return of her old affectionate manner. 'My pleasure, Ginevra. You know that. Let's be in touch.'

They kissed and went their separate ways.

The week prior to his wife's return to London found Jack well into his portrait of Tessa. He had abandoned the idea of the hat in the end, preferring to paint her as she was, a very modern young woman. A bit too modern he was beginning to think sometimes, still conscious of being a step or two behind her all the time. Jack liked country-and-western music, preferably played very loudly. Today's choice was *The Tennessee Stud* which he sang at top decibels, along with the record. Eyeing Tessa's long golden limbs and mindful of the colour of her eyes, he thought, She has the nerve and she has the blood, she's my Tennessee mare. It is doubtful whether Tessa would have appreciated this description, even though, coming from Jack, it was in fact a compliment of a high order.

'Can't you turn that racket down a bit?' she shouted. She herself preferred heavy metal, another bone of contention between herself and Alexander, who was a classical music lover.

'Do try to keep still!' He decided to ignore her request, or, better still, pretend he hadn't heard it.

Wearing nothing at all, except her distinctive emerald wedding ring, she was sitting on the chaise longue, and half reclining against the embroidered cushions. Rather than tackle it head on, Jack had decided the whole thing worked better as a composition from one end of the chair, so the portrait, which was large, was vertical rather than horizontal. Tessa's legs were wide apart, and while one foot was on the floor, the other was on the chaise itself with one polished knee drawn up to her chest. This left nothing to the imagination at all, but then, Jack reasoned, neither did Tessa herself. In one hand she held an apple out of which she had taken a bite, and whose sharp green echoed that of the emerald. Tessa had complained about the apple, which was probably a Granny Smith.

'Couldn't you have chosen something sweeter like a Cox's Pippin?' she had said.

'I've chosen it for its colour, not its gastronomic excellence. Anyway, it suits you!'

She looked mutinous. It occurred to Jack that she had been complaining ever since her arrival at her usual hour of eleven o'clock. Perhaps they should have a break. On the other hand he wanted to press on since it was important that he finished the painting before Ellen's arrival. He would also need somewhere to store it. He was inclining towards giving the whole exercise another half-hour before adjourning for lunch, when she took the decision out of his hands by standing up and stalking into the kitchen. Watching her smooth, unselfconscious progress, he was reminded of long-necked graceful African girls who glided along with terracotta pots on their sculptured heads. This was probably one of Tessa's more useless talents too.

'Oh yuk!' he heard her exclaim. '*What* is that?'

She must have opened the fridge door.

The head had grown as the days had passed, and was threatening to take over the inside of the refrigerator. He had meant to do something about it before she arrived and had forgotten. She shut the door with a bang, having first extracted a bottle of white wine between finger and thumb.

'You'll have to go out and buy some food. I can't be expected to pose on that chaise longue all day if you don't feed me properly.' She bit into the Granny Smith.

Jack was annoyed. 'That's the one I was painting, and you've just eaten it!'

'So what? How old are you? You must know what a green apple looks like at your age!' She was plainly now in a very bad temper indeed.

Unwilling to get onto the vexed subject of age since his next birthday was forty, and aware of the fact that time was slipping away, Jack said, placating her, 'I'll go down to the corner shop.'

'And then you must clean the fridge. I simply can't bear the thought of sharing the kitchen with that grisly relic. It makes me feel quite ill.'

Letting himself out of the front door, burning with martyrdom, he reflected, It will be a miracle if this painting ever gets finished.

All the same, even if he said it himself, it was looking very, very good. He felt he had managed to display Tessa's predatory, youthful beauty, and that he had admirably succeeded in producing a character study of his subject as well as an accurate physical depiction.

When he let himself back into the studio twenty minutes later with a carrier bag full of groceries, it was to find that she had gone. Before doing so she had drunk half the white wine, he noticed.

There was a note: *Jack darling, I suddenly remembered that I had another appointment today. A lunch appointment, which was lucky in the circumstances, wasn't it? I shall come again tomorrow. A tout à l'heure. Tessa.* She had drawn a heart with an arrow through it. It must be his heart, since she didn't appear to have one. Going into the kitchen he unpacked the bag onto the table, and then, very slowly, began to clean the fridge.

Sitting up in bed together that night, James and Victoria were both reading. Or, rather, he was trying to read the day's *Daily Telegraph*, and she was reading her novel and talking to him at the same time, which she was apparently able to do. He had scrutinized the leader twice now, and still had no idea what it was about. Reluctantly putting it aside, he enquired, 'So what have you been doing today?'

'I've just been telling you. You haven't been listening!'

'Darling, I am trying to get a grip on world events.'

'I know!' She kissed him, and then carried on as though he hadn't said it. 'Ginevra came to lunch today. I think she may be about to ditch Kevin.'

'Oh well, I can see that that's much more important than the Lloyds débâcle. Has it occurred to you that if we were on the Outhwaite syndicate, which thank God we aren't, we would be nearly wiped out by now.'

'Really?' She sounded unelectrified. It was exactly the same when he asked her uncomfortable questions about the state of the Volvette, which these days resembled nothing so much as a stock car. 'Anyway, as I was saying, her behaviour was odd.

Distrait, if you know what I mean. At one point she almost appeared to go into a trance. Looking at our wedding photograph of all things.'

A fleeting vision of the aftermath of that Commem. Ball surfaced again, together with a stirring of guilt. Those eyes. Pushing it under the waters of his memory, James said, 'It's hard to see how Ginevra could get any more peculiar.'

'I know she has always been eccentric but this was something different. And when she talked about her husband, there was a quality of detachment about what she had to say that was quite chilling. As though she has already cut him out of her life. I think living alone in the country has caused her to lose touch with reality.'

'Maybe she has someone else.'

'Maybe.'

Without saying it aloud they were separately of the opinion that this was unlikely.

Victoria lapsed into silence, thinking about it.

Hopefully James picked up his newspaper.

'You really have had a week of it, haven't you, what with Tessa and now Ginevra? It will be Alexander next. Perhaps you ought to set yourself up as a psychotherapist. Get a couch.'

Fondly he looked at her. Mainly impervious to nuance, she was, of course, the very last person who should be providing others with advice. In time to come she would no doubt become a magistrate.

'Don't tease! Seriously, though, I wonder whether I shouldn't go and see her.'

He put his newspaper down again. 'Why ever would you want to do that?'

'Just to see the setup for myself. I've never been there, you know.'

'Maybe she doesn't want you to see it. I bet you'll find they're as poor as church mice.'

'That wouldn't bother Ginevra. She has always been immune to her surroundings. Luckily.'

'Besides which, I could do with some help in The Gallery this week. And next week, come to that, if you can spare the time.'

They both knew she could.

'Of course I can spare the time.'

'Oh, and I had a phone call from Maybrick in the States. He's coming over in three weeks' time. With Irma. I thought we might take them out to dinner.'

A Harold and Irma Maybrick evening.

'Can't we dilute them with other friends?'

'I don't think I want to inflict them on friends. Enemies maybe.'

'Inflict them on Jack. He deserves it! Any word from Jack by the way?'

'No word from Jack.'

Turning over and pulling most of the sheet off him in the process, she said, 'I think I'm going to sleep now.'

Bending his head to kiss her peach-coloured shoulder, he murmured, 'Love you.'

'Love you too.'

Feeling free at long last to do so, James addressed himself to his newspaper, thinking as he did so that he probably should pull out of Lloyds, and the sooner the better.

9

The last week in June was to turn out to be one of the hottest on record. The fur-coated Captain Morgan was particularly uncomfortable, and lay lethargically for hours at a time under the pear tree. Ginevra, who had never been to such a place, supposed that it must be even more tropical than this in Saudi Arabia. There had been no recent communication from her husband, and she was beginning to feel as though he had never existed. Since there seemed no point in doing so, she had not written to him at all and the last epistle according to Kevin, scribbled on lined paper torn out of a notepad, had contained a complaint about this. After that there had been nothing.

Because of the airless heat, Ginevra had taken to rising very early and working in the garden, where she sat on one of the ladder-backed kitchen chairs at a small wooden table, marshalling her thoughts on paper before later transferring them onto the computer. Wearing on alternate days the two shapeless shifts, one turquoise and one orange, that she had bought herself as a concession to the temperature, with the straw sunhat on her head she managed to get a significant amount done before the relentless sun forced her to stop.

At this point it was her habit to make herself a cup of coffee as well as feeding the cat, after which she allowed herself some time off in the striped deckchair reading for pleasure in the dappled shade of the tree. Indoors, no matter how many of the tiny windows she opened apart from the few which appeared to be terminally stuck, it was so close that the air seemed almost tangible. In the end she had taken to sleeping in the coppery afternoons and working throughout the cooler indigo evenings, well into the night, starting with the computer, and finishing between the pages of the red and blue marbled notebook after which, satiated, she fell exhausted into her bed. Living totally within her own imagination and meeting no one apart from the odd monosyllabic encounter with local tradesmen, such as Mr

Monk the butcher, was likely, Ginevra recognized, to result in mental slippage if she was not careful. As it was she was uneasily conscious of the increased insistence of the alternate voice, and more often than not during the hot afternoons she had confused, violent dreams in which the main participants were James and Victoria Harting and herself, and at the end of which she awoke trembling, with the knowledge that she had committed some dreadful act, but could not remember what it was.

It was in order to counteract these disquieting symptoms that she decided to take a long early morning walk once or twice a week from now on. It was not as satisfactory as seeing more of other people, but Ginevra had no friends in Little Haddow, and very few in London, most of whom, with the exception of Victoria, could more accurately have been described as acquaintances anyway. Still, it would get her out of the confines of the house and her own mind.

The first morning she did this was very peaceful. The milky sky was high and cloudless, an understated precursor of the sweltering day to come. Rather than hike along the roads first to where the walk properly began, Ginevra bicycled there. It commenced with a chalky, uneven lane, also a bridle path, and wound up hill to a large clump of trees, some of which had fallen down in the hurricane of 1987. At this very early time of the day the air seemed much thinner, with a clarity which would lose definition as the sun rose higher and the shimmering heat increased. For the moment it was exhilarating, and walking, even up hill, was a pleasure. Deliberately keeping her mind as empty as she could of the clutter of her own problems, Ginevra concentrated on her surroundings. With the exception of a solitary rider she met no one. Mistrusting the unpredictability of horses whose size and power she felt to be out of all proportion to their small brains, she stood well back to let them pass. The rider saluted her politely before passing on down the slope, his horse sliding slightly on the chalk.

On either side of the path stretched fields, some of which were swept with drifts of blue flax, and others which radiated the hot yellow of the last of the oil seed rape. Above these were the Downs, and as she got nearer the top of what was a long, slow climb, campion, cow parsley, dog roses and convolvulus proliferated, and in the field cohorts of poppies flared anarchically scarlet.

Eventually arriving at the summit, rather breathless, Ginevra sat down on a bank among foxgloves. It was quiet, unnaturally so. In the profound stillness she gradually became aware of all the tiny sounds which made up the muted murmur of the early morning swelling and pulsating with a rhythm of their own. It was as though she could hear, and even feel, the heartbeat of the countryside and for a brief space it seemed to Ginevra as though the world and herself marked time together. She who had felt herself an outsider during most of her life became all at once an intrinsic and important part of the whole. It was a thrilling and mesmerizing experience.

She had no idea how long she sat there, and as the sensation of timelessness receded, it was as though an angel had passed overhead leaving a marvellous lightness of being in its wake.

Eventually Ginevra reluctantly rose and continued on her way with something of a sigh, realizing that she had been granted, though only evanescently, the sensation of belonging that she had craved all her lonely life. Continuing on her way, she dropped down the hill, along what was hardly more than a track in places, passing the edge of a yew forest on her right before eventually bearing off to the left, calculating that, with luck, this might bring her out further along the same road in which she had left her bicycle. It did. Walking back along the grass verge she saw from her watch that it was seven o'clock. She had been out for nearly two hours.

By the time Ginevra arrived back at Pear Tree Cottage, although she was still very aware that she had been touched by something extraordinary and quite outside her previous experience, the rapture had worn off leaving in its place, but underlined, the customary, acute ache of deprivation. Putting on the kettle with a yearning, starving heart, she proceeded to open the one letter which had arrived while she was out. It was from Ellen Carey.

Dear Ginevra, wrote Ellen, *I am writing this letter from Butterfly Cottage. As you may or may not know, I should have been going to London on the 29th, to live there for the next fortnight with a view to keeping Jack's nose to the grindstone. Unfortunately, or fortunately, depending on how you look at it, I have had to put this off because Mrs Phipps, my domestic help, is currently indisposed, and the upshot of this is that I have spent a great deal of time trying to fathom the computer. Not only have I not succeeded but I am beginning to take personally the fact that it refuses to do anything I ask of it. I have to keep reminding myself that it is a brainless machine, and that I am supposedly in charge. My inferiority complex regarding it and the instruction books (which might as well be in Greek, by the way) grows daily. Unless I take up your offer of help (assuming that this is still open) I may do it an injury. I have written rather than telephone a second time (the first time I rang you, you were out) because, knowing how busy you are, it seemed unfair to ambush you into setting a date straight away. Having said that, if you can do it, sometime this week would suit me, since once I am back in London, sorting out Jack will take up all of my time. I look forward to hearing from you. Love, Ellen.*

PS I shall, of course, come to you. Perhaps I could take you out to lunch? E.

Leaning against the kitchen table reading this, Ginevra became aware that she had burnt the toast and that the kettle was boiling. Lifting it off the flame and turning off the gas, she made herself some instant coffee, and started again with fresh bread. While this was turning into toast, she searched for a tin opener in order to feed the importunate cat, whose single yellow eye followed every movement with rapacious anticipation. By the time she had located it and opened a tin she had burnt the toast again.

'That was *your* fault,' she told Captain Morgan, aiming the two charred offerings at the gash bin, which had long since lost its lid. Giving up on it she peeled herself an orange instead, and picking up her mug of coffee, went into the garden.

Sitting sipping, Ginevra thought about her parents, both of whom were dead. She had not done this for years, and had an odd feeling that it was her hallucinatory experience on the walk which had caused it, and that it had somehow put her in touch with her roots again, reaching back in time beyond her present unhappiness.

Her mother, Ginevra recognized, had been a disappointed woman. Intelligent but largely uneducated, she had worked all her life to supplement the family income, shoring up her tubercular husband who winkled out a very modest living teaching the piano. Watching her embattled mother working all hours of the day, and quite a few of the night too, had made Ginevra decide at a very young age that she never intended to be trapped into any more household drudgery than was absolutely necessary. After winning a scholarship to the local girls' grammar school where she received the sort of education they could never have afforded for her otherwise, she displayed from the beginning a single-minded ambition to succeed academically and, in so doing, lift herself out of the world of sooty little back-to-back houses in which she had been born and brought up.

She had adored her unworldly father, who reared his daughter on the classics which he read her at night until she became old enough to read them herself, along with the Victorian poets such as Tennyson and Browning. In her mind's eye she saw him once again, reciting 'Crossing the Bar' with more gusto and enthusiasm than had ever been evident in his day-to-day life. It was as though he were able to live only through words, not deeds, a very unpractical man, who could have been said to have sacrificed his wife and any aspirations she might have had on the altar of his own inertia.

> *For tho' from out our bourne of Time and Place*
> *The flood may bear me far,*
> *I hope to see my Pilot face to face,*
> *When I have crost the bar.*

Aged eleven, she had declaimed the words along with him, especially the last line, accompanied by the clank of her mother washing up the plates unaided in the Belfast sink in the kitchen. By the time she was thirteen he had crossed the bar sooner than anyone expected, dying in his sleep one night with his exhausted wife dreaming beside him. For his cerebral only child the shock of this imploded rather than exploded.

After that life was never quite the same again. With very little in common beyond the tie of parent and daughter, Ginevra and her mother rubbed along. There was really no other word for it. By now, though without being exactly unpopular, an awkward, solitary, figure at school, Ginevra had been revealed as a very clever girl indeed. The predicted scholarship to Oxford achieved, her mother had contracted pneumonia six months after she left home to go there, and, probably because she had nobody left to look after and no other interests of any sort either, simply faded away in a very Victorian way and also went to meet her Pilot face to face. The sale of the little house, which had been her mother's family home before she married, brought in enough money to see her daughter through Oxford and later fund her postgraduate studies too. In her home town, Ginevra had been regarded as slightly mad. At Oxford, where she no longer stood out as particularly peculiar, this became the much more acceptable eccentric, and her brilliant intellect gave her a cachet she had never had before gaining her admittance to the Harting/Benson circle.

Ginevra put her empty coffee mug down on the grass where a column of hopeful ants began to ascend its side. Somewhere, in a suitcase, she had the old photographs. She must look them out some time.

Turning her mind from the past to the present, she went in search of her address book in order to telephone Ellen Carey.

Two days later, as they had arranged, Ellen drove to Little Haddow, leaving at 7 a.m. Before she set off she went through the Indian jewellery box and selected a silver necklace of barbaric proportion and design from which hung a chunk of amber the size of a large marble. Out of her wardrobe she chose a substantial black silk shawl embroidered with birds and flowers in the same colour and heavily fringed, which she had never worn, and carefully packed both into her carpet bag.

Arriving in the village after a leisurely journey Ellen was surprised at how rural it was. Clearly there would be nothing as sophisticated as a restaurant, but there must surely be a pub. She parked the car and went to look for it. Wearing a low-cut ethnic dress embellished with a heavy silver collar and with flimsy sandals on her feet, Ellen floated, questing, along the

Little Haddow main street, closely watched by Mr Monk's sensibly shod, acrylic queue.

There was a pub, a very small one at the opposite end of the village to Pear Tree Cottage. It stood in a well-kept garden and had tables outside which looked promising, but at that time of day was closed. Undeterred, Ellen walked around the side, and at the back found a pinnied person washing and polishing glasses.

'I wonder whether you could help me,' began Ellen. 'I'm trying to discover if the pub serves food at lunch time.'

Eyeing her curiously and thinking that the questioner looked as though she was in fancy dress, the woman said, 'Ploughman's and sandwiches, that's all. And we stop serving them at two o'clock.'

'What about wine?'

Amazement greeted this. 'Oh no. This isn't London. Beer's good, though. And the cider. Cider's famous.'

A voice inside shouted, 'Freda!' and with no further reference to Ellen at all, not even a valedictory look, Freda dourly departed, still holding a glass cloth and a half-polished glass in her hand. The kitchen in which she had been working was very clean, Ellen noted, which augured well where the food was concerned. She decided that she would propose the pub for lunch, unless Ginevra could suggest anywhere better.

By the time she had explored what there was of the village and had drawn up outside the cottage where she intended to leave the car if possible in the shade, it was ten o'clock.

Standing back to get a better look at it, Ellen decided that Pear Tree Cottage was not only very picturesque but very dilapidated. Racking her brains to remember what Victoria had said about Ginevra's home setup the day she had telephoned to get hold of the Hayes' number, she thought she recalled being told that Kevin was a builder of some sort. If so, it was time he got down to some work here. Gathering up her skirts, she picked her way along the weedy garden path, and achieving the front step knocked on the door. There was no answer, though a large villainous-looking tom-cat with one empty eye socket appeared around the corner of the house and rubbed itself against her legs. The garden was a small wilderness and, judging by the number which had congregated on the ice plants and the nettles, something of a butterfly sanctuary.

'What's your name,' enquired Ellen of Captain Morgan, 'and where's your mistress?'

'Captain Morgan, and she's here,' announced Ginevra who had just pedalled up on her bicycle. Dismounting she pushed it through the wicket gate and leant it against the wall of the house.

'Come on in. Sorry I wasn't here to meet you.'

'Don't worry about it. I've only just arrived anyway.'

Like the outside, the inside of the cottage was shabby and neglected, and, although some of the windows were open, smelt of something indefinable. The kitchen, which was antediluvian with no old world country charm of any sort to redeem this, was quite filthy. Where the wallpaper had peeled off in places, yellowed newspaper was revealed to be underneath it. Ellen read part of it. Dated 1920, it appeared to be all about someone's pig winning its class in the Little Haddow Show. Two large bluebottles, their buzzing loud in such an enclosed space, flew in and out of a full waste bin which seemed to have no lid. In a way Ellen was not surprised. The untidiness of Ginevra's own dress had signalled her to be oblivious to sartorial niceties, and the state of her kitchen was presumably just one step further on from this. Ellen, who was fastidious about that sort of thing thought, Thank God for the pub.

Partially speaking the truth, Ellen said, 'The cottage is charming. Where do you work?'

'In here.' Ginevra pushed open the door to the sitting room, which was altogether more pleasant. Clearly she drew a line between areas of domesticity and areas of study. Books were everywhere. They were all over the floor, on the table and littered the chairs. On either side of the fireplace somebody had put up shelves which were lined with yet more of them including three or four substantial attractively marbled notebooks, Ellen noticed. Perhaps Kevin had commenced his building works in this room before being hauled off to Saudi Arabia, or wherever it was he was supposed to have gone. Like a household god, the computer presided over everything from its position on an oak gateleg table which had been opened out to its full length and stood in the window. On the mantelpiece there was a bowl of the very prickly shell-pink roses which climbed around the cottage door and a clock which had stopped, but no family photographs or memorabilia of any kind. All the furniture, with the exception of the Amstrad, which did not appear to attract it, was covered with dust but, even so, there was an air of purpose within these walls which was conspicuously absent from the rest of the house – or the part that Ellen had seen, anyway.

'I was going to suggest,' said Ginevra, 'that we get to grips with the computer straight away, before it gets too hot to work indoors.'

'Good thinking. And at one o'clock I'm going to take us both to lunch at your local. Unless you know of somewhere better, that is.'

Ginevra blinked. Lunch. The Dog and Pheasant had been one of Kevin's haunts, a favourite darts playing venue. Notoriously indifferent to conventional mealtimes, she had not even thought of lunch and certainly had not got round to buying any for herself or her guest.

'There isn't anywhere else. That's a good idea. Thanks, Ellen.' Ginevra favoured her new friend with one of her rare, transforming luminous smiles and switched on the computer.

Later on, walking along Little Haddow High Street, which was in fact Little Haddow Only Street, openly observed and pointed at by those of the village who were about, Ellen decided that some sort of change had taken place within Ginevra. Firstly, probably due to the morning hikes which she had talked about, she was thinner although the dress she was wearing, which was an unfortunate shade of orange, made her appear to be still hill-shaped. The face though was narrower than Ellen remembered and the sun's light burnish, which became it, had also lightened her hair whose thick straight fringe had grown long enough to be tucked behind each ear, revealing a high and thoughtful forehead. The unbecoming glasses were still in position. Ellen could see that while Ginevra Haye would never be called beautiful or even handsome, it might be possible for her to achieve an almost Roman dignity of bearing which, allied with her formidable intelligence, would be impressive.

Silence fell as the two women entered the pub. A game of

darts was in progress, and one of the participants after a hesitation said pleasantly to Ginevra, while frankly ogling her exotic companion, 'Hello, Mrs Haye. How's Kevin doing? Coming home soon, is he?'

'No idea,' was the unencouraging answer. There then followed a silence which she made no attempt to break.

Left conversationally stranded, Kevin's chum had no alternative but to go back to his game. Attempting to catch the publican's eye, and feeling rather embarrassed, two things struck Ellen, who had never met Ginevra's husband, about this brief exchange, the first being that Kevin was called Kevin but Ginevra appeared to be known as Mrs Haye, and the second being the extent of her complete close-down at the mention of her spouse.

Having ascertained what Ginevra wanted, Ellen ordered for both of them and then said, 'They'll call us when the food is ready, so let's go and sit in the garden, shall we?'

Neither liked beer and, each carrying a large glass of Little Haddow cider, they moved out onto the small lawn where they sat on a partially shaded wooden bench which had a table in front of it. Sipping their drinks, they rested for a while without speaking. Kicking off her sandals, Ellen leant back, raised her face to the sunshine and closed her eyes. To Ginevra she looked suddenly vulnerable and very tired.

Without opening her eyes, Ellen eventually said, 'Does your husband never write?'

'He does write. After a fashion. The one who doesn't is me.'

'Why ever not? Don't you care about him?'

'No, not much.' Ginevra drank deeply.

Alerted by this positive negative, Ellen observed, 'There's no such thing as the ideal husband. I should know. Look at Jack.' Normally she never complained to other people about Jack. It must be the cider. Country cider could be very strong.

Also fortified by the cider, and greatly amazed at her own daring, Ginevra said, 'Have you ever thought of leaving him?'

In the face of such a blunt enquiry Ellen hesitated, and then came out with it. 'Yes.'

'Why don't you?'

'Well, principally because of our sons, David and Harry.'

And then, remembering Jack the day after the Harting lunch, Ellen thought, But if I'm honest with myself it's not just the boys. The other day, in spite of the fact that I was absolutely livid with Jack, I enjoyed our lovemaking. I enjoyed it. It was suddenly like the early days, when he still tried. When, in spite of everything, I felt he really cared about me. Perhaps we could start again. Oh, hell, I don't know! I think one thing one day and another the next.

Aloud, and feeling all of a sudden light-headed, she said, 'It's all complicated by the fact that he's a good fuck.' She finished off her cider. 'I think we should have some more of this, don't you? It's balm for the soul.'

The food arrived at last, reluctantly brought by Freda who had given up trying to attract their attention from the doorway.

'And could we please have two more ciders, as well?'

Freda opened her mouth to point out that she was not here to fetch and carry, and that they were supposed to get their own drinks from the bar, and then, abashed by the determination of Mrs Haye's forceful stare, thought better of it, and went off to do as she was told.

Ginevra turned back to Ellen and was shocked to see a solitary tear slip down her cheek.

'I do apologize. It must be the cider. I don't usually behave like this.'

'Kevin's a brilliant fuck too.' Materializing with two full glasses, just in time to hear this last, Freda nearly dropped both of them.

In spite of herself Ellen spontaneously laughed. 'So what's the problem?'

'He's very stupid. And I mean *very* stupid.'

'Jack's no great brain, you know, though he thinks he is,' observed Ellen, adding after a minute, 'But he is a wonderful painter. That's when he does any.' Adding mentally, Which, as far as everyone else is concerned, is where I come in. I don't appear in my own right at all.

They sat in silence for a minute or two, drinking. Then, pursuing it, Ginevra said, 'But it's a social problem too. Kevin doesn't have hair, for instance, he has a barnet.'

Ellen, graduate of the egalitarian atmosphere of art school, knew what she meant, but could quite see that the Hartings, for example, might be out of their depth here.

'I'm surprised that that matters to you, Ginevra.'

'It doesn't matter to me. It matters to other people.'

Reflecting on the fact that, after all the years they had been married, Mrs Braithwaite had still never come to terms with the fact that Jack's father was a bookie, hailing from Newcastle-upon-Tyne, she said, 'Oh, I see what you mean.'

'Anyway, that's not the whole of the problem. It's compounded by the fact that I've been in love with somebody else for years.'

Ellen was amazed. Of all the reasons Ginevra might have given this was the last one she had expected to hear. She waited. There was no more forthcoming. In spite of the relaxing effect of the Dog and Pheasant cider, Ginevra was aware that she had proffered more than she had intended, and decided to shut down that particular line of communication forthwith. Too tactful to press it, Ellen put down her glass carefully. She felt all at once both tipsy and bleak, a dangerous combination. No more cider. Looking at her watch, she said, 'I'll go and pay the bill.'

As they dawdled back to Pear Tree Cottage afterwards, she voiced some of the confusion she felt.

'There are days when I *know* that leaving Jack is the right thing to do. I think it's mainly because I'm thirty-six and keenly aware of my own life slipping away by default. I only exist as an appendage of Jack. On the other hand, lots of women have successful, selfish husbands and manage to stand apart enough within their marriages to hoe their own row, so why shouldn't I?'

Listening to her, Ginevra was aware that this was a monologue of pros and cons which had taken place many times before within Ellen's mind.

'I think if we could just start again, there might be hope for both of us,' resumed Ellen. 'But not unless he gives up the girls.' Like that slut Tessa Lucas, was Ginevra's mental response to this. 'I simply can't go on feeling loveless and used.'

Feeling hot tears beginning to well again, and brushing them away, Ellen thought, I'm very uneven at the moment. Laughing one minute and crying the next. I really must pull myself together. If I'm going to leave Jack, I should do it, and if I'm not going to then I should stop complaining and get on with it.

Watching her with sympathy, at the same time reflecting, I wonder how many people know about beautiful and outwardly composed Ellen Carey's inner disarray. None, I'm willing to bet, Ginevra pushed open the front door of the cottage which she never troubled to lock during the day. Feeling wrecked, Ellen sat down on one corner of the fraying sitting room sofa. She looked drained.

'Why don't you put your feet up and have a rest?' suggested Ginevra, moving heaps of books and papers and putting them in orderly piles on the floor. 'I normally have a siesta at this time of day anyway. We can go back to the computer later on, when it's cooler.'

Gratefully doing it, Ellen said drowsily, 'Too much cider and sun, in that order.' Lying curled up on the sofa, with one tear-stained cheek pillowed in her hand, she slipped into sleep. After looking at her new friend with compassion for a minute or so, Ginevra went to her bed, closing the door noiselessly behind her.

When she awoke it was late afternoon. The threatening dreams which had been plaguing her recently had not come today, with the result that she felt refreshed instead of worn out by her nap. Downstairs Ellen was already up. She had washed her face and redrawn her eyes. Composure regained, she appeared, on the surface at least, once more mistress of her own situation.

'Ginevra, here you are! My dear, I'm afraid I must be on my way. The drive is a long one and I did promise to look in on Edna Phipps this evening. Will you believe me when I tell you that I'm not normally quite such dismal company?' Here Ellen smiled at her, a bitter-sweet smile, the gallant outward expression temporarily masking the conflict within. 'I'm really grateful for your patience and hospitality.'

Ginevra was suddenly bereft at the prospect of her departure. 'Come again any time. If the computer remains a problem let me know. I'll come to you next time if you like.'

'Before I go I have something for you.' Delving around in her carpet bag, Ellen drew out her gifts.

'This.' Unfolding the shawl, she placed it around Ginevra's shoulders. 'Now turn round,' ordered Ellen, delighted with the result, and slipping on the silver and amber necklace, she fastened its catch. 'And this. Do you have anything as frivolous as a mirror in this house?'

'Full length, no,' replied Ginevra, who never usually took much interest in her own appearance, 'but there's a half-length one in the bathroom. It's cracked though, I'm afraid.'

The crack, which was a diagonal one, cut her reflection in two, causing one side of her image to be out of alignment with the other. Standing in front of it she was surprised by the alteration brought about by Ellen's presents. It was almost as though the tapering, multi-ringed fingers of the elegant donor had passed on some of their own grace. Heart full, she thought, No one has ever given me such lovely things before. In fact, nobody has ever given me anything much before. Her kindness is overwhelming. Then, aloud: 'Ellen, they are exquisite, but I really can't – '

Forestalling her expected polite remonstrance, and at the same time recognizing Ginevra to be a proud woman, Ellen interrupted, 'But you really can! The wrap has importance. It makes you look like a particularly severe empress, and the necklace has the same sort of pagan authority. They suit. There is no more to be said and I'm sure you wouldn't want to spoil the pleasure of the giver.'

Humbly submitting, and under no illusions about her own dress sense, Ginevra said, 'But what should I wear with them? I have no idea about clothes.'

Ellen seized her chance. 'No more mid-calf tents. From now on your choice must be imperial colours, purple or black. Possibly dark green or deep, deep red. No more pink, orange or turquoise. The shapes should be simple, and reveal your legs, which are good.' And then, remembering the thick woollen stockings on the evening of the Harting dinner party, 'Dark, sheer tights would not be at all amiss either.'

Listening to herself, Ellen was all at once aghast. This can't be me speaking. I must still be drunk! I sound like a particularly dictatorial editor of *Vogue*.

Too late now. She had said it, and decided in the light of this undiplomatic fact to go for broke. 'And have you ever thought of contact lenses?'

Her meagre wardrobe and even her glasses having been comprehensively junked in a few well-chosen sentences, Ginevra did not take offence, but intellectually assessed Ellen's views, decided that she was right and resolved to raid the Saudi money in the joint bank account.

Looking at her as she decided all this, with one hand on the front door latch, Ellen said apprehensively, wishing that she could take the words back, 'I do hope I haven't offended you. I can't think what came over me.'

'Oh no, on the contrary, you may have transformed me. Nobody has ever taken that amount of interest before. What about shoes?'

'Medium heels, narrow, classic, probably black. I *must* go.'

They embraced.

Slipping into the driving seat of the car, and winding down the window as she did so, Ellen's last words were, 'Do you think they make their own cider in that pub? Try and find out what they put in it.'

She turned on the engine, waved, and in a cloud of fine white dust, which hung in the air long after her departure, was gone.

10

The anonymous letter said, *Are you aware that your wife is having an affair with Jack Carey?* That was all. In true Agatha Christie style, it was composed of single printed letters cut from newspapers and magazines and pasted down, and had apparently been hand-delivered through the office letter box. On first reading it, Alexander had dropped it as if it were hot. Later on, turning it over in his hand, his first instinct was to ring up Tessa and confront her with it. His second instinct was to screw it up and throw it away, thereby treating it with the contempt it deserved. In the event he did neither, but rang up Marcus Marchant, who was a barrister.

'What do you think I should do?'

Marcus, who had only been surprised by half of this communication, said cautiously, 'What do *you* think you should do?'

'On the basis that anyone who sends this sort of filth is deranged, destroy it and say nothing to anybody. Especially Tessa.'

'Out of interest, what is Jack Carey's situation at the moment?'

'So far as I know, Ellen's back in London making sure he gets down to some work.'

'Ah.'

'She's living at the studio.'

'Well then, that would appear to scotch that.'

The same thought occurred to them both simultaneously: not necessarily.

Marcus observed, 'Quite apart from the allegation itself, the interesting question, to my mind, is who could have sent it.'

'I have absolutely no idea.'

Reviewing the possibilities, Marcus thought, Probably a wife or fiancée of one of Tessa's lovers. But if so, why latch on to Jack. How did the writer find out? I've heard quite a lot of gossip, but Carey's name has never been mentioned once.

There was no way he could tell his old friend what he had heard, which just might be inaccurate anyway – though having picked his information up from several sources, he was pretty sure it was not.

'Perhaps I *should* talk to Tessa.'

'It might be an idea. After all, there is no need to be accusatory. You can tell her on the basis that it's absolute garbage, but you thought she ought to know.'

She would, of course, deny it, but the revelation might cause her to lie low for a while, and maybe even put her back into her marriage. For a while. Marcus was too old a hand at this sort of thing to feel very optimistic about the purification of Tessa.

After he talked to Marcus, Alexander sat at his desk for quite some time mulling over what to do next. Perhaps, after all, his friend was right. His own initial impulse had been to tackle Tessa rather than simply tell her as Marcus had suggested. On balance he now thought he should do it Marcus's way. Looking in his diary, he discovered that he only had one afternoon appointment, which could easily be rescheduled for the following day. Calling in his secretary, he asked her to do this, and then announced that he would be out for the afternoon, without saying where he was going. Before leaving he rang home. Alexander knew why he was doing this: he did not want to risk finding Tessa in *flagrante delicto*. She was not in, as it turned out, but nevertheless the idea of remaining in the office and doing an ordinary day's work in the light of what had happened was intolerable to him.

Outside a low and bulbous sky was the colour of a plum, and heavy, glistening rain had begun to fall, causing the hot pavements to steam and shine like tinfoil. It was as clammily warm as the Palm House at Kew. Because of the sudden cloudburst, there were no taxis immediately available, so Alexander decided to take the tube. Sitting in an end carriage, which was very nearly empty, he changed his mind at least ten times on the way home as to what he should do next. Trying to analyse his own torment, he thought, I know that I should never have married her. And yet it doesn't make any difference to my feelings. What on earth is the good of my Oxford-educated brain if I'm incapable of implementing what it tells me?

In his present dilemma there was no answer to this.

Having changed on to the District Line at Embankment, he finally alighted at Parsons Green. By now the rain had stopped, and the air smelt of soaked, scorched earth. Walking along the grey London pavement, without knowing he had done so he passed a restaurant in which the day before Tessa had had lunch with one of her lovers.

He arrived at the house and let himself in. Even in the hall, he knew from the undisturbed quality of the silence that it was empty. He went into the sitting room, and then the bedroom. Tessa had evidently changed her mind several times before deciding what to wear. Shoes, knickers and dresses lay abandoned. It looked like a last-minute panic. She must have been late. Alexander suddenly realized how little he knew about his wife's routine when he was not there, that is, if Tessa operated around anything as mundane as a routine. Today, for instance, he had no idea what her plans were.

He fixed himself a drink, aware that according to his own view of such things it was really much too early for this, and then moved around the flat restlessly sipping it. Stopping by the bookshelves, he took down a volume of John Donne's poetry. He turned to 'The Broken Heart', the third verse of which always made him think of Tessa and the tyranny of his physical passion for her and began to read aloud:

> *'He is starke mad, who ever sayes,*
> *That he hath been in love an houre,*
> *Yet not that love so soone decayes,*
> *But that it can tenne in lesse space devour;'*

enjoying the sound of the words and his own voice declaiming them. He had just reached:

> *'. . . what did become*
> *Of my heart, when I first saw thee?*
> *I brought a heart into the roome,*
> *But from the roome, I carried none with mee:*

when her arrival to collect something she had forgotten
interrupted him.

'Who is that?' Finger poised over the panic button, Tessa was
understandably jumpy.

He had been so engrossed in his own recitation that he had
not heard her key in the lock. Materializing in the doorway, he
said, 'It's okay, it's me.'

His wife, who had had a fright, was correspondingly less
welcoming than she otherwise might have been.

'Why are you home at this time of day, talking to yourself?'

'I was reading John Donne aloud, which is what should
happen in poetry. Don't I get a kiss?'

'John who? Yes, all right.'

She kissed him. Very perfunctorily.

'What's going on? You haven't had the sack, have you?'

'No. Well, not yet anyway.'

'So what *is* going on?'

Without a word, he handed her the letter. Tessa read it, and
handed it back.

'So what?'

'*So what!* You are being accused of having an affair! With Jack
Carey! Doesn't that bother you? Clearly not!' In spite of
Marcus's advice, and all his good resolutions, he could feel
himself becoming volcanic.

Remembering the contents of his fridge, Tessa said almost
truthfully, 'I wouldn't touch Jack Carey with a barge pole.'

Recalling with an effort his friend's sensible advice, *no need to
be accusatory*, Alexander made a heroic effort and almost
succeeded in damping down the fires of his own doubt.

'Of course I never believed it for one minute.'

Unimpressed by this and feeling herself to be besieged, Tessa
decided to lead with a charge.

'I think you did! Otherwise why ask me about it? Why not just
throw that poisonous letter away?'

'I thought you ought to know.' This sounded lame, and he was
acutely conscious that it was all going awry.

107

'Well, now I do know. And now,' looking in the mirror she re-outlined her lips in red, and then blocked in the shape, 'now I'm going out again.'

Alerted, and suddenly extremely jealous, he said, 'Where to?'

She was crisp. 'Alexander, that is none of your business. Normally you aren't here at this time of day and believe it or not I do have my own little life to lead.'

Feeling his aggression start to build up again in the face of hers, he ordered, 'Put them off, whoever they are. I'm going to take you out to lunch.'

'Another day, yes, today no.' She picked up her bag and her Filofax (not a good idea to leave that lying around), and as she did so he noticed that her wedding ring was not on her finger.

'Where's your ring?' Rage escalated. Aware that once he had lost his temper, he would have put himself firmly in the wrong, Tessa, who knew perfectly well that the emerald was sitting on the side of the wash basin in the bathroom, shrugged. 'No idea!'

Finally losing control, he shouted, 'It's your wedding ring, God damn it! Doesn't that mean anything to you at all? Evidently not!'

> *(Mine would have taught thine heart to show*
> *More pitty unto mee: but Love, alas,*
> *At one first blowe did shiver it as glasse)*

He caught hold of her roughly causing her to drop the overstuffed Filofax, which exploded on contact with the floor in a sunburst of days of the week and business cards. Swooping on them with the same alacrity as if a wad of bank notes had suddenly been scattered all over the carpet, Alexander spread out the ones he had collected and, like a hand of bridge, began to classify them. There was not, he noticed, a single female of the species, and right in the middle was that of Jack Carey.

Unusually for him when the phone rang in his studio, Jack

picked it up. His sixth sense told him that it might be Tessa. It was her, very tearful.

'Jack, Alexander's on his way over to see you. He has thrown me out!'

'You didn't tell him about us, did you?'

'Of course not. Jack, he hit me. He's absolutely enraged, he's convinced that we are having an affair.'

'We *are* having an affair.'

Listening to her talking, Jack let his eye run over the studio. So far as he could see the only sign that she had ever been there was the painting, which he had been working on when she telephoned. He would have to store it somewhere.

'When did he leave?'

'About ten minutes ago.' It would take Alexander at least thirty minutes to get to Docklands, and probably longer, depending on the traffic. Jack, who had seen off outraged husbands before, was confident in his ability to do it again.

'If you didn't tell him, how the hell did he find out?'

'Somebody sent him an anonymous letter. And then he found your card.' Her voice was beginning to rise. She sounded hysterical. 'He went right over the top. One minute he was reciting poetry, and the next minute he struck me.' She omitted to tell him that she had hit Alexander first, and hearing her Jack himself doubted that it had happened quite the way she related it. Keeping a careful eye on the time, he observed, 'An anonymous letter! I don't understand it. So far as I'm aware, nobody knew about us!'

Disregarding this, Tessa said, 'Someone must have known. I have to pack. I'll let you know what my new number is when I know what it is.'

It occurred to Jack that Tessa without the inhibiting influence of a husband was a loose horse.

'Do you have any idea where you are going to go? If you do go, that is. He will cool down, you know.' Thinking: They all do in the end.

'I'm not staying here whatever happens.' Peering at the mirror as she said this, Tessa saw that her cheek was rainbow hued, and beginning to swell. She would not be able to go out for at least a week, possibly longer. 'I must go.'

After she had rung off, Jack lifted her portrait off the easel, and stowed it carefully behind a couple of virgin canvases which were eventually destined to be Maybricks.

He foresaw trouble.

In Chelsea, Tessa dropped to her knees and began to re-assemble the Filofax. She looked up S and rang Cecilia Storrington.

'Ceci, it's Tessa.'

'Tessa! How are you?'

'Not so good. Ceci, Alexander and I have had a cataclysmic row. Could I possibly come and stay with you for a while? Until it blows over.'

To Cecilia, who like Marcus had heard rumours of Tessa's colourful lovelife, this intelligence was not entirely unexpected. But, more to the point, she had shared a flat with Tessa before the latter's marriage and was not at all certain that she wished to repeat the experience, in spite of a rather malicious desire to hear at first-hand all the details of what had plainly been an epic quarrel even by Lucas standards. In the end, unable to resist it, she decided to bite the bullet.

'Of course, but how long for?'

With her foot now in the door, Tessa said, hedging her bets, 'Not sure.' She had been toying with the idea of leaving Alexander anyway, and maybe she would do just that, regardless of whether he wanted her back or not. It would rather depend on Jack.

An undefined stay. The worst of all possible worlds.

'I only ask,' lied Ceci aloud, 'because as you know there is just one spare room, and in a fortnight I have my mother coming to stay,' reflecting, as she spoke these words that the most memorable of the fireworks should be over by then.

Hearing the intake of Tessa's breath, she forestalled the inevitable, 'That's all right, I'll move out to a hotel when she arrives and back in when she's gone,' by adding, 'For an indefinite period.'

'I thought you and your mother didn't get on.'

'We don't, but she's still my mother. So what time shall I expect you?'

Looking out of the window, Tessa made the unwelcome discovery that Alexander had selfishly driven off in the joint car to have his confrontation with Jack. She would have to order a taxi.

'In about an hour, I should think.'

Waiting for the arrival of Alexander at the studio, Jack decided to improve the shining hour, and start a Maybrick. The letter from Ellen, who had given up on his telephone, had arrived a few days ago, informing him that Mrs Phipps was ill, and since the cats had to be fed, and those fruit and vegetables which were in season had to be picked, she would be unable to leave until Edna was back on her feet again. This news, which threw The Gallery into paroxysms of despair, had no such effect on Jack, who looked forward to an unexpected extension of his fancy-free existence, though even Jack was becoming aware that time was running out.

There was a knock on the door. Opening it, he found, as he had expected, Alexander Lucas on the step. In debating with himself how to handle this, Jack had decided to tell the truth where he could, since this made things simpler all round, especially if for any reason he had to repeat what he had said later on. In court, for instance.

Driving to Docklands, Alexander felt that he had calmed down to the point where he could just about have a rational discussion.

'This is an unexpected pleasure,' said Jack urbanely. 'What brought you in this direction?'

'Do you mind if I come in?'

'Not at all.' Jack led the way into the studio. 'Have a seat,' indicating the chaise longue, where more had lately happened between himself and Tessa than, hopefully, her husband would ever know about. 'Can I get you a drink?'

'Thanks, but no thanks. Is Ellen here? Because if she is I should prefer not to say what's on my mind in front of her.'

'Ellen should be here, but has had to postpone her journey to London because her Sussex factotum is ill.'

Jack poured himself a single self-denying finger of whisky.

'Now what can I do for you?'

'Are you having an affair with my wife?'

'Chance would be a fine thing,' said Jack unoriginally, and then, lapsing into avuncular mode, 'Only wish I was, old son. What makes you think I am?'

'This!' Alexander proffered the letter. 'And the fact that she has your visiting card in her Filofax.'

Studying the letter with interest, Jack enquired, 'What does *she* say about it?'

'She denies it!'

'And you prefer to believe the writer of this muck to your own wife?'

Alexander ignored this.

'Why would she be in possession of your card, if there is nothing going on between you?' The memory of her blatantly flirting with Carey at Victoria's dinner party came painfully to haunt him.

Appearing to cast his own mind back, Jack eventually volunteered, 'I think I gave it to her when we last saw you both at the Hartings. She's a beautiful girl. I thought she might like to pose for me.'

'Pose for you!'

'All right, don't get het up. She declined. She's a good girl, Tessa. And anyway it's years since I painted a nude.' That much was true at least.

Against his better judgement, Alexander was beginning to feel something of a fool. Whatever the truth of the matter, he was getting nowhere with Carey. Declining another offer of a drink, he stood up. Feeling a successful conclusion to be imminent, Jack rewarded himself with two fingers of Scotch this time. Seeing Alexander to the door, he said, 'Take my advice and don't do anything hasty. Sleep on it. Preferably with your lovely wife.'

Driving inconclusively home, Alexander thought, I've been conned. Or have I?

When he finally got home to Mimosa Street and re-entered the house, it was to find that Tessa had obeyed him for once and left, but not before tearing all the pages out of the John Donne and strewing them all over the bedroom. In the centre of the pillow on his side of their large double bed she had left her wedding ring, whose flashing green eye caught, and held, his own.

11

The news that Ellen had been obliged to postpone her London good deed for a week, coupled with the fact that no news of any sort was forthcoming from the studio caused James Harting to decide that desperate measures were called for.

'I simply can't stand the suspense,' he stated to Victoria, stopping his ceaseless pacing up and down in front of their own Jack Carey. 'Here we are, into July, and I have no idea what the man is doing. He may not be doing anything at all. In fact he probably isn't!' James ran his fingers through his hair. 'I'm sure my blood pressure is up. Is it worth it, I ask myself!'

Watching him with sympathy, and thinking how fraught he looked, his wife suggested, 'Why don't you just go there?'

'I have, I have. Nobody answers the door. Either he is there and simply lying low, or he's out on the town, heaven knows where, doing heaven knows what. Whatever he is doing you can bet your bottom dollar it's not what he should be doing.'

James began to pace again.

Reflecting that trying to eat one's supper with someone marching restlessly up and down at the same time was very unrelaxing, Victoria said soothingly, 'Why don't you sit down, darling? It must be bad for you to eat on the hoof.'

He complied and then almost immediately stood up.

'I feel I must have done something awful in a previous life to deserve this. Do you realize that the other day I rang him, and actually got through without being intercepted by that fucking answering machine? And do you know what he did? He said, "I'll ring you back," and, when he'd done it, he then announced that there was someone at the door, laid down the receiver at his end and then apparently went out, with the result that The Gallery telephone was out of commission virtually all day.'

'You really must try to calm down.'

'I know, I know!' This last was delivered as a controlled shout.

Victoria, who had news of her own to impart, could see that

now was probably not the moment. On the other hand, the way things were going there never would be a moment until the 1 September Rubicon had been crossed. She decided to tell him anyway, and was just framing the words, when James said, 'I think I'm going to fire Carey. Tell him to find another gallery if he can. I've absolutely had it.'

It was hard to know what to say at the end of this apocalyptic utterance. After regarding her husband in silence for a minute or so, she said, 'I'm pregnant. We're going to have a baby.'

This did not receive the expected euphoric response. James put his head in his hands.

'Oh Christ! Oh no! Then we can't *afford* to let him go. There will be school fees. Nobody can pay those out of income these days. Carey and I are stuck with each other. Like the old man of the sea, I'll never be able to shake him off.'

Regarding him with disbelief, Victoria said, 'James, it isn't even born yet!' And then with gathering frustration, 'Don't you care about your own family any more? It seems to me that all you can think about is bloody Jack Carey and The bloody Gallery. God, I hate that man!' Tripping over a snoozing Ho on the way, she ran out slamming the door.

Also tripping over Ho, he went after her.

'Darling, I'm sorry! Of course it's wonderful news!'

Turning a tear-streaked face towards him, she said, 'You are happy about it, aren't you? I simply couldn't bear it if you weren't.'

Suddenly very emotional, and at the same time full of wonderment, he kissed her. She looked exactly the same as she always had, and at the same time was quite different. There was no mistaking his sincerity when he said, 'You're a clever girl. I'm thrilled.'

She smiled at him through another surge of tears. 'I know we didn't plan to start a family quite yet, but I thought you would be.'

Kissing her again, he said, 'I adore you. When shall we tell the rest of the family?'

'Not yet. Let's keep it as our secret for the time being.'

Left alone while Victoria washed her face, he made a decision vis-à-vis The Problem of Jack. He would go to the studio taking with him Mr Peck, The Gallery's handyman, along with Mr Peck's tool kit and drill and, failing all else, they would break in. Anything would be better than the awful suspense he was being forced to endure at present, though probably it would be better that Victoria did not know what his intentions were.

Mr Peck, who was seventy, had the philosophical attitude that comes with age. He was a small nut-brown man who looked like a refugee from someone's rockery and whose father and grandfather had both been handymen too, many of his tools having been handed on, including his hammer, which down the years had had its wooden handle replaced at least three times. Retirement never entered his head, for his job was his *raison d'être*.

Sitting beside James, whom he still called Mr Harting, in spite of all the years he had worked for The Gallery, just as he himself was still referred to as Mr Peck and never Bill, he wondered where they were going. All he had been told was that the expedition was something to do with Mr Carey. Mr Peck had seen quite a bit of Mr Carey during his long association with Mr Harting and The Gallery, and disapproved of most of it. Himself a conscientious workman, Mr Carey's haphazard, slapdash ways were anathema to him, though through it all he continued to regard Mrs Carey as a saint, and it was his personal view that he himself could have turned out one of Mr Carey's so-called abstracts, no trouble at all, and nobody would have known the difference.

'Have you ever been to Canary Wharf before, Mr Peck?' asked James as they drove along it.

Looking at the tower, though not with admiration for it was much too new-fangled for him, Mr Peck said no, he couldn't say that he had. He was much more interested in the *Financial Times* printing plant, which they also passed, and through whose cloudy glass front he could see the massive presses, though at this time of the late afternoon these were not yet in motion. Useful, was Mr Peck's approving verdict. The mystery tour continued, and finally they drew up beside what looked as if it were an old warehouse.

Getting out of the car, James said to Mr Peck, 'Have you got your tools?' Mr Peck nodded. It was his habit to carry them around in a hemp holdall with leather handles. At the entrance to what was in fact a complex of offices and studios, James pressed the bell labelled Carey. There was, of course (as he expected) no answer. In succession he pressed the others and finally struck lucky.

'Who is it?' said a voice over the intercom.

'Parcel for Mr Carey,' replied James. 'I've been told to leave it outside the door to his studio if he isn't there.'

'Then you're fortunate that *I am* here,' said the voice, impatient, but letting them in.

'Now what?' asked Mr Peck, struggling up the stairs after James's tall figure.

'Breaking and entering, Mr Peck,' came the unreassuring answer. Even Mr Peck's seventy-year-old composure was shaken by it. 'Got your jemmy ready?'

In the event, to his enormous relief, there was no need for such a drastic measure, since it appeared that Jack had left his own front door ajar.

They went in. A probable clue to the open door in the shape of a half-empty whisky bottle was the first thing James noticed. The next was a very large nude still on the easel, though apparently finished.

'Good God!' ejaculated James.

'I didn't know Mr Carey could do real pictures,' observed Mr Peck with interest. Moving closer he put his glasses on and, as the whole thing shifted into focus, received a shock. It was Mrs Lucas, the way he had not seen her before and probably never would again. Embarrassed, he turned away and began to polish his spectacles which were unsurprisingly showing signs of steaming up.

James stood in silence looking at the painting. It was extraordinarily good. Very much herself, his sister stared uncompromisingly back. Everything was there, beauty, will, stupidity and lust, with a masterly trace, but only a trace, of the naivety of the younger, softer Tessa. It raised the question of whether Jack shouldn't be going back to his roots, artistically speaking. Lost in speculation he became aware that Mr Peck was speaking to him.

'If you don't mind, Mr Harting, I'll wait for you outside. I could do with a breath of air.' It was certainly true to say that a second furtive glance at the portrait of Mrs Lucas had made him feel a little faint. Modestly he wondered how it would be possible to look her in the eye the next time he met her.

'Of course, Mr Peck, no problem. I won't be long.' And he probably wouldn't be either since there appeared to be nothing else to look at. Rooting around he discovered a cache of drawings of his sister. Almost all as explicit as the painting, they were sensationally good. Jack's carnal enjoyment of his subject was obvious, made manifest in the languorous curve and easy sweep of his line. Self-evidently these drawings were a celebration of his sister's sexuality.

Mindful of the fact that Jack might soon return, James continued his search. From here on, unfortunately, it was downhill all the way. Among the canvases stacked against the wall he discovered one and a half possible Maybricks. Superficial and slick, James decided, looking at them. These would not even fool Harold.

Picking up the telephone receiver, he rang his wife. Without preamble he said, 'It's worse than we feared!'

'What is? Where are you?'

He had forgotten that he had deliberately kept his plan from her.

'I'm in Jack's studio.'

'Oh! Presumably things can't be that bad if he actually let you in.'

'He didn't let me in. In fact Mr Peck and I came here with the express intention of breaking in. Or rather I did, old Peck knew nothing about it until we arrived. In the event there was no need because Jack, careless slob that he is, had gone out leaving his own front door wide open.'

'So what *is* there?'

'A wonderful though decidedly pornographic nude of my sister, some similar drawings, and one and a bit thoroughly second-rate Maybricks.'

There was a sharp intake of breath at the other end. Before she had time to utter, hearing a commotion downstairs, James said, 'I think he's back. I'll have to go.'

On his return to the studio, Jack had been amazed to find Mr Peck sitting disconsolately on the step. Bonhomously tanked up, Jack was nevertheless immediately alerted. Eyes on the car he said, 'Right! Where is he? Where is Harting?'

Refusing to be cowed, Mr Peck said with dignity, 'If you mean *Mr* Harting, he's in your studio.'

'Oh *shit*!' To Mr Peck's enormous relief, without saying anything else his interlocutor lurched up the stairs. James was standing contemplating the Maybricks. He did not turn round when Jack made his entrance.

Determined to bluff it out if he could, Jack said, 'Pretty good, eh? What do you think?'

'Substandard is what I think.' James was acid.

'Oh right! Well, maybe they do lack depth.'

'They lack a lot more than depth. You may think Harold Maybrick is a prat, but even he wouldn't be taken in by these!'

Jack looked sheepish. 'Maybe you're right.'

'You know I am. Anyway, *faute de mieux*, I think this one should be exhibited.'

'You can't do that old son.'

'Why not?'

'It's your sister. Her husband wouldn't like it.'

'I don't care if it's Mickey Mouse. There isn't anything else that I can see.'

Even Jack was sobered by this prospect.

'Tessa has a pathologically jealous husband. He'll kill her. You know that.'

'He's much more likely to kill you. Anyway, that isn't my affair. It's yours. You got yourself into this!'

Throwing up his hands, Jack said, 'Yes, yes, all right. I give in. I'll get on with it.'

'When does Ellen arrive?'

'As soon as Edna Phipps is back on her feet. Could be any day now.'

'Okay. Here is what is going to happen. When Ellen does get back, I want her to ring me, and thereafter I want a progress report once a week. In one month's time there will be a meeting here to assess what you've done so far. If I'm not satisfied then I'm going to cancel the exhibition and, with it, our contract. Is that clear? And,' gesticulating in the direction of Tessa, 'I should get rid of that before Ellen appears too.'

He went.

Jack, whose skin was too thick for him to be offended, spread out the drawings of Tessa on the top of the plan chest. He would have to ask her to store both them and her own portrait. Sitting down on the chaise longue he dialled Cecilia Storrington's number.

Driving back to Chelsea via Balham in order to drop off Mr Peck, James enquired, 'Do you want to ring Mrs Peck to let her know that you are on the way back?'

Regarding the car telephone with suspicion, and aware of the fact that tonight was Marjorie's ladies' darts night and that his dinner would be in the oven anyway, Mr Peck declined.

After watching him dodder up his front path and let himself into the house, on impulse James decided to make another detour and visit Alexander and Tessa on his way home. Quite what prompted him to do this, he could not have said exactly. To reassure himself perhaps. Crossing the road on his arrival, having been forced to park some way away because Mimosa Street was full, he noticed that all the house lights appeared to be on. Very typical of my extravagant sister, thought James. Their car was parked outside.

Grasping the door knocker, which was itself in the shape of a brass hand, he rapped twice. It was Alexander who appeared.

'Oh James. What a surprise. Come in.'

He led the way into the sitting room.

'Can I get you a drink?'

Feeling as though he needed one, James said, 'A glass of dry white would be marvellous if you've got one open.' Suddenly feeling grubby, he said, 'Do you mind if I wash my hands?'

'No, go ahead. You know where the bathroom is.'

Passing the open bedroom door on his way his attention was arrested by the fact that what looked like the pages of a book were scattered all over it. Back in the sitting room he remarked, 'I couldn't help noticing that you appear to have been purging your bookshelves.'

Handing him a glass, Alexander said, 'That was Tessa.'

'Tessa?'

'Yes.' He put his head in his hands.

'Are you all right?'

'No, not really. She has left me. Or rather I told her to go, and she did.'

'Where has she gone to?' thinking: If he says to live with Jack Carey, I'm going to shoot myself, 'and when did all this happen?'

'A few days ago. She's staying with Ceci Storrington. She left her wedding ring behind.' He sounded bleak.

James's view of the Lucas marriage was very much akin to that of Marcus Marchant. With exquisite understatement he observed, 'You've had rows before. It will blow over. They always do in the end.'

Looking at his brother-in-law properly for the first time, he saw that Alexander was unshaven and had dark circles under his eyes, which made him look even more poetic than usual.

Alexander handed James a piece of paper.

'Someone sent me this.'

Reading the letter, James thought, I *am* going to shoot myself!

Giving it back and making up his mind to say nothing of his visit to Jack's studio, he observed, 'Surely you aren't about to take any notice of trash like this?'

'That's what Carey said when I went to see him.'

Ye gods!

Aloud, and with commendable calm in the circumstances: 'Oh, you've been to see him?'

Alexander sounded wretched. 'Yes, but it didn't get me anywhere.' (No I'll bet it didn't!) 'When I got back she'd gone.'

James noted no mention of the painting, so it couldn't have been there. Obviously Tessa must have tipped Jack off. He would have to go and see her next, in order to have a full and frank discussion about what the hell she thought she was doing. He could see he was never going to get home tonight.

'Try not to get too depressed. She'll come round when she has cooled down.'

'That's partly the trouble. I don't know if I want her back.'

Eyeing him, James thought, Alexander is suffering from withdrawal symptoms. Poor devil, he's physically addicted to Tessa. But that's all. Nobody could be addicted to Tessa's brain, since for all intents and purposes she doesn't have one. No wonder he doesn't know what to do.

'I have to go. Victoria will be wondering what's happened to me. Look, why don't you come and stay with us for a few days? Until things settle down again.'

'Thanks all the same, but I think I'd rather remain here.'

He saw James to the door.

'By the way, was there something special you dropped in to say?'

'No. No, just passing. Where does Ceci live these days?'

'Walpole Street.'

'Oh yes, I know. *Courage*. I'll give you a ring in the morning.'

Driving back at last to Chelsea, feeling depleted, he decided to go and see his sister in the morning.

12

When Ellen arrived at the studio two days after James's visit, she found more or less what she had expected. On the easel was a fresh canvas, though with absolutely nothing on it. Jack was plainly in his About To Start mode. Everything was thick with dust, even the plant. There was no sign of her husband. Deciding to make the most of this fact, she elected to do a whisky trawl now, while he wasn't there to make a fuss about it. She discovered three half-bottles, all partly drunk and all secreted in different places, and poured the contents away. Every single dish in the kitchen was dirty, and nothing had been put in the dishwasher. He had simply gone on using plates until they ran out. Rather to her surprise, the inside of the fridge was relatively hygienic. A cleaner was clearly going to be a high priority. Since Jack, understandably, objected to anybody hoovering around him while he was trying to work, it was Ellen's plan to ring a firm such as Scrubbers and get them to clean the place from top to bottom in the course of a day. After that, until the next purge, she herself would keep on top of it.

She was dragging the plant, which was too heavy for her to lift, across the floor to the bathroom in order to spray the leaves with the shower, when the phone rang. Ellen picked up the receiver.

'Hello. Ellen Carey speaking.'

There was a long silence at the other end, during the course of which she could hear soft breathing.

'Hello,' intoned Ellen again.

A click. They had hung up, whoever they were.

Going back to the plant, she managed to tilt it over the bath and then proceeded to dowse it with lukewarm water. It responded gratefully by suddenly becoming a vibrant and completely different green.

'You poor old thing,' said Ellen. 'He really is a bastard, isn't he?'

'Who's a bastard?' Jack had entered without her hearing him over the noise of the shower.

'Hello, darling. You are. I don't believe you ever water this.'

Unabashed, he agreed. 'No, I don't.'

'Would you mind heaving it right into the bath for me so that I can give it a good soak.'

He did.

'And while I'm doing this, you can unload the car.'

It had not, of course, occurred to him to offer. Reluctantly he went. When he returned with her bags, one of which felt quite heavy, she had finished.

'Now, come with me. If we tackle the kitchen together, it shouldn't take too long. Unless you want to go and engage that canvas. If you do, then I'll cope with this little lot by myself.'

He did not want to do either. Giving her a mournful look, he said, 'I'm feeling rather tired tonight. I thought I'd start tomorrow.'

Ellen thought, *Plus ça change*, but if he thinks I'm going to skivvy here while he sits about like a sultan, he's got another think coming.

Jack thought, I remember when Ellen used to be one of those pliant girls and now look at her. She reminds me of my mother. Like many Northern women his mother had been a coper and a doer, and extremely bracing with it. He and his father had done as little to help as they could get away with, and over the years had been castigated as idle and useless. Usually she had found it quicker and certainly more efficient to do whatever it was herself.

'Oh, all right.' This was delivered with the air of one who makes a great concession. 'What do you want me to do?'

Putting on an apron, she handed him a dish.

'That's a dish and that,' she pointed to it, 'is a dishwasher. You have to put the dish in the dishwasher. Then you put in another one and another one until it is full. If you are feeling especially creative, you may want to fill the top with glasses. After that comes the hard part. You have to turn it on. Then I thought you might like to take me out to dinner so that we may enjoy one last convivial evening before you go on the whisky wagon for the duration. What do you think?'

'I think therefore I am. Where would you like to eat?'

'What about The New Friends?'

'Done!'

When they had finally finished they smiled at one another. All of a sudden it felt like the old days, days of beer and penury. And, for quite a bit of the time, happiness.

Meaning it, Jack said, 'I'm glad you're here, Ellen.'

Looping up a stray tendril of hair which she secured with a comb, and wondering at the same time whether this might not be a fresh start for them both, she smiled at him a slanting, seductive smile.

'So am I. Shall we go?'

When they returned it was still only 10.30. Walking back through the violet evening, holding hands with her husband, Ellen asked herself, Am I mad to think that I can resurrect this? They were both slightly drunk.

Inside the studio Jack found himself desiring his own wife.

'Take your clothes off. I want to see you.'

'You'll have to help me with the buttons at the back.'

She turned her back to him and, like a very young girl, stood head bowed patiently waiting for him to undo them.

Performing this potentially interesting task, he enquired, 'How on earth do you do them up in the first place without help?'

'It takes forever. You have to be a contortionist.'

Raising her arms she pulled the crimson dress, whose long light skirt floated upwards with a breath of air from the open window, over her head, revealing a body which was both slender and ripe at the same time. With her painted eyes and air of mysterious containment there was a quality of Cybele about her. Within the bedroom the only illumination came from an old-fashioned streetlamp outside. Wanting to see her better, but by the softest and most old-fashioned of light, Jack the artist struck a match and lit the large beeswax candle which topped a five-foot French flea market torchère in one corner. Delicately pale its flame stole tentatively around the bedroom and kindly it enveloped Ellen's body, throwing into relief the cheekbones and highlighting the silver collar and the rings on her fingers.

'Don't remove the collar, but just let down your hair. Now come here.'

As he kissed her, the prelude to all sorts of other delights, she thought, It's the first time for ages that he hasn't tasted of whisky.

Although it was his wife's view that he should have done so, James did not ring Tessa first before going to see her. His objection to doing this was that Tessa could normally spot an oncoming lecture a mile off and was therefore likely to avoid the sort of confrontation which might conceivably lead to one. 'That's all very well,' Victoria had pointed out, 'but what if Cecilia's there?' In fact, as it turned out, she was not. There was, he thought, an air of defiance about his little sister.

'James.'

'Tessa.'

They kissed. Sitting down on one of Ceci's button-backed chairs, he was wondering how to broach the subject of her liaison with Jack, when she saved him the trouble.

'I gather you know all about Jack and me.'

'If by "all about Jack and me" you mean the squalid little affair you have been having such as he has already had with dozens of others, yes I do.'

'There's no need to be so judgemental.'

'I'm not being judgemental, merely stating a fact.'

'There's no comparison. I intend to marry him!'

'Oh really.'

'Yes, really.'

'Tessa, you already have a husband.'

'I don't want the one I've got. I want a different one.' It took him back to their childhood fights over toys in the nursery.

'What the hell's the matter with you. Alexander is good-looking and clever. A lot of women would give their eyeteeth to be married to him.'

'Well, I'm no longer one of them. He may be clever but he's no fun. What's the point of having a brilliant brain if you aren't entertaining with it? No point I'd say.'

Trying another tack, he said, 'All right, let's for the sake of argument say that you and Alexander *are* all washed up, but couldn't you leave the Carey marriage alone? What about Ellen? And the boys?'

'That's his problem. Anyway, look, you don't care about Ellen. Or the boys come to that. All you care about is your forthcoming exhibition at The Gallery!'

James was silent. She had him there. Much as he adored Ellen it could not be said that her welfare was the real reason for his visit.

'Tessa, you never used to be this hard-bitten. It really doesn't suit you.'

'Oh trust my big brother to take the moral high ground.'

Looking out of the window with a set expression, he decided that it wasn't so much that he had mishandled the interview as that she appeared to be able to see neither to the right nor the left of her own way.

'For what it's worth, I don't think Alexander is one hundred per cent convinced that you have been having an affair with Jack. I mean I think the whole thing is salvable, if that's what you want.'

'Oh big deal,' was the unpromising reply.

Eyeing her with exasperation, and thinking that what she needed was a bloody good hiding, he got his revenge: 'So when did Jack ask you to marry him?'

'He hasn't yet. But he will. You wait and see. He will.'

Not if he knows what's good for him, thought James. It appeared that there might yet be hope.

Wearily he stood up. 'I must go. Thank you for the coffee.'

'Coffee? But I didn't . . . Oh, very amusing.' Then defensively: 'Maybe if you hadn't come round with the express intention of delivering a rather sanctimonious lecture, I might have been more welcoming.'

'You might. Anyway, try to think over what I've said. Goodbye, Tessa.'

'Goodbye, James.' He was barely off the front doorstep before she had shut the door.

Walking back to his car, it was clear to him that Tessa had lost her way. *Au fond* he loved his sister, though manifestations of his concern usually received scant thanks. If he himself had not been so beleaguered, his immediate instinct would have been to have taken her out to a good lunch and to have told her so, amid the sort of convivial surroundings that she enjoyed. For the present, however, at least until after 1 September, the thought of supervising Tessa's moral welfare was more than he felt he could cope with.

Jack began to work. As usual, once he had been forced through the starting gate, he became surprisingly disciplined. Watching him getting under way, and enjoying himself as he did so, Ellen was reassured. As requested, she rang James.

'He's off!' she announced, 'and I think he has enough impetus to last him through the week that I'm at home with the boys.'

Mindful of the very unsatisfactory interview he had had with Tessa, James said, 'What do you do in the evenings?'

Extraordinary question. 'What do we do? Well, I cook dinner here, and we usually split a bottle of wine. No whisky, though. And then he works on through the night. I think you'll be pleased with what you see.'

James knew this to be understated Ellen-speak for he's starting to produce some very good work. It was a pity that she had to leave town for Sussex quite so quickly.

'Ellen, you're a sweetheart! And you really think there's no need for me to come and check up on what he's doing while you are away?'

'My advice would be to let him get on with it, but of course you must make your own decision.'

'Sure. When are you off?'

'Tomorrow, I'm afraid. He has provisions, including, most importantly for Jack, plenty of Marmite. And he knows he's up against it. Oh, and I'm taking the car, so to all intents and purposes he's grounded.'

But Tessa isn't.

'I'll probably take your advice.' After all what else can I do? 'Meanwhile enjoy your trip. Perhaps we should have a meeting at the studio after you get back.'

'I'll make contact as soon as that happens.' She rang off.

For several minutes afterwards James sat in silence pondering the Tessa problem. He could either warn her off, which in her present recalcitrant mood would be tantamount to an invitation to do the opposite, or he could keep quiet about Ellen's departure in the hope that by now Jack was so engrossed in what he was doing that he would forget all about Tessa. It was unlikely that she would drop in while she still believed Ellen to be in situ, but then Jack had only to pick up the telephone to tell her that for the time being this was no longer the case. Thank God Ellen was only away for a week. In the meantime prayer was probably his only hope.

Finally on her way to Sussex with both boys quarrelling sotto voce in the back seat of the car, Ellen reviewed the past week. It was true to say that she and Jack were getting on much better, but, as usual, this was because her own life had been subjugated entirely to his. Quite apart from the fact that her husband was so time-consuming, there was literally nowhere for her to work in the studio. The thought of living like this until September suddenly seemed insupportable, and, although it was only for another six weeks or so, was threatening to be the last straw. Because, Ellen thought miserably, it's more of the same and I just don't want it any longer. My heart is, quite simply, no longer in this life style, and Jack will never change now.

The quarrel in the back seat began to escalate. What could they be fighting about? After all, they hadn't seen each other since the last exeat. Breaking into her own train of thought, Ellen shouted, 'Shut up, both of you. I've had enough!' At the end of this there was dead silence for something like four miles before it began to rumble on again.

Going back to her own troubles, she decided to print up the first five chapters of the novel and to send them off with a synopsis to three different publishers. She might as well find out now if what she was doing possessed any commercial appeal. The next question was who to contact. It occurred to Ellen that the obvious person to ask for advice was Alexander Lucas. All of that could be accomplished during the coming week.

And the other thing I'll do, she decided, is to ring Edward Montague and ask him what my legal and financial position would be if I left Jack.

Making up her mind on these two fronts, although for

different reasons she dreaded doing either, brought a sort of peace to Ellen, and she resolved to tackle both as soon as they arrived at the cottage.

Alexander Lucas was working at his office desk when his secretary buzzed through.

'I have a Mrs Carey on the line. Shall I put her through or would you prefer to phone her back later?'

'Put her through.'

She must be ringing about Tessa and Jack. He could not think of any other reason for her call. Bracing himself, he said, 'Ellen! How are you?'

'I'm fine, thank you. Do you have a few minutes?'

'Yes.'

'Look, I could do with some advice. I'm in the process of writing a novel.'

Of all the things she might have said this was the least expected. A novel. Alexander's eyes glazed. It was probably hopeless. In the course of his working life he had encountered many such, quite often written by friends, and most of them were.

'Don't worry, I'm not asking you to have anything to do with it. It's just that I wonder what to do next. I'd like an opinion on whether it is any good or not, and thought of sending what I've done so far off to two or three publishers. I'm not sure how these things work. What do you think?'

This was a relief. Alexander marshalled his thoughts.

'First, what sort of a novel is it?' She told him. 'Right. If you send it cold to a publishing house it will probably join the slush heap which is a vast collection of unsolicited books and it may be months before you hear another word, that's if you ever do. I think you'd be better advised to try to get yourself an agent. I can send you some names if you like. At least that way you'll get an opinion, and if he or she likes it and is prepared to take it on, they'll hawk it around for you.'

Ellen was grateful. 'Oh, would you? Thank you, Alexander.'

'Where shall I send the letter to?'

'The Sussex address.'

Immediately alerted, he said, 'I thought you were in London with Jack.'

'Mainly I am, but not this week. The boys have just broken up for the summer.'

'I'll get those names off to you today. No doubt we'll meet in London before too long.'

'No doubt. Goodbye, Alexander, and thanks again.'

'My pleasure. Goodbye, Ellen.'

Listening to Edward Montague's telephone ringing, Ellen decided that he must be out and was just about to hang up when he answered.

'Edward, it's Ellen.'

'Ah, Ellen. Could you possibly hold on a minute?' To her acute ear he sounded fussed. She could hear what sounded like lapping noises. Surely he couldn't be in his bath? His voice sounding far away, as though he had the receiver gripped between shoulder and cheek and was using both hands to do something else at the same time, he eventually said, 'Now what can I do for you?'

'I need your advice on a rather delicate matter.'

'Getting divorced, eh?'

He must be psychic. 'How did you guess?'

'The way you phrased it. Besides which I've met your husband.'

His voice receded again. 'I'm going to have to put down the receiver for a moment. Don't go away.'

Patiently she hung on. There were sounds of stirring this time, and more lapping. Eventually he came back.

'Sorry about that. Now where were we? Ah, yes. Divorce. Yes. Carry on!'

'Edward, I sense that this is not the moment. Do you mind if I ask what you are doing?'

'Not at all. I'm cooking an oxtail. I have a lady coming to dinner tonight. Do ladies like oxtails?'

On the whole Ellen thought they probably did not. Too late to say so now. The guest was coming and he was cooking it.

'Yes, I should think so. Look, why don't I phone you tomorrow when you aren't quite so embattled?'

He wouldn't hear of it. 'No, no. I can stir and listen. What are the grounds? Do you like oxtail, by the way?'

'No, I don't, but I'm probably in the minority. Endless infidelity.'

'Good Lord, is that all?' Edward Montague had himself been relentlessly unfaithful, as three successive Mrs Montagues, the last of whom had been very blonde indeed, could have testified, and had never been able to understand the inordinate fuss made about this particular habit. 'People go on putting up with a lot worse than that you know. What about physical violence? Does he knock you about at all?'

Astonished by his response, Ellen replied, 'No, he doesn't.'

'Keep you short of money?'

'No.'

'What about mental cruelty?'

Disregarding this last, Ellen observed, 'Surely adultery is one of the most common reasons for divorce?'

Grudgingly he said, 'Only if people want it to be. If I were the judge and that's your *only* reason you wouldn't get one off me.'

Thinking: Thank God you never will be. Strikes me there are enough dotty judges around without you swelling the throng, she said, 'No, I've got that message. Anyway, assuming that you aren't, and that I do, what sort of financial settlement could I expect?'

Edward Montague found himself forced into professionalism. 'Broadly speaking half, and custody of and maintenance for the boys. But I'd like to think about it. You work, don't you? What happens to the money you earn?'

'It all goes into the common pool.'

There was a silence, punctuated by chopping noises.

'Have you definitely decided that you want a divorce?'

'No. But it's certainly on the cards.'

'I should think long and hard about it before taking such a drastic step. Give me another ring tomorrow. I'll be here between twelve and one.'

'I will.'

Ellen spent the following morning playing some tennis with David and Harry and at eleven o'clock left them having a lesson with the coach. Carey tennis was vicarage standard and lessons were an effort on her part to try to raise everybody's game.

Back at the house she began to print out three copies of the book. This was an interminably slow and very noisy operation. At 12.30 it was quite a relief to stop and telephone Edward Montague. More strange sounds, masticating sounds plus the odd noisy swallow. This time he must be eating it.

'How did the oxtail go down?'

He did not reply to this.

'As a matter of fact I'm having an early lunch and eating some now. There's quite a lot of it left.'

Probably half of it at a guess.

'Have you had any further thoughts concerning our conversation of yesterday?'

'Not really. I think that what I told you you could expect is probably about right. That is, unless he cuts up very rough, but you won't know that until you start. Now tell me the real reason why you want to leave.'

'I have. And I want to lead my own life.'

Aware that he had finally flushed her out, he pounced. 'Ah! Feminism! That explains it. What a lot that has to answer for!'

'Nothing to do with feminism. I simply want the time and space within which to make my own contribution as another member of the human race. I'm fed up with being submerged by Jack. It has nothing to do with being a woman.'

'But you *are* a woman, Ellen, and a very attractive one if I may be allowed to say so. Don't you think that's a bit much to expect? After all, your husband needs you.'

Picturing him with a Kitchener moustache pointing at her out of a poster bearing this legend and reflecting that he was even more of an unreconstructed male chauvinist than Jack, Ellen decided to draw the conversation to a close. Before she could do so he finally went too far.

'Your mother wouldn't like it, you know.'

By now very irritated, Ellen said, 'Oh, fuck my mother!'

She heard him choke on the oxtail before she slammed down the receiver.

13

Walking along the Fulham Road with a leaden heart and a carrier bag full of groceries, Alexander Lucas wondered if he would ever be free of the image of his wife. Given the pain Tessa caused him when she was there, he decided that he must be some sort of masochist to suffer in this way because she was not. The evening was fresher than it had been of late, and a skittish wind indicated that the weather was possibly about to break. In the west, where the sun was on its way down, banked sulphurous clouds were rimmed with gold and, in spite of the fact that it was still only the end of July, there was a distinct chill in the air. This fact only served to underline his mood. Since she left they had not contacted one another. Countless were the times that Alexander had dialled Cecilia's number only to replace the receiver without saying a word when one or other of them, usually Ceci, answered. What his wife might be doing with her time consumed most of his morbid waking thoughts, and it had occurred to him to take Cecilia out to lunch to discover. In the end he did not do this, reasoning that Ceci was Tessa's friend more than his and would be unlikely, therefore, to divulge any of her secrets.

Here he was wrong. Cecilia would have liked nothing more. Although just about as intellectual as Tessa herself, she had nevertheless always found Alexander attractive and secretly envied her chum's marriage. Now that it was beginning to look as though the whole thing might be over, given the chance, she would not have been above making a pass at him herself. Moreover, loyalty to Tessa was being severely strained by the daily trial of living with her. For one thing when she was in, she was hardly ever off the telephone, and when she was off the telephone, she was in the bath. Thank Christ I don't have a portable phone, thought Ceci, because if I did she would be endlessly in the bath on the telephone. Men came and went, but mostly took no notice of Cecilia, which was very bad for morale, and when the one or two who were her very own called to take her out, they eyed Tessa when she happened to be around with more interest than Ceci found acceptable. On top of all that the eagerly anticipated fireworks had not materialized. There had been neither hide nor hair of Jack Carey, and Alexander himself had not been in evidence either. It was becoming apparent to Cecilia that she was going to have to wheel out her mother sooner than she had anticipated.

Then the painting had arrived. Ceci had come home from the Foreign Office, where she worked as a secretary, to find it propped up in her sitting room.

'What do you think?' asked Tessa, who, it transpired, had just brought it home from Jack Carey's studio with the aid of a mesmerized taxi driver.

What did she think? There was no doubt that in her chintzy, button-backed little sitting room, where it was practically the size of the door, it looked vast, and, well, (here Ceci searched for the *mot juste*) erotic. She foresaw the few admirers she had left defecting if they were allowed to see this.

Lost for words, Ceci eventually came up with, 'It's very *frank*, isn't it? I definitely think it's one for the bedroom myself. Has he given it to you?'

'Sort of. Rather, I have custody of it while his wife's in town.'

'Why don't I give you a hand with it?'

'You don't like it where it is?'

It was obvious that instant clarification was necessary if she was not to be bulldozed into leaving it there.

'No, I'm afraid I don't.'

Giving in for once without a fight since she was shortly going out for the evening and wished to make some telephone calls prior to having a bath, Tessa said, 'Oh. Okay.' Together they carried it into her bedroom and propped it up beside the wardrobe, where, thankfully, it could not be seen from the open door.

Reaching his front door, Alexander let himself in. As always he paused just inside, hoping against hope that while he had been out at the office she might have returned. Going into the bedroom, where the pages of John Donne's poetry which he had been too dispirited to pick up were still scattered, he loosened his tie and took off his jacket, throwing it on the bed. Marcus had been quite right when he had said that there was no point in leaving Tessa until he was absolutely sure that that was what he wanted. 'Otherwise you will just keep leaving and going back and you will drive each other mad.' Prophetic words. Alexander groaned aloud. It seemed that he couldn't live with her and he couldn't live without her. Deciding to end his purgatory he dialled Cecilia Storrington's number.

It was she who answered.

'Oh Alexander, it's you. I thought it might be the idiot who keeps ringing and then hanging up as soon as one of us answers. How are you? So sorry about the contretemps between you and Tessa.'

'I'm all right. I don't suppose she's there, is she?'

'No, I'm afraid she isn't. You've just missed her.'

Though very tempted, Ceci forbore to say, as was the case, that she had gone to visit Jack Carey.

There was a short silence, and then he said, 'Could you possibly tell her that I called, and would like to talk to her urgently?' He sounded very disappointed.

'Yes, of course. I don't expect her back until late tonight so I'll leave her a note.'

When he had hung up he went into the kitchen and opened a can of baked beans. Going to the cupboard under the stairs which was where they kept the wine in the absence of a cellar, he discovered that there was none of the cheaper variety left. Selecting a bottle of Château Latour, Alexander thought, To hell with it. If I'm going to be miserable, I might as well be miserable in style.

Jack's message on the answer phone had said, 'Tessa, can you drop round to the studio tomorrow evening? And bring a bottle of whisky when you come, there's a love.' He had not bothered to say who he was, obviously just assuming she would know.

Old reprobate, thought Ceci, who had arrived home before Tessa and switched on the machine straight away. There were no messages for her. All the same, it looked as though things might be hotting up again. Ellen Carey must be away.

Going to Docklands by cab, since her husband still retained the joint car, Tessa resolved not to go to bed with Jack tonight. It was important that he be made to understand that by no means was she at his beck and call. There were, however, some important things she had to say to him. On her way there she bought only half a bottle of malt, reasoning that if he became paralytic he would have forgotten everything she had said by the following morning.

The moment she entered it, it was obvious to Tessa that the studio was transformed. The plant now looked like a real one again, instead of a dusty plastic imitation, and the whole place had obviously been cleaned from top to bottom. Handing Jack the whisky, she said, 'There you are. Don't drink it all at once.'

Only half a bottle. That wouldn't go far. Never mind, it was better than nothing. Pouring them each a glassful, Jack raised his. 'To us, Tessa.'

Not missing a trick, she came back with, 'I'm glad you said that because it's us I've come here to talk about.'

Warily he looked at her. Usually when women delivered that sort of statement it meant that pressure of some sort was about to be applied.

'I think we should get married.'

'Hang around. I've got a wife and you've got a husband.'

'Don't be obtuse.' This had been one of her father's favourite expressions, usually applied to Tessa herself. It was very gratifying to be able to belabour someone else with it. 'People get unmarried every day.'

She had a look of terrifying determination.

Desperately Jack said, 'But what if I don't want to?'

'But of course you do. We can be a dazzling social couple, and enjoy sublime sex together every night as well. I'm making you an offer you absolutely can't refuse.'

He wasn't sure about that, but was beginning to perceive that shaking off Tessa was not going to be easy. The word 'work' he noticed did not appear to be part of her vocabulary at all. He did not think that, with the possible exception of his mother-in-law, he had ever encountered quite so much will. It had been his intention to make love to her all evening, for after all he felt he had earned some time off. On the other hand it was just that activity that had got him into this.

Changing the subject he said, 'What have you done with the painting?'

'It's in my bedroom in Cecilia's flat.'

'I'd prefer that nobody else saw it for the time being.'

'I gather my brother already has!'

Jack looked startled. 'Oh, he told you, did he?'

'Not in so many words, but I just put two and two together. He knows that we are having an affair, so I thought that he must have.'

'Let's hope he doesn't tell your husband.'

'Since I've quite made up my mind to leave my husband, I can't see that it matters if he does.'

'It might matter to me,' said her lover, through gritted teeth. His desire for her was evaporating as they talked, though treacherously this revived when she announced, looking at her watch, 'Heavens! Is that really the time? I must go!' when it became apparent that she did not want him anyway this evening.

'How are you getting back?'

'By cab. Alexander has the car, which is a real bore. It's waiting for me outside. Think over what I've said.' With a wave she was gone.

Going back to his work, a glass of Scotch in one hand, Jack found himself thinking longingly not of Tessa but, rather to his surprise, of Ellen, enigmatic, beautiful Ellen. Remembering the dense floating cloud of her hair and the planes of her body by candlelight, its lights and darks interchanging as she moved towards him through the shadows of the bedroom, naked except for her rings and the heavy silver collar, he was reminded of haughty, seductive Etruscan ladies such as they had both seen depicted on vases and pottery one year in the Roman Villa Julia. Mysterious and unfathomable, she was all at once attainable and unattainable. For the first time it occurred to Jack that perhaps he did not know his own wife very well at all.

'What the hell *am* I doing with Tessa Lucas?' he asked himself out loud. There appeared to be no answer to this. It was to be hoped that, as had happened so often before, Ellen's presence would see this his latest, no, this his *last*, mistress off. He was about to be forty. Time to call a halt. From now on Ellen would be the only one.

The Maybricks' visit was imminent.

'Whatever shall we do with them?' fretted Victoria. 'I don't think I could bear to see *Cats* again.'

'Harold's the intelligent one. I think *Starlight Express* is more Irma's level, and it's probably her turn to choose this time, so brace yourself,' replied her husband. 'Actually, I thought we might entertain them at Langan's Brasserie one evening. Harold likes to feel himself among celebrities.'

'What about asking Jack along? He could be our very own celebrity. And Ellen if she's back.'

'It really depends how much work he's done, and of what quality. I don't honestly think I could stand a whole evening of Jack bullshitting an admiring Maybrick on the subject of nonexistent paintings. According to my diary they arrive on the seventeenth and Ellen should be coming back to London on the eighteenth, after which, hopefully, we'll have her for at least two productive weeks. It's also a question of whether he should be allowed out.'

'Don't you think a sniff of the Maybrick dollars is just the thing to motivate him?'

'Maybe. I'll see what Ellen thinks. She's the one I trust.'

In Sussex Harry brought Ellen her morning cup of tea in bed.

'I would have made it a whole breakfast but I wasn't quite sure how to do it,' he apologized. 'Here's the newspaper.'

'Anything in it?' she asked, opening it up. If she had thought about it, it was a silly question to have asked ten-year-old Harry, who was only interested in the sports pages. As it was she got the answer she deserved when he replied, 'Yes, Arsenal won.'

'Any post?'

'Yes, there is.' He produced it. Just coming upstairs it looked as though it had been in the bottom of a satchel. There was one letter from Alexander Lucas, presumably with the promised names, and a rather longer one from James Harting. She quickly scanned both.

'I'm going to have to work for most of today. Do you think that you and David can amuse yourselves?'

'Yes. We're going to play some tennis and I want to have a swim. Are we going to see Daddy before we go away?'

'Possibly, possibly not. He's working very hard at the moment. You'll see plenty of him once the exhibition's over.'

Actually we won't because we'll be back at school by then, was Harry's mental response. However, because he was of an age when the presence of his mother was still more important than that of his father, he said equably, 'Oh. Right!' Then, on a completely different tack, 'He promised to take us skiing after Christmas. Do you think he will?'

'Really? Are you sure he said skiing? He doesn't know how to do it.' Her husband had a horror of physical exercise of the sporting variety. He must have been drunk when he promised that. Intent on averting disappointment later on, she enquired, 'Does the school organize a skiing trip? It might be better for you both to go on an *organized* excursion first time around, so that, by the time you hit the slopes with Daddy in tow, at least two of you know what you are doing.'

Noting the light emphasis on the word organized, and recognizing that to his father the whole concept of organization was foreign, Harry thought that this probably made sense.

'I think there's an Easter one. I'll check it out.'

'Yes, do that. And get David to do the same, would you, darling?'

Like a witch's cat, Casimir slid into the room. Standing by the bedroom door he fixed Ellen with an unblinking green gaze. When the cats were desperate enough to come in search of her Ellen knew it was time to get up. Throwing back the bedclothes, she said, 'If you don't mind feeding the cats, I'll feed both of you. Go and find your bro.'

Later, sitting in her work room while the printer noisily printed, she penned a note of thanks to Alexander, and then, after rereading his to her, another one to James.

Dear James, wrote Ellen, *Thank you for your letter. I shall be back in London by the 18th, unless something totally unexpected happens. On balance, if Jack has continued to work with the same dedication that he was displaying when I left, I feel it would be A Good Thing for him to have dinner with Harold and Irma. I think it might concentrate his mind still further. And no doubt you would be grateful if we were there to leaven the Maybrick lump. Presumably you will let me know venue and time in due course? Love to you both, E.*

They did go to Langan's. A famous drinker, Jack was greeted with smiles by the management, and shown to a prominent table. All bowed reverently to Ellen. Harold, who was tightly buttoned into an expensive and ill-cut double-breasted suit, pulled out Victoria's chair for her with a flourish. Chic in black, she felt all at once very sick. Morning sickness was a nuisance, but morning and evening sickness really did threaten to be a cross.

'*Mrs* Harting,' he said gallantly, faintly flirtatious.

'*Mr* Maybrick,' she replied, in kind, fighting nausea and thinking, This evening is going to be endless.

Watching, Irma, who as usual was overdressed, in electric blue with sequins, bridled.

'Honey, could you please take my wrap?'

The wrap changed hands. Now he had it instead of her. Casting around for a waiter, he eventually got rid of it. They all sat down.

Clothed in a suit made of what looked like mattress ticking, but still not above sartorial criticism of someone else, Jack in barbed though courtly vein turned to Irma.

'May I congratulate you on the very brilliant blue of your dress?'

Mentally unsophisticated and therefore unsuspicious, she sent him an arch look. 'Why thank you, kind sir!'

From her seat beside James Ellen heard it, caught her husband's eye and frowned at him with an almost imperceptible shake of her head.

Harold was staring in a very unsubtle way in the direction of a bald-headed man at an adjacent table.

'Say, isn't that Bela Lugosi?'

Startled, Victoria followed his gaze.

'No, I don't think it can be. It doesn't look like him, does it? Anyway, he's dead, isn't he?'

Losing interest, Harold said, 'Oh, really?'

'Shall we order?' suggested James.

They did.

'How's the car business, Harold?' asked Victoria desperately, into a prolonged lull. Harold had made the Maybrick money out of cars. While doing this he had been aided considerably by the first Mrs Maybrick, an intelligent, thrusty partner, who, when the first million had been made, had been expensively dismissed for saying 'You're wrong, Harold', once too often. Irma, then his secretary, had become the second Mrs Maybrick. A compulsive agreer, she was prone to reiterating, 'You're right, Harold!' which phrase had evolved along with their relationship from the more secretarial 'You're right, Mr Maybrick.' More often than not following this up with, 'He *is* right, you know!' which was reassuringly addressed to the assembled company.

The waiter arrived with their food. As they ate it there followed a monologue which they had all heard before which was How Cars Are Made. Throughout Irma nodded.

Victoria thought, If she goes on doing that I'm going to fall into a hypnotic trance. That marriage is suffering from a severe case of arrested development.

Deprived of his whisky and demoted, as he saw it, to premier cru claret, Jack interrupted.

'Tell us all about the Maybrick Collection, Harold. What's the point of it in the middle of Texas?'

Missing the point, and out of habit, though unconsciously original with it, Irma observed, 'He's right, Harold. Tell us all about the Museum.'

And, brick by brick, he did. Two hours later they were all propping each other up on the pavement outside.

'We need a taxi, Irma.'

Pre-empting Irma, whose mouth was open already preparing to deliver the usual response, Victoria said, rallying at the prospect of the end of the evening, 'No, no, he isn't. You don't. We'll drop you off at Grosvenor House. It's on our way back, after all.'

Turning to Jack, Harold shook his hand. 'Good to meet you

again, Jack. We leave for Paris at the end of this week. Is there any prospect of seeing the work you're doing before we go?'

Suavely, James stepped in. 'I think Jack and I should probably have a conference about that. Why don't I ring you tomorrow evening, Harold, when I've had a chance to see what he's got? Our car's over here.'

'Sure. Let's be in touch, Jack.'

They went their separate ways.

Alexander decided to meet Tessa on neutral ground. A very fashionable restaurant of the sort she liked was the obvious terrain.

When she eventually arrived, twenty minutes late, the sight of her made him catch his breath in common with all the other male lunchers. After a great deal of thought about what to wear, Tessa had decided that More In Sorrow Than In Anger was the look she wanted to project. Accordingly she was wearing black, a long-sleeved scoop-necked dress made of some sort of silken material whose short skirt flirted only four inches above the knee. The same colour ran down her long legs in the form of the sheerest of Lycra tights and ended in narrow black suede pumps with gold buckles. Round her neck she had tied a black velvet ribbon from which was suspended a large, flat heart, also golden in colour. The heart, which was made of brass, was striking but worthless, being something that her husband had bought her in the Portobello Market thinking, rightly, that she would like it. In its present position there was no denying its effectiveness, nostalgic and otherwise. Conscious that she had achieved an all-but-flawless blend of beautiful fragility and wronged womanhood, Tessa took her seat opposite her husband, knees decorously together, the better to act her part.

Marcus Marchant, who happened to be eating in the same restaurant with his wife, both of them effectively screened from the Lucases by a large palm, and who had not yet made his presence known to his friend because he was curious to see who Alexander's lunch companion was going to be, whistled under his breath.

'Good God!'

'What is it?' enquired Jane.

'Tessa the nun! Though more like one of the Loudun variety than Mother Theresa.'

'What are you talking about?'

'Darling, you've met her. Tessa. Alexander's wife – estranged wife, I should say – who has more heart-shaped scalps hanging from her belt than any other woman in London, is sitting over in the corner dressed from head to toe in black, with her hair in a French plait, looking as though butter wouldn't melt.'

'I thought you told me that was all over!'

'Christ, no! There's a lot of emotional mileage in that marriage yet, mainly to be covered by my friend, I should guess.'

'Shouldn't we make ourselves known?'

'Yes, of course, but not now. When we leave.'

They went back to the menu.

Unaware that they were being watched, Tessa and Alexander studied theirs too. When they had both chosen and the waiter had gone, Alexander took his wife's hand. Ringless it lay lifelessly within his own. Slipping his other hand into the inside breast pocket of his suit, he drew out the emerald and slid it onto her finger.

'Regardless of what happens to us, I want you to have this back.'

Eyes modestly downcast, she looked at it. Today it seemed to have lost its usual green fire, and appeared a lacklustre, sulky stone. Perhaps it had disliked being separated from its energetic custodian.

Able to stand her composure no longer, Alexander said urgently, and against his better judgement, 'Tessa, come back. I can't bear the house without you. I love you!' conscious as he did so of a small voice within his head querying this rash statement: love her? You don't love her! You just want her back at Mimosa Street because she's currently living somewhere else. You can't bear to let her go. That's obsession, not love.

But watching his wife with desire as she ate her first course, these thoughts receded.

She did not make the mistake of telling him that it was his own fault that she was no longer there since he had told her to leave. Recrimination was not the name of the game, but retaining a second string to her bow was. Gravely composed she said, 'I love you too, but it's not as simple as that.'

For the life of him he couldn't see why not. 'Why isn't it? If we love each other we should be together.'

'I need time. Time to,' here she hesitated wondering what to say next, before vaguely resuming, 'time to sort my mind out.'

Her mind? Now they were in uncharted, dangerous territory. Tessa had never bothered overmuch about her mind before. Alexander was aware that it took some people years to sort their minds out once they had embarked on such a course, and hers was particularly rusty.

'Why can't you sort it out and live with me at the same time?'

For the first time returning the pressure of his hand which still held her own, she said contritely, 'Try to be patient with me, darling. I *am* doing my best. I'm afraid that last row we had shook my confidence in us. I need some mental space to get my equilibrium back. So that we can start again.'

Baffled, and feeling himself unable to express displeasure when such good intentions were being expressed, Alexander found himself forced to back off. It occurred to him that although there was a submissive, even chaste air about his wife, she had not actually submitted to anything, and seemed to be constantly, though nicely for a change, saying no.

He was just about to propose that they should forget about ordering a pudding, put all this atypical soul-searching aside and go home and go to bed, when Marcus and Jane came over on their way out.

'Alexander! Tessa! What a surprise!'

Watching her husband expressing amazement reinforced Jane's view that she was married to a devious man.

'Why don't you join us for a drink?' Having proffered the invitation, Alexander earnestly hoped they would not take him up on it, and to his relief they did not.

'Thank you but no, we do have to go. I have an appointment with my gynaecologist, and Marcus is due in court. Perhaps we'll see you both at Marchants before too long.'

His arm around her shoulders, they left. Turning his attention back to his own wife Alexander wished he was taking her clothes off, rather than finishing his *paupiettes de veau à la crème*.

Calculating that a month should just about be long enough for her to get a commitment out of Jack, prior to making the smoothest transition possible in the circumstances from one husband to another, Tessa said, 'Could you be very understanding and allow me one month on my own? Without making a fuss about it. Please, darling?'

It seemed to Alexander that he had very little choice in the matter. Reluctantly agreeing, he said, 'Would you like a pudding? Or shall I just order coffee?'

14

With Harry now at sailing school on the south coast, remembering, she hoped, to wear his life jacket, and David grumbling his way around the remains of classical Greece, Ellen was at last able to devote all her attention to supervising Jack. In the event this was not as trying as it might have been, since he now seemed to have acquired his own momentum and was obviously enjoying himself. The upshot was some wonderful work. Sustained by the odd pint of draught Guinness, and plenty of Marmite, he painted tirelessly, often late into the night after they had eaten their evening meal.

To Ellen's surprise he evinced no desire to stray at all, the reason for this being that he was afraid to go out. After their last interview, during the course of which she had been so ruthlessly uncompromising and sure not only about what she wanted but about what he wanted as well, he dreaded meeting Tessa again.

Knowing nothing of it, Ellen congratulated herself on the way things were going, though she did advise against a potentially disruptive Maybrick visit to the studio. 'Just let him get on with it and don't interrupt the flow,' was Ellen's view expressed to James. 'A surfeit of Maybricks will only make him cantankerous and upset his concentration. And we don't want him reaching for the whisky bottle, do we?'

No, they didn't. James fobbed off Harold and Irma, but, because of this, felt compelled to organize a theatre evening. They all went to see a revival of *The Sound of Music* (Irma's choice) and then once more out to dinner afterwards, during the course of which a history of the Maybrick family practically from the time of the Pilgrim Fathers was the chosen monologue. With luck, thought James, stealing a look at his watch while picking up his napkin which had slid onto the floor, it will all have been worth it.

At the studio, that same evening, mindful of the success of his portrait of Tessa, Jack said to Ellen, 'I'd like to paint you again.

Without clothes or, rather, mostly without clothes. Have you got that purple wrap with you? The one with the dramatic sleeves?'

To begin with he decided once again to do some preliminary sketches. For the first two or three of these he did not bother with the robe, wanting to feel his way on paper around the whole of her body to begin with. He was interested to discover that the sensuality of line which had informed his drawings of Tessa was still with him, though these studies were by no means as explicit. If asked why not, Jack would probably have said in a rather prudish working-class way, 'Because one's my wife and the other's my mistress.' In fact it was instinctive, for it was Jack's genius to paint character as well as form, and understatement rather than vulgar display had always been his wife's way.

The purple robe was one which Ellen had used from time to time both as an evening coat and a glamorous housecoat. Reminiscent of a kimono, although not one, its voluminous sleeves tended to get in the way while performing such mundane tasks as making coffee, and lighting the gas could be hazardous. Its collar was high at the back.

'I think I should loop my hair up, don't you?'

Currently looking around for props, Jack agreed.

'And I want you to wear that silver collar. We need something else though. But what?'

'The lilies?'

Ellen had bought two dozen of them the day before and had arranged them in a tall rectangular vase of very stark, modern design through whose clear glass their long slender green stems could be seen crisscrossing each other. There was a *fin-de-siècle* aura about the flowers which were still fresh enough to have retained their creamy, waxen perfection. From them emanated a fragrance both heady and indefinably sinful.

'Brilliant! The lady of the lilies. Why don't you arrange yourself while I get organized?'

When he returned, it was to find her ready for him. She was half lying and half sitting on the chaise longue (Useful that chaise longue, thought Jack), and the purple coat with its massive sleeves was thrown open displaying her breasts and the length of her lissom body. In one hand she held two of the lilies and the rest of these in their glass vase stood on a small, high antique table which she had placed behind the sofa. This inspired marriage of formality and nakedness was enough to tempt a saint, and Jack did not even try to resist.

Falling on his knees before her, he kissed first her mouth and then each rosy nipple.

Languorously Ellen sighed.

Running his hands down her body, he gently parted her legs.

Unbuttoning his shirt, she said, 'What about the painting?'

'Later. Meanwhile keep that coat on.'

And later he did get down to work, thinking as he drew: I've looked at Ellen practically every day since we married, but looking and seeing are quite different. Now I feel that I'm seeing her properly again for the first time for years. Suppressing a desire to make love to her again, he painted on. He had every intention that this should be his masterpiece.

Invitations to the Jack Carey private view were sent out. In Little Haddow Ginevra found hers on the doormat when she returned from one of the early morning walks. Since their last meeting there had been no word from Victoria. Ellen had rung but only to say that she had her hands full with Jack.

Hiking along, Ginevra had reflected on her isolated state. Early in the morning, when her head was still clear and she was not bedevilled by the alternative voice, which was at its most vociferous during the long brandied evenings, she was almost at peace. In the fields on either side of her the harvest was well under way, and flocks of wheeling, darting birds followed in the wake of the farm machinery, bright white against a dark sky. A few days previously the weather had temporarily broken with high gusting winds and sluicing rain, causing the drooping gardens and parched countryside to revive. Walking, which had been hard on the soles when the earth was like iron, now became easier, and before the drought resumed its stranglehold there was even, very briefly, something of a turf-like spring underfoot.

During the many times she had done this since then, rather to her disappointment, there had been no repetition of the strange experience she had had the first time. Recognizing that possibly one of the reasons for it had been that when it occurred she had been deliberately trying to keep her mind empty, thereby opening herself up to other, usually more elusive, sensations, Ginevra had attempted to repeat the circumstances and therefore the same happening, but without success.

There had been no further word from Kevin, whose reappearance in her day-to-day life Ginevra frankly dreaded where once she had dreaded his absence. By now she was well into the third of the marbled notebooks, and since just reading earlier entries was enough in these days of deprivation to give her an orgasm, she deemed her husband to be superfluous. At least on paper it was possible to have an intelligent affair as well as a very carnal one. Marching along towards her parked bicycle which was now in sight, Ginevra realized that she was shortly going to have to decide what to do. He was not going to be away for ever. The fact that Pear Tree Cottage had been purchased in both their names, and that the remains of her own money had gone into buying it posed a problem. And so did moving out and renting somewhere else, since Ginevra had no cash coming in, and until and, more to the point, unless, the book was sold, no prospect of any. With her usual discipline where work was concerned, she continued to research and write in the mornings and, now that the weather was cooler, frequently worked on into the afternoons. The warm indigo evenings were reserved for her notebook, and as she covered page after page, so great was the intensity of her feeling, it seemed impossible to Ginevra that James Harting should not have been aware of her passionate obsession.

At first, seeing the large envelope lying by her feet, she had thought it must be a letter from Kevin, though judging by its size it was too grand for that. Nobody else wrote these days. Picking it up and turning it over, she recognized Victoria's spikey black hand. *Jack Carey Paintings*, said the invitation, under a coloured reproduction of one of them, *Private View, 1 September, 6.00 p.m. – 9.00 p.m. at The Gallery.*

She would certainly go, and she would wear, for the first time, the shawl and the silver and amber necklace which would mean purchasing a dress, tights and shoes as designated by Ellen. Suddenly feeling that she had something to look forward to again, Ginevra sang as she put the kettle on and fed the cat.

As she had always said she would, Ellen spent the week beginning 2 August with her sons in Sussex, and it was arranged that Jack, who had not seen his children for some time and, truth to tell, had not missed them either, should join his family for supper on the Saturday night before they went to spend a week with their grandmother.

Watching his parents that evening, it seemed to Harry that there had been a change. For the first time for a very long while they were openly affectionate with one another, and, with the perspicacity which even very young children have where such a thing is concerned, he knew that this was not being enacted just for the benefit of David and himself.

'So what are you going to do with Granny?' asked Jack, trying to take an interest and thinking, Thank God it isn't me who has to go and stay with her.

'She said in her letter she wants to spend at least one day in London taking us to the Science Museum and the Natural History Museum, if there's time.'

'Oh grim!' said David, whose face was resolutely set against all things educational after two relentless weeks of it in Greece.

'With McDonald's in the middle,' added Harry encouragingly.

'Is she taking us to any films? And anyway how come you know so much about it?'

'*I* answer her letters,' came the virtuous and therefore irritating reply.

'Don't be pi, Harry,' said his mother.

Making a resolution to beat his little brother up later, David reiterated, 'Well, is she?'

'Yes, she is. Granny's brilliant about that sort of thing.'

She was too, Ellen saw. It was almost as though a talent for parenting and generally empathizing with the young had skipped a generation. Given how hopeless Jack was in terms of backup, this was very useful.

Beginning to clear away the plates, Ellen enquired, 'Are you two packed ready for tomorrow?'

'No,' they chorused complacently.

'Have you still got the lists I gave you?'

'Yes.'

'Well then, go and do it! Right now!'

When they had reluctantly gone, Ellen turned to Jack.

'Do you want to go up by train tomorrow morning, or do you want to wait until Mother has picked the boys up and then drive up with me?'

'Drive up with you. I love you, Ellen!'

'Do you, Jack?' Smiling her mysterious smile, she nevertheless sounded doubtful.

Even as he kissed her, he wondered how he could persuade her that this time he really meant what he said.

The middle of August found James, Ellen and Jack in the Docklands studio looking at what he had completed so far. James was dazzled. This was Jack at his very best. He said as much.

Gratified, Jack said, 'I've been such a good boy, I think I deserve my first whisky for weeks. But I don't suppose there is any, is there, Ellen?'

They both knew there was. He had found a quarter of a bottle the other day in the back of one of the plan chest drawers where he had earlier secreted it and forgotten it. Discovered holding it by his wife, prior to having an illicit swig, he had been shamed into promising that if she did not throw it away, he would not drink it until the exhibition was finished. Ellen had then removed it and hidden it. Try as he might he had not succeeded in unearthing it.

Deciding to indulge him, rather as though he was a child, Ellen said, 'Oh, all right. But just one! Can I get you a drink, James?'

More in the interests of keeping it away from Jack than because he liked spirits, James nodded. 'Thanks, Ellen.'

How Jack had managed to produce so much marvellous stuff in the time was more than he could begin to comprehend. Other artists worked sometimes for years before producing as much. It seemed that Jack was able to dissipate and incubate at one and the same time so that when push came to shove it was all there in his head ready for the production line.

While his wife was in the kitchen, Jack said, 'And that's not all!'

'Isn't it?' James was surprised.

'No it isn't. Let's see what you think of this. This is the *pièce de résistance*!'

He drew out the canvas of Ellen and set it on the easel. James stepped back a pace, the better to appreciate what he was being asked to look at. Without saying anything, for they could both hear Ellen returning with the drinks, he contented himself with merely rising his eyebrows ironically at Jack.

Assessing it, he commented, 'I think it's quite simply one of the best paintings you've ever done. I hope you're prepared to exhibit this.'

Tessa wouldn't like it, of course. The memory of his sister made him frown. She had rung up twice lately to enquire about the whereabouts of Ellen, once while Ellen had been in Sussex. Feeling that there was nothing else for it, James had lied, something he hated doing, and had said that Ellen was in London.

'Sure I am.'

'Would you mind, Ellen?' She handed him an amber glass.

'No, of course not, though my mother will probably have a fit.'

Mindful of the last such exercise of Jack's he had seen, he said, 'Do you have any of the preliminary studies? What we might do, since the rest are abstracts, is to make a feature of this painting by displaying it in the small room off the main gallery, together with the drawings. What's your view?'

'Okay by me.' Drinking his whisky Jack felt at one with the world and himself. It was also unexpectedly enjoyable to be approved of for once. 'It's not for sale, though. Everything else can go, but not that one.'

Reflecting that this was a pity, but one couldn't apparently have everything in this life, James raised his glass.

'Congratulations, Jack. To the exhibition.'

15

Having successfully put her husband on hold, as she thought of it, Tessa found herself unable to contact, and uncontacted by, Jack. When she quizzed James concerning the whereabouts of Ellen she suspected her normally veracious brother of not telling her the truth. In the end she wrote to Jack, asking him to telephone her. When there was no reaction to this of any sort, there was nothing for her to do except bide her time, and wait for a gap in the line such as the departure of Ellen for the country. How to find out about this was the problem, for the Hartings closed ranks, refusing to talk about the Careys, and Jack was not to be seen at any of his usual watering holes where it was murmured, in the sort of hushed tones usually reserved for those who have passed over, that he was working. It was beginning to look as though the next time they would meet would be at his own exhibition when, doubtless, he would have his wife in tow.

Infuriating! And inexplicable was Tessa's view, looking at herself in the mirror. Still, it appeared that there was nothing to be done, and the frustration of will occasioned by Jack's silence (He might just as well have been in purdah, thought Tessa crossly) caused the angelic forbearance which had been on display for her husband's benefit over lunch to be eclipsed by rather more usual behaviour.

On 22 August, Ellen collected both the boys from her mother's house, and drove on to Sussex to get them ready for the return to school. Her absence from the studio was a closely guarded Carey/Harting secret which, with luck, could be contained until her return on the twenty-seventh.

Concerning Jack, James no longer had any misgivings. Jack appeared to be both motivated and in tune with himself and his wife for a change. For once the threat came from outside, and James was under no illusions concerning the havoc Tessa was capable of wreaking given half a chance.

Ceci, and she was not the only one, wished her friend would go back to her husband. Disaster had struck where her mother's proposed fictitious visit was concerned when a postcard had arrived stating her parent's intention to spend the next four weeks with her other daughter who lived in Australia, and who was pregnant with what would be Mrs Storrington's first grandchild. Reading this announcement at breakfast time, prior to her departure for the Foreign Office, Cecilia was going to put it quietly away without saying anything, when Tessa, never very scrupulous about reading other people's mail, said, 'I'll bet you're relieved you aren't going to be saddled with your ma after all.'

As the implications of this sank in, Cecilia visibly wilted.

'Oh you saw Mummy's postcard.'

Thinking of her difficult mother without affection and wondering why she couldn't write letters like other people instead of using the inconveniently public medium of the postcard, Ceci saw that dislodging Tessa was going to prove almost impossible.

'What's the current state of play between you and Alexander?'

'No play for the present,' was the disappointing answer, 'while I consider my options elsewhere.'

'How did you manage to swing that one?' Cecilia was aware that she sounded sour.

'Elementary, my dear Watson. I simply informed my darling husband that I needed to sort out my mind.' Like Alexander before her, Ceci was amazed by this emphasis on the cerebral.

'And he fell for it? Just like that!'

'Just like that.' Looking at the invitation to his exhibition at The Gallery, with her mind on the elusive Jack Carey, Tessa appeared more complacent than she actually was. Alexander had intimated the last time they had had lunch together that he was not prepared to wait longer than the previously agreed four weeks for her return home. So it was therefore a pity that all this valuable time was being wasted.

Looking at her watch, Cecilia swallowed her coffee.

'Must go. See you tonight.'

Left alone Tessa rang the studio and got the answer phone, with Ellen's cool, even voice inviting her to please speak after the tone.

No point in doing *that*.

'Oh, sod it,' said Tessa, banging down the receiver.

Although it was early days, Victoria, who had expected to take pregnancy in her capable stride, felt almost permanently not well but not exactly ill either. This unaccustomed state was accompanied by an unnerving sensation of precariousness, as though something was about to go adrift. It was probably, she told herself, all to do with the tension surrounding the run-up to the exhibition. As soon as that was over it would all settle down. Meanwhile, she did not look pregnant, nobody, with the exception of her husband, knew she was and so she felt herself required to carry on as usual.

When she mentioned the way she felt to her fashionable gynaecologist, she found herself patronized, rather as though because she was now engaged with the slow and, she was beginning to think, tedious process of reproduction, her brain was diminishing as her waistline prepared to expand.

'Tired, Mrs Harting! I expect you're tired.' He wagged his finger at her. 'You're probably about to move house. All pregnant women move house. They shouldn't, of course. But they do.'

Surely he wasn't about to deliver a dissertation on the nesting instinct?

'Well, this one isn't.' Her tone was tart.

Scenting disenchantment at such an early stage, and aware that this might turn into insubordination later on, thereby making her one of those difficult patients who thought for herself and even consulted the books with a view to tripping him up, he reprovingly pointed out, 'A positive attitude is all important in pregnancy.'

Nettled she replied, 'I really don't think I have an attitude problem. I just feel odd, that's all. Not at one with myself.'

'Well, there are two of you now!'

Disbelieving she stared at him. The man was an idiot.

'I know that. But the second one of us seems to be causing disruption out of all proportion to its current minuscule size.'

'Hormones in uproar, my dear Mrs Harting, hormones in uproar. Nothing to worry about I assure you.'

It seemed to her that his response to her attempt to tell him that she thought something might be the matter was to mug her with a paragraph of verbal chloroform.

Writing the word *neurotic* down in her notes, he was uneasily aware that the reverential approach, which as a celebrated consultant he had come to expect from his female clients, was sadly lacking here. Deciding that demotion to flat on her back and an internal was one way of getting her into line, he proposed this. It was almost impossible to be combative in quite such a one-down position. Lying submitting to an undignified examination, and feeling in the process like a piece of meat on a slab and just about as interesting while he ummed and ahhed, Victoria thought, I'm not sure I can stand another seven months of this and him.

Eventually desisting, though without having passed any concrete information of any sort on to her, he said, in a lordly way, 'That's all. You may get dressed now.'

Sitting opposite him when she had done this, she watched while he wrote at length in her notes. He did not utter. It was impossible to decipher his crab-like hand upside down.

'May I see what it is you have written?'

Shocked, he replied, 'Out of the question. These are The Notes. I'm afraid The Notes are private and confidential.'

Hardly state secrets though. What on earth was the matter with him? Perplexed but determined, she persevered. 'But the notes are about *me*.'

Triumphantly avuncular and probably only ten years older than she was, he agreed. 'Quite so, my dear Mrs Harting! But for my eyes only. All you need to know is that in my professional opinion there is nothing the matter here that a long rest every afternoon won't cure.'

A long rest every afternoon? He clearly encountered a great many women who had nothing whatever to do. Sensing her irritation, and feeling ruffled by her extraordinary inability to concede that he was in charge, he sent her a charismatic smile in an attempt to recharge his own vanity and stood up to denote that the meeting was at an end.

Eyeing his carnation and wishing it would wither, she shook his hand, after which he showed her as far as his receptionist where she was supposed to make another appointment. Deciding not to do this, and pleading the fact that she did not have her diary with her, Victoria left it that she would ring up.

Driving home, she thought, I'll talk it over with James first, of course, but my instinct is to get rid of that man. He's creepy. Perhaps I'll ask Ellen. She might know a good one.

The Hanging Committee consisted of James, Victoria and Jack with Mr Peck, who would do it all, in attendance. The side room into which it was proposed to put the painting and drawings of Ellen was not exactly a room with a door as such, but had floor-to-ceiling shutters right across so that it could be pressed into service as an extension of the main gallery as and when it was needed. The dominant wall colour for the exhibition was white, this being deemed the best background to set off Jack's large, rich canvases. For other artists a paint job was sometimes necessary. The Gallery itself, although part of a large Victorian building with lofty rooms and fine, acanthused cornices and ceiling roses, was very modern in terms of its decoration, with spot lighting, and a tobacco-coloured highly polished parquet floor, which had a long, sparely elegant, white-cushioned steel banquette running down the middle of it. The only other colour until the paintings themselves should be properly displayed was provided by two enormous potted palms which stood greenly graceful in either corner at one end in lobed blue and white Chinese jardinieres. Apart from this there were two other rooms, one of which was a small reception area, and the other a split-level arrangement with a white cast-iron spiral staircase from one floor to the other, usually used for showing smaller more intimate art, such as lithographs or etchings.

The paintings were all placed around The Gallery, occupying the positions which would be theirs though, for the time being, propped against the walls on the floor. Broadly speaking the committee were in agreement as to what should go where. All, with the exception of Mr Peck who was frankly disappointed in Mrs Carey, though he did not say so, thought the portrait of Ellen to be the highlight of what promised to be a brilliant show. Although he did have to concede that even without most of her clothes on Mrs Carey still managed to remain a lady, which Mrs

Lucas definitely did not. Mr Peck had not told his wife about the painting of Mrs Lucas, being uncertain how to put into words what he had seen without shocking her and himself all over again.

Turning to Victoria, James said, 'Are the catalogues in yet?'

'I'm collecting them from the printer tomorrow.'

'What about replies?'

'It's a high acceptance rate, around eighty per cent so far, and the press are very interested.'

'Good!'

Suddenly alerted by the prospect of some money and mindful of a recent spate of letters from the bank which had at first tactfully claimed to be memory joggers as to the state of his overdraft, and then had become plaintive and finally stern, Jack enquired, 'Are the Maybricks in town yet?'

'Tomorrow,' replied Victoria with something of a sigh. Still, at least she was being let off another stupefying evening of Harold's reminiscences since the Maybricks had suddenly decided to go and bore for America in Scotland during the few remaining days before the exhibition. All the same there was still a great deal to do. She looked at her list, adding *Flowers* to the end of it, and then wrote another note to the effect that she must check with the caterer that all was in order. Looking at the painting of Ellen, it was obvious to Victoria that the flowers must be white lilies. Nothing else would do.

'When is Ellen back?' she asked Jack.

'She is back. We drove up together the day before yesterday.'

Well, that was reassuring, thought both Hartings at the same time. With Ellen in the offing, and the paintings safely finished and delivered they were surely home and dry.

Feeling suddenly depleted, Victoria sat down on the banquette with the pretext of sorting out her notes. The odd sensation of physical instability reasserted itself and during the short time of its duration was unnerving. Resolutely rising to her feet, Victoria chastised herself for imagining things. After all, although she might not like her gynaecologist there was no reason to doubt his competence and he had categorically stated that there was nothing the matter. Once the exhibition was over she would make an effort to take things more easily.

'Right,' said James, who had just finished briefing Mr Peck, 'I think we are almost there. Nothing else for you to do, Jack, but turn up on Thursday at the witching hour. Victoria and I, and Mr Peck, of course, will be here all day to field anything unexpected which might crop up.'

Noticing that his wife looked uncharacteristically tired, he reflected that it was a pity he had just lost his competent factotum, a girl who had been with The Gallery for the last five years. Although he had recently acquired another, it was James's view that she was too new to the job to be asked to shoulder all her predecessor's responsibilities quite so soon, which meant that Victoria must step in. Putting his arm round her shoulders and giving her a reassuring smile, he said, 'All right, darling?'

'Absolutely,' she replied, since by now she was.

16

Because his own car was being serviced, the morning of the private view found James being chauffered to The Gallery by his wife. Darting and weaving and missing the rest of the traffic by inches, Victoria drove *con brio*, magnificently oblivious to the cacophonous accompaniment of outraged car horns. Sitting sweating beside her, James felt as though he were part of the Royal Tournament. Able to bear it no longer as she sliced straight across three lines of traffic, missing the shining snout of a black cab by millimetres, he remonstrated, 'Steady on, darling.'

'But we're very late, James, and I do feel it's all my fault.'

'I'd rather arrive late and alive than dead and even later!'

To his relief she slowed down fractionally, but then the habit of a driving lifetime reasserted itself and, unable to resist it, she accelerated, taking the Piccadilly exit on two wheels at Grand Prix speed.

'Point taken,' said Victoria. Watching the Royal Academy streak past, he wondered what point she had in mind. If anything her speed seemed to be escalating in spite of the traffic lights. Next time he would drive.

On their arrival at The Gallery he said, 'Nothing to be gained by looking for a meter since we are going to be here most of the day. Why don't you go in and sit down, and I'll take the Volvette to the car park?'

Feeling suddenly shaky, but not mentioning it, she complied. Walking round to the other side of the car, James reflected that he must find a way of taking her driving in hand. Maybe an advanced motoring course was the answer. Maybe.

Inside the air-conditioned gallery, Victoria felt better again. Mr Peck was sitting on one of the chairs in the reception area, patiently waiting with his hemp tool bag at his feet. When she appeared he stood up.

Looks washed out, was his concerned verdict on Mrs

Harting. Not like herself at all. Then, mindful of an equally washed out Marjorie in the early days: Wonder if Mrs Harting's in the family way.

'So sorry to have kept you hanging about, Mr Peck. The traffic was simply awful. Nobody seems to know how to drive these days.'

Mr Peck, who had been traumatized by Mrs Harting's driving more often than he cared to remember, decided a noncommittal murmur was the only inoffensive reply to this. They settled down in companionable silence to wait for James.

Having parked the car, James strode towards The Gallery. Although the weather was still benign, there was a different quaity to the air. The milky blandness of summer had gone, probably for good this year, and, due to an autumnal drop in temperature, there was now a zesty, sharp edge to the paler sunshine, which caused him to step out with pleasure. It always seemed to James that autumn restored his sense of purpose. Of all the seasons it was, perhaps, his favourite. Walking along, he thought of his wife with affection. When tonight's show was over he would make sure that she took things more easily. Soon, he reflected, the leaves would begin to change, a particularly rich and beautiful time to be in the country. Perhaps he would take her to Scotland for a couple of weeks then. He was still mulling it over when he reached The Gallery.

Inside, Victoria, who had deputed the new receptionist, Hilary, to go and collect the previously ordered lilies from the florist, was now on the phone to the caterers, and Mr Peck was sorting out his tools. The exhibition was half complete. The old familiar excitement gripped James. Not in the least creative himself, it thrilled him to be the medium through which somebody else's talent was revealed. Two large canvases remained to be hung, plus the portrait of Ellen and the drawings. Victoria intended to arrange the flowers herself.

It was while James was finalizing with Mr Peck the height and position of Ellen and the relative placement of the satellite pencil drawings around her that Victoria fainted. Without a sound she simply slipped to the floor. Mr Peck, who saw it happen, pointed wordlessly. She came round almost immediately, as they lifted her onto the reception room sofa.

'So sorry, darling,' murmured Victoria the coper. 'I'll be all right in a minute.'

Her colour was dreadful. Fighting back panic, James was wondering what on earth to do next, when Mr Peck announced, 'Beg your pardon if I'm wrong, Mr Harting, but if her condition's what I think it is, you should get her into hospital double quick!'

Of course! What an ass he was.

'I'll get the car!' Running along the street followed by curious looks, he realized suddenly and conclusively the importance of this unplanned child. His child. If she lost it he would never forgive himself. On his arrival back at The Gallery he and Mr Peck installed Victoria in the back of the Volvette.

'Now don't you worry about anything,' was Mr Peck's unruffled instruction. 'I know what you want doing, and I'll do it!'

Remembering that the Volvette did not have a car phone, James said, 'Could you possibly ring St Mary's and alert them to the fact that we are coming? I'll be back in touch as soon as I get to the hospital.'

With a racing start worthy of his wife he set off across London. His last view of The Gallery in the rear-view mirror contained a diminishing Mr Peck waving his hammer in eccentric stalwart salute.

With his wife safely stowed away in a private room, undergoing tests, one and a half hours later found James grappling with the antediluvian hospital phone, which took ten-pence pieces but was extremely particular about which ones, choosing to spit out identical coins several times before eventually capitulating and accepting them. This all took an inordinate amount of time and under the dispirited gaze of a lengthening queue, he rang first Jack. No answer, just that damned answer phone. 'Oh, fuck it!' said James. Then he rang Alexander. No answer again. Lunch time. Heaven knew when he would get away from here and it was imperative that someone, other than Bill Peck in his leather apron, was on hand to greet the guests when they began to arrive for the private view. Beginning to feel desperate, he rang Tessa.

She was in. Explaining the situation, he said, 'I know we've had our differences lately, but I'd be so grateful if you could get over there early and hold the fort. Oh, and don't tell anyone about Victoria's pregnancy. We don't want to announce it yet.' There might, after all, be nothing to announce.

Tessa, who had been wondering how to occupy herself all afternoon anyway, graciously agreed. 'I'll get a cab right away and I'll take my party dress with me.'

Feeling that he had done her an injustice in their last interview, and thinking, She may have a funny way of showing it, but her heart's in the right place, James said, 'There's nothing to do, Tess, except arrange the flowers. It's the same Cordon Bleu team as usual and they know the ropes. And Bill Peck knows exactly what to do as well. No need to interfere, just let him get on with it. And be on hand to greet the guests if I don't make it on time.'

'I will.'

He was about to elaborate on his gratitude for her co-operation when there was a staccato tap on the glass of the booth. 'Hurry UP!' mouthed a furious face on the other side of the glass, causing it to mist over. James signalled back optimistically and received a glare by return.

'I'll have to go! Thanks, Tessa, you're wonderful.'

Avoiding the black looks of the besiegers, he left the kiosk and made his way back to the ward, reflecting as he did so that it wasn't a satisfactory solution but it was better than nothing.

Sitting in the taxi, Tessa checked the contents of the small holdall. Minimal red dress, tights, silver shoes, earrings, necklace, silver bag, makeup and scent. It was all there. She looked forward to being queen bee in the hive of chic social activity which was a Gallery private view, and most of all she looked forward to meeting Jack again. Time was running out, Tessa recognized, and if she were to concentrate Jack's mind on herself and their life together it would have to happen soon, otherwise she might end up with no one.

When she arrived at The Gallery she found that Hilary had already had the common sense to arrange the flowers, which task she had completed with artistry and flair. Having nothing else to do for the moment, Tessa decided to go and plague Mr Peck. She found him cloistered behind the shutters in the little room off the main gallery where he had just hung the portrait of Ellen Carey, which was flanked by two massive vases of waxen scented lilies. Her curdling displeasure at the unexpected sight of the painting was so concentrated that the air became all at once dense with it.

Sensitive to this and smiling to himself, Mr Peck said, 'Good afternoon, Mrs Lucas,' through the screw gripped between his teeth.

Her next words removed his grin. 'Take that down, please.'

'But I've only just put it up,' he protested, removing the screw.

'I expect you are aware that Mr Harting has put me in charge until his return from the hospital.' Mr Peck, who had been informed of this unwelcome fact by telephone, just before Mrs Lucas turned up, had no option but to say that he was.

'Well then, when I tell you that Mr Harting has had second thoughts about exhibiting this and has instructed me to ask you to put another one in its place, I'm sure you will make no objection.'

Phrased like that he was sure he wouldn't either, though it did cross his mind to wonder whether she was telling the truth. Since there was no way of checking up on her, he felt he could not very well refuse. Sulkily he asked, 'Well, where is it? The other one. Where is it?'

'In Chelsea. I have to go and collect it.'

Watching her as she telephoned for a taxi, he thought, She's bold, that's what she is. And no better than she ought to be either. Thinks herself a lady. Lady Muck more like! Noting how she found time to bully Hilary over some minor omission on her way out, Mr Peck exuded deep disapproval. Neither Mr nor Mrs Harting would have spoken to an employee like that. But then they've got class, was his biting verdict on Mrs Lucas.

Cow, was Hilary's.

It was four o'clock by the time Tessa got to Ceci's flat, which meant that time was short.

'I wonder whether you would mind helping me carry something?' said she to the cab driver. Dazzled by her soignée beauty, and the shortness of her skirt, he replied that he would not, and together they carried the canvas, mysteriously wrapped in one of Ceci's sheets, down to the vehicle.

'Oh, I have to collect one more item,' remembered Tessa, 'and then we can go.' Locking the front door with the drawings under one arm she thought, With any luck, and provided that James doesn't get back in time to stop me, by the end of this evening Ellen will have left her husband, and Jack will be with me.

'Where to, ma'am?'

'Back to The Gallery,' she instructed, settling back to read Ceci's copy of September *Vogue*, which had arrived that morning after her friend had left for work. When they finally drew up, and she had paid the fare, they both carried the painting into the reception area.

The usefulness of the driver was at an end.

'Thank you!' said Tessa, dismissing him. Giving her one last lascivious look, he went. 'Hilary, could you and Mr Peck please carry this into the little side room?'

They did so, and it was at that point that the caterers arrived. Having sent Hilary off to deal with them, Tessa closed the shutters, and exposed the painting of herself for the delectation of Mr Peck.

He had been expecting it but, nevertheless, the sheer explicitness of the thing shocked him all over again. And worse was to come. She had a series of drawings which he had not seen before. Between them they positioned the canvas, and then, while he held it, she stepped back to check the height.

'Yes, that will do.' Leaving him to get on with it, she began to tackle the drawings. Those of Ellen were exactly the same size as those of herself and had been glassed and clipped. Nothing simpler than to effect a swap. She did. Standing back again to assess the result, she viewed the lilies with distaste.

'I suppose it's too late to change those.'

Peering at his watch, which told him that the time was five o'clock, Mr Peck was quite sure it was, but did not deign to reply. Leaving him to go in search of Hilary and the caterers, she pleasantly observed, 'I hope you aren't going to go on sulking, Mr Peck.' With his loyalty to the Hartings and The Gallery now

under severe strain, Mr Peck pretended that he had not heard
her and pointedly closed the shutters after her.

17

At six o'clock the first guests began to arrive. Shortly a few became a multitude as what Victoria called the glitterarty mingled with critics and prospective buyers. James had rung to say that he hoped to arrive by seven. As yet, typically, there was no sign of Jack, and until he and Ellen arrived it was Tessa's intention to keep the shutters closed. At the door where she was greeting the guests, she encountered Marcus and Jane Marchant. Giving her a kiss on each cheek and then taking a glass of champagne, he enquired, 'Where's James? And', looking over her blonde head into the room, 'Victoria?'

'Victoria's ill. Nothing serious. James will be here soon.' Though not too soon, she hoped. 'Meanwhile I'm in charge.'

'*You're* in charge?' He gave her a speculative look, at the same time intuiting that this did not all add up. Stung by his evident surprise, Tessa bridled and said, 'Yes, *I'm* in charge. Oh, there are the Maybricks. I must go. Excuse me.' The Marchants moved off into the main body of the gallery, where they encountered Alexander Lucas who had apparently arrived just ahead of them.

'Your wife appears to be in charge of this extravaganza,' observed Marcus, sipping his drink. 'What's going on?'

'Search me. She's so busy I've hardly had a chance to speak to her. We look like getting back together again, by the way.'

'I'm so glad for you both,' said Jane the warm-hearted. Her husband digested this depressing information in silence, deciding to keep his own counsel. No point in being a spectre at such a feast, which might prove to be of very short duration anyway.

Changing the subject, Marcus said, 'I notice that Carey hasn't yet put in an appearance at his own exhibition. Or, if he has, I haven't spotted him.'

He let his eye travel round the room. The gathering was eclectic, an animated chattering combination of the press, the ultra chic and the ultra arty, most of whom had apparently felt it necessary to make creative statements through the medium of the clothes they wore and some of whom looked quite extraordinary, like a random sample from Central Casting.

On the other side of the room, Tessa was finding it very hard to dislodge the Maybricks. Limpet-like Irma clung to Harold, and both clung to her. Neither appeared to wish to fend for themselves socially. Integrating them at this sort of occasion was a task which normally fell to Victoria. The minutes were ticking by. In desperation, she said, noticing Ginevra standing stonily alone like a monument on Easter Island, 'Time I introduced you to some other people. Come and meet Ginevra Haye.' Descrying from a distance Ginevra's uncompromising mien, Harold was by no means sure that this would be a wise move. Stately in black and wearing a silver necklace from which depended a chunk of amber the size of a pigeon's egg, he divined her to be the sort of intellectual woman who might be interested in abstract ideas, but never, in a million years, in cars. Feebly he began to protest, but Tessa would not be gainsaid. Watching this little scenario with amusement from within another group, Marcus noted that Irma, in daffodil yellow with more sequins, looked tawdry beside the imposing and clever Mrs Haye, whom he knew to be an old Oxford friend of Victoria's. The introductions completed, Tessa left them to it.

Still following her progress, Marcus saw her stop stock still as Jack Carey entered the gallery with Ellen on his arm, and then appear to issue some sort of urgent instruction to the girl called Hilary, who was apparently James's new personal assistant. Aha, she's up to something, thought Marcus. Whatever it was, he had a hunch they would soon find out. Taking his wife's elbow, he said, 'Come on. Let's make a tour of his work before it gets any more crowded.'

With now only seconds to go before she pulled off her *coup de théâtre*, even Tessa had sudden doubts as to the wisdom of the course she was pursuing.

Standing beside her husband who was wearing his favourite mattress ticking suit, Ellen was stylishly and dramatically Bohemian, wearing a tubular floor-length black dress of spectacular simplicity embellished by the silver collar and its matching equally barbaric earrings, and the purple coat which

Tessa recognized from the painting, now relegated to the cellar. For a brief moment her kohl-clouded eyes met and dispassionately engaged those of Tessa, and then she looked away. A spontaneous burst of clapping greeted their appearance, followed by the clicking and flashing of cameras. Enviously eyeing them as they talked to the social diarist of the *Tatler*, Tessa thought, I should like to be the centre of attention like that, and I will be.

The sliding sound of the shutters being opened by Hilary warned her that now was the time to make herself scarce, and slipping out through the reception area, which was luckily empty, Tessa gained the street and, still in her party finery, went for a conspicuous walk around the block.

By this time Ginevra had shed the Maybricks and was talking to the Marchants, and because she was facing that way she was one of the first to see the unveiling of Tessa. Following the direction of her transfixed gaze, Marcus turned round and saw it too. So that was it! Aware that there was now a crisis to be averted, he scanned the room for his old friend, and, in order to prevent a murder if possible, for Tessa. She was nowhere to be seen. As more and more people realized what was in the little room, a hush pervaded The Gallery. All at once Marcus saw Alexander shouldering his way through the crowd to the front. It was too late to stop whatever was about to happen.

Marcus watched Alexander achieve his objective and then stand, face livid, studying in ominous silence first the painting of his wife and after that, one by one, the drawings. Then turning to a waitress who was standing beside him, mouth open, gaping at the painting with a full tray of drinks in her hands, he said, politely and unexpectedly, 'Why don't you let me help you with that.' Amazed she handed it to him.

'Bitch! Rotten, bloody bitch!' shouted Alexander, and hurled the whole lot at the canvas. Openly weeping with the pain and betrayal of it all, he turned to his mesmerized audience and announced to the room at large, 'That whore is my wife!' Champagne mixed with shards of glass poured off Tessa's image. For the second time flashbulbs popped, and it was at this point that Jack arrived on the scene, his interviews with the press completed and Ellen in his wake, to find out what was happening. He was only halfway to the scene of the action when he collided with Alexander storming out. Scarcely breaking his stride, Alexander hit Jack very hard and continued blindly on his way to the door. Beckoning to Jane to follow him, Marcus ran after him. Lying on the floor, consciousness coming and going, Jack wondered what he had done to deserve such treatment at his own show.

From her refuge in the telephone box across the road opposite The Gallery, Tessa saw her husband's enraged exit, which was more or less what she had expected. He was closely followed by Marcus and Jane Marchant, who caught up with him further along the pavement. There was some sort of discussion, after which Jane hailed a cab and they all drove away in it. Cautiously letting herself out, Tessa walked across the road and back to The Gallery.

Inside it, leaving her husband where he was, Ellen moved forward to discover what the fuss was all about. Amazed to be confronted by a portrait of his latest mistress instead of herself, she stood frozen into shocked immobility. How could he have done this to her? Her predominant emotions were those of furious disbelief and then overwhelming grief for the end of her marriage, for now, Ellen saw clearly, it would have to end. I will never be able to trust my husband. Never. And this public humiliation is the last straw, she thought.

In silence and with great dignity she turned and walked back through the throng, which parted respectfully for her, to where Jack still lay. Slipping off the purple coat with disdain she dropped it on the floor beside him and, turning to go, found herself face to face with Tessa.

For several seconds Ellen stared haughtily at her adversary, who was forced to avert her eyes in the face of such arctic contempt. Finally, into a dead silence, she said, 'You can have him. I've had the best of Jack. And in a curious way, I think he has had the best of himself. I suspect it's downhill all the way from now on.'

Put like that he did not sound like much of a bargain.

Oh no, Ellen, no! On the parquet floor Jack was dimly aware that his wife was giving him away, and tried to rouse himself enough to beg her not to do it. Lapsing back into unconsciousness, the last sound he heard was the light, inexorable tap of her steps receding as she made her exit.

It seemed that the drama was over. A subdued murmur broke out among the guests, some of whom prepared to drift away although it was still only 7.15. Heart bleeding for Ellen, Ginevra slipped out after her, determined to see that she got home safely, wondering as she did so what on earth could have happened to James Harting.

In the reception area, and also preparing to leave were the Maybricks. Mouth turned down puritanically and eyebrows drawn together, Harold said, 'Say, I had no idea Jack Carey painted that sort of thing! What's your view, Irma?' So seldom did he ask her for her view of things that Irma was stumped. Disgusted, Dallas, was her own reaction to what she had just witnessed but, mindful of the way in which Harold, seared by the experience of his first assertive wife, came down like a ton of bricks on any member of his family who appeared to be indulging in the dangerous practice of thinking for themselves, she carefully replied, 'I'm not sure, dear. I think I'd like to hear yours first.'

'Irma, I'm disappointed in you,' was his ungrateful response to the sort of deference he normally demanded. 'You of all people, the mother of children. American children! *My* children! Where's your judgement, Irma?'

Flustered, since it now appeared that she was in even more trouble than Jack Carey, Irma was just about to try to field this when James Harting appeared, out of breath but secure in the knowledge that both Victoria and the baby appeared to be all right.

'Harold! Irma! Not going already surely? Where is everybody? What's going on here?' And then, with a sudden flicker of foreboding, 'And where's Tessa?'

With only the clothes she stood up in and her ticket paid for by Ginevra, Ellen took the train to Sussex. The thought of returning to the studio to which Jack would surely also return was anathema to her. I shall never set foot in there again, she decided. 'Come and stay with me,' Ginevra had urged, but Ellen had felt unable to face it. Going home she realized that the depth of her disappointment was founded on the unrealistic hope she had allowed herself to nurture that they might after all have begun again. Tears filled her eyes, and then there was guilt.

Harry and David will be devastated, agonised Ellen, but there's nothing I can do about it. I've done my best and I simply can't go on like this any longer.

She would have to go and see them. Or maybe it would be less traumatic to wait until the next exeat, when they were both due to come to the cottage. On balance she thought it would. Better to have some days at home with her after the receipt of such upsetting news than to be told and then pitched straight back into school where they would have to cope with it as best they could on their own.

When she finally got back to Butterfly Cottage, the telephone was ringing. It was probably her husband. Let it ring. As she had promised she would, Ellen called Ginevra and then she went to bed.

Victoria was still in hospital where she was due to remain for at least one more day, so the next morning found James eating a solitary breakfast and poring over as many newspapers as he had been able to acquire. As he had expected, most of the qualities' critics had not had time to file their thoughtful copy yet. That would probably appear tomorrow or, in some cases, on Monday. The tabloids with a rather simpler message to put across had moved quickly. It was all there with photographs. James groaned. Among the less offensive headlines were: *Fine Old Art Fracas* and *Poet Goes Ape In Art Gallery*. The *Daily Telegraph* appeared to be the most restrained with *Private View Disturbance*, followed by a more or less factual report of what had apparently happened when he was not there.

Reflecting that he and Tessa, with whom he had had a cataclysmic row, looked like being on non-speakers for the rest of their lives, but that at least he hoped he had managed to salvage the Maybrick connection during the course of an interminable dinner, James got out of bed and found himself a couple of aspirin. Watching these dissolve in water in a cloud of healing bubbles, he pressed his poor aching head against the cool glass of the bathroom cabinet. Jack, he remembered, had gone rushing off in pursuit of Ellen and Christ knew what had happened to Tessa. Or Alexander for that matter.

The telephone began to ring.

'Mr Harting have you any comment on last night's . . .'

'No comment,' said James, smartly cutting off the caller in mid-sentence. He replaced the receiver. It rang again.

'Mr Harting, have you . . .' This time he left it off the hook and went off and had his shower. Damage limitation was now the name of this particular game, and the sooner it started, the better.

18

Ellen struggled into consciousness the next morning through the mental swamp of a black depression. Her heart felt like a stone. For a few moments she lay there, hoping that this was only the legacy of a bad dream and then, slowly, the events of the previous evening paraded themselves before her inner eye. Her limbs felt leaden. Dragged down by inertia, she wondered if she could bring herself even to get out of bed. In the wake of what had happened the night before there seemed no point in doing anything any more, and Ellen, normally an early riser, went on lying where she was, staring into space, painfully reviewing her marriage.

Her conclusions were sombre: I see now that when I talked about leaving Jack I was deluding myself. Since the decision has been taken out of my hands, I am quite simply heartbroken. This is real. The other was fantasy, and I'll bet old Edward Montague realized it too. I always believed that, *au fond*, Jack loved me. Of course we have been married for a long time, and I knew about, and mainly turned a blind eye to, his philandering, which I probably shouldn't have done, but I never thought he would ever do anything as gratuitously cruel and insulting as he did last night. I shall never forgive it.

The telephone on the bedside table began to ring. Ellen ignored it and after a while it stopped, only to recommence a few seconds later. In the end she picked up the receiver and, holding it gingerly a couple of inches away from her ear, she listened without saying anything. Jack, for he it was, was clearly in a panic.

'Ellen, darling Ellen, thank God I've got you at last. Ellen, it's all a dreadful mistake. That bitch, Tessa Lucas engineered the whole thing. You do believe me, don't you, Ellen? Ellen? Ellen?' The last was a shout. He sounded desperate and close to tears.

Ellen rotated her arm so that the receiver was poised four inches above the rest and dropped it back into place with a clang.

She hoped it burst his ear drum. It didn't matter a jot who had engineered what. All the time he had been assuring her that from now on his sexual allegiance was to her, he had been not only bedding Tessa but also painting her. Inured to infidelity as Ellen was, this was probably the hardest thing of all to condone, a worse betrayal than the other, for as she had stood looking at her rival she had felt as though by painting Tessa's image he had painted over her own, obliterating her very being. Sometimes, thought Ellen, I wonder whether I'm really here at all as an individual, or just a convenient cooking, childbearing extension of my husband's personality.

With a determined exercise of will, she got out of bed. She felt physically weak and her legs shook as though she had just recovered from the flu. Drawing back the curtains, she noticed that her hands shook too. Emotionally dehydrated and feeling as though her body was a husk within which nothing very much resided any more, Ellen stared bleakly out at her garden. No more tears. She had wept enough tears to last a lifetime during the course of her marriage to Jack, and there was literally nothing left to shed. No more tears.

The phone started up again. Pulling the plug out, she could still hear its forlorn echo purveyed by other extensions in far reaches of the house. Eventually she would have to speak to her husband, if only to stop him rushing to Sussex to see her. At present Ellen did not feel up to such an emotionally battering interview as this was bound to be, and thought it possible that she never would. She turned on the news and found it hard to believe that, notwithstanding the profound change in her own life, outside the world was carrying on as normal. The main thing, Ellen instinctively felt, in spite of her chronic unhappiness and despair, was not to let standards slip. Sitting down in front of the pine washstand, which doubled as a dressing-table, she made the effort to brush her hair and then picked up the oval hand mirror and, pulling her makeup bag towards her, began very slowly to design her eyes.

'This will sound mawkish, but I honestly had fallen in love with my wife all over again.'

Listening to Jack, James thought it did sound mawkish,

especially in the light of the way Jack had treated Ellen down the years.

'And now, now she says she wants a divorce. She won't see me. She doesn't want me to come near her. I've begged her to reconsider, *begged* her, and she won't.' He poured himself another finger of whisky which he drained at a swallow. James, who had come to make sure that he was all right and to deliver the glad tidings that, in spite of the adverse publicity, or possibly because of it, the exhibition had been a sellout, feared that his friend might be about to cry.

'Have you heard from Tessa?'

'Endlessly. I can't shake her off.' Here Jack put his head in his hands. 'Can't you talk to her? She's your sister.'

'No, I can't. She's your mistress and you'll have to sort it out.' James was quite decided. 'Besides which, we aren't on speaking terms. And probably won't be for some time.'

'Perhaps,' resumed Jack, without much conviction, 'I could appeal to her husband.'

Reflecting that another punch on the jaw might be the upshot of such a misguided move, James observed, 'He doesn't want her either!'

'I wish to God *she* didn't want *me*.'

'On the contrary, it strikes me she's absolutely determined to have you.' James did not feel like being kind to Jack. Standing up, he said, 'I'm afraid I have to go. Let me know when the wedding is, and don't drink any more whisky. You'll need a clear head for the trials in store.' Seeing Jack's fugitive, wretched expression, James relented. 'Look, why don't you go and see Ellen, in spite of what she says. Take a prayer rug with you.'

When he had gone, Jack reread Ellen's very severe letter. As he did so, he pictured her in the country, presiding over Butterfly Cottage and her garden, or sitting in the bentwood rocking chair reading a novel with one of the cats on her lap, probably Casimir the favourite. Lastly, and hardest to bear, he pictured her silkily naked in their marital bed, shortly to be her bed alone if she really meant what she said.

Jack,
I have never told you, wrote Ellen, *but now you should know,*

that I have been thinking of leaving you for months. It seemed to me that our marriage had run its course and that there was nothing left in it for me, although clearly it was convenient for you to have a wife on hand to run your houses and your children. And you, come to that. Although no doubt a housekeeper would have done just as well. Nevertheless, probably because there was, in spite of everything, some residue of our early love left, I was prepared to try again when I sensed, or, rather, thought I sensed, that suddenly, for reasons now beyond my comprehension, you appeared to want to reinfuse our relationship with some of the passion which indubitably did exist in the early years. Though even in those days, besotted as I was and flattered (I'll be frank) to be married to so much talent, I was well aware of your shortcomings. But then we both had those. The trouble is, Jack, that you have never grown up and far from being the exciting, unconventional Bohemian painter of your twenties, you are now about to enter your forties as that most depressing of prospects, an elderly swinger. I could have overlooked the treachery of your affair with Tessa Lucas – after all you have conditioned me over the years to accept that sort of thing, and, before you say it, I'm well aware that albeit reluctantly and principally because I felt I had no choice, I did condone it. Whether you would have been prepared to take the same behaviour from me as I have been expected to stomach from you is another matter. What I could not forgive was the cynicism of your hollow promise of a fresh beginning. I have known for years that I am married to a self-indulgent hypocrite (well, after all, nobody is perfect, are they?) but to learn at this late stage that you are, on top of that, a manipulative and cruel bastard has finished it.

One more thing I should mention in the interests of honesty and fairness, having listed all your transgressions, and that is that, very discreetly (and I'm willing to bet you never knew this) I have had lovers of my own (quite a few of them) throughout the course of our marriage. So now you do know. Please do not attempt to contact me for at least another week. I am aware that we shall at some point have to meet and talk, but since the boys' exeat is not until the 26th, which is when I will tell them that I intend to divorce you, there is a little time in hand and I need that to come to terms with what has happened. With regard to ourselves, I am sure that I am doing the right thing. With regard to the boys, I feel desperately guilty and sad, and am well aware that both, and probably Harry in particular, will suffer. That being the case, I hope that we can bring this marriage to a close with the minimum of acrimony and emotional disruption.

Ellen.

Self-analysis had never been one of Jack's favourite pastimes, but now it was beginning to look as though there was no help for it. Pulling in his stomach, he decided that he disliked the phrase 'elderly swinger' in particular. And looking for a way of coming to terms with another piece of unwelcome information, he decided to make himself more comfortable about her lovers by rationalizing and taking the stance that it would be bourgeois for him to object to his wife's adultery. Yes, bourgeois. So that was all right then.

On the other hand, the notion that his wife had been unfaithful not once but apparently many times brought out a level of sexual competition in Jack that he would not have suspected existed, and raised the unnerving question of invidious comparisons. Also unnerving was the realization that for most of his marriage he had been living with someone he did not know. Holding her letter, Jack reflected what a bugger it was that after all those years during which he had needed Ellen without really wanting her, except intermittently and usually between mistresses, now he did, she did not want him. All the same he was confident that he could win her back. To reinforce this confidence he poured himself another glass of whisky and looking across the studio at her portrait, which had been restored to its former position on the easel, having been located in The Gallery cellar, he said, 'I love you, Ellen!' Enigmatically beautiful, but mute, his wife stared back at him.

In the country Ellen went through the motions in the week that followed of living a normal life. Today, for instance, she was discussing the vegetable garden with Mr Phipps.

'I think we've got a mouse run here,' he was saying in his Sussex burr. 'I'm goin' to have to put down a trap or maybe two.'

'But what about the cats?' objected Ellen. 'They walk through the vegetable garden and I'd hate Merlin, who's getting very old, to get his paw caught.'

Mr Phipps replied with scorn, 'He won't get his paw caught,' adding heartlessly, 'worst that can happen to him is that it'll jump up and hit him on the ear.'

Ellen smiled, in spite of herself. 'I don't think he would like that either, Mr Phipps.'

'No mebbe not,' he agreed. 'Now them gorgettes,' here he pointed, 'them's over the top!' He made them sound like a row of geriatric tap dancers. 'And them beans too, Mrs Carey. You pick the last of them and I'll get rid of 'em.'

'I will, Mr Phipps,' said Ellen in the obedient way she knew he liked where his precious vegetables were concerned. 'I'll do it after lunch.'

And so it was that the mild and balmy September afternoon found Ellen, with a trug hooked on one arm, cutting the last of the courgettes and picking runner beans. As she pursued this peaceful occupation, she thought of Jack. Since she had written to him he had not attempted to contact her. It was, of course, true to say that she had asked him not to, but all the same Ellen was piqued. What had happened to the desperation on parade earlier in the week?

She picked on. Runner beans were crafty. They ran secretly down behind the canes and generally displayed a talent for invisibility. Accordingly, she picked a trugful in the course of the first trawl, and was just embarking on a second to catch the recalcitrant remainder before calling it a day, when she became aware of a car coming slowly up the drive.

Standing looking at her as she pulled a last handful of beans before turning to come and greet him, Alexander was suddenly aware of how very pretty Ellen was. Her face beneath the wide brim of her straw garden hat was dappled with its shade, and her creamy ankle-length cotton dress, which had a low-necked high-waisted bodice, billowed slightly as she came towards him, putting him in mind of eighteenth-century country girls, all of whom, he felt sure, must also have walked like fallow deer.

'Alexander! What a surprise!' Holding the trug in front of her, she smiled up at him.

She's absolutely charming, he suddenly realized. How come I've seen Ellen Carey many times before, and yet I've never noticed it? He could think of no answer to this.

'I've come to apologize.'

'*You've* come to apologize? But why?'

'Let me give you a hand with that.' He took the trug off her and followed her into the house.

Inside, in spite of the Aga, it was very cool. In deference to the clement September day all the windows were open, letting in a smell of leaves and grass and late flowers.

Ellen tipped the beans and courgettes onto the work surface and then hung the trug back on its hook.

'What can I get you? Tea? Coffee? Sinful glass of afternoon wine?'

'Sinful glass of wine, definitely.'

He watched her as she poured it, with her cats weaving serpentine around her, no doubt hoping for food. Ellen poured herself one as well.

'Now, explain yourself. And why don't you sit down while you do it?'

'I'm afraid my wife has wrecked your marriage.'

'I can assure you that my marriage has been wrecking itself for years without any help from your wife. What about *your* marriage?'

'That's had it!'

'Perhaps Jack and Tessa deserve each other!'

Thinking, Not even Jack Carey deserves Tessa, Alexander said, 'I'm told he doesn't want her.'

'Really! Well, it's no longer any concern of mine what he wants.' Remembering that she was still wearing the straw sunhat, she took it off and hung it on the back of the door. 'However, be that as it may, it is true to say that those two are both children and left to their own devices would destroy one another. Each needs to be married to a grown-up in order to function at all. Which is the most awful cross for whoever lands the job.'

'Don't I know it!' Alexander spoke with feeling.

'Are you still in love with her?' As she asked this, Ellen tried to avoid putting the same question to herself vis-à-vis Jack.

'I can't forgive her.'

'Love and forgiveness don't necessarily go hand in hand.'

'It makes living together a bloody sight easier if they do.'

'I suppose so. I can't forgive Jack either.'

'You've been married a long time. Won't you miss it?'

'Some of it,' said Ellen with a sigh. 'It's Harry and David I'm most worried about. And then there's the question of how I support myself. I suppose if the book worked it might be easier.'

Admiring the lines of her lissom figure as she leant against the massive old butcher's block which stood in front of the Aga, he decided not to tell her how slim were her chances of being published by anybody at all in these recessionary times.

'Did you write to any of the agents whose names I gave you?'

'Yes, I did, but nobody has written back as yet.'

Getting up, he walked over to the bay window and stood for a few minutes looking out at the garden. He and Tessa could simply go their separate ways, each taking half a car and half a house. She had a private income. He had a job. But Ellen's case was quite different, he recognized. Perhaps, after all, she was better off with Jack.

Turning to face her, he moved across the room and put his empty wine glass down beside her intending to suggest this. Instead, looking at her upturned face and moved by an irresistible impulse which he could not explain and made no attempt to control, Alexander lifted Ellen up onto the butcher's block and kissed her.

Later, although not much later, in the airy country bedroom they made love to one another kindly and with circumspection, each fearing to wound again where so much injury had taken place already, and when they finally came together it was with a mutual sigh of instant pleasure mixed with distant pain. Afterwards, exhausted, arms around each other, they fell asleep and when Ellen awoke it was six o'clock. Propped up on one elbow beside him, she looked at Alexander in the same way as she had looked at other lovers over the years. Probably sensitive to her gaze upon him and just beginning to stir, a faint frown between the fine brows, he opened his eyes, Celtic eyes of an unexpected dark blue, and drew her towards him.

'Witch! How long have you been looking at me?'

Drawing her ringed finger down his aquiline nose she said, 'I may have been looking at you but I wasn't thinking about you.'

'I really think I have fallen in love with you, Ellen.'

Love.

'I really don't think you have, Alexander, though I am enormously flattered to hear you say it.' This was said gently, but with certainty. She smiled at him, a slow, luminous smile, the memory of which would linger with him, along with the scent she wore, for a very long time to come. 'Oh, I'm not saying that wasn't wonderful. It was. But only a respite. A brief, healing fusion of two social casualties, if you like. I'm afraid the action for both of us is elsewhere.'

But even as she spoke the words, she thought, In another incarnation I could have fallen in love with you. Too late in this one, though, now that I have been so comprehensively emotionally fucked up by my marriage. Oh, Alexander, you're sensitive and kind and so attractive. A true romantic! Not many of those about these days. And best of all, you punched Jack! Otherwise the way I was feeling I would have had to do it myself.

For the first time since the previous Friday, Ellen laughed out loud.

'I'm glad you find my protestations of passion so amusing,' he said, slightly miffed.

She kissed him. 'No, not you. Jack. Lying on the floor of The Gallery, out cold! What happened to the painting of Tessa, by the way?'

'When James finally arrived and found out what had been going on, apparently he and she had a monumental row, during the course of which he told her to take it with her when she went and she did. Jack, by the way, didn't know anything about the substitution. It was all her idea.'

'What did you do after you stormed out?'

'You'll have to ask Marcus and Jane Marchant. They took me with them when they went out to dinner afterwards and by the end of the evening I am informed I was legless. I dimly remember the doorman helping to ladle me into a taxi saying, "Does he often do this?" and Jane replying, with ladylike English understatement, "No, hardly ever, but he's just had some very bad news." When I woke up I was in their spare bed together with a crashing headache and no idea how I got there. More I cannot tell you.'

'And why was Victoria not at the opening?'

'Mystery surrounds that. Nobody seems to know.'

'Shall we get up?'

'Only if you allow me to make love to you again before we do!'

Somewhere else in the cottage the phone began to ring.

'That will be Jack. Take no notice.'

As he was finally leaving, Alexander said, 'Please don't send me away, Ellen!'

Firmly she replied, 'I must. One day you'll thank me for it.'

'Maybe.' He kissed her hand, repeating without conviction, 'Maybe.' And then, on impulse, still holding her hand and wanting to do something for her, he said, 'Why don't you give me a copy of the synopsis of your book, plus whatever you've written so far. I have a great many contacts in the profession, and can think of at least one who may be prepared to take a flier on a first novel, if he likes it.'

As Alexander drove himself back to London with her manuscript on the seat beside him, the whole episode began to take on a dreamlike insubstantiality. And yet, at the same time, he knew himself in some indefinable way to have passed out of Tessa's sphere of influence. Dipping his headlights in the face of some oncoming traffic, he reflected, Perhaps Ellen's real gift to me is that now I can begin again.

19

In Little Haddow Ginevra pursued her familiar daily routine. The frustration of not encountering James Harting at the Carey private view had been intense. Exactly what had happened, Ginevra had no idea, though someone, probably Ellen, had told her that his absence was due to the fact that Victoria had been taken ill.

Now that the weather was cooler her work pattern had changed again and the early morning walks were, for the moment anyway, a thing of the past. Ginevra tended to spend the mornings researching and collating, and the afternoons writing. The day of the exhibition had been her last trip to London, and she had combined this with a morning in the library, and a visit to Covent Garden in order to purchase another of her favourite marbled notebooks. There was none in stock. This was a blow, since, irrationally for her, she could not conceive of writing her love affair with James Harting in anything else. In the end she placed an order for two of them, which would be sent to her when they came in, and had to content herself with reading back pages in bed with her brandy at night.

There had been no communication of any sort from Kevin, apart from a dog-eared postcard, which looked as though it had been carried around in the back pocket of his jeans for several weeks before finally being sent. It was purely factual, with no endearments of any sort, and baldly purveyed the news that it should not be too long now before he was on his way home though he did not give any dates. Tearing it into tiny pieces, and hoping as she did so that he would never come back, Ginevra dropped these in the bin. The money was still arriving and although she had dipped into it for clothes to wear at the Carey show, and one or two other things besides, there was still a substantial amount left.

Mentally she felt herself to be in a disquieting state of

suspended animation. The dreams, more often than not erotic and frequently frightening, still occurred, though not as often as they had during the stifling, claustrophobic heat of the summer when they had tormented her almost every night. Like all acutely lonely people, Ginevra talked to the cat and, more and more frequently these days, to herself, and it had come as something of a shock to her one day while standing in the queue in the Little Haddow one-cashier bank to realize that her under-the-breath mutterings were attracting curious looks.

Her only friend in the world, for Ginevra had long since stripped Victoria of that title, was Ellen, with whom she spoke once or twice a week, and whose uncertainties concerning her future Ginevra knew all about. On Ginevra's advice Ellen had managed to stave off a visit from her husband until the night before the boys were due to come home from school. Ellen had strong, independent days and weepy, fearful days, and, in Ginevra's opinion, was in no fit state to take any final decisions about her future. Shoring up Ellen was just about the only worthwhile thing she felt she did, and was also her only current contact with reality.

The telephone call from Victoria came as a bolt from the blue.

'Ginevra? Victoria here. How are you?

'Okay. How are you?'

'Blooming! Never better! Look, I wondered if I might drive down to see you, maybe towards the end of this week. It's too long since we've seen each other.'

Not that long and not just coming to see me either. She must want something, Ginevra surmised.

Watching her knuckles whiten as she gripped the telephone receiver hard in trepidation at the prospect, Ginevra was at a loss as to how to refuse, especially in the light of the many invitations she herself had accepted to Victoria's house. Mentally reviewing the meagre contents of her fridge, she said after a pause, 'Yes, all right. When?'

'Whenever it suits you, though looking at my diary,' here there was the sound of leafing, 'I see that it will have to be Thursday as I'm busy every other day.'

So why claim to be suiting me? Listening to it, Ginevra was irritable and, therefore, ungracious.

'I suppose Thursday's all right. What time?'

Mindful of the fact that her friend's cooking was famously awful, Victoria responded, 'What about after lunch?'

That's a relief anyway. 'Fine. See you then.'

'Yes, see you then.'

She rang off, leaving Ginevra wondering what on earth she could possibly be after. Thoroughly unsettled at the prospect of a Harting in Little Haddow, she decided to make herself a calming cup of tea only to discover when she opened the fridge, closely watched by Captain Morgan's single eye, that the milk was off.

'What a very monosyllabic conversation! If I didn't know her as well as I do I might have got the impression that she didn't want me to come!' said Victoria to James when she had hung up.

'Well, you have to admit that Ginevra has never been exactly what you might call talkative. In the social sense, I mean.'

They had both just got back from The Gallery. Throwing into heaps the sofa scatter cushions, which Mrs Pond had left in a spaced out uniform row like a series of breast pocket handkerchief points, Victoria was forced to agree.

'I have to say that I'm not happy about you driving around the countryside at this moment in time. What happens if you are taken ill again? Why don't you ask Ginevra to come here for lunch or something?'

Oblivious to the fact that it was not the quantity of driving she was about to undertake that worried him but the quality of it, Victoria said, 'Oh I'll be all right, darling, you worry too much. It's really not that far. Besides, Ginevra is one of my oldest friends, and do you realize that I've never even seen her house? And I have to say if I'm going to I'd prefer to do so before Kevin comes back.' Reflecting that she probably was better off driving in the country where there were fewer cars to crash into rather than in the teeming city, he capitulated.

'Okay, but do take it easy. What's your real reason for going?'

Victoria was unabashed. 'Apparently she and Ellen have become very friendly. I want to know what the state of play is in the Carey marriage. And so should you. Without Ellen he won't produce a thing.' That much was certainly true, unless,

187

supposing they did divorce and Jack remarried, he had the sense to go for an Ellen mark two. On the whole James doubted it. Sense had never been one of Jack's predominant characteristics.

'Why don't you just ring Jack? Or, better still, Ellen, if you're that desperate to find out?'

'I have. Rung Ellen, I mean. She's not answering her phone at the moment. Besides, she's a very private person, and I think I'm more likely to get the whole story off Ginevra.'

He was sceptical, but contented himself with saying, 'Try to resist the temptation to interfere.'

'As if I would!' was her ambiguous reply.

Standing by the window and thinking afresh about the urgent need to rehabilitate his star painter's reputation after all the recent adverse publicity, James suddenly had a brilliant idea. So obvious was it that he wondered why it had never occurred to him before.

'Do your remember those two critical appraisals Ginevra wrote three or four years ago?'

'Yes, of course. The art intelligentsia all stopped quarrelling with one another and sat up and took notice. Those pieces are still remembered as being very impressive, you know. She ought to do more of that sort of thing, make a name for herself.'

'Perhaps nobody asks her.'

'They do from time to time, but she's too taken up with the book. That's one of the reasons I've kept in contact with her: if the book makes her reputation she might be useful to The Gallery.'

'Exactly!' He was exultant.

'What?'

'Well, there's no doubt we need to polish up Jack's tarnished image in the light of the bad personal press he's been getting since the exhibition. Underline his well-deserved fame rather than his even more well-deserved notoriety. So, why don't you ask Ginevra if she's prepared to do a sympathetic in-depth profile of Jack? How the intolerable pressures and insecurities of the creative process are bound to cause behaviour lapses from time to time, you know the sort of thing. But these are as nothing when set beside what he paints. And,' warming to his theme, 'ending on a laudatory note to the effect that the wonderful work he produces is a triumph of genius over psychological shortfall.'

'Put like that I hardly recognize the old goat! I don't know why you don't write it yourself!'

'Nobody would listen to me. But they will to Ginevra.'

'Absolutely. Why don't you give Robert Wilmot a ring? Ask him if he's prepared to run it in *Modern Art*, and if he says yes, as he's almost certain to, I'll sound her out tomorrow.'

Thursday was a close day, and it was under a dark sky that Victoria drove to Little Haddow. Beside her on the passenger seat snoozed Ho, and as she piloted the car she listened to *The World at One*. At 1.30 they stopped at a pub for a sandwich lunch, and then resumed their journey at two o'clock. As they travelled further out into the countryside, the advance of autumn became altogether less tentative, and extrovert shades of yellow, russet, burnt orange and deep red were conclusively overtaking the shyer green of the season before. Provided the weather held up, the next two months would celebrate the end of an exceptional summer with a tinder-dry salvo of mellow beauty before the dreariness of the English winter finally set in.

Turning off the motorway, Victoria drew to a halt in a lay-by and consulted the map. Fearing that a walk was in the offing, Ho opened one apprehensive eye and they lay very still. Apparently, to his great relief it was not to be, or not yet anyway, for, after much draughty unfolding and flapping and folding, she finally put the map away and they set off again. At first the highway was dual carriageway, but after about twenty minutes they took a minor road and then a still more minor road, after which any pretence at macadam dwindled away into a series of large country lanes. Victoria was just beginning to think that this was a bad idea and that she should probably have taken the train, when they came across a sign for Great Haddow. It stood to reason that where Great Haddow was, Little Haddow could not be far behind, and with a feeling that at last she might be about to arrive, Victoria pressed on.

Although violet, lowering clouds still massed, several shafts of pale September sunshine succeeded in striking through them all at once, transmuted into a darker shade of richness by the sumptuous colours of the trees. Appreciating this as she drove, Victoria looked forward with anticipation to the holiday in Scotland which James had promised her when all the loose ends of the Carey show were finally tied up. On her left she passed a small railway station with flowerbeds, and rightly decided that it must be from here that Ginevra took the train to London. Must be very close now. After driving along several lanes, she turned a corner and there it was.

As had Ellen before her, Victoria went into the pub, leaving a relieved Ho behind in the car. Wearing pearls and refined tweeds, for, after all, the country was the country, Victoria succeeded in immediately catching, and holding, the eye of Freda who was behind the bar that day. Recognizing money and class when she saw it, Freda prepared to be accommodating, civil even.

'What can I get you?'

'Nothing, thank you.' Sizing up Freda in her turn, Victoria spoke in her 'my good woman' tone of voice. 'I'm trying to find Pear Tree Cottage. Mrs Haye.'

Looking at her interlocutor with curiosity, and reflecting that this one was nothing like the weirdo in the floating draperies of the other day, Freda obediently delivered directions.

'Thank you so much.' Expensive leather shoulderbag swinging and narrowly missing four cider glasses, the visitor turned and strode out.

Crawling through the village, Victoria was struck by its minuteness. In her view the country was for weekends, preferably in someone else's large house. How anybody could want to spend all their days in a place like Little Haddow was beyond her. Pear Tree Cottage then came as another depressing revelation. It was . . . well, it was shabby. No getting away from it. And run-down. Practically falling down, in fact.

Hauling a reluctant Ho out of the front seat of the Volvette, and collecting his water bowl as she did so, Victoria shut the car door without troubling to lock it, and then picked her way up the weed-clogged path to the peeling front door. She was uncomfortably aware as she did so that if she had known that Ginevra lived like this she would not have come, or, rather, would have come if invited but would not have invited herself. James had been right, and she had been a fool not to listen to him. Too late now. She rang the bell.

There was a clatter of feet descending what sounded like uncarpeted stairs, and then Ginevra opened the door. They did not kiss as they normally would have done. Looking back on it afterwards, Victoria decided it was simply because neither of them made the move. At that point, her old friendship with Ginevra definitely took a small but telling step backwards.

'Come in. Oh. You've got the dog with you.'

Heavens, another error. Like most dog owners, Victoria Harting tended to assume that wherever she went her pet would be equally welcome.

'I have a cat, you see.'

'I *am* sorry. It never occurred to me that you might have. Look, could I tie him up in the kitchen, with a bowl of water?'

Ginevra shrugged. 'Of course. It's in here.'

The kitchen was something else again. It was quite filthy. Luckily the window was open, allowing in some fresh air, but even this could not conceal the smell of something rotten, possibly in the bin, or maybe under the floorboards. Mentally holding her nose, and deciding to shampoo Ho when they got home, Victoria settled him down and then followed her friend into another room, closing the door behind her as she did so.

Left behind, Ho, who was very thirsty, had a long and extremely noisy drink of water and then sat down on the floor and looked around. Tied up as he was there was no opportunity to explore. Normally, *force majeure*, a clean, silky dog, he would have liked to investigate what smelt like a promisingly rancid gash bin, but – he tried it – the lead did not stretch that far. Feeling neglected, he began to whimper. Finally, when his mistress did not come, he lay on the floor and prepared to doze off.

Fifteen minutes later, a large mouse in his jaws, Captain Morgan came through the window like a feline commando on an assault course. Dropping the mouse on the work surface as a present for Ginevra, he jumped with a soft-padded thud onto the lino and found himself unexpectedly confronted by what looked like a large, stuffed toy. Sensitive to the vibration of his landing, Ho opened one sleepy eye. Suddenly sleepy no longer, he opened the other. Captain Morgan spat. Combative and territorial, he arched his back and his fur bristled into punk-like points as though a powerful electrical charge had shot through him from head to spikey tail. His one yellow eye bulged with menace. Catilla. Ho, who hitherto had only encountered languid, well-bred Chelsea cats with velvet collars, yelped with fear, and forgetting that he was tethered to a cupboard door nearly garrotted himself trying to run away. Tied up. No escape. On tiptoe, his sinister tormentor balletically skipped backwards, and then, turning so that his right side with its horrible empty eye socket was towards the petrified Pekinese, he launched an erratic sideways run at his victim, spitting as he came.

In Ginevra's work room where, by dint of moving a large pile of books off the sofa, she had finally been found somewhere to sit, Victoria could not hear the commotion in the kitchen and was therefore oblivious to the ongoing martyrdom of Ho. If her last encounter with Ginevra had been stilted, this one verged on hostile.

Waiting for her to get to the point of her visit amid a welter of inconsequential small talk, Ginevra thought, Victoria Harting does not look particularly well. She has lost that healthy bloom she used to have. And (noticing that the skirt button of the tweed suit was undone) she has put on weight. Aloud she said, 'Why weren't you at the Carey private view?'

'I was ill,' was the unilluminating response. 'James had to take me to the hospital.' So much Ginevra already knew. 'I assume you saw the rather embarrassing scene which took place, all masterminded, I gather, by Tessa.'

' "Rather embarrassing",' said Ginevra, 'has to be the understatement of the year. There was mayhem.'

Skirting around asking an actual question, Victoria essayed, casually, 'I wonder how Ellen's taking it.'

So that was it. 'Don't you know?'

'I have rung her several times. She doesn't appear to be answering her phone. I'm concerned about her, that's all.'

Poppycock! You're avid for all the gossip. And aware of the fact that, if she goes for good, Jack as a source of revenue will probably dry up.

'I expect, if she had wanted to talk to you, she would have rung you.'

In the face of this unhelpful rejoinder, it was difficult to know what tack to take next. After a short baffled silence, Victoria decided to sail on with indirect surmise in the hope of eliciting an informative answer.

'Still, you and she are quite close. She has you to confide in.'

'Yes, she does.'

'Well, that's all right then.'

Ginevra was suddenly fed up with it.

'I'm afraid that if you have come all this way to extract news about Ellen Carey, you have had a wasted journey.'

Flushed out, but at the same time determined not to admit it, Victoria said lamely, 'No, no, not at all. It only seemed to me that in all the time you have been here I have never once visited you in the country, and I really felt I should.'

Disregarding this speech as though it had never taken place, or perhaps simply treating it with the contempt she felt it deserved, Ginevra continued, 'You see, Ellen is my greatest friend, and, as such, I could never betray her confidences to anyone.' Waiting for the words *not even to you*, Victoria was to be left waiting, for they did not come. 'Now, shall we have a cup of tea or do you have to get back?'

It was, quite clearly, time to leave. 'Well, there was just one more thing I wanted to sound you out about.' Victoria was conscious of disastrous timing, but at a loss as to what to do about it.

'Really. What is that?'

'I wondered, that is James and I wondered, if you would consent to do a positive profile of Jack Carey and his works. The point being that, although the exhibition was a sellout, he has been the victim of a great deal of prurient press attention, which has upset some of The Gallery's more conventional clients, such as the Maybricks, more than somewhat, to the point where James feels that rehabilitation needs to be the next step. Robert Wilmot says he would be keen to publish, but only if you do it. He trusts your judgement.'

Instantly making up her mind that she would do it but only for the sake of James Harting, Ginevra nevertheless decided to make Victoria suffer. 'I'll think about it. Cosmetic journalism is not, after all, my habit. In fact, I despise it. You can tell Robert Wilmot that I'll telephone him when I've made my mind up.'

In the face of this snub of snubs, there seemed little left to do except to withdraw with whatever pride she had left.

'Thank you, Ginevra,' said Victoria, humbly, preparing to leave.

Incarcerated within the kitchen, a demoralized Ho heard the sound of her footsteps and began to howl in anticipation. Going in, Victoria found her pet the subject of a violent terrorist attack which was being mounted by a hideous and very aggressive tom-cat. In his abject terror Ho had apparently fallen into his own water bowl. Apart from the indignity of this, the only injury inflicted appeared to be a deep scratch on his nose, where the blood was already beginning to congeal. Ginevra's cat, it seemed, was more into psychological warfare than grievous bodily harm.

As she was leaving, a dripping dog under her arm, in a last and desperate attempt to ingratiate herself once again with her erstwhile chum, Victoria said on impulse, 'By the way, I wasn't going to tell anyone yet, but we are such old friends that I would like you to know. I'm pregnant! Outside the family, you're the first to hear it. James is delighted.' It was an unwitting revenge but a very potent one. Halfway between reality and the dream, Ginevra felt as though, prune-like, her heart had shrivelled.

James is delighted. The ultimate betrayal. How could he?

Pulling herself together with a supreme effort, she said, 'That's wonderful news. Congratulations.' The words sounded lifeless. Looking at her face which was all at once apparently openly smiling and, at the same time, shut, Victoria once again experienced uneasiness and an odd intuition that something was very wrong. Dismissing it as a figment of her imagination, she said her goodbyes. This time they did kiss.

When she had finally gone, Ginevra did something which she had not done since her father died. She sat down on the sofa in her work room and, putting her head in her hands, wept.

'Christ, I loathe her,' she cried aloud between sobs. '*Loathe* her! Oh I'll write their profile for them, but it won't be what they're all expecting, and I'll dish that bastard Carey in the process too.'

In Sussex, Ellen drifted wraithlike around her house. The September weather faltered with a few days of rain, and then rallied and stabilized into a brilliant summer finale whose light warm breezes began to blow away the leaves of the trees. To protect herself against the well-meaning enquiries of concerned friends, she bought herself a telephone answering machine, and the only calls she returned were those from Jack, mainly to make sure that he was not about to turn up on the doorstep, and Ginevra, whom she trusted to be discreet.

The boys' exeat was now a week and a half away and Ellen dreaded her confrontation with her husband almost as much as she dreaded revealing to her sons that their parents' marriage was over. It would also be necessary to tell her mother what was happening. Probably fortunately, Olivia Braithwaite had been away on a cruise and so had missed the press jamboree over the drama at The Gallery, which she would very much have relished had she been around to enjoy it. Consulting her diary, Ellen saw that she should have returned two days ago. Better get it over with, was Ellen's view. She lifted the telephone receiver and dialled the number.

Olivia intuited almost immediately that something was amiss.

'Is there something you aren't telling me, Ellen?'

'No, mother, no. Or, rather, yes. Yes, there is, but . . .'

'Well, is there or isn't there?'

'If you could just let me get out a whole sentence you might learn something.'

There was an atmospheric silence at the other end of the line, and then her mother's huffed voice said, 'As you wish.'

'Very well, what I was going to say was that there is something the matter, but I would rather tell you face to face than over the telephone.'

'Can't you give me a clue? You aren't ill, are you?'

Disregarding this last, Ellen said, 'Why don't I drive over tomorrow?'

'Certainly. Although I'm bound to say the day after would suit me better.'

'All right, the day after.'

Some ten minutes after she had put the phone down, it rang

again. Automatically picking it up, rather assuming it must be her awkward parent wanting to alter the arrangements they had just made, Ellen found herself talking to her husband, her maudlin and slightly slurred husband who probably had a glass in his other hand.

'I've decided I'm going to drive down to see you regardless of what you say. I'm going to woo you all over again, Ellen.' There was the unmistakable sound of whisky being poured, quite a lot of it.

Woo me again! Oh heavens, anything but that! 'Jack, please don't. I'm just not ready for it. Please, *please*, don't!'

'Nothing you can say or do to stop me. I love you, Ellen, and I'm going to prove it to you.' There followed a long swallow.

'You're very drunk!'

'Had one or two, that's all. What do you expect me to do when you won't see me or speak to me? I'm lonely, Ellen. Lonely without *you*! I know you want to punish me, and you're right to want to, but don't be too hard on me.' There was an audible escalation of that most unlovely of emotions, self-pity.

Ellen felt close to desperation.

'There is no point in your coming to Butterfly Cottage since I won't be here. I'm going away.'

A thoughtful silence followed this utterance, and then the noise of a cascade of spirits hitting the bottom of an empty glass. Finally, enunciating with difficulty, he said, 'Well, I'm going to come anyway, and when I do I'm going to – '

She cut him off, and when the line was finally clear immediately rang her mother.

'It's Ellen again. Look, I know it's inconvenient, but could I possibly come tomorrow after all, and stay for a few days? I really need to get away from here.'

Consumed with curiosity, Olivia decided not to cavil for once and graciously consented.

'How very mysterious you are, Ellen. All right. Shall we say in time for lunch? Yes? Very well, I shall expect you at twelve.'

Lastly Ellen rang Mrs Phipps. After her call Mrs Phipps said to her husband, 'Mrs Carey. She's goin' away for a few days. Wants me to look after the cats. Somethin' funny goin' on there if you ask me. She hasn't been herself lately at all.'

Mr Phipps, who hasn't asked her, without taking his eyes off *Match of the Day*, merely grunted. It would be a good opportunity to get those traps down in the vegetable garden.

20

Before Ellen left the next day, the post arrived. There was only one letter, which politely informed her that the literary agent concerned felt that he could not handle her book but wished her good luck with it anyway. Throwing this away, Ellen cheered herself up with the thought that there were still two more to go. All the same, she felt depressed. Good news was required at the moment, not bad.

She took very little with her. The effort of organizing herself away for a few days proved almost more than she could cope with. She seemed to feel exhausted all the time just lately. Suspecting her intention, the cats hung around her mournfully, aware that, while she was away, they would be fed but not pampered.

The taxi arrived and at the same time the telephone bell started to peal. It was possibly Jack, although this seemed unlikely at such an early hour in the light of what had clearly been limbering up to be a heavy drinking session the night before. Letting herself out and shutting the door with resolution, Ellen reflected that a ringing phone was just about as impossible to ignore as a crying baby.

The arrangement she had made with her mother was that she would take the train, and then another taxi at the other end.

If I continue to live in the country, thought Ellen, I shall have to have an old banger of some sort to get around. I can't keep taking taxis everywhere.

The prospect of the future was a dismal one, and was likely to be even more dismal if Jack refused to play financial ball. Ellen briefly toyed with the idea of asking her mother for a loan to tide her over, and then dismissed it. In the generous face of the very expensive educations she was underwriting for both boys, it seemed too much to ask. And anyway, how would she pay it back?

Her mother lived in a small modern semi-detached house

which was probably just the right size for one forceful widow, but gave Ellen claustrophobia. Or, maybe, it was her mother's dominating presence that did this. Mrs Braithwaite opened the front door wearing an apron one of the boys had given her for Christmas one year, which bore the legend 'You may kiss the cook'. Ellen did so.

Scrutinizing her watch to make sure that it was not too early for such a thing, Mrs Braithwaite said, 'Why don't you pour yourself a sherry, Ellen?'

'Thank you, Mother, I'll just take my bag upstairs first.'

The appetizing smell of roast lamb cooked by someone else drifted up the stairs after her.

Ellen lay down on the bed.

I need looking after, she thought to herself. I'm so very tired. I want to feel safe, to step off this draining, unhappy treadmill which I've been on for years. I have no resilience left. Nothing to draw on. And if Jack won't leave me alone then I'll just have to go to ground until he does.

'Ellen!'

Wearily she descended the stairs.

'No time for an aperitif, it's ready. If you look in the fridge you'll find half a bottle of white wine.' Mrs Braithwaite did not drink red at all, having at some time in her life conceived the odd idea that white was more dietetic. Ellen found it. Lying beside it was a plate on which reposed an orphaned pork chop wrapped in stretch and seal. Divining this to have been earmarked for her mother's lunch until the agenda had changed as a result of her own telephone call gave Ellen a depressing insight into the single life.

If I go ahead with what I'm planning, she reflected, the solitary chop and I will become inseparable lunch companions too, except when David and Harry are at home, which is going to happen less and less as they get older.

Pouring out two glasses of wine, Ellen carried them to the table and sat down. Or rather, her mother noted, sank down. Managing to watch her daughter narrowly as she carved, it was Mrs Braithwaite's view that Ellen, like an unsteady tightrope walker, was keeping her equilibrium, but only just. An organizing personality with a good brain, who usually knew what she wanted from herself and, more importantly, from others, Olivia Braithwaite, though a bracing parent, was not, *au fond*, a hard-hearted woman. She clearly saw that for the moment she was her daughter's safety net, and prepared to spread herself.

Aloud, she said, 'Where is Reginald?'

'Not with me. We are currently separated. It's my intention to ask him for a divorce.'

There, now she had said it. A lonely tear fell onto a sprig of rosemary on her plate where it briefly glistened before disintegrating through the spikey leaves.

'I'm afraid I have to say, depending on what he's done I suppose, that I don't think that is a very good idea at all!'

Ellen looked at her mother in astonishment.

'But, Mother, you've *never* liked Jack!'

'No, I never have.'

'Well, then!'

Mrs Braithwaite, who was an atheist, nevertheless found the Good Book a useful fund of appropriate imagery, and now waxed biblical.

'Well then, nothing Ellen! You have stayed with that marriage throughout all the lean years, and now the fat years are here you want to leave it. Why? I can't believe Reginald has changed that much. He never was one to try to conceal his faults after all.'

'He hasn't changed, I have.'

'Please don't wave your fork around, Ellen. Why can't you, what's the modern expression, Do Your Own Thing within the marriage? Knowing Reginald as I do I should be very surprised if he even noticed.'

'Thank you very much, Mother. Let's get this straight. Are you telling me that I should stay with him for his money?' Here Ellen looked severely at her grasping parent.

Unembarrassed came the answer, 'Yes, I am!'

'And what if I tell you that he has humiliated me not only in private, which he's been doing for years by the way, but now in public, in front of all our friends?'

'I don't wish to pry but are we talking about infidelity? Are we? If so I think you are being very self-indulgent, Ellen. What does a little bit of adultery here or there matter as long as you are his wife? He doesn't want to marry anybody else, does he? *You* have the title, Ellen! Make the most of it.'

She made it sound like being the Queen of England. Remembering Edward Montague, Ellen thought, It must be a generation thing, this business of treating adultery as though it's a tiresome irrelevance. Their attitudes were so similar that she found herself wondering whether Edward and Mother had ever . . . Oh no, surely not!

Picking up the carving knife and fork in hands which had grown more and more like the claws of an armadillo with the passing of the years, Olivia Braithwaite flexed her elbows. 'And have you thought about the children? More lamb, Ellen?'

Afterwards they sat in her small sitting room drinking coffee. It always felt odd to Ellen in this alien interior to be surrounded with a distillation of the furniture and pictures among which she had grown up. Contraction to accommodate her present circumstances had forced her mother to rid herself of a great deal of personal paraphernalia, though the sepia photographs of her as a young woman, which had stood on the mantelpiece in the old house, stood on the mantelpiece here too. These had always fascinated Ellen. Broad shouldered and with an uncompromisingly level look, her parent stared out of the silver frames, the seeds of the physical present already firmly planted. It was interesting that her legs, which in her youth had clearly been spectacular, remained trim today, even though the body which they supported had become stout. In her wedding photograph she was magnificent, not to say triumphant, accompanied by her new husband who was not quite as tall as she was and, trussed up in his morning suit, stood diffidently beside her with a plethora of photographically transfixed relations all around. Jack unfairly called this one the spider and the fly.

Breaking into her reverie, her mother announced, 'I'm afraid I do have to go out this afternoon for a couple of hours, Ellen.'

If anything this information came as a relief.

'That's all right. I'll cope with the washing up and then I think I'll have a rest. I really feel done in.'

'You look it!' Mrs Braithwaite enunciated around the lipstick with which she was painting her mouth vampire red as they talked. It was interesting, thought Ellen, watching her mother give herself a liberal floury dusting, but not surprising, how powder compacts had gone totally out of fashion. Rouge was then superimposed, each hectic dot carefully blended in, underlining a well-preserved but masklike appearance. Baring her teeth at her own reflection in the compact mirror, Olivia Braithwaite was evidently satisfied with what she saw, for she then closed this with a click prior to dropping it, together with the rest of her makeup, into the depths of her large leather handbag. This she shut in its turn with a smart snap, putting Ellen in mind of the closing of a steel trap. Seeing her energetic mother out, Ellen made a resolution not to start taking afternoon rests, and decided to write the weekly letters to the boys instead.

Sitting in the little Fulham house at the end of what had been an extremely busy day at work, Alexander wished he was still at the publishing house. At least constant action kept introspection at bay. He had neither contacted Tessa nor been contacted by her and he had not missed her. Nor, oddly, although he thought about her constantly and with gratitude, did he pine for Ellen. It had all been too complete. Emotional hyperspace. A lifetime of knowing her in an afternoon. Already he could feel the poetry he was to write forming itself out of their briefly perfect union, which would remain perfect because it would never be repeated, at least in the physical sense. Ralegh had summed it up in four marvellous lines:

> *Butt Love is a durable fyre*
> *In the mynde ever burnynge:*
> *Never sycke, never ould, never dead,*
> *From itt selfe never turnynge.*

Just such was his unalterable love for Ellen, which would coexist with any other attachment he might form, enhancing but never spoiling.

A wonderful and totally unexpected sensation of light-heartedness engulfed Alexander. He thought, Ellen has altered my perception and given me a point of reference which has taken me way beyond my obsession with Tessa. For the first time since I married her, I am free of her.

A celebration in verse of this momentous knowledge was the only truly valuable return he could make, and pulling a notebook towards him, Alexander began to write, slowly at first, and then with more lyrical fluency and originality than had been at his disposal for years.

While this creative rebirth was taking place in Fulham, Jack Carey, whose head had felt as though it was full of loose ballast the morning after his conversation with Ellen, was still, six hours later, *hors de combat*. Unwise precipitate movement caused a vibration between the eyes which slowly, and exquisitely painfully, spread itself all around the interior of his skull, and felt as though it was buffeting his poor atrophied brain. Paracetamol made no inroads into this cranial chaos, which brought Jack to the brink of deciding to postpone his dash to Ellen's side to the following day. Until he took Tessa's telephone call. So far he had successfully managed to avoid her by dint of having his answer phone on all the time and refusing to answer his own front door. Last night he had forgotten to switch the machine on, and this afternoon, on automatic pilot, he had actually picked up the receiver when it rang and announced himself.

'Jack! At last!' She sounded vibrant, and not at all offended by all the times he had failed to respond to imperious messages to call her back. 'If I didn't know you better I would think you were trying to avoid me.'

This was the opening. The heaven-sent opportunity to speak. Jack wished he felt up to it. There was something about the sheer power of Tessa's will which sapped his own. In his mind's eye he saw her once again naked in his studio, her firm high breasts like apples and her reclining body perfectly tensioned, like a drawn bow. Tessa the Huntress. Tempted all over again, in spite of himself, Jack mustered all the willpower he had.

'I *was* trying to avoid you.'

'But why? Your wife has left you. There is no impediment now. We can do as we please.'

This was a dialogue of the deaf. His head began to throb with an insistent, regular rhythm.

'I think you have forgotten how good we are together. Why don't I come over and remind you? Now.' She sounded coaxing, insidious. Regretting it, and at the same time thinking, Why can't she settle for just being a mistress the way everyone else has to, then we wouldn't have a problem, Jack said, 'There's no point. I'm just on my way to Sussex.'

'Don't go.'

'Look, Tessa, it wouldn't work between us. A marriage, I mean. I have to work. Contrary to what you might think, my life isn't one long party. You would get very bored.' There was a profound silence at the other end of the line. Desperately he rationalized on. 'An affair is one thing but a marriage is another discipline altogether. We both know that.'

'Are you saying that I'm for amusement only?'

'No! Yes. In a way.' This was a minefield. Why on earth hadn't he written the standard letter, the way he always had before?

'You bastard! Do you realize that I've left my husband for you?' Although they both knew that this was not strictly accurate, she sounded so furious that Jack did not feel like arguing the toss. He decided to try to bring this unsatisfactory conversation to an end by getting off the telephone as quickly as he could. Maybe light-hearted breeziness was the answer.

'Look, I'm afraid I have to go. It was great while it lasted. I'd like you to keep the painting . . .'

It was not.

'Fuck the painting, and fuck you too!' This last was delivered with such force that the earpiece of the receiver and Jack's head both reverberated.

'Tessa, I'm really sorry –'

'You will be!' The crash, as she hung up, reactivated the headache which he hoped had been about to subside. The main thing now, he recognized, was to get on the road before she arrived on his doorstep. Forty-five frustrating minutes later, having finally located his car keys which had apparently spent the night in bed with him, and after a furtive glance around to make sure that the coast was clear, Jack slammed the door of the studio behind him and set off in search of his wife.

*

The cottage was empty. The moment he drove up to it he could see that. She had meant what she said. All the curtains were drawn, and as he got out of the car both cats, who had access to the garage via a cat flap when the Careys were away, appeared through it and, with muted delight since he did not usually feed them, began to circle him. Ignoring them, Jack let himself in and when he had turned the alarm off, went in search of clues as to where she might have gone. Nothing. There was a note for Edna Phipps, however, on the kitchen table together with an envelope presumably containing her wages. He dialled the Phippses' number. Busy. Quicker to go and see them.

The Phippses lived in a small house in the village. In front of it were flowerbeds, and behind, a vegetable garden and a fruit cage. Mrs Phipps's bicycle leant against the wall by the door. Jack rang the door bell, which was the sort which played half a tune.

'Wonder who that is,' speculated Mrs Phipps in surprise putting aside her knitting.

Without moving a muscle her husband observed, 'Why don't you go and open the door and then you'll find out.'

The sight of Mr Carey on her doorstep reinforced Mrs Phipps's surmise that all was not as it should be in the Carey household. He was unshaven, she noticed, and his shirt looked as though he had slept in it. Pulling herself together, she said, 'Mr Carey! Nothin' wrong I hope.'

'Who is it?' shouted her husband from the sitting room.

'If you get up and come out here, you'll find out,' called back Mrs Phipps, who was not above this sort of small revenge.

'No, no, nothing wrong. It's just that my wife has gone away for a few days and has forgotten to leave me a note, as she promised she would, with a telephone number where I can contact her. I just wondered if she had written one down for you.'

Mrs Phipps was not deceived by this, and also was in something of a quandary since Mrs Carey had asked her not to tell anyone where she was, although without specifically mentioning her husband in this regard. Mr Carey was her employer, but, on the other hand, so was Mrs Carey of whom she saw a great deal more. Better be safe than sorry.

'I'm afraid she didn't,' said Mrs Phipps, reflecting that this was strictly true as it was she herself who had written the number down.

'Did she say how long she would be away?' Jack decided to abandon all pretence.

'No. She just said to go on feedin' them cats until she got back, and do the house as usual.'

'Oh, right!' At least it sounded as if she were coming back. 'Thank you very much, Mrs Phipps, sorry to bother you.'

Mrs Phipps watched him go, and then went back to the sitting room and her knitting, which she picked up and resumed without uttering.

'Who was it?' asked her husband for the second time.

'Nobody as you'd want to know about,' she replied, deciding to be cussed about it.

In order to stop them badgering him, Jack fed Merlin and Casimir, and then sat down in the kitchen. Even that was unwelcoming since Ellen had turned the Aga right down before she left. What to do next was the question. To say that Jack wanted his wife badly would have been an understatement. Her absence was much more potent than her presence, and he would have given much of what he had if life as he had known it since they married could be resumed. In order to achieve this, he first had to find her. On impulse he dialled his mother-in-law's number.

'Hello?' said Olivia Braithwaite. Since he wanted something, it seemed unwise to get into the 'Granny' charade, though he dared say he would be forced to endure 'Reginald'.

'Olivia, it's Jack.'

'Ah, Reginald! How are you?'

'Fine, fine. How are you?'

'Never better!'

'Good, good.'

This ritual dance over, he felt he could get on with what he really had to say and more or less reproduced what he had said to Mrs Phipps with the odd change here and there for credibility. She heard him out without saying anything, and it was not until he got to the end that she revealed her hand.

'Ellen is here. I gather she has left you. I know all about it, though I'm bound to say that I don't entirely recognize your version of events.'

Feeling, as he was no doubt meant to, a fool, Jack thought, Well, why didn't you say so in the first place, you silly old trout? when she followed this up with, 'I have to say that I don't approve at all.'

Here was a totally unexpected ally. 'Don't you?' he ejaculated, amazed.

'No, I don't. I think Ellen's place is with you, her husband, not sitting around here like a tragedy queen.'

Wondering if his wife was sitting listening to this devastating plain speaking, Jack enquired, 'Where is Ellen now?'

'Upstairs, asleep. She seems to be very rundown.'

'Do you think she would agree to speak to me?'

'I'm afraid not. I have been deputed to do that.' Readjusting the cushion in the small of her back to make herself more comfortable, Olivia prepared to enjoy herself with some emotional power broking.

Deflated, Jack said, 'What do you think I should do?'

'Ellen needs time to reassess, and I think you should give it to her. Finite time though, otherwise this will drag on for ever. According to her she asked you for that, and your response was to pursue her up hill and down dale. I have to say I think you would be wise to give it to her. Don't follow her round the country like a lapdog. I'm sure she'll come round. After all, what else can she do? And you may be sure, Reginald, that I shall do my bit at this end. Incidentally, while you both are in a state of separation, you might care to reflect on how all this came about in the first place, and perhaps make the odd small adjustment here and there to your own behaviour. I have to say she seems very fed up with things as they are. And then, when all this is over, I suggest that you take Ellen away on holiday!'

Discovering, for the first time, that to have Olivia Braithwaite for you rather than against you was a very significant advantage, Jack was beginning to see that this was all going to take some time, and that his desire to get back to normal as quickly as possible was not necessarily going to be realized quite like that.

'Perhaps I should go back to London?'

'Perhaps you should. Just for a while. And now my

programme is coming on the television, and if you would excuse me, I should like to watch it.'

When he had hung up, curious to know what this was, Jack checked it out in the daily paper he had brought with him.

Mastermind.

In the light of this constructive exchange Jack went back to the studio by train, in a rare burst of thoughtfulness leaving the car for his wife, even remembering the keys. He wrote to her to tell her that he had done this. Two days later, with a feeling of great relief, Ellen went home.

Putting her on the train, Olivia also felt relief, reflecting that although Ellen was her daughter and, as such, she loved her, they really did not have that much in common.

Her arrival was greeted with ecstasy by both cats. Opening her mail as they rubbed against her legs, purring, among the usual crop of bills and circulars, Ellen found a second literary agent's letter, again politely, but definitely, saying no.

21

Because she was nothing if not intellectually disciplined, in spite of the way in which the news of Victoria's pregnancy rocked her mental foundations, Ginevra continued to work on her book. This took care of the days, but the nights were another matter. Almost totally isolated, apart from the odd telephone call from Ellen, Ginevra grew to dread them and the long yearning empty evenings which preceded them, during the course of which she read and reread the fictional account of her erotically inventive affair with James Harting. An important component of her life at the moment was brandy. It made orgasm as she read easier to achieve, and, in her more lucid moments, when she knew the whole thing to be the product of her own imagination (which were fewer and fewer these days), it deadened the pain of unrequited love, as well as helping her to sleep. Although, when she did, the dreams, in which her erstwhile friend Victoria featured, returned in full force, almost medieval in their violence and cruelty and sometimes, when she woke up, Ginevra found her pillow wet with tears. Curiously, within these nocturnal adventures, James himself was merely a remote presence, a detached observer of the struggle for sexual power taking place between Ginevra and Victoria.

These days Ginevra found it hard to think of Victoria without a shudder of disgust. Even the plausible, alternative voice had been silenced temporarily by the incontrovertible fact of the pregnancy, with all its confusing possible implications of betrayal within the shifting images of what was fantasy and what was not. There was still no sign of the ordered red and blue marbled notebooks. Perhaps if these had arrived, and Ginevra had been able to write on and rationalize, this would have constituted a safety valve of sorts. As it was, with no other outlet, the pressure built up within her mind, threatening to loosen for good her increasingly tenuous grip on what was real.

It was on just such an evening, while rummaging in a drawer, that she found Victoria Harting's scarf, the one which she had inexplicably put in her bag. Holding it in her hands, Ginevra considered it. It was rainbow-hued and fringed, not the sort of thing Victoria, who normally gravitated towards Hermès and horses' heads, usually wore. It smelt faintly and elusively of scent. An evening scarf perhaps. As she stood irresolute, wondering whether to throw it out or, maybe simply to return it quietly, should she ever go to the house again, the idea of a symbolic scotching of her rival entered Ginevra's head. The pregnancy. Those dreadful dreams. An exorcism was clearly what was needed.

Thinking about it, she put a record on her ancient player, listening to the faint crackle before the music actually began. It was Wagner. On impulse she took down the corn dolly which had sat in the same place on the mantelpiece for as long as she could remember. Blowing some of the dust off it, Ginevra began to wind the scarf sari-like around and around, securing it with pins which she drove hard into the figure itself. Although the coloured silk was flimsy, there was too much of it, and after a certain amount of indecision as to whether this would make what she was about to do less potent, she decided after all to cut it, and did so, allowing the redundant fragments to fall to the floor where she left them. Listening to 'The Ride of the Valkyries', she went into the kitchen and returned with the Swan Vestas. Kneeling down, she placed the little figure in its finery within the otherwise empty hearth and, with a swift flourish, lit a match and set it alight.

'Purification by fire,' murmured Ginevra.

The silk did not burn but shrivelled with the faintest hiss. As its evanescent beauty disappeared, the flame shot through the tinder dry corn dolly and consumed it, shedding a surprising amount of light all around as it did so.

Purification by fire.

Ginevra got to her feet. Outside it was now dusk. As the winter advanced and the days grew shorter the evenings would grow even longer and more claustrophobic. She turned the record over and, trembling slightly with the knowledge that she had performed a symbolic yet powerful and irrevocable act, sat on in her darkening sitting room listening to it.

That night there were no dreams.

22

Harry was devastated by David's letter. Tears welling, he read it over and over again under his duvet that night, with the aid of his pocket torch. Then he read the newspaper cutting, which was from a tabloid gossip column. *JACK CAREY AND HIS WIFE SEPARATE* said the headline, underneath which was an old picture of them both in which his mother looked about twenty. There then followed an account of the private view débâcle, and some not very oblique references to his father's colourful private life. Right at the end, inset into the text, was a photograph of Tessa, whom Harry dimly remembered from the Butterfly Cottage lunch party. *When asked whether they intended eventually to marry, Mrs Tessa Lucas, Jack Carey's constant companion, said no comment.* The self-satisfied smile on the face of Tessa's very up-to-date photograph indicated, even to ten-year-old Harry, that she thought they would. He remembered David saying, as they sat in the play tree, 'I think he's having it off with that blonde.' Thinking, I hate her! Harry was unable to stifle an audible sob.

There was a movement in the next bed as Charlie Penrose turned over.

'Are you all right, Harry?'

More smothered sobbing. Harry was well aware that to be found blubbing was more than his dormitory life was worth.

Mouselike, Charlie got out of bed very quietly, and sat on the end of Harry's in silent sympathy.

'It's my parents, they've split up. At least, I think they have.'

Charlie, who had been seared by his own parents' blistering divorce, and who had had to grow up very fast during the course of it, to the point where, watching them quarrel, he sometimes thought he was more adult than they were, was sensitive to Harry's grief.

'How do you know?'

'My brother sent me this.' He passed the cutting together with the torch over to Charlie.

'N-n-newspapers aren't always right,' was Charlie's doubtful response after he read it. 'Why don't you ring your ma?'

'I have tried to ring her, but she never seems to be there. And all I get at Daddy's studio is the answer phone. She wrote to me this week but she didn't say anything about it. I really want to see her.' As he spoke the words, it was obvious to him that that was the answer. If he could only get to see her, he felt sure that he could persuade her not to do it. There was, he knew, an exeat coming up, but by then it might be too late.

'I think I'm going to go tomorrow!'

'You'll never get p-p-permission.'

'I'm going anyway. We've got that outing, to the museum. Who's taking us?'

Charlie thought for a moment. 'Old Petherbridge, I think.'

'That's all right, he's dozy. I'll just bunk off. Trouble is, I haven't any money.'

'I've got some. I've got a tenner I can lend you.'

Wondering if ten pounds, which was a lot of money to Harry, would get him home, he whispered, 'Wow, thanks, Charlie!' Planning to do something about it, rather than just enduring the suspense of waiting to find out made him feel suddenly much better.

They began to discuss the logistics of how to go absent without leave without this fact being noticed. As the conspiracy got under way, their voices rose with the excitement of it. A slipper flew through the air from the other end of the dormitory, narrowly missed Harry's head and hit the wall behind him. 'If you two don't shut up, I'm going to come and duff you up! I need my sleep even if you don't.'

Charlie made a rude gesture in the direction of the speaker, saying under his breath as he did so, 'Up yours, Oliphant,' and then crept back into bed.

'L-l-let's talk about it in the m-morning.'

'Okay. Goodnight, Charlie.'

Exhausted, Harry slid steeply into sleep.

The Weald and Downland Open Air Museum was situated in a

park, and consisted of vernacular architecture previously under threat of demolition on its original site which had been carefully dismantled and rebuilt here, thereby providing a design development sequence to this sort of dwelling.

'You will see that daub and wattle has been used here to fill in the timber frame construction,' proclaimed Mr Petherbridge, consulting the admirable guide book. They were standing in Winkhurst House.

Daub and what? In common with the rest of the boys, Harry was there in body rather than in spirit, though it was true to say that he had more on his mind than most. The Open Air Museum was ideal for what he had planned, though, and, unaware of what a large county Sussex is, he believed it was probably quite near home.

With Mr Petherbridge in full flow at the head of the straggling group of thirty-five boys, they all trailed from house to house. It was a close, dull day, much too hot for the regulation tweed sports jackets which were *de rigueur* on this sort of trip. Finally, he handed out questionnaires.

'I want you to go your own separate ways now, and find out the answers to as many of the questions on the sheet as you have time for. At four o'clock we will reconvene here. Is there anyone who does not have a watch?'

Nobody spoke. 'Right, off you go then, and remember you are representing your school. Politeness at all times. No misbehaviour and no ragging.'

What a very unrewarding day, was Mr Petherbridge's view, watching them all fan out before taking himself off for a reviving cup of tea. He didn't believe any of them had listened to a single word he'd had to say, except maybe Oliphant, who was something of a swot. However, no doubt the questionnaires would sort out the sheep from the goats.

'This is it,' said Harry to Charlie as they wandered off. 'Do or die.'

'Here's the tenner.' This had been folded over and over so many times that it was the size of one of the inky pellets they were wont to flick across the form room with the aid of a springy ruler when the master's back was turned.

'Good luck!'

'Thanks, Charlie!'

Putting the money in his jacket pocket, Harry set off without a backward glance in the direction of the Charcoal Burner's Camp. It was his intention to conceal himself within the museum grounds until the coach had gone, in case there was an immediate hue and cry. To pass the time until this happened he dutifully filled in the roneoed sheet like everyone else. At four o'clock the boys began to drift back to the appointed meeting place where stood Mr Petherbridge talking to the driver of the coach which would convey them all back to school.

With a clipboard in his hand to which was attached a list of all the participants, he began to check them off.

'Andrews.'

'Here, sir.'

'Atherton.'

'Here, sir.'

'Bennet.'

'Here, sir.'

This was tricky. Charlie had assumed that they would simply get on the coach and drive away. Thinking quickly, he ran around the group until he was standing behind the master.

Mr Petherbridge ploughed short-sightedly on down the list.

'Canford.'

'Here, sir.'

'Carey.'

'Here, sir,' said Charlie, determined to triumph over the stutter which might have given him away, and succeeding.

'Cummings . . . Mulholland . . . Oliphant . . . Penrose . . .'

Finally he reached the end of it. Watching the coach from his hiding place as it left the car park, Harry felt suddenly very lonely and not a little apprehensive. He wondered when they would discover his defection. It also occurred to him that he had no idea where to go from here. The Open Air Museum appeared to be in the middle of nowhere, with no sign of anything as helpful as a railway station or even a bus stop. Unwilling to ask the way in case he drew attention to himself, in the end he climbed over a fence and struck out through some woods, and walked and walked until the light began to fail, realizing, too late, that he was a wombat not to have fixed himself up with a map first.

The news that Harry was missing shook Ellen to the core. It was clear from the tenor of the conversation with the Headmaster that he had hoped to find her son at home with her. Ashen and suddenly freezing cold with fear, Ellen's voice sounded to her own ears as though it was far, far away saying, 'How long has he been missing?'

'His absence was first noticed when he failed to turn up for prep. We now think that he did not return with the other boys from this afternoon's outing.'

'What outing?' Ellen dimly remembered receiving a piece of paper asking her to sanction the cost of it and give her permission for him to go.

'The Weald and Downland Open Air Museum. It's in Sussex. Singleton to be exact.'

Feeling as though she might faint, Ellen spoke the awful words: 'Have you informed the police?'

'I'm just about to do so. I wanted to speak to you first. Mrs Carey, can you think of any reason why he might have run away to try and see you?'

So far as Ellen was aware, Harry knew nothing about the marital upheaval she and Jack were currently experiencing, and so, apart from the fact that she was his mother, she could not. Alerted nevertheless by his question, she fudged it, saying, 'Not off hand, but why do you ask?'

'His friend Charles Penrose says that Harry was very distressed last night. Apparently he had received a letter from his brother. It contained a newspaper cutting.' He waited, in the face of the stricken silence at the other end of the line, to hear whether she had anything to say to this.

Ellen remembered Charlie Penrose, whose parents had indulged themselves in such a spiteful divorce that it had even made the newspapers. Poor little Charlie, she had thought at the time, and Charlie, a mop-headed, rather serious little fellow with a stutter, had come to stay one holiday when the Penrose parental behaviour had been at its fraught worst.

Into the verbal void, and deeply ashamed, she said, 'My

husband and I are currently separated. It's my intention to ask him for a divorce. I fully intended to tell the boys during the next exeat.'

'It sounds as though a gossip column may have got there before you.' His delivery was dry, but he was, in fact, furious. Furious with the old duffer Petherbridge who apparently couldn't count up to thirty-five, and furious with Mrs Carey who had not alerted the school to what was going on.

'Shall I drive to the school?' She sounded dazed.

'I think it's better if you stay where you are, since it seems likely that Harry may be making for home. With your permission, I shall now ring the police. Do you want me to contact your husband?'

'No, I'll do that.'

He hung up.

Looking through the windows whose curtains were still undrawn, revealing the night, Ellen saw that it was starless. Harry, an unsophisticated ten, was out there unprotected, somewhere in the dark countryside, alone and probably frightened. To sit here and do nothing was inconceivable. She rang Jack. And got the answer phone.

'Oh, Christ!' shouted Ellen to nobody. 'That's typical of my useless husband! When I don't want him he's bloody well there, and when I do want him he bloody well isn't.'

Breathing hard and getting a grip, she dialled Edna Phipps's number.

'Mrs Phipps, it's Ellen Carey. Look, we have a slight crisis at this end. Harry has got himself lost in Singleton, we think, and I'm going to drive there now to look for him. Would you mind coming and waiting here until I get back. Just in case he turns up at Butterfly Cottage?'

Aware that this really was above and beyond the call of duty, but noting at the same time the tremor in Mrs Carey's voice, Edna folded up her knitting, put it in her knitting bag, and went to get her coat.

The sight of her imminent departure captured her husband's attention.

'Here, where are you goin'? What about my supper?'

'Emergency,' said Edna without elaborating. 'You'll have to get your own. Won't do you no harm.'

'Now see here –'

'No, you see here, I'm goin', and that's that.'

Getting her coat off the peg, she accidentally dislodged his favourite flat cap, an orange and brown hound's-tooth check, which fell to the floor. With some satisfaction Edna did not pick this up but stood on it instead while she put on her jacket, and then she kicked it into the corner, causing it to rise and, like a tossed pancake, turn itself over in midair before it fell with a soft plop onto the dusty floor.

'See you later!' She slammed the door, muttering under her breath as she put her knitting in the basket and mounted her bike, 'Bad-tempered old sod!'

The drive to Singleton took an hour. As she drove, Ellen played Bach very loudly in an effort to keep her spirits up and to hold morbid thoughts at bay. With forethought she had brought a powerful torch with her, and would need it since the night was a cloudy one which obscured even the half-moon. Taking the turning to the Open Air Museum, she drove the car as far as she could before being stopped by a locked gate. Here she parked and got out. There was no wind at all, and it was quiet yet at the same time unquiet, though all the sounds were small ones, mainly rustlings, probably of little animals, and the hooting of owls. Following in the wake of her beam of light, Ellen climbed a fence, tearing her skirt as she did so, and set off into the grounds of the museum. As she walked she called Harry's name, pausing to listen every so often in the hope that he might answer. Light, warm rain began to fall. Not heeding it, Ellen stumbled on. Her searchlight picked up the eyes of a wild animal in the bushes, probably a fox judging by the height of the eyes from the ground. It broke cover and she saw that it was a fox, a large one, probably a dog. Unconcerned by her presence, he loped along the footpath ahead of her for a few yards before slipping off to the left among the trees. While he was there, Ellen desisted from shouting for her son, but strained her ears instead.

By now the rain was falling steadily, hitting with a soft rattle the leaves of the trees beneath which she passed. Ellen left the open ground and, unconsciously following in Harry's footsteps, began to make her way through the woods.

Eventually she stopped, and leant against a tree.

'Harry!' she cried desperately, 'Harry! HARRY!'

No answer, only the drumming of the rain.

This was hopeless. A mad enterprise. She realized that she was soaked to the skin and beginning to shiver. Passing a hand across her eyes, Ellen turned and began to retrace her footsteps. Several times she lost her way, which did not augur very well for Harry either, but finally she emerged from the dripping woods and managed to navigate back to the car. Weary and drained and dreadfully worried, she drove home.

Being lost in the country made Harry appreciate two things. The first of these was grub, which normally appeared with miraculous regularity, as though a wand had been waved. Although a good-natured little boy, Harry had been known to complain about his food, especially at school. Never again, was his current view in the light of the fact that he was absolutely starving. The second was the inestimable security of a warm bed. The first problem was easily solved by scrumping some apples, although steak and chips would have filled the bill better, but the second less so. By now he was glad of the tweed jacket, which had been such a bore earlier in the day, and for the first time in its history, he even did up its one remaining button.

The barn, then, or what Harry thought was a barn, came as a welcome refuge. It stood in one corner of a large field, and faced away from the direction in which he had come. Walking up to it and then round it to get to the front, he was suddenly petrified by a stamping sound. There was something or someone in it. Determined to be brave, though frankly terrified, he crept silently round the corner and discovered that the barn was in fact a stable, which contained one medium-sized horse. Harry and the horse, a grey, looked at each other. The horse blew gently, rolling its mild dark eye in his direction.

'Aren't you smashing!' said Harry, ever sociable. Fishing in his pocket he found an apple core, and gave it to his new acquaintance. The thought of spending the night with something alive and friendly in the immediate vicinity was enormously reassuring. Exploring further, he discovered a hay store to the left of the stable just beyond another door which was locked, and probably belonged to a tack room. The hay smelt lovely, and was dry and warm. By now Harry was so tired he could practically have slept standing like his stable companion. His last act before curling up comfortably within a gap between the bales, was to take his school shoes off, at which point he discovered that he must have trodden in one of his new friend's droppings. 'Oh, rank!' said Harry, deciding to sort it out tomorrow.

Ellen got back just before midnight. She let herself in and went straight through to the kitchen where she had left Edna Phipps sitting, placidly cabling her way through some large turquoise garment by the Aga.

'Any sign. . . ?'

Edna shook her head. 'There have been some phone calls, though. One from Mr Carey, who says he's drivin' down by way of the school tomorrow mornin', and could you ring him back whatever time you get in, and one from the police, but' – seeing the look of hope on Mrs Carey's face – 'they did say as they had no more news. Oh, and the school headmaster rang. He'll telephone again tomorrow mornin'.'

'Oh thank you, Mrs Phipps, I honestly don't know what I would have done without you.'

'You're done in,' said Mrs Phipps kindly, thinking that Mrs Carey looked as though she might be sickening for something. 'I'll make you some cocoa, and then I'll be on my bike.'

'No cocoa, thank you,' replied Ellen, who felt more in need of a stiff drink, 'but I'll run you home and we'll organize the bike back tomorrow.'

'Bless you, I wouldn't hear of it.' Mrs Phipps was in stalwart mode. 'I'll see you in the mornin' as usual.'

When she had gone, Ellen put the heating onto constant and went and got a blanket, which she wrapped around herself. Then she lifted Casimir off the rocking chair, and sat down herself in his warm place, putting him on her lap as she did so. Stroking his old head for comfort, she prepared to sit up through the watches of the night in case her son should come home.

The silence and the darkness were oppressive. She looked at the American wall clock, whose uneven tick had moved along the time in Butterfly Cottage for years. Half-past midnight. Using the portable phone, which had been one of Jack's favourite toys until everyone got one, she dialled the number of the studio.

23

Unaware of the drama unfolding in Sussex, Alexander arranged to have lunch with Marcus. That same day he also had an appointment to see Tessa in Mimosa Street, the purpose of which, as far as he was concerned, was to start winding up their marriage. He had not seen his wife since The Gallery catastrophe, and had not wanted to. However, emotional considerations apart, there were still certain practicalities to be considered, such as the house, for example. Alexander, who liked it and who, now that Tessa had been exorcised, felt that he would like to go on living there, hoped that she might feel disposed to let him buy her out. All this had to be discussed. His emerald he did not want to see again. He had told her she could keep it and, in the light of the life it had led while encircling her wedding finger, did not intend to change his mind, even though it was a family heirloom and valuable.

Marcus arrived cock-a-hoop. Jane had given birth to a son. After two daughters, both of whom he adored, he now had an heir for Marchants. Alexander ordered champagne.

'It's a double celebration after all, the birth of your son, and the death of my marriage.'

Eyeing his friend as he drank it, Marcus thought, That last remark could have been cynical, but I think it wasn't. There's something different about Alexander. A sort of liberation, as though Tessa's chains have finally fallen away.

Aloud he said, 'So you've finally decided to finish it.'

Clear of brow, Alexander said, 'I'm meeting her this afternoon to talk things through. Unfortunately it looks as though she will be on her own, since Carey isn't prepared to make an honest woman of her.'

Reflecting that nobody would ever make an honest woman of Tessa, Marcus observed, 'How can he? He's got an absolutely delicious wife already.'

'Apart from that, what do you think of Ellen?'

'She's a born muse. It must be maddening for her, because I know she's a creative person in her own right, but my perception of Ellen is that it's through her that others, such as her slob of a husband, produce their best work.'

Mindful of the fact that he was writing poetry again, and good poetry too, and that he felt this to be in some magical way an off-shoot of their brief encounter, Alexander said, 'I think she's a goddess.'

'Very few of those about, but I know what you mean. There's a grace and luminosity about Ellen, and the sort of warmth which, alas, is not much in vogue these days.' Warmth was one of the qualities of his own second wife, and Marcus, who had had a chilly first marriage, was not about to underestimate it. Curiously, he looked at his chum. Clearly something had gone on there, between Ellen and Alexander, though heaven knew what. He waited to see if any more was forthcoming, but apparently it was not.

Changing the subject, he enquired, 'What do you think Tessa will do now?'

'No idea. Worries me a bit. The thought of her on her own, I mean.'

Thinking as he spoke, God preserve me from ever being a romantic, Marcus observed robustly. 'She won't be on her own for long. I predict that Tessa will marry a duke, and quite soon too.'

'What! Do you know something I don't?'

'Not at all. I've just watched the way she operates, that's all. It's what you might call a logical progression. Shall we order?'

The sun was high in the sky when Harry awoke. For a moment he could not think where he was, but was aware that something was tickling his nose. Hay. A companionable snort reminded him of the horse next door. Getting up, he searched for his shoes, and then remembered that they were covered in horse dung. Gross!

He was very hungry. Not so the grey, which was placidly tucking into a full hay net. Someone must have arrived this morning and fed it, but had not spotted Harry who had bedded himself down between two bales.

'It's all right for you,' he told his friend, trying unsuccessfully to wipe his shoes on the grass.

For the first time in his life, Harry would have liked to wash his face and even clean his teeth. Now it was light, he saw that, during the course of his travels of the night before, over and under fences, he had torn his trousers and his jacket, both of which were covered in mud. Small darts of hay were everywhere and proved well-nigh impossible to remove except individually. In the end Harry gave up. Reaching into his pocket, he searched for Charlie's tenner. For one awful moment he thought he had lost it. Locating it with relief wedged into one corner, he decided to flatten it out and put it folded only in two into his breast pocket where it should not be so easy to mislay it.

Pausing to pat his placid stable mate on the nose, Harry resumed his odyssey, though general dampness from the rain of the night before, coupled with acute hunger pangs, could be said to be taking the edge off this. All the same, with sunshine came optimism, although he still had no idea where he was. As he walked, he had a debate with himself as to whether he could afford to buy some breakfast and still have enough money left to get home. Even Harry, who had very little idea what things cost, thought the answer was probably no.

Eventually he came to a sizable country road, and asked a man walking along it with his Labrador the way to the nearest village. Perhaps, when he got there, he would buy himself a doughnut. The village turned out to be another couple of miles' hike. On his way he passed a phone box, and sensibly decided to try to ring Mummy reverse charges, which would have been a good idea except that this turned out to have been vandalized and was out of order. It seemed that there was nothing to do but plod on.

The village was tiny, but it did have a shop, which did sell doughnuts. In a fit of extravagance Harry bought two. As he paid for them, he asked the lady behind the counter whether she knew where he could get a train or a bus to Hocking. Looking curiously at his dishevelled little figure, and thinking that he seemed a very small boy indeed to be travelling about on his own, she told him that he would have to get a bus to the nearest town and then a train.

Sitting on a seat in the churchyard, eating, it occurred to Harry that, in order to conserve his money, the best way of getting to the nearest railway station was probably to try to hitch a lift. Accordingly, when his breakfast was over, he carefully put the redundant paper bag into a litter bin, and set off, thumbing as he went, the way he had seen people do in films.

Several cars passed him before one of them, a battered Ford, stopped. Running to catch it up, he was dismayed to find that it was being driven by a single man.

'Jump in! Where do you want to go to?'

Very tempted, Harry still hesitated. He remembered Mummy's strictures on the subject of not getting into cars with strangers. Instinctively he knew that a lady would have been all right. Once or twice when he had had to travel by train by himself, with Mummy putting him on at one end and Daddy taking him off at the other, his mother had scoured the platform for an elderly lady, preferably tweedy with a large bundle of knitting, who had been prepared to take him under her wing.

'Well, come on!'

Flushing scarlet, Harry said, 'I'm very sorry. I don't think I want a lift after all.' Disconsolately he started to tramp on. Rather to his alarm, the car cruised along beside him.

'What's the problem? I'll take you wherever you want to go.'

That settled it. Harry knew that people who picked up hitchhikers, unless unusually saintly, took them as far as they could in the direction they themselves were going, at which point there was a parting of the ways. Deciding that to get out of the orbit of this persistence was imperative, he suddenly darted left, jumped the ditch, climbed the bank and, tripping over a tree root, rolled down the other side of it where he lay, winded, for a few seconds before getting to his feet and running off across the field.

The driver of the Ford, who was the local vicar in mufti, was saddened by this panicky reaction, though not very surprised. It was, he thought, a sad reflection on these Godless times that the very young, and therefore vulnerable, had to be so cautious. Perhaps he would construct a sermon around this for his little congregation, which numbered twenty on good days and half that number if the weather was bad.

Unaware of his interlocutor's impeccable credentials, Harry congratulated himself on a lucky escape. He gave it ten minutes before returning to the road, where he resumed his hitching, preparing to take the same evasive action should this be necessary. The next person who stopped could have been tailor-made for Mummy. Mrs Heathcote and her red setter were on their way into the nearest large town to shop.

'You look as though you've been in the wars,' remarked Mrs Heathcote, motioning the dog, which had been sitting in the front seat like a human being, although without a seat belt, into the back of the car. 'Where are you making for?'

He told her.

'So you want the station. You're in luck. We're on our way to the game shop and we go right past it. Hop in.' Pressing her Hush Puppied foot down on the accelerator, at the same time letting out the clutch, she gave him a sharp look.

'What's your name?'

'Harry.'

'Aren't you a little young to be travelling around the countryside on your own, Harry?'

'I'm on my way to meet my mother.' There was a pause. Anxious to get off the tricky subject of his own programme, Harry said, 'What a brilliant dog!' And then, knowing the answer perfectly well, 'What sort is he?'

Mrs Heathcote, who was a widow, and whose only son lived in America where she went once a year, waxed enthusiastic. 'She. She's a red setter. I breed them, you know. Such intelligent dogs. And kind too . . .' On and on, she went, with Harry interjecting another question whenever it looked as though she might be about to dry up. In this fashion they finally drew up outside the station.

Letting him out she said, doubtfully, 'Are you sure you'll be all right? You wouldn't like me to ring Mummy for you to tell her that you're on your way?'

For a moment Harry considered it and then decided against, since, hopefully, he was on the last leg of his journey now.

'No, I'll be okay. It's all arranged. Thank you very much, Mrs Heathcote.' He held out his hand and she shook it. Turning away, he walked in the direction of the ticket office. Watching his muddy back retreating she thought, Goodness me, you could grow mustard and cress on that jacket. His mother won't be very pleased.

Inside the station there was no one behind the counter, but there was a blackboard with a misspelt message informing the general public that, owing to illness, there was nobody on duty and tickets would have to be bought at the other end. The indicator, a surprising piece of up-to-date technology in what was otherwise a very old-fashioned station, told Harry that his train would be the next but one. Patiently, he sat down to wait.

Jack, who was not feeling very happy himself, did his best to shore up his distraught wife. There had been no clue concerning Harry's whereabouts, and a police search in the grounds and surrounding countryside of the Open Air Museum had not found him either. Tomorrow it would all be in the newspapers, together with a photograph. Meanwhile, there was nothing to do but sit and wait. Finding himself for once in a position of responsibility, Jack surprised himself by rising to the occasion, and it was he who dealt with the police, the school and the newspapers, and he who drove to David's school to tell him what was happening.

David was shamefaced.

'Dad, this is all my fault. There was a story in the newspaper, and I sent it to Harry.'

Jack, who did not allow himself to believe in the existence of guilt because if he had he would at the most have been forced to retire to a monastery and at the very least to have been faithful to his wife, dismissed this. 'No recriminations. Question is what we do next.'

'What if something has happened to Harry?' David's voice shook. His little brother often got on his nerves, especially since Mum seemed to have an especially soft spot for Harry, but the prospect of a world without him was still not to be borne.

'Here's a copy of the cutting.' He handed it to his father. Jack stared at it in silence. Tessa. Tessa had given an interview both coy and self-promoting to the newspaper. He rued the day he had ever met her. On the other hand meeting her had not necessarily meant that he had had to indulge himself in an affair with her as well.

Uncomfortably in touch with himself, Jack said to his elder son, 'It's not your fault. If it's anybody's fault it's mine.' He put his arm around David's shoulders, and, wishing he felt as sure as he hoped he sounded, said, 'He'll be all right, you'll see. Come on, let's go and have some lunch.'

Sitting in the train, Harry said politely to the gentleman opposite, 'Excuse me, could you please tell me what time this train gets into Hocking?'

'I'm afraid it doesn't,' came the disconcerting reply. 'Only the front four coaches go there. The back half, which is where we are, peels off and goes somewhere else entirely.'

Harry's heart sank. For the first time he began to doubt that he would ever reach home. His anguish was so evident that, putting his paper temporarily to one side, his fellow traveller enquired, 'Didn't they tell you that when you bought your ticket?'

'There wasn't anybody in the ticket office where I got on. Just a notice saying that you had to pay your fare at the other end. Thanks anyway.'

Harry was beginning to feel that there was a limit to how long he could go on being brave. What had started out as an intrepid adventure was turning into a nightmare. Nothing was going right. He got up and went to stand in the corridor looking out of the window at the wrong countryside flashing past. His eyes filled with hot tears. By the time he had paid his fare to wherever it was they were finally going to end up, he would have no money left to pay for where he really did want to go. A sudden overwhelming longing for Mummy and home made him feel sick with apprehension. He was beginning to feel that he would never see them again.

Some fifteen minutes later, the train, which by now was almost empty, stopped outside a country station. After five minutes it was still static. On impulse, and just in time before it slowly took off again, Harry opened the door, plummeted down onto the track which, without a platform, was a surprisingly long way to fall, and losing his balance careered down the grassy bank beside it, bursting the remaining button off his tweed jacket as he did so. It looked like being another famished, itinerant night.

Once again refusing to go to bed, in spite of Jack's protestations, Ellen sat up in the rocking chair. At one point, despite herself, she did sleep and dreamt that Harry came home, and when she woke was briefly and cruelly suffused with thankfulness and joy.

The day, a grey and drizzling one, brought disillusion and the newspapers, a quality and a tabloid, both of which had a large photograph of Harry on the front page. Missing. Every mother's nightmare. There seemed nothing for her and Jack to say to each other. As if in separate worlds they moved quietly about the house, blaming themselves, not each other, and each, in different ways, grieving. The phone rang constantly, mainly journalists, sometimes the police. Mrs Braithwaite threatened to arrive.

'Please head her off, Jack. I know she's worried too and wants to help, but I just can't hack it at the moment. Tell her the moment there's any news she'll be the first to know.'

'Leave it to me!' Jack rather relished the unusual feeling of being on top of things for once.

His wife lifted down the trug. 'I'm going to cut some cabbages. I won't be long,' thinking as she did so, it's crazy. I'm not eating at the moment so why do I want to cut cabbages? Because it gives me something to do, and because there is solace in a garden. She cut six, which was at least three too many, and as she straightened and looked up, she saw Harry, travel-stained and clearly very, very tired, just as she had seen him in her dream, coming up the lane.

Ellen stood for a moment disbelieving her own eyes, and then, throwing down trug and cabbages, she flew through the garden gate and raced down the drive towards him, skirts streaming, arms outstretched. Laughing and weeping at the same time, and heedless of the mud caused by the rain of the interminable night before, she fell on her knees and took her son in her arms.

Under a monochrome watercolour wash of a sky, Alexander walked along the Fulham Road towards the house he had shared with his wife. He felt no emotion about the interview to come, only a desire to draw his marriage to a close so that he could get on with his new life unfettered at least by the material complications of his old one. Emotional chains were, of course, another thing, and though he presently felt these to be vestigial, he was aware that he might be deluding himself, and that it might be some time before the real extent of these became apparent.

He arrived to find that, atypically early, she had got there before him. Tessa was sitting on the sofa by the window and was back to black and the French plait.

'Hello, Tessa. I hope I'm not late.' Aware of sounding formal, Alexander recognized that this was in fact an outward manifestation of a profound inner change.

'Hello, darling. Don't I get a kiss?'

Warily he kissed her on the cheek, and then sat down opposite her in the armchair by the bookshelves. They looked at each other across a great deal more than just the room in which they sat. Tessa was the first to speak.

'I'm afraid this has all been a great mistake.'

'It doesn't matter. We don't have children. It can be easily undone.'

'That isn't what I meant.'

'Oh?'

'I meant our separation. I have come to ask you to forgive me. I should like us to start again.'

The words he had longed to hear such a short time ago now were powerless to move him. The emerald on her wedding finger glittered as she moved her hand. There was no point, he recognized, in building up false hopes.

'Of course I forgive you, Tessa, but starting again is out of the question.'

Turning her head sideways, she stared out of the window, presenting him with a pale and all but flawless profile. A cameo. His newly dispassionate gaze detected the faintest of lines beneath her eye.

> *But beauty vanishes; beauty passes;*
> *However rare – rare it be . . .*

Age would defeat Tessa more comprehensively than he ever could. Gently he said, 'I'm sorry.'

'So there's nothing to be done.'

'Nothing.'

There was a silence.

'What will you do?' asked Alexander.

'Do? I'll think of something. You're probably right, by the way. It just seemed a pity, that's all, to throw away all those years together.'

'Nobody's throwing them away. They still exist for both of us. It's just that we as a couple are played out. There is nowhere for us to go together from here.'

Suddenly disconcertingly practical, in a way which convinced him as nothing else could that she had been preparing to use him as a staging post all over again, she asked, 'What do you want to do about the house? And the car?'

'Take the car. But I'd like to buy you out of the house.'

'All right.' She stood up. 'You'd better get it valued. Oh, and I should give you this.' Taking off the emerald, she held it out to him on the palm of her hand. Its smouldering green stone reminded him of nothing so much as jealousy and betrayal.

Kissing her on the cheek, and smelling her sharp, seductive scent for the last time as he did so, Alexander said, 'Keep it.'

Harry was ravenous, and so fatigued that he nearly fell asleep over his egg and chips. In answer to his mother's anxious questions, he told them that he had spent the previous night in an outhouse, prior to hitching another lift across country and finally achieving the right train. On his arrival in Hocking, with no money left at all, he had walked from the station. Watching him with solicitude and guilt, Ellen decided to ask no more until tomorrow. The main thing was that he was home safely. That night she slept properly for the first time, but only until six o'clock. Waking up, she knew, or thought she knew, that Harry was safely back. Remembering her dream of the night before when she had also woken up to the certainty that he was back, Ellen got out of bed and walked quietly past the spare room, where her husband lay, and into Harry's den. He lay rosily asleep on his back with one arm around his head, his breathing so soft that she could not hear it. His hair, which was thick and could probably do with a cut, spread in a dark blond aureole around the ten-year-old face which still retained its childish peacefulness. The crescent-shaped sweep of his dark lashes touched her deeply, perhaps because sleep is one of the greatest expressions of trust. Sitting down beside him, love welling, Ellen stared at her son.

It therefore came as a surprise when the unconscious one said, 'Hello, Mummy.'

'Harry, you naughty boy, I thought you were asleep!'

'I was.' Sleepily he smiled at her. 'Mummy?'

'Yes?'

'You won't leave Daddy, will you?'

'Is that why you ran away?'

'I only thought that, if I could just see you, you wouldn't do it. Although Charlie Penrose says that newspapers are often wrong.'

'I'm so sorry that you saw that, Harry. I had no knowledge of the existence of such an article.'

'David sent it to me.'

Oh, well done, David, thought his mother.

'But you won't, will you? Please say you won't!'

Anxiety replaced tranquillity. Mentally despairingly beating her wings against the cage of her marriage, Ellen finally replied, after a fractional hesitation, 'No, I won't.'

'Promise!'

'I promise.' She kissed him. 'Go to sleep now.'

The next morning her third rejection arrived through the post, this time a three-liner. So that, it appeared, was that.

24

Sitting in his Soho office studying the schedules, Robert Wilmot said to his assistant, 'Any sign of Mrs Haye's Carey profile?'

'None, I'm afraid. Do you want me to ring her up?'

'No, I'd better do it. It's just that we're very close to the deadline and I'd like a chance to see it in advance in case anything needs editing.'

When he telephoned, Ginevra was in the act of sharpening her pencil.

'I've nearly finished it. I'm just going through it now, pencilling in the odd alteration. With luck, I should be in a position to express it to you tomorrow.'

Relieved, he replied, 'That's great. I look forward to reading it.'

Her typescript did not, in fact, arrive until three days later, by which point he was beginning to panic all over again. Settling down to read it straight away, since by now time was very short indeed, he instructed his secretary not to put through any telephone calls for the next thirty minutes.

When he had finally finished, Robert felt as though he was in shock. What on earth had she thought she was doing? He had always assumed her to be a close friend of the Hartings. The article was closely reasoned, elegantly written, as he had expected, and pure vitriol, as he had not expected. A demolition job. If pressed on the matter he might have admitted that he agreed with a good bit of it. Like her his view was that the end, especially in this case, did not justify the means, and Robert had long held the private opinion that Jack Carey was a shit, with what might well prove to be an over-inflated reputation. All the same, *Modern Art* also had a reputation, which was for fairness, and this was right over the top, the stiletto spareness of the prose making the whole thing even more lethal. Although without a doubt it would sell copies if only on the grounds of thought-provoking iconoclastic aggression, he felt that it would be impossible to run it as it stood, and not just because of his friendship with James Harting. Writs would fly.

After a pause to marshall his thoughts, he rang the Little Haddow number.

'Mrs Haye?'

'Yes.'

'Robert Wilmot speaking.'

'Oh, yes. Hello. Did the article reach you?'

'Yes it did, thanks very much.' There was a pause. 'I have to say it wasn't quite what I was anticipating.'

'It's my considered view. I'm not in the business of writing anodyne essays to flatter the egos of over-promoted celebrities.'

He was tempted to say A lot of it is my considered view too, but did not. Instead he replied, 'No, quite so, but it's very caustic. I'd like you to consider toning it down a bit. Maybe dwell rather more on Carey's positive points.'

Waiting for a flat refusal, he was taken aback by her next utterance. She said, 'All right. When's the soonest you can get it back to me?'

This was easier than he had expected. Gratefully he said, 'I'll put it on a train this afternoon, if you could arrange to pick it up at your end. You'll have to turn it round almost straight away though.'

'When's your ultimate deadline?'

He told her.

'You'll have it.'

Greatly relieved he rang off and summoned his assistant.

Later that day, as she had promised, Ginevra bicycled to the station and bicycled back again with the parcel in her basket. Extracting this on her arrival, she took it into the sitting room where she dropped it into a drawer without even opening it. The day after tomorrow, on the eve of his deadline by which time it would be too late to do anything about it, she would send it back. Exactly as it was.

The typescript spent its allotted time in the drawer and then, at the eleventh hour, was sent back to the offices of *Modern Art*.

Ginevra tried to put the whole episode out of her mind and, watching the weather begin to break, went back to her book. By now the trees were becoming bare, autumn seeming ready to call it a day and yield to winter, and streaked lurid sunsets began to replace the milder evening skies. It became significantly colder for a time, and for several mornings in a row before the rain set in again, there was a thick and hoary frost. She still walked, but because of the rain, it was slippery underfoot with wet leaves and mud, and she was forced to buy herself some Wellington boots.

There had been no word from Victoria since their last encounter, which was hardly surprising, but Ellen had rung with the disturbing news that she and Jack were back together again and were shortly to go away for a week or so. Disturbing because, Ginevra recognized, now that they were once more a couple, the article she had written would hurt Ellen as well as her husband. 'I'll come and see you when I get back,' Ellen had said. Ginevra, who did not take a daily paper, had known nothing of the drama of Harry's disappearance until Ellen told her. To Ginevra's sensitive ear Ellen did not sound ecstatic, as one whose marriage had been dragged back to safety from the brink of the abyss might. Ellen sounded resigned.

Without much hope in her heart, Ginevra rang Robert Wilmot.

Sounding furious, and thinking as he spoke, I honestly think this woman is mad, he said, 'You're right, it's much too late to do anything about it. It's gone to press. You should have altered it while you had the chance. As it is, I'm afraid you're stuck with it.' And could not resist adding, 'However, since you tell me that it is your considered view, there's surely nothing the matter with that.' There was, of course, everything the matter with that, for he was stuck with it too.

There was another halting letter from Kevin. Kevin sounded very fed up, and there were no endearments of any sort. It intimated that he might be coming home at last, but there was no indication of when. All the same, as she threw it in the bin, Ginevra experienced the uncomfortable sensation that he was getting nearer by the minute. The prospect was not a pleasant one.

The once longed-for marbled notebooks still had not arrived, but since the burning of the corn dolly, in an odd way, Ginevra had felt the mental pressure to be off, as though some sort of exorcism had indeed taken place. These days, twice a week at least, she travelled up to London to research and work in the library, and although Ginevra spoke to nobody and nobody spoke to her, the illusion of being in company was still therapeutic.

In Chelsea the Harting household had more or less returned to normal. At the suggestion of Alexander Lucas, Victoria got in touch with Jane Marchant in order to sort out the vexed question of which gynaecologist. Supplying the answer to her first question, Jane's response was, 'Oh him! He's a good consultant, by which I mean he knows his babies, but otherwise he's a complete prat. Likes his patients to fall down and worship. I have a brilliant one who knows that women have the vote. Got a pen?'

Victoria wrote the name down. 'Do you see much of Alexander and Tessa these days?'

'Since they split up we see either Alexander or, very occasionally, Tessa, but mainly Alexander, since he is an old friend. You probably see more of her, don't you?'

'Not really. I'm afraid she and James haven't spoken to each other since Jack's exhibition.'

'Yes, she did rather go to town, didn't she? And nearly capsized the Carey marriage in the process I gather.'

'That was the whole idea. And then there was that awful business of Harry running away from school. James just can't forgive it.'

'Ellen must have been frantic! Hopefully it will all have taught Jack a lesson.'

'He probably thinks it has at the moment, but it's my view he's too old to change. I fear Ellen's stuck with him, warts and all now.'

'Sounds as though it's mainly warts!'

'Quite. Anyway, look, thanks for giving me the name, Jane. I'll let you know how I get on.'

The September exeat came and went, and after another prod in the form of a letter from his mother-in-law, Jack booked an out-of-season holiday for himself and Ellen in Venice. Their last visit had taken place when they were both students and followed much the same pattern as this one except, Ellen reflected, as she followed Jack around, outwardly smiling and compliant and inwardly desperate, that then she had been much happier. Much less well off and not staying in the Cipriani, but still much happier. Apart from the fragility of her own mental equilibrium, the sexual side of their marriage, hitherto good, had become a problem, and, although they now shared a bed again, Ellen endured her husband's lovemaking rather than enjoyed it, as had once been the case. This was a pity in one of the world's most romantic cities, and privately she thought that perhaps it was too soon for a vacation such as this, and that they would have been better slowly picking up the pieces in the familiar surroundings of home.

They spent most of the time walking, and one day revisited the Accademia Hotel, where they had stayed before, and then went on to the Ca' Rezzonico, in which the Brownings had once lived. The Ca' was large and gloomy and possessed not one but two paintings of a triumphant Judith holding up the head of Holofernes, and yet another of Orpheus being torn to pieces by the Thracian women. Ellen identified with them all. She thought, Maybe I'm depressed because I'm so angry. Maybe cutting Jack's head off would solve my problem too.

The following afternoon, well wrapped up against the cold, they hired a gondola. Eel-like it slid along, interestingly slipping the wrong way along *senso unico* canals, and turning right or left when this was prohibited and, while Jack talked to the gondolier, exhausted Ellen watched carmine, rose and terracotta houses with their flowered ornate balconies and weed-trailing watery steps pass her by. Birds nested in holes in the walls, occasionally flying upwards with a clatter of wings which was magnified by the narrowness and height of the channels through which they glided. The water was green. *Green as a dream and deep as death*. No, not deep as death, only two metres, she heard the gondolier helpfully informing Jack, who must have asked.

Why can't Jack shut up for five minutes, wondered Ellen irritably. Why can't we just drift along in blissful healing quiet for a while?

Emerging into the Grand Canal, she noticed with disappointment that the beautiful façade of the Ca' d'Oro was boarded up. Such a shame. She supposed that, like the Browning apartments, it must be the victim of some endless Italian repairs. On their return to the hotel, Ellen lay on the bed and slept. Ellen slept a great deal of the time, noticed Jack, publicly sympathetic and privately exasperated.

Four more distant days passed in this desultory fashion and, on the evening of the fourth, Jack took Ellen out to dinner in one of the little restaurants behind St Mark's. When they finally left it was late. Outside there had been a very heavy shower, and drops of rain like tears hung in trembling rows from the balconies in the alleys. Finally emerging into the splendour of the square, opposite the Doges' Palace, they found it to be almost deserted. Shining sheets of water reflected the old-fashioned streetlights and the golden mosaics of St Mark's, and although the doors of the cafés were open, under the awnings the tables were empty, and thus abandoned had the forlorn air of poor relations in a mansion. A solitary pianist was playing, and listening to the haunting, melancholic melody floating on the night air, Ellen recognized the music from *Jeux Interdits*. Sad! Sad! So sad! It defined with clarity Ellen's own mood to a point where she could no longer even attempt to rise above her own pain. Standing in St Mark's Square, she began to weep.

It was not until he had been walking for five minutes, declaiming about the architecture with the aid of the *Blue Guide*, that Jack suddenly realized that his wife was not with him. It had just begun to rain again. Going back to look for her, he discovered her standing alone, arms crossed over her chest as though to protect herself, her silver dress clinging damply to her slim body. With remorse, and a sudden recognition of the scale of the damage, Jack took her in his arms and they stood there in the pouring rain embracing one another.

'It's too late, Jack, much too late.' She appeared to be unable to stop crying. Holding her hand he led her to the boat. Two days later, on the advice of the hotel doctor, he took her back to England.

25

Without prior warning, Ginevra's computer went wrong. Incomprehensibly it announced: *Write section buffer failed.* Turning to the manual, she received the unwelcome instruction to consult her dealer. In Little Haddow and the depths of the country this was easier said than done.

'Blast!' said Ginevra. The prospect of writing it all by hand until some sort of repair could be effected was not an enticing one. On impulse, and not expecting to receive any response, since she understood them to be away for at least ten days, but intending to leave a message on the answer phone, she rang Ellen. To her surprise, her friend answered.

'Ginevra!' Ellen sounded warm but faint. 'How are you?'

'How are *you*? I thought you might still be away.'

'We should have been. I'm afraid I've been under the weather, with the result that we came home early.'

Ginevra, who had never been to Venice or indeed anywhere very much, could not imagine anybody wanting to come home early from such a trip.

'I'm sorry! Nothing too serious I hope.'

'Depends what you call serious. They tell me I've had a minor nervous breakdown. I'm currently being chaotically nursed by Jack, which is enough to make it turn into a major one. Actually that's not fair. I'm much better than I was. By which I mean I don't cry all the time now, only half the time. Anyway, never mind about that. How are you?'

'Stumped. My computer has broken down. I'm having to write in long hand until I can somehow organize a repair, and then I'll have to transfer all the handwriting onto the hard disk, so it's all going to take twice the time. I almost feel like giving up on the book until it's in working order again.'

Ellen said, 'Why don't you come and spend some time here at Butterfly Cottage with me? Jack has to go to London for a few days to sort out some details with James Harting, and he's very unhappy about leaving me alone. So much so that he's threatening to invite my mother to come and occupy the position of Florence Nightingale while he's away. You haven't met her, of course, have you? All I can tell you is that she has many talents but nursing is definitely not among them.'

Lonely, and now effectively unable to work as well, Ginevra leapt at the idea. 'I'd love to! But when, exactly?'

'Jack's going to London on Monday, and will be away until Thursday, so why don't you come for those four days if that suits?'

'It does suit.' Ginevra felt her heart lift.

'Oh good, then that's settled. If you want to check the times of the trains and let me know when you're arriving, I'll come and pick you up.'

After she had replaced the receiver, Ginevra sat for a while staring out of the window. This sort of visit to a friend, something most people took for granted, for her was a highlight of her repetitive and narrow life, and, rather like a child with a forthcoming treat, she made up her mind to savour the prospect as well as the actual event. Captain Morgan pushed his tattered head into her dangling hand.

'I expect you want to be fed,' said Ginevra. Agreeing with her, he emitted a loud twanging miaow, which sounded more like a feline battle cry than the well-modulated domesticated voice of a pet. Getting up and preparing to organize it, she wondered what on earth to do with him while she was away.

'I'll leave you several bowls full, but after that it's down to you. Decimate the rat population. That's the answer!' Watching his dish, globe-like, descending he stood briefly on his hind legs, and then, as she put it down, he ran at it and began to eat ravenously, scattering food as he did so.

Sitting opposite James Harting in his Chelsea sitting room and clutching a large whisky, Jack felt more at ease than he had for a long time.

Sorting out his own drink, James enquired, 'How's Ellen now?'

'Not too good, but better than she was. Ginevra Haye is keeping her company while I'm away.'

Ginevra. Again James had that disquieting echo from the past. Those eyes. Deep blue almost purple eyes in which a man might drown. With it came an odd, clairvoyant intimation that a wheel of some sort had not come full circle, but might be about to. Absurd. He dismissed it.

'Do you ever see Tessa these days?'

'You must be joking!' Jack swallowed some whisky for fortification. 'More than my life's worth. She's one hell of a girl though, your sister.'

For one tantalizing moment he saw her again making love to him, she in the dominant position and for once almost modest, her breasts veiled by the rippling curtain of her hair. He and Ellen had not made love since their return from Venice. Currently without his oats, as his father would have said, Jack lamented the fact that Tessa had wanted to regularize their relationship. If she had been content to settle for an affair all the ensuing catastrophes might not have happened, and he could still have been secretly enjoying her superb body on the basis, vis-à-vis Ellen, that what the mind doesn't know about, the heart doesn't grieve over.

'What about you?'

'She may be my sister but I simply can't condone her behaviour. Even her husband has finally seen the light and he really was in thrall. It's my opinion that Tessa needs to go into social orbit with a member of the jet set. Then she could sleep, or whatever that sort of person does, all day, and party all night. Anyway, be that as it may, the answer to your question is that I expect we'll get over it in time, but at the moment we're incommunicado.'

What an old puritan James is, thought Jack, watching him sip his wine.

'Still, at least Ellen has apparently forgiven you.'

With sudden gloomy perspicacity, Jack said, 'We're together again, sure, but all the same I don't think she has. It's possible she never will.'

His thoughts dwelt for a moment on the mistress before Tessa. What had her name been? Zoe was it? Zoe? Yes, Zoe, that was it. He found himself briefly wondering if she was still available, and then rejected the idea. It occurred to him to wonder if Tessa's expertise and lack of inhibition coupled with her startling beauty hadn't perhaps spoilt him for anyone else. Given the fact that in common with everybody's her looks would eventually fade – though everybody did not start off from such a high threshold, of course – he was glad that he had immortalized her on canvas, in spite of the mayhem which had resulted.

'Does Tessa have anyone else?'

'Tessa *always* has someone else.'

'Where's she living now?'

'Still with Ceci, but not for much longer. According to Alexander, Ceci's had enough too.'

Jack looked ruminative and, at the same time, regretful. Eyeing him keenly, James said, 'If you'll take my advice you'll steer well clear of Tessa in future. She may be sexual dynamite, since she's my sister I wouldn't know about that, but as you rightly pointed out at the beginning of this conversation, she's sure as hell marital dynamite. You're too bloody impatient, Jack. Give yourself and Ellen a chance.'

He's right, of course.

'You're right old son. I know that.'

All the same, he thought, one last time? Why not? Before I finally become a model husband.

The front door shut with a crash, making the glasses jump and causing an updraught which blew all the invitations off the mantelpiece. Gathering them up, James replaced them. They heard Victoria saying, presumably to Ho, 'Who's had a lovely long walkies then?' and minutes later he staggered into the sitting room and collapsed into his basket.

'Who's knackered then?' was Jack's genial enquiry, watching him.

She called upstairs.

'Hello, darling. I'm afraid I . . .' The rest of what she was saying got lost as she apparently walked off into the kitchen in mid-sentence. Coming back, still talking, they heard '. . . the car.'

James got the drift.

'Which bit?'

'Back bumper, I'm afraid. Quite a large dent. Panel beating job probably.' Then, adroitly changing the subject, 'I'm just putting the kettle on. Would you like a cup of tea?'

'I've got Jack here with me!'

'Oh, well, *he* definitely won't want a cup of tea.' She sounded tart.

'Sometimes I think your wife doesn't approve of me,' was Jack's complacent response to this.

Sidestepping it, James said, 'She's very fond of Ellen.'

'Aren't we all.' With a sudden pang, Jack wished his wife was better, and that the old irresponsible days were back. If he didn't fuck somebody, soon, he might as well call carnality a day.

Ginevra found Ellen to be better than she expected. Grace under pressure, was her view, watching her friend moving within the even, familiar rhythms of Butterfly Cottage. Ginevra had never lived in a house such as this, and she was surprised at the tranquillizing effect of being surrounded by pretty things. It was all so easy on the eye. Even the cats appeared to be affected and, unlike the predatory, buccaneering Captain Morgan, sprawled and lazed, peaceful drones in this kingdom where their mistress was queen of the hive. In Ginevra's opinion, which approximated to Olivia Braithwaite's, Ellen would be mad to give this up. But then, thought Ginevra, my existence has been conspicuously lacking in this sort of comfort and taste. I'm aesthetically starved, whereas Ellen has probably never known anything else and therefore, paradoxically, feels herself able to do without it. On the other hand, it was probably true to say that someone with her flair would be able to make a bower out of a mud hut.

Sitting companionably together after dinner, each holding a glass of red wine, Ginevra brought the subject up.

'Don't you think you'd miss all this if you left it?'

'There is no longer any question of me leaving it.' Ellen stared into the fire. 'Oh, at one point I thought I would. Thought I *could*. I don't think that any more. I now see that to go would be to sacrifice Harry. And I couldn't do that.'

She sounded sombre.

Ginevra was intrigued by a significant omission.

'What about your elder son?'

'They are quite different. It's probably partly due to age, though by no means entirely. If push came to shove, David and a stepmother would probably rub along, that's provided Jack wanted to marry again, and, on the whole I think he would. Jack needs a framework within which to misbehave. But I don't think Harry could ever divide his loyalties in that sort of way. Anyway, I promised him that I wouldn't go.'

Reflecting that by the time Harry, who sounded a sensitive little boy, was old enough to realize how tyrannical he was being it would be too late for Ellen, Ginevra said, 'What about the book?'

'A nonstarter. Nobody's interested.' The tone was unemotional, disappointment carefully concealed. 'It's probably just as well. That sort of success might have made me very restless, and it's no use. I can't escape my responsibilities here, and was mad to think I could. In a phrase I'm locked into it.'

Thinking of her own book in which no agent or publisher of any sort had ever expressed any interest either, Ginevra was silent. Shortly she would have her own marital affairs to sort out when confronted by Kevin's arrival home, which she frankly dreaded.

Picking up on her friend's thought, and noting a troubled frown, Ellen castigated herself for concentrating on her own woes to the exclusion of those of her guest.

'What about you?'

A look crossed Ginevra's face which could only be described as a dispassionate summing up of where she was at. The answer, when it came, was forthright, though not comfortable.

'I *have* to leave. There's nothing to keep me. Funnily enough, if he hadn't gone away, I think the whole thing would have drifted on. The trouble from my point of view was the break in continuity. Quite simply I couldn't sustain it and that has sent me off in a direction which is incompatible with living alongside Kevin any longer.'

Noting the unusual use of the word 'alongside', Ellen ventured, 'You once told me you were in love with someone else.'

'Unobtainable. And anyway the whole thing was a fantasy.'

Ginevra was amazed at the ease with which she was able to utter these words, so recently unthinkable. And there was no sign of the insidious alternative voice either. Lately she had been conscious of a miraculous lightening of being which, she felt sure, dated from the corn dolly auto-da-fé, during the course of which symbolic exorcism had apparently translated itself very satisfactorily into actuality. Perhaps, thought Ginevra, I will burn those notebooks, and cancel the order for the new ones too. On the other hand, the thought of resuming life as they had known it with Kevin was unthinkable, which left her facing the same sort of void as Ellen. Namely that of where to go and what to do and what to live on. Perhaps I should move out before he gets back, she thought.

Unobtainable? Odd word to use. He must be married, Ellen decided. Stroking Casimir's glossy black head, and drinking her wine, she said, 'I've had a brilliant idea. Why don't you borrow my computer until yours is mended? I'm not using it at the moment so I'm hardly going to miss it. I could drive you and it to Little Haddow.' She smiled her slow, incandescent smile. 'What do you think?'

26

Kevin arrived back in England very early one morning on an unsociable flight. Brick red from Saudi, his ruddiness was pointed up by a light silvery frost. Kevin revelled in the extreme blue cold, breathing it in with pleasure. He felt that he had had enough of heat and abroad to last him the rest of his life, although conceded that he might have been prepared to stretch a point where ten days in Majorca was concerned since there, his mates reliably informed him, were fish and chips. Feeling like treating himself (for, after all, hadn't he earned it?) he took a taxi from the airport.

Because of the hour there was no one about, and it was still quite dark in Little Haddow when they arrived. The moon was full and pale and his footsteps rang on the glittering path as he walked up it to the front door, brushing past the overgrown and tangled shrubs whose leaves were delicately and formally etched in white. Letting himself in, Kevin was assailed by a famished, shouting Captain Morgan. It was even colder inside the cottage than outside it.

Going into the kitchen, he found the window open a cat-sized crack and six empty bowls on the floor plus a small collection of dead mice in various states of stiff decrepitude. Although it had to be said that Gin had never been much of a housewife, it was her habit to throw these small bodies out as and when they occurred, so this was therefore a substantial advance on the usual quota, and by now it was beginning to dawn on Kevin that perhaps she was not there. This was unusual for his wife, he knew, had very few friends, and those she did have were not of the overnight stay variety. He supposed he must have turned up in advance of his own letter, but, even so, her absence was surprising. Captain Morgan watched his every thought with a voracious eye, preparing to trip Kevin up should he try to leave the kitchen without doling out some food. Catching his eager amber orb, Kevin opened the cupboard in which the cat food was kept and found one half full, very mouldy tin, which had evidently been forgotten about and which he threw away.

'Aw, for Pete's sake, Gin!' said Kevin, reproachfully, nostalgically recalling his mother who had been a real house-wife, a paragon of kitchen virtue who would probably have passed out had she seen this one. He opened another large tin, and left the cat wolfing down its contents as he climbed the stairs. The bed was made and the bedroom empty. Pulling the curtains, Kevin decided to stop speculating about where his wife might be. That could wait for the morning when she would probably turn up anyway. Right now he needed some sleep.

As the sun came up, the frost retreated, so that only pearly pockets of it were left in sunless sheltered corners of gardens. Bicycling sturdily along from her cottage to the village post office which she ran, Mrs Trigg hummed to herself. Having parked her bike in its usual place, she let herself into the back of the shop by lifting up a hinged segment of the counter, and put on the kettle for some tea.

Waiting for it to boil, she examined the parcels which awaited delivery that day. There was one for Freda at the pub, one for Mrs Monk the butcher's wife and one for Mrs Haye. She picked up the one for Freda and shook it. It rattled slightly, and when squeezed felt spongy. She examined the postmark to see where it had come from. For Mrs Trigg every day was Christmas Day, and the parcel game made her feel like a sixty-year-old little girl again, opening her stocking. Giving up on Freda, she turned her attention to Mrs Monk. Mrs Monk's packet was altogether less secretive, helpfully pronouncing itself to have been sent by a firm who made surgical stockings. Of course she does have awful varicose veins, poor thing, thought Mrs Trigg, whose own legs were in good shape, although her waistline had given up the fight long ago.

This only left Mrs Haye's package, which was large and flat and surprisingly heavy. Assessing it with an expert Holmesian eye, she ran her thumb along three sides of it and then the fourth. Three indented, the last did not. Books, was Mrs Trigg's verdict.

By now the kettle was steaming. Putting the parcels to one

side to deliver later should none of the addressees come into the post office before then, she lifted it off the gas and commenced to make what she called her morning cuppa, over which she normally scrutinized the letters before opening up.

Kevin slept right through until the afternoon and, when he finally woke up, could not at first think where he was. Remembering and putting an exploratory sideways hand towards his wife's side of the bed, he remembered that she was not there. This was a great deprivation. In Saudi the memory of sexual pleasures shared with Gin had comforted him in what had proved to be a physical desert, and, although the fact that she had never written once had offended him, Kevin, who had long ago recognized that when sexual intercourse stopped social intercourse did not take over where he and she were concerned, the way it apparently did with other people, had eventually been forced to assume that this must extend to letters too.

Going into the bathroom, which was freezing, Kevin looked at himself in the cracked mirror. His hectic sunburn, a product of his sandy colouring, looked incongruous in this stark room but would soon fade down to something less strident, and the beer belly which he had taken away with him had practically gone. These days he looked almost athletic. And well hung. Definitely well hung. But, as of this moment anyway, redundant. Where the fuck was she? For the first time since his jet-lagged return Kevin began to feel mildly aggrieved. More to protect himself against hypothermia than anything else he got dressed, and then, feeling that he could murder a cup of tea, went downstairs. There was no sign of Captain Morgan, though the ritual mouse was on the work surface. Having first opened the front door in order to throw this away, he went in search of the caddy. Naturally there was no milk though he did find a battered box of what looked like antediluvian tea bags and also half a jar of Coffeemate. After boiling the water he assembled these ingredients and then, clutching the resulting unappetizing brew, he made his way back up into the bedroom to see if he couldn't find a clue as to where his wife had gone.

*

Ellen and Ginevra loaded the computer into the back of the Carey car.

'You did remember to park the heads, didn't you?'

For Ellen this always conjured up a surreal image which made her want to laugh. Lately she had felt herself to be better, as though, by dint of a tremendous effort, and with the help of Ginevra's tactful company, she had managed to lever herself over the threshold of her own depression and was fully aware that it was imperative not to slip back.

'Yes I did, though I have to say that I don't know what it means!'

'Nor do I, but apparently it is important.'

'What time do you think we'll get there?'

'Late afternoon I should think, maybe early evening. Depends what time we actually get started.'

'I'm practically ready now.'

'Yes, so am I, apart from organizing Edna Phipps to feed the cats. We might drop by there on our way.'

On opening the door of their joint wardrobe, Kevin received a surprise, for within it he found certain items he had not seen before. On the floor was a pair of narrow black medium-heeled shoes of a sort that he had never seen Ginevra wear. Hanging up above them was a black dress within an embroidered shawl which was magnificently weighty and thickly fringed and, even to Kevin's untutored eye, looked expensive.

''Struth!' said Kevin.

He fingered it, wondering to whom it could belong. Certainly not Ginevra, surely, who had never been interested in clothes and often went forth attired from head to foot by Oxfam. Investigating further, in one of the twin top drawers of the chest, he discovered the silver necklace with its dramatic amber drop. He held it up to the light, where the amber glowed dully, and the silver shone. It was very heavy and had probably cost a mint. What the hell had been going on here? In the same drawer were several pairs of very sheer black tights. Tarts' tights was Kevin's disapproving view of these, reflecting that his mum would not have approved either.

A further search turned up nothing else of interest in the

bedroom. By now Kevin felt thoroughly unsettled by the discoveries he had just made during the course of his snooping. For starters, where was she? He felt the dead silence of the empty house beginning to get him down and decided to descend the stairs again, during the course of which he nearly fell over Captain Morgan who had reappeared and was determined not to let Kevin out of his sight until the bowl should be filled. Ignoring the animal, for there was no more cat food left anyway, he went into the sitting room.

The computer stood in its usual place in front of the window. Open beside it, at a section headed *Troubleshooting*, was one of the manuals. He looked around the room, which otherwise appeared to be its customary dusty self. On the mantelpiece was a bowl of roses which were so old and so dead that they had turned a papery brown, with only the very faintest vestige of their original colour left. Beside them was propped a sepia photograph which Kevin had never seen before. Picking this up he peered at it. It depicted an old geezer sitting down with an open book on his lap, behind whom stood a woman whose face bore a resemblance to Ginevra's own. It must be her parents. This was odd too, for Gin never talked about them, much less put up pictures of them. Kevin replaced it. Something was different about the mantelpiece too. Trying to put his finger on what this was, he finally remembered the corn dolly, which he had won at darts, and of which there was no longer any sign. Looking around the room and not seeing it, he decided that she must have thrown it away for some reason.

By now he was hungry and noticed that outside the light was beginning to fade. Picking up a couple of large handsome notebooks in order to sit down on the sofa, he laid these on his knees instead. Idly turning the pages of one of them which were covered in Gin's orderly script, he supposed that it must constitute part of the work she was doing. Kevin, who had difficulty in stringing more than five written words successfully together, was in awe of The Book. He was just about to put them to one side, mindful of the fact that, if he wanted to eat, he would have to purchase a pie for his supper from the village shop, when, halfway down the page, a four-letter word caught his eye which even Kevin did not think could be part of any research

Gin might be doing. Going on, he found another. And then, further down, yet another and, laboriously following each line with one finger, he slowly began to realize that what he was reading was a highly sexually explicit account of an affair which was apparently currently taking place between his wife and her lover. With something between a groan and a sob, Kevin turned to the beginning where it all started with the words *My Darling James*.

Two hours later he laid down the third notebook, which ended in the middle of a sentence. Kevin had not got the heart to get up and see if there were any others, and anyway what did it matter? There was nothing they had not done. He had been working and sweating in fucking Saudi and all that time she and he . . . ! He felt like weeping, and was conscious of a gathering headache. Worst of all, in the whole chronicle there was no mention of himself, not one. It was as if he had never existed! Kevin, whose gifts were not analytical, nevertheless perceived himself to have been ignored as a person in his own right and finally, and most woundingly, treated as a creature of no importance. In its way, this was worse than the physical betrayal because it shafted him where he was most vulnerable. He knew he was good news in bed, because all his girlfriends prior to Ginevra, and Gin herself, had told him so. On the other hand, all his life Kevin had been designated dim, from infants' school, where he had been a very late reader and writer, onwards when he had continued to labour away at the bottom of the inner-city sink school in which he had ended up. *Kevin is good with his hands*, was the most constructive remark on his dreaded school reports, and had pointed the way to leaving at sixteen and going into the building trade. Marrying Ginevra then, had gone some way towards allaying this intellectual inferiority complex, although his mum, he recalled, had prophesied that it would all end in tears. 'She's not your sort, Kevin,' Mum had said. 'You want a pretty girl who'll make you a nice home.' In sexual thrall to Ginevra by then, he had ignored this advice.

Anger festered into rage, and the headache worsened. He got up and went out into the passage, automatically switching off the light in the sitting room as he did so. On the floor of the hall he noticed what looked like large, coloured fragments of some silken material, as though she had cut something up. Disregarding them, he went to the cupboard under the stairs where he kept his tools and extracted a claw hammer. Then he went back to the sitting room where he sat down in the dark to wait for his wife to come back, and, in the process, to let his fury feed upon itself.

Owing to a particularly convoluted roadwork hold-up which culminated in a diversion, Ellen and Ginevra arrived too late for the village shop.

'The pub might be able to let me have some milk,' said Ginevra, who found the prospect of a cold, tealess morning depressing.

'I'll go on if you like and unload the Amstrad.' Noting the hour Ellen was anxious to get on with it, since she had the journey back to confront.

'No, it's heavy. Comes under the heading of hod-carrying. After all, you're doing me a favour so I think I should do it.'

'Oh well, as to that, being married to Jack I'm quite used to hods and, besides, I know how to set the whole thing up. Just.'

'So do I!'

Ellen glanced at her watch a second time, aware that friendly banter was taking up time. 'Look, let's toss for it.'

She spun the coin.

'Heads or tails?'

27

Leaning her bicycle against the garden wall of Pear Tree Cottage, Mrs Trigg took the parcel out of the basket and made her way up the garden path. It was very, very cold. Clearly there was going to be another hard frost. To her surprise the door was ajar.

'Coo-eee!' called Mrs Trigg and then, receiving no answer, she pushed it open and stepped inside.

Within the hall there was an odd smell and also a curious noise which Mrs Trigg could not at first identify. Not sobbing and not whimpering, it was a low-pitched moaning lament. The sitting room door was wide open and the light was on. On the floor lay a body, whose feet pointed upwards, and whose skull had been cracked like the dome of a breakfast egg. There was blood everywhere. As if within the detachment of a dreadful dream, she noticed that one of the dead hands was clutching what looked like the remnants of something rainbow-coloured and silken. A scarf perhaps?

Mrs Trigg's first impulse, which was flight, was stayed by the terrifying vision of being pursued along the hall if she did so, and knocked down in her turn by the person who sat, head in hands, and apparently oblivious to her presence, by Mrs Haye's computer. Petrified she stood stock still and then, small noiseless step by small noiseless step, began to back away along the passage.

She heard the unmistakable creak of the garden gate. And stopped. Kevin Haye neither moved nor ceased his dreadful keening. Understanding none of it, Mrs Trigg finally achieved the front door at the same time as the newcomer. Trembling, her eyes dilated with the shock of what she had seen, she stretched out one arm, barring the way.

'I shouldn't go in there if I were you,' said Mrs Trigg, in a whisper. 'I'm afraid there has been a terrible accident.'

28

Victoria organized the memorial service. It seemed to her that, in the circumstances, it was the least she could do. The tiny Chelsea church was full and looked rather as though the Carey exhibition guests had transplanted themselves in the same outré clothes, having first all fallen into a vat of black dye. Sitting in the front pew, with a husband-sized space on her right, she wondered where James was. It would be too bad if he were late for an occasion such as this. Twisting around in her seat she scanned the congregation. No sign. Further along her own row and splendidly isolated since, presumably out of respect for relations and friends, those who were neither had avoided sitting in it, was Jack, who was even wearing a suit which looked almost like anybody else's despite the fact that it was an unusual shade of aubergine. Leaning forward, elbow on knee, head in one hand and order of service, which, she noticed, he had covered in drawings, dangling from the other, he was staring morosely at the floor. He looks shattered, and no wonder, Victoria thought, eyeing him with some sympathy for the first, and probably last, time. Behind her, and at opposite ends of the same pew, were Tessa and Alexander, safely segregated from each other by six or seven self-consciously sober-hued glitterarty.

She consulted her watch. Five minutes to go. Quietly, almost circumspectly, the organ struck up. It was a Bach cantata, one of the favourites, whose evocative cadences unwound themselves poignantly through the lily-scented air causing tears to well in her eyes. Victoria tipped forward her large hat, shook her hair over her face and dipping into her bag for one of the three handkerchiefs which she had brought with her, prepared to indulge herself in a discreet sob.

Softly the choir began to sing. Mindful that, left to its own devices, this was normally a charismatic church, Victoria had sternly quizzed the vicar about the choir. Was he sure that they were musically up to what she was proposing? After all, the subject of the service had been a musically literate person, and she, Victoria Harting, would be mortified to be confronted on the day by a collection of upper-crust flats, rattling tambourines. Nettled, the vicar ran his eyes down the proposed service, and was further put out to descry no opportunity to display his own guitar playing talents. Stiffly, he replied that his was a competent choir.

'Oh, only competent?'

'*Very* competent,' he had quickly amended.

'Well, if you're *absolutely* sure,' had been her doubtful response to this. An attempt to suggest that they lighten things up a little on the musical side had been briskly dismissed with the one word: inappropriate.

Walking up the aisle, he was still aware of unchristian irritation, though for once his church (for so he thought of it) was gratifyingly full. Arriving at the lectern, he turned around to face them all.

He had got as far as, 'We are gathered . . .' when, heralded by a blast of freezing air and the sound of a police car siren, James Harting scudded in, a magazine under one arm, and, in the face of a long, reproving, ecclesiastical stare, contritely wedged himself into a small space at the back.

The vicar allowed another ten seconds for gravitas and their full attention before resuming.

'We are gathered here today to mourn the death and celebrate the life and work of . . .'

Unbelievable! The door had opened again, letting in yet another frosty draught coupled with the roar of the outside traffic, though not, heaven be praised, the shriek of a police car this time. Through it came the figure of a woman, swathed from shoulder to ankle in a black cloak and wearing a broad-brimmed hat with a veil. A buzz of appreciation greeted this dramatic materialization. Aware that he had been comprehensively upstaged, he pointedly desisted until she should be seated. To his surprise, the latecomer did not unobtrusively slip into the nearest gap, but made her way towards him, arresting her progress for just long enough to incline her head minimally in his direction before proceeding to the front pew where she sat down beside Mrs Harting.

Watching her raise the dusky veil, which glistened with tiny sparks of jet, and struck, as she did so, by her extreme pallor, he recommenced in a competitive rush, this time achieving the end of his sentence: 'We are gathered here today to mourn the death and celebrate the life and work of Ginevra Haye.'

Afterwards the Hartings, the Careys, the Marchants and even the Lucases, who had apparently raised the tone of their social intercourse to the level where they could be civilized with one another now that they were on the point of divorce, left the church together. All except Tessa, who deemed it politic to depart with Sam Jessop, intended to make their way back to the Hartings' Chelsea house, where tea and coffee and sandwiches were on offer.

Waiting on the steps outside the church while his wife was shaking hands with the vicar, at the same time giving him a critical assessment of his choir's performance, James caught sight of Robert Wilmot.

'Robert!'

'Oh, James!' He looked unaccountably put out, and it occurred to James that Robert had hoped to leave without speaking to him, though why on earth he should want to do that when they had known each other for years, James could not begin to guess.

'Awful business this, isn't it!'

'Awful.' Then, gesturing, 'I see that you've got the latest issue.'

'I'm going to read it tonight. I hope it has Ginevra's valedictory article in it?'

'Yes. Yes, it has.' There was an awkward pause, and an indefinable sense of something left unsaid.

'Why don't you come back to the house with us? Victoria has organized some sustenance, and I'm sure one more won't make any difference.'

By now frankly fugitive, Robert said, 'No, no I'm afraid I can't. I have another appointment.' He began to descend the steps and then, apparently on impulse, turned back.

'Look, I'm really, really sorry. I tried to persuade her to take a different tack, and I thought she had, and when I found out she hadn't it was too late to do anything about it. And then suddenly, don't ask me why, she wanted to change her mind after all. No chance! By then we were well past the deadline. It's all extremely embarrassing. An epic cock-up.' His eyes wandered in the direction of a passing taxi. 'I'm afraid I absolutely *must* go.' Then, seeing her approaching, 'Give my love to Victoria.'

Too late to do anything about what? Frankly baffled as to what his drift was, James replied easily, 'I shouldn't worry about it, whatever it is. Anyway, don't let me hold you up.'

'No. Well, goodbye then.' Clearly very uncomfortable, for whatever reason, he finally went as Victoria arrived.

As she set out the sandwiches Victoria reflected that it was hard to believe in the reality of Ginevra's death. She wondered what would happen to Kevin, and supposed that in the fullness of time there would be a trial, another horrendous ordeal for Ellen to face. And not just Ellen either. In the light of those notebooks presumably James, and possibly she herself, would be called upon to give evidence. It was unnerving, thought Victoria, that someone as intellectually incisive as Ginevra, whom she had known for years and regarded as a close friend, should have apparently been sliding into madness and none of them had noticed. Nothing to be done about it now, alas.

'Milk?'

Pouring, she noticed that James, who was talking to Alexander, had a copy of *Modern Art* under his arm. It must be the latest one in which Ginevra's laudatory piece was due to appear. Next month it would be her obituary. So anxious was she to see it that Victoria was tempted to press-gang someone else into ministering – Jack, for instance – and go and take it off him. She resisted this impulse, and deciding to be more subtle about it, instead bore a plateful of sandwiches in the direction of her husband.

'Smoked salmon?'

Alexander refused, and then, seeing Ellen on her own at last, said, 'Would you excuse me for a minute? I have something I must say to Ellen.'

'Of course!' Watching him make his way towards her, and wondering what it was he wanted to say that had obviously had to wait until Jack was no longer in the room (and, by the way, where *was* Jack?) Victoria said, indicating the magazine, 'Is Ginevra's profile in it?'

'Yes. I saw Rob Wilmot and he says it is, but with all this going on I haven't yet had a chance to look.'

Like an excited child she couldn't wait. 'Do you mind if I have a quick peer now?'

Amused, he replied, 'Not at all. You can tell me what it says!'

'Congratulations. Jane tells me that you're pregnant.' The speaker was Marcus Marchant. Turning to face him, Victoria reluctantly put down *Modern Art*. James was probably right. Now was not the moment.

In a corner of the room with the ethereal blues of the Carey painting behind them, Alexander and Ellen faced one another. Ellen had looped back the veil, which draped itself gracefully around the crown of a matador-style hat, beneath whose dramatic brim her face was in partial shadow.

Suppressing a desire to take her chin between finger and thumb, tilt back her head and kiss the cupid's bow of her mouth, today painted a surprising red, and the hell with what anybody else thought about it, Alexander said instead, 'Your novel. The publisher I sent it to likes it. He thinks it has distinct possibilities and he wants you to go and see him. If you have no objection perhaps I could give him your telephone number and he could talk to you direct.'

Disbelieving, she looked up at him.

'But what about the others who didn't rate it? Three agents weren't prepared to give it the time of day.'

'So what? It happens all the time in the book world. Anyway, it's like selling a house, you only need one buyer. And once you've got yourself a publisher, take it from me, you won't have too much trouble finding an agent. I think you may be on your way.'

To his consternation he thought that she might be about to weep. Smiling at him through brimming tears, she clasped her hands together. 'It's quite simply the most marvellous thing that has happened to me ever. I'm so grateful, Alexander.' To hide her discomposure she partially lowered her veil.

Gallantly he handed her his handkerchief.

'Thank you. I feel *such* a fool. Why am I crying when I should be ecstatic? When I *am* ecstatic.'

Moved, and thinking, I wish she would let me look after her, he replied gently, 'You deserve some good news. It's been a very tough time for you, Ellen. And I suppose that, with the trial to come, it will get worse before it gets better.'

'Oh, but this will sustain me. It's something to work towards. It's the prospect of a life of my own. You have given me more than you'll ever know. I shall never be able to repay it, never.'

Aware by now that their absorption in one another was attracting a certain amount of attention not least from Jack, who had re-entered the room looking flushed, Alexander decided to ignore this. Lifting her ringed hand he kissed it, and quoted:

> *'Thy firmness makes my circle just,*
> *And makes me end, where I begun.'*

'Nothing *to* repay,' said Alexander.

At last Victoria and James and *Modern Art* were alone together. Deciding to leave the clearing up for Mrs Pond tomorrow, and glad to take her increasing weight off her feet, Victoria settled herself into the wing armchair nearest to the fire, thumbed through the magazine until she found Ginevra's article, and began to read.

Also available in Arrow by Elizabeth Palmer

The Stainless Angel

When wealthy bachelor George Marchant marries the exotic Camilla Vane while on secondment to Rome, his friends and family are astonished. Camilla's motives are entirely pragmatic: her rising debt and a largely forgotten small son. But to her horror, accommodating George proves stubborn in one thing: he insists they live at his family estate back in England.

From the moment Camilla arrives, nothing at Marchants will ever be the same again. Within the first year one of the family has attempted suicide, one marriage has ended, and one son is dead. As she sweeps through the corridors plotting her return to Rome, Camilla is oblivious to the destruction and heartache she leaves in her wake – but she has not reckoned on the one person who will stop at nothing to save the family inheritance . . .

'Full of wit, family entanglements, death and deceit, it is beautifully executed.' *Today*

Read on for the first chapter of
THE STAINLESS ANGEL

CHAPTER ONE

His friends sometimes speculated on why, aged forty, George Marchant had never married. Good-looking and rich enough to be considered a catch, he plainly liked the girls and they apparently liked him back. The truth of the matter was simply that he had never wanted to. In the past his girlfriends had been upper-crust English girls, mainly country blondes of the horsy variety, who had eventually got tired of waiting for him to make a permanent commitment and had drifted off to other partners. George hardly noticed. It was true that he liked to have a woman in his life, preferably on a long-term basis, since this meant less effort all round, but he had never felt the remotest desire to legalize any of his liaisons. Then, in Rome, on secondment from his firm, he met Camilla Vane. Her blend of Italianate chic and striking looks coupled with a mind which many admired for its brightness and just as many dismissed as superficial, dazzled George and, in his forty-first year, he married her.

Like him, Camilla was English, and the daughter of diplomatic parents, both of whom were dead. She fitted seamlessly into the Italian scene and, George was to discover, had a spectrum of acquaintances which ranged from the respectable to the raffish. At thirty-four Camilla had been around. George, who was beginning to feel as though he had been asleep for years, rather enjoyed all this, and certain things which he probably would not have condoned in London seemed in the rather louche atmosphere of Roman society, and in particular of Camilla's set (or those of them he was allowed to meet anyway), to be acceptable. Of course, George had been around too but not, it could be said, with Camilla's avid curiosity and lack of scruple. George was really very conventional. For her part, having once decided that, if she could, she would marry him, she was careful not to expose George to more than she thought he could stand. It was not until they had been seeing each other for some time that she invited him into her bed, after which exotic happening George was lost. Her sensuality and appetite were counterpointed by a feline reserve both mental and, at times, physical, and an unpredictable intermittent coolness which, at the height of what had become, certainly for George anyway, a very hot affair, was at once fascinating and unsettling. When she finally told him of the existence of her son, Anthony, and her first marriage, the upshot was a very unpleasant quarrel. George, for years such a lethargic suitor, found himself tortured by possessive jealousy such as he had never encountered before. Of course he knew that there had been lovers prior to him, but a husband and child were something else again. In his calmer moments he tried to understand why he was so upset. Perhaps it was because she had only just thought fit to tell him. Whatever the answer to this was, it put him in touch with himself and his real feelings. He discovered that he could not bear to be away from her. At the end of a separation which lasted a week and nearly killed him, he asked Camilla to marry him, and she accepted. When they finally had a rational talk about it, it transpired that her son was at an English prep school, and the former husband was dead. She was a widow. This made the whole thing easier for George. It had a finality and respectability about it which put an end to further discussion. Obsessed as he was with making her his wife, his mind veered away from how much he did not know about Camilla, and, if he had only been prepared to think about it in those terms, how much of her past did seem to be (literally) buried. As only those can who have fallen violently in love late, he put all of this to the back of his mind and concentrated on the entrancing present.

For her own part, Camilla was well satisfied. At thirty-four it was definitely better to marry for money than to be unmarried with no money. Of this she was quite sure. As usual, though, there were two sides to it, the upside being that he was rich enough (just), presentable and besotted with her, the downside that not infrequently he bored her and, furthermore, she recognized a probity about George and his dealings which could seriously cramp her style. *Still, nothing is for nothing*, thought Camilla. *I'll just have to put up with that. For a while.* And, just as she had had to gauge the right moment to tell him about Anthony's existence, she would have to pick the right time to tell him about her debts. After that, maybe, certain old friends kept for the moment right out of George's orbit in the interests of a stainless image might begin to filter back.

It was while all this was happening that the news of his father's death arrived. Because of this George suggested to Camilla that they should marry quietly and at once, which they did. He did not, however, go into the other implications of his father's demise, the principal one of which was that he would inform the firm that it was no longer possible for him to continue working in Rome and they would go home to England. When he did tell her she was thunderstruck. It had never occurred to her that they would leave Italy. Equally it had never occurred to George that they would not eventually return. The matter had not been discussed during the course of their affair. It was the one thing concerning which the usually malleable George was absolutely immovable. Camilla felt trapped and infuriated. Essentially an urban animal, the prospect of English country life filled her with panic and gloom. Most of this she concealed by means of a great effort of will, and with her customary calculation settled back to play a long game, at the end of which she hoped to get her own way. Even so, she had not come to terms with the new turn of events enough to feel like accompanying him to his father's funeral. It was a small revenge but she decided to take it all the same. Accordingly she went to bed with what she described as an August fever.

Sweetly she said, 'I'm so sorry, darling, but do give my love to all your family, and tell them how much I look forward to seeing them in September.'

So George went alone, with a feeling that although she was not reconciled to her new life at present, she soon would be. After all, she was his wife and where he went she would have to go too.

George's mother was at home when he finally arrived at the house. Sarah looked tired and strained but was not distraught. Osbert had been ill for some months and his death had not been unexpected. She had had time to prepare herself for the inevitable.

She kissed her son. 'How very sad that Camilla couldn't come with you,' she said. 'The family are dying to meet her. We're so happy for you, George.

George could imagine. He knew perfectly well that they had all given up hope that he would ever marry, and that speculation concerning Camilla and what sort of a person she was must be intense. He looked forward to the day when they would all meet her for the first time. Meanwhile, Sarah was saying, 'Tell me all about her. Where did you meet? What are her family like?' Typical Mother, that last question. She had always been a great believer in the importance of family. Answering the first was easy, the second less so and after the words 'dead' and 'diplomatic' service', he rather ground to a halt. Both of them were suddenly struck by how little he seemed to know about her, although neither put it into words. Sarah experienced a faint flutter of apprehension.

'Does Camilla work?' she asked, getting off the unsatisfactory subject of family. This was, in fact, another poser for George since Camilla apparently lived off thin air. Well, no, not quite. Camilla earned herself some money advising well-heeled Romans on the decoration of their houses and palazzos. What her qualifications were for doing this sort of thing he had no idea, and it could never have been called anything remotely like a full-time occupation and certainly couldn't have funded Camilla's life-style, never mind Anthony's education. George, child of the upper class, supposed she must have some kind of private income, and said as much in those terms to his mother. Sarah was amazed that her eldest son, normally so punctilious about that sort of thing, should know so little about his own wife. She decided to drop the matter. After all, in a few weeks' time she would meet Camilla for herself and could make her own assessment. The talk turned to arrangements for the funeral, after which George was flying straight back to Rome to settle his affairs.

Her husband having finally left for Fiumicino, Camilla lay in bed in the flat in Trastevere. The faint hum of traffic came through the open window across which the heavy curtains were partly drawn. In the half-light the pretty things she had collected from the Porta Portese and various antique shops while searching out more exclusive treasures for her clients stood upon the polished dark wood floor and decorated the old rose of the walls. Her favourite possession, a carved and gilded angel the size of a small child, stood on an apple wood chest in one corner beside a large jug filled with scarlet flowers. With its pageboy hair and sightless eyes, the angel faced Camilla across the room, wings furled. A pencil of light from the window traced the golden outline of its full, sensuous mouth and the folds of its robe and formed a nimbus around its head. Looking at it, Camilla had an idea. On impulse she picked up the telephone receiver and rang an old friend.

'Julius? Camilla. Yes, I know it's been a while. Look, George has gone to London and I'm here by myself and very bored. Why don't you come over and amuse me?'

He must have said that he would for she got up, checked that there was a bottle of champagne in the fridge, put on the lightest touch of make-up and scent and then rearranged herself on the bed, heaping up her soft pillows against the rococo mirror which formed its head, before lying back luxuriously framed by the dark cloud of her hair. Half an hour later Julius let himself in, still having a key from the days when he was one of Camilla's regular lovers. Since her marriage he had seen virtually nothing of her in the interests of discretion and landing George. Being a penniless descendant of old Roman aristocracy, he had perfectly understood this. Without preamble he walked across the room and sat down upon her bed. Without hesitation he kissed her hand, kissed her lips, kissed each shoulder and then, very slowly, slid down the thin silk straps of her robe and kissed her white breasts. With a sigh Camilla gave herself up to the intense pleasure of making love to a man who was not her husband.

How desirable she is, thought Julius, looking at her as they lay in bed afterwards, sharing a joint and talking. But not to be trusted. A ruthless, worldly woman who knew what she wanted. In spite of her beauty one could not on reflection say that Marchant was a lucky man. Devoid of hypocrisy concerning matters like this, the reasons for Camilla's marriage were obvious and perfectly acceptable to Julius. Eventually he himself would have to do something similar and marry for money. But not yet. He wondered how long it would be before she reverted totally to type and, try as he might, he could not imagine her in an English country setting, though it was easy to see how her life with Marchant could have been conducted here.

Eventually he prepared to take his leave. When he was ready to go he once more bent his sleek head over her slim hand adorned with George's large generous emerald. His key lay at the feet of the angel and he stretched out his hand towards it. As he did so, Camilla got there before him, picked it up and dropped it into her small crocodile handbag, whose little golden jaws she shut with a snap. Nothing was said. He looked at her with a mixture of chagrin and admiration. So that, for the time being at any rate, was that.

'*Ciao*, Julius,' said Camilla, and saw him out.

When he had gone she went back upstairs. Standing before the angel she drew her red fingernail down the classical nose stopping at the curved lips where she let it rest a minute. Then she dressed and went out.

Two days after this interlude had taken place, George arrived back. By this time another bottle of champagne lay coolly in the fridge, replacing the one drunk previously by Julius and Camilla, and the smell of Julius's interesting cigarette had quite disappeared. George kissed his wife, opened the champagne and raised his glass. 'To going home,' he said, and began to talk about his journey. As he spoke she stood looking at him, her mind in furious turmoil her face inscrutable. There was, she knew, no point in saying anything. They had been over it all before. Camilla had been too subtle to let George see the true extent of her loathing for the whole idea, but had done her best both in bed and out of it to dissuade him. All to no avail, it seemed. To a cosmopolitan nomad such as Camilla, George's ingrained Englishness and strongly entrenched family ties were quite incomprehensible.

'The family' (he made them sound like the Mafia) 'were very disappointed that you couldn't come,' George was saying. 'I've told them to expect us back in roughly three weeks' time. The idea is that Mother will move into the Dower House, though probably not until after Christmas since a lot of work has to be done on it first.'

It was all she needed, thought Camilla crossly, the prospect of sharing a house with her mother-in-law. She stared moodily into her drink. By this time George had woken up to the fact that she had not uttered for the last twenty minutes. Wisely, he decided to drop the subject. They were going and that was that. He would have given Camilla anything within reason, but on this front he was absolutely inflexible. There could be no question of not going home to take up his inheritance. Besides which the house needed a face-lift and Camilla would enjoy doing that. She would also do it very well. A little time was all that would be needed, he felt.

He looked at her. She stood by the fireplace sipping her drink, one elbow on the marble mantelpiece. Apart from her silence and the faintest of shadows between her eyebrows there was no outward sign of the anger within. She was wearing black, which suited her. Around the stalklike neck, just below the chin, a satin ribbon was tied in a bow and secured with a pearl pin. Above the bow the face reflected in the old grey glass of the overmantel mirror was not merely that of a pretty woman, but that of a beauty with all the aloofness and finely drawn severity that this implies. The dark hair swept shining back from a pronounced widow's peak and fell to the shoulders, framing a face that was notable more for its strength than its softness. Camilla's eyes were grey, her nose straight and her cheekbones high. The mouth then came as a surprise being full and curved and painted very red. There was a hint of cruelty and appetite about it reminiscent of certain classical statuary. A pagan mouth. A man who had taken the trouble to understand women in a way George never had, a man like Julius, for instance, would instantly have seen Camilla for what she was – a formidable woman, and, if thwarted, quite possibly dangerous with it. All this passed George by. He adored her.

Putting down his glass he walked across the room and took her in his arms. With inward rebellion and outward compliance Camilla let him. 'Darling,' was all she said. George picked her up, carried her into the bedroom and laid her down among the embroidered cushions on the bed. Here he slid her sheer black stockings down to her painted toenails, and kissed her narrow feet, then very slowly he undressed her until she wore nothing but the black satin ribbon and the pearl pin, and began to make love to her. In spite of her bad temper, it seemed wise to respond and Camilla did so.

Lying in his arms when it was all over, it was clear to her that now was the time to tell him about her debts. He might, after all, never be this much in thrall again. She got up, put on her robe and went to fetch the remains of the champagne. Then she sat on the bed beside him and said in a faltering, contrite voice, 'George, I have something to tell you.' He listened indulgently, his mind half on something else, until she got to the actual amount, at which point he was quite shocked.

'Good God!' said George. Five seconds at least passed, during the course of which he did not, as she had hoped he would, immediately take her into his arms again. He looked grim. By the time another five had elapsed she could see that drastic action was needed before stupefaction and disapproval became active condemnation. Camilla took a deep breath, put her face in her hands and began to sob. George had never seen her cry before, and was not seeing her cry now though he did not know this. He gathered her to him. What a brute he was. It was not as though he did not have the money to bail her out. He said as much. Her sobs began so subside and finally ceased altogether to his great relief. She turned her face up to his. Kissing her, he noticed with some surprise that, despite her distress, there were no tears.

Eventually she got up and went into the bathroom, where he heard her turn on the shower. Lying on the bed, the flicker of unease signalled its presence again. Why had she not told him all this at the beginning? It occurred to him to wonder what else he didn't know about his wife. He stared at the angel and the angel looked ironically back. Suddenly unwilling to confront this particularly uncomfortable line of enquiry George got up and hastily began to get dressed. He looked at his watch. Time for dinner. Drawing back the curtains he found it was already dusk outside. Leaning through the open window he breathed in the spiced warmth of the indigo Roman evening. Like her, he thought, he would be sorry to leave. Eventually turning back into the bedroom, he was disconcerted to find Camilla silently watching him. She had lit the tall church candles on either side of the angel. The pale light burnished the rosy interior of the bedroom, gilding the flowers and delicately highlighting the gold thread of the cushions. Camilla was wearing something high necked and black, and above it her face appeared to float in the dark, a third oval flame. A light air from the window caused the candles to flicker and almost go out and as the shadows were tossed around the room, it seemed to George for one startling moment that the angel laughed.

AN ISLAND APART

Lillian Beckwith

Kirsty MacLennan is the cook-general at 'Islay', a respectable guest-house in a Scottish suburb. When her kindly employer retires, and the fractious Isabel takes her place, Kirsty decides it is time to leave – but where shall she go?

Her dilemma is unexpectedly solved by one of the guests – Islander Ruari MacDonald, who has come to the city to seek a bride. Accepting his proposal, Kirsty leaves her old life behind and takes up residence in the crofthouse on Westisle, an idyllic small island uninhabited but for the brothers MacDonald.

As Kirsty joyfully rediscovers her Hebridean roots, and adapts herself to the mysteries of marriage and the challenge of a rigorous new working routine, only one thing stands in her way: the silent, brooding presence of her brother-in-law . . .

A haunting story of love and loss, *An Island Apart* is one of Lillian Beckwith's most magical and elegiac evocations of Island life.

LIGHT A PENNY CANDLE

Maeve Binchy

'Thanks heavens a thoroughly enjoyable and readable book'
The Times

Evacuated from Blitz-battered London, genteel Elizabeth White is sent to stay with the boisterous Irish O'Connors. It is the beginning of an unshakeable bond between Elizabeth and Aisling O'Connor which will survive twenty turbulent years. Writing with warmth, wit and great compassion, Maeve Binchy tells a magnificent story of the lives and loves of two women, bound together in friendship.

A timeless bestseller.

'The most enchanting book I have read since *Gone With The Wind.*'
Irish Independent

'A marvellous novel which combines those rare talents of storytelling and memorable writing' *Jeffrey Archer*

CROSS STITCH

Diana Gabaldon

Claire Randall is leading a double life. She has a husband in one century – and a lover in another . . .

On holiday with her husband just after the Second World War, she walks through a stone circle in the Scottish highlands and into a violent skirmish taking place in 1743.

A wartime nurse, Claire can deal with the bloody wounds that face her: it is harder to deal with the knowledge that she is in Jacobite Scotland and the carnage of Culloden is looming. Marooned amid the passion and violence, the superstition, the shifting allegiances and the fervent loyalties, Claire is in terrible danger from Jacobites and Redcoats – and from the shock of her own desire for a courageous renegade.

A passionate, unforgettable love story crossing two hundred years of Scottish history.

LAST GUESTS OF THE SEASON

Sue Gee

'A subtle and revealing look at human interaction . . . three stars' *New Woman*

After years out of contact, Claire and Frances, once fellow students, meet again by chance. Both are now married, with children: impulsively, the families agree to go on holiday together.

The house in Portugal is set in a garden of lemon trees. Inside, it is cool and dark; outside, the valley shimmers in the heat and cicadas sing. In an atmosphere of watchfulness and longing, secrets are revealed whose intensity threatens to tear both families apart, and the night is full of terrors. As events move inexorably toward tragedy, no one sees who is to be the real victim.

Haunting and beautifully crafted, this is a novel which illuminates the darker side of family life and the salvation that is found in it.

'Careful, evocative writing full of touching observation' *Woman's Journal*

THE WILDER SIDE OF LIFE

Diana Stainforth

She was a woman who seemed to have it all – until she chose to reject the illusion.

Francesca Eastgate appears to have it all – good looks, a blossoming career, a successful marriage and an immaculate home. But when charismatic ex-convict Jack Broderick appears on the scene, the illusion is soon shattered and her life thrown into turmoil.

Rejecting her oppressive husband William and flouting social convention, she escapes London's elegant Inns of Court – first to Broderick's dog track in Richmond and then to Las Vegas. There among the cut and thrust of the casinos and their poker tables, she learns to take control of her own life, and to decide where her heart really lies . . .

'I came to Las Vegas with nothing. It was sink or swim and I learnt to swim. This town gave me a fresh start. It taught me that I can survive on my own if I have to. It's made me strong.'

OLD SINS

Penny Vincenzi

POWER

Two clever, stylish and ambitious women are fighting for control of a multi-million cosmetics empire.

MYSTERY

What is the secret that lies behind its charming ruthless, mysterious creator, Julian Morell – and why when he dies does he split the inheritance between his family and a complete stranger?

GLAMOUR

Here are the designer interiors, the jewels, pictures, cars and to-die-for couture of the rich and the super-rich – the glittering fabulous world Julian created for himself, and the six powerful women who loved him.

PASSION

A love story, poignant, sexy, tempestuous, spanning thirty years, a mother, a mistress, a wife and a daughter, but always overshadowed by . . . old sins.

'A superior three star novel. An impressive, silky smooth saga, which explores the boudoir and business lives of a mega-rich family' *Sunday Telegraph*

BESTSELLING FICTION
available from Arrow

☐ An Island Apart	Lillian Beckwith	£3.99
☐ Dublin Four	Maeve Binchy	£3.99
☐ Light a Penny Candle	Maeve Binchy	£4.99
☐ The Lilac Bus	Maeve Binchy	£3.99
☐ Silver Wedding	Maeve Binchy	£3.99
☐ Victoria Line, Central Line	Maeve Binchy	£4.99
☐ Cross Stitch	Diana Gabaldon	£5.99
☐ Last Guests of the Season	Sue Gee	£4.99
☐ The Stainless Angel	Elizabeth Palmer	£4.99
☐ Old Sins	Penny Vincenzi	£5.99
☐ Friends and Other Enemies	Diana Stainforth	£4.50
☐ Indiscretion	Diana Stainforth	£3.99
☐ The Wilder Side of Life	Diana Stainforth	£4.99

ARROW BOOKS, BOOKSERVICE BY POST, PO BOX
29, DOUGLAS, ISLE OF MAN, BRITISH ISLES

NAME_____

ADDRESS_____

_____

Please enclose a cheque or postal order made out to Arrow Books Ltd,
for the amount due and allow for the following for postage and packing.

U.K. CUSTOMERS: Please allow 75p per book to a maximum of
£7.50

B.F.P.O. & EIRE: Please allow 75p per book to a maximum of £7.50

OVERSEAS CUSTOMERS: Please allow £1.00 per book.

Whilst every effort is made to keep prices low it is sometimes necessary
to increase cover prices at short notice. Arrow Books reserve the right to
show new retail prices on covers which may differ from those previously
advertised in the text or elsewhere.